CHROMA CROSSING CHRONICLES
BOOK I

BLOOD
MOON

Part 2

S. Yurvati

Cover art and design by Melissa Gannon
www.melissagannon.com

This is a work of fiction. All names, characters, places, brands, media and incidents are either the product of the author's imagination or are used fictitiously. Any resemblance to actual persons (living or deceased) is coincidental. The author acknowledges the trademarked status and ownership of various products, brands and/or restaurants referenced in this work of fiction, which have been used with due veneration, but without permission. The publication/use of these trademarks is not authorized, associated with, or sponsored by the trademark owners.

The following story contains mature themes, strong language and sexual situations, and is intended for adult readers.

Chapter One
Thorne

She'd said she had *nothing* to trade with.

At Candy's words Thorne had wanted to laugh—wisely he had not. Never had he seen a prettier female, and Candy had plenty of fine attributes to trade with. She was undoubtedly innocent of how her words sounded to a man's ears and affected a man's groin.

Admittedly, her declaration had certainly encouraged his trade enthusiastic throbbing shaft. He'd bargain much simply to touch her pretty face, to meet her lips with his own, to . . . Enough of such senseless thinking!

The point to be considered was, there was not a single man who would not eagerly accept what she had to bargain with, and be keen to 'exchange' with her. Hopefully she now understood the error of her words and would not offer them freely again. Not that he would allow any man to barter with her in any manner whatsoever.

How strange to come upon this foreign woman while hunting in the wilds. And even stranger was when, against his better judgment, he'd made a foolish promise to her. Doing so had been imprudent and a task for which he should not have committed. The influences of the 'needing moon' were too great to escape and how was he to proceed?

He remembered back to his first 'needing moon' when he was thirteen, though barely a man, yet he'd felt the effects and had clumsily acted on them. The need outweighed reason at such a time. Looking back he suspected he'd been bungling back then, but soon found that practice improved all skills.

Candy was seated in front of him as they made their way to his village. Her curious green eyes darted everywhere as if soaking up a newness that Thorne did not truly see or understand. But then what did he know of her world? Mayhap this village was unique unto her eyes.

To him it was just a bigger village than some, smaller than others. The village beheld the same dirt and cobbled roads, the same thatched rooftops, the same wood and stone homes. Indeed the same look for the past hundreds of years. Only now, it was also a village in a realm robbed of color for the past decade. This locale did not appear so unique unto his eyes.

As he passed villagers, they called out his name and bowed their heads while crossing their right hand over their chest. He gave a quick bow of his head in response. Playful children with smudged grinning faces and missing front teeth ran into the street to meet him with laughter. Upon seeing the woman seated in front of him, they were stunned by her colorful clothing.

The villagers clearly recognized that Candy was not from their realm and they stared at her as his war-horse passed. Some children pointed at the foreign woman, however parents quickly lowered their children's arms. Thereafter they bowed their heads, as if shamed by their child's discourteous behavior. It became obvious that Candy was going to merit many questions from many superstitious people.

Thorne leaned against her ear, "Lassie, tell no one, and I truly mean *none*, from whence you are from. Answer only that you came from a village far south of here and your path went astray whilst traveling."

"Am I in some kind of danger? I haven't done anything, have I?"

"You are yourself, and such is enough to cause much trouble if anyone were to learn the truth of it. The villagers are distrustful of things they cannot explain. Heed my words on this. And tonight, you must not let others know you are ignorant of the festival, only that you do not wish to partake while in a village other than your own."

"Partake? In what? If you don't tell me how am I supposed to know how to respond?"

Thorne let out a deep sigh and nuzzled her ear. As he spoke his breath caressed her lobe, and his deep voice sounded entirely masculine.

"Do you wish to join the village in the effects of the 'needing moon's' ecstasy, join bodies as they writhe in lust, mayhap couple with any man who wants you? If not, you must follow my advice. However should you decide to participate—"

"Uh, no, absolutely no. I've never done anything remotely like an orgy and don't plan to. Ever!" Candy's blush became an intense shade far beyond pink.

Aye, this female he had come upon was ignorant of the Moon Goddess, though how was such possible? Perchance they had other deities in her land? Yet how could Candy not know of the Moon Goddess and her powers? The goddess traveled the heavens nightly and was of the trinity of deities he paid tribute to, beneath the *Creator of All*. How could she not know of the goddess?

With his head leaning against Candy's golden hair he spoke in a low sensuous voice. "You can choose a single partner if your need becomes too great. There would be many men to choose from... should any please your eyes."

"You're talking about sex, right?"

"Aye, that I am." His words caressed her hair and he felt when a shiver ran through her. Obviously she felt something—

"Would you be one to choose from?" Her face pinkened further at her realization of what she'd just asked.

Ah, her blushing bespoke a rare innocence.

He liked that about her, though Candy looked to have regretted her forward manner, and the words were likely spoken because of the 'needing moon's' influence. Mayhap she was neither immune to the Moon Goddess, nor to him?

The wee female was a beauty, and if she decided to partake he would want her and eagerly take her as his woman. He would gladly pleasure this woman until she screamed his name. The pressure within his leathers kept reminding him how he was more than eager to do so.

Alas, she'd said she would not, and he needed to push such thoughts aside. This was neither her land nor her ways, and she was not his, though he would very much like to change that. Even for a 'needing moon' he found his increasing desire for her to be strangely unfamiliar, and consuming beyond his nature. Truly, this feeling was damn unsettling to him.

He would not force his attentions upon any woman, and Candy had said she had no wish to participate. That in of itself should be enough to dissuade him, nonetheless, as the hours on horseback passed his craving for her intensified. The yearning went deep, and his sac ached for release into her. Never had he felt desire for a specific female before, as one comely face served as well as the next when it came to the physical release of sex.

Most unsettling.

He leaned in to explain. "The need for us is too great to deny, tis both a blessing and a curse from the Moon Goddess. As a grown man I choose not to be part of any group. A lover should be enjoyed in a more private environment without such chaos. And never do I share the woman I lay with."

His words were so softly spoken she barely heard them although his voice made her quiver in low places and her stomach began doing backflips.

The war-horse and packhorse started up the cobbled incline leading to the House of Rule, their clomping hooves loud enough to bring the attention of stable help. A young groom ran forward to grab the reins of the second horse.

He should think it good to return home, but felt otherwise. The end of the journey also meant he'd no longer remain in such close proximity to this female, and that thought made him feel strangely empty. How odd that word, still it felt true enough.

Without doubt, this would grow into a most trying meeting with his jealous sister who considered herself the most desirable woman not only this village, but also the entirety of the land.

Although Levenia was truly beautiful, sadly she long ago lost any look of purity or innocence. A feature that Candy's beauty sustained. Nay, his sister would not take well to him bringing a comely female under their roof. Of this he was certain. Levenia was far too jealous regarding her vanity and her brother's affections.

Several men ran to greet Thorne, readied to take charge of his war-horse. The venison was carried off and to be cooked for the night's festivities, and already preparations were noted in the courtyard. Tents were being set up while large tables were being carried to fill them.

It was obvious that the riding had been physically uncomfortable for the wee female saddled in front of him. Clearly Candy was not accustomed to being on horseback, as her buttocks had forever bounced against him. Her petite frame would require a smaller horse to carry her, but why was he thinking as though she would be in need of one?

As if this small woman held a place in his land and by his side. On the other hand, would she not require a means to return back to her home, wherever it might be?

Aye, a smaller horse would be needed to return her to her own land, he told himself.

Thorne dismounted then reached up to help Candy down. His war-horse was much too wide for her small figure and the woman was entirely too short to jump from such a tall horse. He also suspected Candy's legs would not support her after such a long ride.

In this he was correct. As Candy let herself be lifted down, her legs gave way, and it was only by his hold on her that she did not collapse into a heap onto the ground.

How difficult he found it to not smile at her useless land legs, as she resembled a newly birthed colt trying to stand. He tried not to let her see his humor at her ungainliness.

Candy was so fragile looking it called to his protective nature.

"You will feel better soon Lassie, however at this time I think you require need of me to carry you."

Thorne scooped her into his arms without waiting for her response. So light of weight, easily a third the weight of the stag he had shouldered, and he did not mind carrying her in the least. In fact he enjoyed her soft womanliness beneath his hands—overly so.

As was becoming all too common, her proximity led to him hardening beneath his leathers. He needed to think about far less fleshy thoughts least Levenia see him thus. Never would he allow that, as his sister would choose to comprehend the cause erringly.

"I'm embarrassed, but thanks for your help. Who lives in this place or is it a hotel of some sort?" Candy's eyes were traveling the expanse of the dwelling.

"Thus is called the House of Rule. My family resides within."

Though he tried to focus on those *unfavorable* blood relatives who resided within—in order to rid himself of the rigidity within his leathers—it was a futile task with the soft woman he desired within his arms. It seemed ceasing carnal thoughts of the beguiling female he carried was far easier sought than done.

"You're married then?"

Had he truly heard disappointment in her voice? Did she find him to be of some interest? "Nay, never have I taken a wife. A few of my family live within. You shall meet them all too soon I fear."

Candy was studying the vast structure in front of her. "Is it going to be alright for me to stay here?"

Thorne fully expected this to be a taxing meeting with Levenia. That would be followed by a tortuous night of denial of the wee woman he carried and desired. "It shall be, as you are my guest."

She must think him merely a hunter, and that he would somehow slip her through the back door. Mayhap she thought he'd provide a cot for her in the kitchen. Thorne found this both amusing and rare—to come upon a female who held no predetermined agenda. Candy knew naught of him and held no expectations. That was as refreshing as her innocence within his world.

"Your relatives won't mind?" Her voice sounded uncertain, as if she thought to be intruding.

Oh aye, his sister would most certainly mind.

With a crooked smile he responded. "Truly Lassie, none will question such a thing."

Chapter Two
Candy

The quaint village sustained the basic-beige color scheme.

In fact it resembled a rendition of a Thomas Kincaid painting, minus the clever lighting changes the artist had been famous for. And of course, everything was in tedious beige. No reds, blues, yellows, or even pastels.

Thatch-roofed cottages, some with fences, dotted the landscape and even the cobbled roads and walkways added unique charm. Many of the rooftops were curved rather than peaked. The scenery was picturesque to say the least, and certainly reminiscent of a lifestyle from a bygone era. No cars, just a sprinkling of horses and wagons. Nor did she spot any unsightly (although technologically useful) electrical lines.

Nothing looked familiar and again she wondered where she was . . . and what year was this anyway?

People were dressed in simple clothing with women wearing long skirts or simple dresses that went to their ankles. All the clothing was of similar shades of boring-muted-beige.

The repetitious monochromatic color scheme was unsettling to her as both an artist, and a female. Imagine a closet full of *beige*? All the fun would be sucked out of shopping.

This observation made her feel as though she stood out like a decorated Christmas tree. No wonder the children were staring. The situation made her feel like a flaunting male peacock amid a flock of wrens, and didn't enjoy being the center of attention.

When Thorne had said those things about the festivities and 'needing moon' she had started to panic. Thank goodness he said he'd protect her, and Thorne seemed an honorable man who would most certainly keep his word. She didn't really know him, but he extruded a confident and commanding air, giving her the feeling if he said something he meant it. If she was going to feel any sense of security she had to believe that about him.

Take one thing at a time in this new land, she reminded herself, *don't panic*. The words came to mind easily, her confidence didn't.

As the horses trotted up the cobbled ramp to the enormous stone structure on the hill, Candy noticed the massive three-story stone building. Some of the turrets rose to create a fourth story. Series of curved rooflines appeared to be covered with slate rather than thatch. Parts of the roof spiraled, while others appeared softly rounded. The building was unique and aesthetically pleasing to the artist in her.

Several of the beige walls had equally beige ivy climbing the stone, which added a feeling of old worldliness to the immense and beautiful edifice. She couldn't imagine how many square feet this building had, but if she guessed it would be at least twenty thousand. Candy couldn't help but think how this place would blow Liam away, to see a structure this atypical. Was it a gigantic residence or something else?

Thanks to her misplaced cell phone she couldn't even take photos. What a pity. She really needed to find a way to keep her phone on her body instead of wherever she'd left it . . . *again!* At least she might be able to sketch it for Liam.

A young man wearing leather breeches, boots, and a loose fitting linen shirt ran out to meet them. Additional similarly dressed men milled close by to assist the hunter and retrieve the stag from the second horse.

When she thought to climb down from Thorne's horse, Candy came to the harsh realization that 'beige-land' probably had gravity, and she had zero strength left in her thighs. Gratefully Thorne whisked her from the saddle and carried her as if she weighed nothing.

Having men carry her was becoming a little too common, however, the feel of his hands on her wasn't anything to complain about . . . not in the least. He was strong yet gentle with her and his bunched biceps didn't escape her eyes. *Hmmm*, maybe being carried was an optimal transport means after all, certainly her ovaries weren't complaining.

While being held close to his chest she wrapped her arms around his corded neck, because where else would hands go when you were being carried? And even after all the dirt and grime of travel he had the audacity to smell sensually desirable, while she no doubt smelled like last weeks garbage. Even his two-day stubble looked incredibly alluring. It required her restraint to keep from touching his face, to feel the texture of his skin.

His booted footfalls reached the entry steps and Thorne effortlessly ran up them two at a time, carrying her to the doorway of what the hunter had called the House of Rule.

Despite their brisk pace she noticed how the double doors, made of heavily carved wood, were a good foot thick. Unfortunately, Thorne was moving too quickly for her to take notice of the designs as he passed through those doors, which were now being held open for his arrival.

Apparently he wasn't the hired help after all, he really did live on the property.

Whisking through the doors, Thorne tread onward into a grand expanse of hallway. Candy figured with the way she probably smelled he was hurrying so he could put her down. The hunter, named Thorne, really was a brave and selfless man because she was in desperate need of a shower.

As he carried her through an immense anteroom, which led to an even larger room, she noted the vast area had proper cathedral high ceilings, hanging tapestries and polished stone floors. The space appeared opulent, in a beige kind of way. At the far end stood a raised dais with three big, plush, and ornate looking beige chairs.

Having never been in such a majestic place before, her eyes were busy trying to absorb it all. She wondered if her eyes were flickering as fast as her mind was. The interior looked stunning, but the lack of color seemed to steal some of the luxuriousness from the dwelling.

Again she wondered, what kind of place was this? It was massive inside. Maybe Thorne's family ran a bed and breakfast lodge.

The walls were dotted with an abundance of ornate oil-fueled sconces. There was a massive fireplace faced with gold-veined marble. The fireplace mantle was hand-carved, reminiscent of what artisans had created for old European castles. Certainly nothing available now, and the cost to reproduce such quality would be astronomical. Even a very high-end antique store would unlikely possess such a fine piece. She would love to get the opportunity to study the design of that exquisite detailing later.

When Candy's eyes lifted, she saw the immense breath-taking domed-glass ceiling. The crystal-like structure was remarkable, and the arched ceiling height easily reached fifty or more feet at the pinnacle. In the center of the glass dome was a large clear circle that probably extended greater than fifteen feet across.

Etched glass pieces surrounded the center glass piece, and the framing pieces looked as if they represented phases of the moon. The domed ceiling enclosure was stunning to her artistic sense of admiration. She couldn't imagine how difficult to complete that extensive hemispherical glass structure, and to construct the whole in a manner to maintain the fortitude to defy gravity—and by the looks of it, apparently the dome had done so for a good amount of years.

When Thorne set her on her feet, it was on a handsomely polished limestone floor. Even though she felt a little wobbly, Candy managed to stand. She might not be able to walk, but at least for now she could support herself and remain vertical. It was a positive start.

A beautiful woman glided fluidly to greet Thorne. Her hips swayed with a grace and sensuality that Candy envied. Thorne quickly bowed his head and folded his arms, palms open, across his chest. The woman mirrored his actions before they engaged in a hug.

A clingy possessive type of hug, as the female practically groped him! She'd clung to him like cat hair on black slacks.

When the woman hesitated to release the embrace, Thorne took her hands in his and stepped back, putting himself closer to Candy, and distancing himself from 'Miss Clingy'. While Thorne frowned and shook his head, the woman's expression flickered annoyance. Quickly her expression was replaced with a Cheshire-Cat smile.

Her dress was floor length with a low-cut draping bodice revealing her décolletage. Candy couldn't help but feel a little jealous. Not that she was by any means flat chested, but definitely not as endowed as this female. Not unless she wore a Wonder Bra. At that moment Candy held no illusions of her own looks being anything other than what the cat . . . or gargoyle as it may be, drug in.

Thorne took another retreating step seemingly much to the woman's disappointment.

"Ah sister, you look beautiful and well, as always Levenia."

"And you my dear brother are always in my heart. What have you brought back with you? A gift, for me? A new servant?" Levenia's brow and lips puckered as if in distaste. "Is *it* a male or female?"

With a *tsk* Thorne shook his head. "Levenia, what of your manners? There is no doubt she is a comely woman, despite her unusual manner of dress. I present Lady Candy, from a village far south of our territory. She became lost within our hunting grounds and near ended up a causality of my arrow."

"A *misspent* arrow, from you?" Levenia sounded as if she couldn't fathom such a failing from Thorne. Still her stare kept returning to Candy and somehow Levenia had made the phase sound rather sordid.

He shook his head, "My shot held true, but this female was near and I had no knowledge of such."

Hello, I'm right next to you guys.

This beige-land might be off a bit, but she wasn't invisible—even though that sister of his was trying to look right through her. Levenia's assessing gaze measured Candy as though she was of no consequence. His sister's expression was familiar, unfortunately it was a look Candy recognized all too well from her father's wives.

Oh yes, little Candy—that child, and inconvenient afterthought.

Ono chose that moment to fly into the great hall and land on her shoulder. "I was wondering where you were," she whispered to her baby gargoyle.

Levenia looked taken aback by Ono and turned her attention back to Thorne. "How did *she* come by a gargoyle?"

"She is a Lady in her own court, and Ono is her companion, as Kemp is yours." Thorne shrugged it off as of little importance, hardly worthy of discussion.

Meanwhile "she" was wishing "she" could get to a less demanding physical position before "she" started wavering and fell down. His sister would probably find that very amusing. Hadn't the introduction been long and uncomfortable enough? It sure had been for her, as "she" struggled not to sway on her feet.

And as if sensing his name had been spoken, Levenia's rather large and robust gargoyle flew into the room and landed on her shoulder. Now Kemp and Ono could eye each other as easily as Levenia did with Candy.

The comfort level between the gargoyles seemed to match what Candy was feeling with Thorne's sister. Obviously out-of-towners weren't really welcome here. That probably ruled out the Bed and Breakfast theory. How nice, landing in a foreign color-impaired land and being an unwelcome houseguest as well.

Regrettably this situation was entirely too reminiscent of her childhood and her stepmothers' responses.

Unwanted. Excess baggage.

None of it should really matter anymore. Certainly she was long past expecting anyone to love her and would only be here until she figured a way back home.

When the silence became uncomfortable Thorne spoke up. "Lady Candy will be my guest until I can lead her back to her own territory."

"I see. Welcome to our House of Rule and betake and enjoy all our festivities tonight. Surely some man will find you . . . pleasing."

As Levenia turned to leave the room her hips swayed and her dress swished behind her as she began calling out orders for the placement of tables and pallets for the night's festivities.

Yessiree, 'Miss Clingy' was used to getting what she wanted and having Candy here wasn't on her wish list. Wasn't that all warm and fuzzy feeling?

B-itch!

Smugness crept over Candy as she considered that for all the beauty and obvious resources Levenia seemed to have, her fine silk dress was still *mundane beige*. No woman looked good in that hue—not even beautiful Levenia.

"She doesn't seem too fond of visitors," Candy murmured as she thought about how his sister hadn't emitted one ounce of hospitality.

"Levenia is fond enough, if they are young virile men," he sighed. "I shall accompany you to a guest room. You likely wish to get cleaned up as badly as I."

"It sounds heavenly. What I wouldn't give for a shower or bath."

Thorne stopped mid-stride. "Are you willing to barter yourself Lassie, because as a man I would more than willingly accept your manner of coin?" His eyes wandered across her figure before his eyebrow rose, as if asking if she was certain she wanted to pay him by using her body as trade.

Blushing with embarrassment Candy rephrased her words. "I would love an opportunity to get cleaned up." When she managed to look at him he nodded.

"On a night such as this, beware your tongue. Even I will only dismiss your words so many times before I will seek payment *starting* with your lips, and I would hardly be stopping there." His eyes perused her body as if punctuating his meaning.

It was effective, Candy felt totally stunned by his words. Did she really sound like a she traded for sexual favors? Certainly she hadn't ever thought so, until now.

Obviously this was something to work on because being flirtatious or provocative was not in her nature. And didn't he just say he would *start* at her lips? About fifty butterflies bounced with joy on her stomach's interior trampoline. Some were doing Olympic worthy triple somersaults.

Glancing up to him she wondered if *his* full lips felt as decadent as they looked and what kind of kisser he was? By the looks of him, a darn good one.

Really? For shame, for shame, Candy. He's your host, not a prize for show and tell.

Thorne took her arm and guided her toward the staircase. Ono chose to ride on his shoulder, no doubt thinking the hunter looked more stable on his feet than Candy. Ono was right. Plus, Thorne smelled a whole lot better too.

"Your room is a staircase up. Have you need, I shall carry you."

Need? *Maybe.*

Want? *Oh yeah. Definitely.*

As she glanced up the winding *long* staircase, she saw dozens of steps to challenge her exhausted and twitching muscles.

"I'll give it a try." Candy took three steps up before her thighs gave out.

As she began to sink southward the hunter simply picked her up in his arms and carried her to the top landing. While he climbed the stairs, Candy's eyes took in the ornate metal railing depicting curling and twisting vines with grape leaves, grape clusters and an occasional small bird. The lovely artistic ironworks encircled the entire second floor.

The workmanship was impeccable, clearly hand-made, and one of a kind. The railing was as impressive as the view into the great room below.

Thorne didn't put her down until he'd passed through the doorway to what Candy assumed was to be her guest room. The hunter carried her to the bed and set her down gently. The situation seemed a little intimate, being laid out on a bed, so she quickly scooted over to sit on the edge.

The linens beneath her hands were embroidered and felt like Egyptian cotton with a million-thread count. Linens like these could totally spoil a girl and she might never want cheapo poly-blends again.

The room was spacious and had two large windows. They were open and the curtains billowed from a slight breeze. There was a lovely white marble wood-burning fireplace. Likely each room had one for heating, since it didn't appear this land she'd been propelled into offered any electricity or gas lines. Apparently, beige-land was technology challenged.

Although the bedroom was pretty, like everything else here it featured a beige palette. The space was decorated with fine antique looking furnishings. All the pieces looked quite usable and not at all frail. Thankfully nothing looked like it would break if you dared to sit on the piece.

When a young pretty girl entered the room carrying towels and what appeared to be soap, Candy knew a bath was so close she could almost feel the coveted clean water on her skin.

"Will you be bathing with your Lady?" the girl asked.

His eyes scanned Candy while a tilted smile hinted on his lips. "Regrettably not, Celcee. I require my own bath drawn. See to it Lady Candy has anything she might need for tonight, including clean clothing befitting her standing."

"Certainly, as you wish."

Thorne turned to Candy. "I will meet with you later and show you about. Celcee is my devoted servant and will serve you well and attend to any needs you and Ono require until I return. Pull the cord hanging by your bedside if you have additional need of her."

"This is a really lovely room, and you've been really kind to me. I don't even know how I'll ever repay—" Candy stopped mid-sentence noticing his arched brow and slight smile to remind her to take care in her choice of wording.

She nodded her understanding.

He rewarded her with a wink, a darn sexy wink—in fact an utterly smoldering wink. Who knew the movement of an eyelid could be so insanely hot?

As he left Candy didn't know what else to say. Everything was totally surreal; the tall and seemingly magnetic hunter, this architecturally superb mansion, the surrounding sepia color scheme and now even a servant. So much to process, but she did know the first thing on her list was to get washed up. A clean body would provide clearer thinking as well. At least she hoped so.

The bathing area was placed to the side of the bedroom where there was an alcove with hanging sheer curtains. These were draped, pulled to the side, and held in place with little bird shaped hooks. The effect was romantic and almost fantasy-like.

Meanwhile, Celcee hummed as she got the water ready in a big freestanding tub that was lined with decorative mosaic glass tile. The interior design consisted of swirls reminiscent of stylized water or maybe wind. Candy wandered over to a group of gracefully shaped bottles on the antique appearing dresser top.

"Those would be oils for you bath, if my Lady would care to choose some."

"Do any help with pain from riding an entire day on a huge horse?"

Giggling, Celcee picked one up and added it to the water. "This shall help some. Do you wish to choose another, as a pleasing scent for him?"

"You mean Thorne? We aren't . . . well . . ."

"Oh, I saw him carry you. Did I think mistakenly of you two? Surely for tonight you will want him, every female does, and you would be the envy of all."

The girl seemed a good resource in regards to 'Pheromone Man', so Candy decided to glean Celcee for tidbits of information.

"Why do they all want Thorne, I mean he is big and muscular and all"—*actually pretty much perfect if you liked huge, buff, rugged men, which her hormones apparently did*— "but he seems rather daunting as well. It seems to me he could be a really dangerous man."

Celcee laughed. "Indeed he is as you say. My Lord is a great warrior with many battles and kills to his name. Both a proud man and unbeatable with his skills with blades, arrows, and most adept with his fists as well." Celcee let out a sigh at what she obviously comprehended as great manly attributes.

"And though my Lord acts as though he notices naught of his influence upon women, he can be totally charming when he so pleases. Tis doubtful any woman would dismiss his advances. Either way, charming or harsh, he is a most desired man. And then of course he is also of the House of Rule, so who would not want to mate with him?"

Oddly enough, the ability to kill or maim wasn't on Candy's list of dating criteria. No doubt an omission that most dating sites wouldn't bother to inquire about.

It didn't surprise Candy that she wasn't the only female who considered Thorne as eye-candy. There was no doubt the man was hotter than a curling iron, and could probably burn you just as easily, leaving blistering scars on your heart.

"What does that mean, of the House of Rule? Where I come from we must call it something different."

"He and his sister Levenia, by his delegation, rule us. Thorne is a most powerful man. Do you not find him of interest?"

"Then is he like a mayor or governor?"

Celcee looked bemused. "He is much more, Thorne is our *King*."

Holy moly, this was one heck of a fantasy, except as impossible as it seemed Candy knew this *wasn't* a dream. Maybe 'king' meant something different here. Or maybe he was 'King of Hunting', or possibly 'King of Pheromones' or 'King of Sex Appeal'.

"I do find him of great interest as you say, but I hardly know him. Does he date a lot of females?" What a ridiculous question to ask. He was a man after all, and a man like him could have any woman. Why should she even ask or care? So what if he was the sexiest male she'd ever laid eyes on, it wasn't like she was going to be getting cozy or naked with him.

"Date? A fruit?"

"Sleeps with?"

Celcee shook her head. "My Lord always sleeps alone."

Candy tried for another word. "Bedded?"

"Aye. I hear he takes females frequently. Though some say no woman gets his cock past a single night, no matter how they attempt to use their charms to keep him. However, my Lord remains most discrete, never speaks of such things. Tonight, my lady, if you know each other in the best way possible then upon the morrow mayhap you would share lustful details with me."

Celcee offered up a smile before reaching her hand out. "Hand me your soiled clothing and I shall send them to be washed whilst you soak."

A man like Thorne would be a complete player and man-whore. Exactly what Candy avoided—a one-night stand.

During their chatting Candy had picked one bottle of scented oil she favored and poured some into the bath water. It smelled fresh, not heavily perfumed. The scent was reminiscent of lemongrass with the added touch of sweet mint, like a spa product that she'd never be able to afford. She was going to feel totally spoiled.

Peeling off her clothing she handed the items to Celcee and saw the young woman's confused expression. Candy thought it was probably the pink color of her tank top.

"You wear this harness in your village?" Celcee was holding up Candy's bra. "Does it signify you are someone's property and they keep you trussed like a stuffed pheasant in such?"

Okay, Candy could kind of see the correlation now that it was put in that particular context. "Where I come from it's a garment women wear under their clothing."

Evidently women weren't 'trussed' here, both interesting and somewhat discomforting to learn.

"Why would you wear such, surely this is most uncomfortable?"

Good question. Candy remembered how awkward it had been trying to learn to be comfortable with it on, but a bra had been an absolute necessity as far as being a teenage girl in those dreaded gym classes. Girls were not kind about slow development, and a bra was a rite of passage.

It had been her father's second wife, also referred to as the 'inebriated stepmom', Bitney, who had finally and *begrudgingly* taken Candy to purchase her first bra. Apparently the requirement to be semi-sober when driving your stepdaughter to the mall had piqued her. Public safety frowned on driving while totally incoherent, some silly thing about the dangers to others, and all that.

Imagine the nerve of a stepdaughter actually needing something requiring an adult to be present! No doubt her intoxicated stepmom would've preferred Candy jog the twenty miles to make the purchase on her own. If only she could have, thereby avoiding the *stepmom-from-hell* bonding, humiliating experience. Outings with Bitney never fared well for Candy.

Of course if her alcoholic stepmom had been completely sober (as if that ever happened) and used an indoor voice (also never happening) it might have been less embarrassing.

Candy had wished the floor would open and swallow her when said stepmom called out to the elderly salesclerk. Bitney was waving a blushing-pink bra above her head (like a flag for the 'State of Intoxication') and yelling out "does this come in a smaller size?" The temptation to hum the national anthem was quickly replaced by Candy wishing she could become internationally invisible.

Once the question had been callously called out, every customer and her curious child had gazed to Candy's small budding bosom; after all, everyone had now been included in the biggest event of the day—the *Bra Quest*.

Candy tried to step back, hoping to retreat, only to stumble into a rack of panties. The rack teetered and then went tumbling. Itty-bitty hangers flew everywhere leaving a trail of colorful lace strewn panties like confetti on New Years Eve.

The scene reinforced every customer's renewed interest in watching the spectacle of *The Bra Quest*. The event promised more action than watching a *Real Housewives'* episode.

The elderly saleswoman assured Candy every-thing was "fine sweetie" and the hundred strewn tangled panties on those silly little plastic hangers (who even hung bras and panties on those confounded hangers that only salesclerks could master?) certainly didn't present a problem. With the clenched expression as the woman mumbled the word "arthritis", while her knees creaked and popped as she lifted the rack up from the floor— Candy didn't quite buy into it being fine.

Why had such a humiliating moment made Candy feel like she'd single handedly championed global abuse against the elderly?

Probably because ninety-nine panties remained for the geriatric salesclerk to bend and pick up while she waved Candy back from the mess.

One passing customer, Mrs. Gilmore, had her teenage son, David, the math whiz with her. Yep, the kid who could master the Rubik's Cube in eleven point two seconds—

with his eyes closed. David, the vice-president of the chess club, also president of their class, a letter holder on the track team, and the very same David who instead of looking like a geek had dark curly hair, an arresting smile and was the cutest boy in school. And of course *this* was the very same David who was seated across from her in algebra class.

They shared an uncomfortable moment when their eyes slowly met through a rack of lacy bras, right before the catastrophic crash. Mortification didn't begin to describe how she felt.

No doubt he'd been filling in the math equation as to what size Candy should be looking for:

If 'X' = small, then 'Y' = 'A' cup

At that embarrassing moment, the color candy-apple-red pretty much described her face and neck, maybe even radiated to her budding bosom. It was that all too familiar hue that blossomed whenever she was embarrassed beyond humiliation.

To this day Candy never stepped into a Macy's again for fear that same saleslady had transferred to the city where she lived. The woman was probably ninety now, but unless that salesclerk had Alzheimer's and/or was retired, that department store was omitted from undergarment shopping options. Steeped in guilt, Candy also donated to the annual Arthritis Foundation Fund.

Undoubtedly the saleswoman probably felt just as uncomfortable about Candy as well. And if she ever spied Candy again she'd likely try to run the other direction. Except Candy was pretty sure with those arthritic knees, the woman would more likely be shuffling with aid of a walker.

She was too kind hearted to ever want to make the woman suffer like that again, so the department store was out and Internet shopping was in when it came to bra replacement.

"Well, in the beginning it's uncomfortable but females get used to it, and we consider a bra proper to wear under our clothing."

Celcee was correct in that it was restricting with straps of elastic . . . actually it really was very similar to a bridle or harness.

Wonder why I never thought about that?

"So you wear such for what reason?"

Candy thought about the question then used her hand movements to help pantomime the concept. "So the 'girls', also referred to as 'boobs', look perky, but covered."

"Yet you hide the natural softness of your breasts?" The expression on Celcee's face indicated total confusion.

"I suppose we do, now that you mention it. We cover our breasts so the nipples don't show and we stay put, but at the same time we push them up and out like we're showing them off. Kind of a paradox I suppose."

Not looking convinced, Celcee held up Candy's panties next.

"Oh for pity sake, please do not tell me you don't wear those here either?" This place was going to embarrass the daylights out of her.

"These are quite pretty with the lace, though most small," murmured Celcee.

Yeah, they're bikini style, thought Candy.

"Only virgins wear covering until they are broken at their first mating. The covering represents a token of purity. Mayhap you are a virgin then?" Celcee was still holding her dog-gone panties and Candy was going to die, right there, right now.

"Not really, but we all wear them where I come from." *Maybe not Cherry Ann, come to think of it.* "Or most of us anyway."

"No matter my Lady, we will return them to you clean. I shall provide what you need for this night. Soak and relax."

Geez Louise, someone was actually going to wash her underwear! Uncomfortable to say the least, but Celcee had already tucked them in with the other dirty clothes. If she made a big deal out of grabbing them back, Celcee would really think she was eccentric.

Since Ono appeared to be settled in for a nap on a shelf with her tail curled around her and looking very comfortable in her surroundings, Candy planned to enjoy soaking as Celcee had suggested. A good long bath would make her feel so much better and was a luxury she seldom took time for. Showers were so much quicker, but not nearly as relaxing.

When Candy heard a small cough her eyes sprang open. Thorne was standing in front of her holding a towel.

The man was clean, shaven and . . . wow. That hunter cleaned up mighty fine. Then comprehension hit and embarrassment seeped in. "Hey, I'm not dressed, haven't you learned to knock first?"

Thorne extended his hand with the towel. "So I see, but you have been soaking long enough to become waterlogged. The skin on your fingers and toes has wrinkled. And where is Celcee?"

Fingers and *toes!* He obviously saw right through the water. Where were her soap-suds-friends? Candy was trying not to ogle the cleaned up hunk while making sure she was covered by dwindling soap bubbles, which seemed to have diminished during her extended soaking time. There had certainly been copious bubbles earlier.

Unreliable little traitors!

Her artist's eyes were trained to notice details and right now they were noting every aspect of the hunter. Like how Thorne was wearing a clean pair of leather pants with leather lacing not just up the front, but also down the entire length of the sides. The construction left an inch of skin showing through the side seams from his muscled calves to his awesome glutes!

Tearing her eyes away from his peeking thigh (ouch, it felt like her corneas had been sprained) she also noticed he now wore a much more ornate and open vest. It had stitching and leather lacing through it as well, but no shirt beneath.

Neither did those naked muscled arms elude her sense of appreciation one bit. How could they while so splendidly taunting her hormones?

His still damp sandy-blonde hair was curled up at the ends. He was clean-shaven—no more wilderness stubble. All of him looked exceedingly, undeniably, delectably, desirable. His chest peeked out from behind his vest and she felt her mouth water.

My-oh-my, how enticing was that?

Thorne's abs exhibited a solid six-pack, or was that an eight-pack? However many 'packs' he had, the muscled ridges looked magnificent. The man's perfect physique would honor any piece of clay or granite in an artist's hand. With him as a model, it would be tempting to take up sculpture. Just hand her a chisel and hammer because she felt inspired.

Oops, was he waiting for her to answer him?

Time to quit drooling Candy.

Using the sponge to wipe the saliva from her chin she replied, "I think she went to find clean clothing for me. So just how long have you been standing there anyway?"

"Are you ready to dry off Lassie?"

"*Hmph.* You don't like to answer certain questions do you?" *Typical man.* "Please turn around for me so I can get out."

Why was it men thought they could just use omissions in lieu of honest answers? And how long had he been standing there anyway? She suspected long enough to see whatever he intended to. No doubt he was in league with the disappearing bubbles.

Even though Thorne ignored her question, he thankfully was gentleman enough to turn away from her. As she stood and quickly wrapped the towel around herself she met his reflected eyes in a tall easel mounted mirror, which stood directly in front of him. Candy's embarrassment resulted in turning a deep shade of rose.

"You asked me to turn about, you did not say I could not enjoy your reflection. This fine mirror is directly in front of me, and truthfully, you can only ask so much of a man." He shrugged as if it made perfect sense.

Her face turned further on the color palette, quickly bypassing scarlet and heading directly to a brilliant crimson. Obviously far too late to change the situation, she tried to pretend she hadn't just shown all of her nakedness to him.

Humiliation won't kill you Candy, you're proficient at it.

Just then Celcee returned with a large tray containing several items, including folded clothing.

So now she shows up! And Celcee couldn't have been here five minutes sooner, why?

"I shall wait outside your door. And may I say, your lovely womanly figure pleases me ever much." Thorne gave a subtle bow and a quick wink to Candy as he left the room. A mischievous smile played across those full and inviting lips.

Celcee beamed at Candy. "So you do fancy each other. I brought you a dress for the evening's festivities. Also wine, bread and fruit for you, and some tasty items for your adorable young gargoyle as well."

Candy was flustered by what he'd said. That man had known full well she hadn't wanted to be seen naked. Funny, she hadn't even noticed the full-length mirror before, but it was clear as day now. Wait, Celcee thought Ono was *adorable*? This place was definitely weird, because buck-toothed and drooling gargoyles were not adorable. Now kittens, *they* were adorable.

Peering at the stoneware cup on the tray, she wondered what was in it. Of course it was basic beige, what wasn't? "What's in the little cup with the lid?"

The servant girl looked up at Candy with surprise. "Why tis your 'needing moon' honey pot of course."

Silly me, I should have known.

"What do I do with it, put it on bread or the fruit slices?"

"So different in your land," Celcee was shaking her head. "Tis to use so you do not beget a child tonight, unless you desire a babe. If I were fortunate enough to share a bed with Lord Thorne I would gladly give him a babe. Of course I only fantasize such things."

"So if I eat it, it provides birth control?"

The girl laughed and opened the stoneware lid to show inside the cup. "Use within your womanhood to prevent a man's seed from taking. Worry not, all men know how to use it, and I have heard they enjoy any excuse to put their fingers into a woman."

The contents looked a lot like average bee spit, but with the addition of darker flecks, possibly herbs. Although a little uncomfortable with the topic, Candy remained too curious not to ask.

"Does it really work?"

"Aye, but you must reapply with each mating. Tis why the cup holds a few applications, in case your man has 'needing' for more of you." Celcee's giggles indicated she obviously liked that idea.

"Do you participate in this whole 'needing moon' thing?"

"I am now mature enough to bleed as a woman and my breasts are fair enough in size for a man to enjoy, so if the Moon Goddess sends me the 'needing' then I shall gladly partake. This may be my first 'needing moon', though I will not know until the moon rises, and see if the Moon Goddess calls the hunger to me. Our first 'needing moon' represents a special right of passage for us."

As Candy picked at the tray of color-deprived fruit, she enjoyed the sweetness of the cut pieces. She pretended the kiwi was green and the strawberries red, and maybe that was a pear or apple slice. Color would certainly make it easier to identify the items on the plate.

"Are you still a virgin?" It wasn't a question Candy should be asking but it popped out of her mouth without thought.

"I have teased some of my cousins, but have yet to be broken by a male. I wanted to wait for my first 'needing moon', for the change from a child to a woman. Do you not have the same where you come from?"

"Not really, no." Goodness, she'd been eighteen when she had her first sexual experience. It had been so disappointing and physically uncomfortable that she hadn't been eager to retry sex again for two years.

"What about venereal diseases, if this moon causes such a degree of lust, doesn't that present a problem?"

Celcee's expression showed complete confusion. "Do you mean illness?"

"Well, yes." *This was awkward.* "Illnesses spread because of messing around. Or do the men wear condoms over their, you know what?" She was pointing to where a condom would go on the male anatomy.

Celcee's brows creased. "Messing . . . ah, fucking?"

"Uh, yep that would be the word." *Embarrassing!*

"We have no such illness, as why would the Moon Goddess or Earth Mother punish us for what is natural and a gifted pleasure they bestow upon us? A man and woman are to meet, not have some covering between. What a shame to not feel the man's hot seed as it fills you. I am looking forward to the feeling."

Apparently so, by the expression on Celcee's face. Candy nodded while trying to imagine the notion. Use of condoms meant she'd never felt a man's 'hot seed' either and wondered how it felt.

It certainly wasn't her place to decide what was right or wrong, and by the sound of it, the populace had little choice in the matter when the 'needing' began. Nor was it anything she'd be participating in.

The dress Celcee brought her was a color best described as almost cream-color, with a hint of mocha. She was trying to be optimistic—in reality the fabric was simply another shade of beige. As Candy slipped it on, the feel of the soft silk against her bare skin felt luxurious. The fabric draped at the neckline and went to her ankles. It pulled in slightly at the waist following her figure, then flared from her knees to her feet.

The fabric and fit showed off too much of her figure in her opinion, but she needed something to wear. At least it wasn't sheer and had a nice weight to it, providing Candy a pseudo-sense of modesty. Without underwear she felt a little naked and a lot self-conscious, but Celcee reassured her this was the custom of this land. To not hide the gifts from the Earth Mother overly much, but to embrace and be thankful for them.

Realizing how her pep talk hadn't really helped, Celcee handed Candy a cup of mead to sip. The sweet wine rolled down Candy's throat and she would swear it landed in her pelvis warming her. Another sip. Candy enjoyed the sweetness and liquid courage it provided. Two more sips and Candy wondered who needed underwear, anyway? Totally overrated and one more item to launder.

The clothing situation here seemed reminiscent of Cherry Ann's recent couture choices. On the other hand, the fabric of the dress was so soft that if she wore anything under it then the underclothing would be more than obvious, in a land where underclothing was foreign.

Well when in Rome and all that—she'd give it a shot as long as she stayed somewhat modest looking and this dress did provide that. Another sip of mead helped to settle it. Still, Candy couldn't help but wonder if her derriere would jiggle too much and if Spanx might be available here.

Yeah, right. They didn't even wear underwear, so Spanx was totally not happening.

When Celcee left, Thorne walked back into the room. "Why are women so slow to done a simple garment?" Despite his words a hint of a smile was on his face.

His eyes wandered over her as if assessing every inch of her. That warm feeling in her stomach moved lower. Between the mead, and this man, she could easily dissolve into an estrogen pool.

"Well, we try to look nice and it takes a little time I guess. Plus Celcee was sharing girl talk."

Candy was trying to fluff her hair a bit. This place didn't seem to have any mousse or hair products to help with the task. She shuddered to imagine how her hair would behave on a humid day without hairspray. Frankenstein's bride would have nothing on her.

"My Lady," Thorne gave a nod of his head, "nice does not compare to how enthralling you look. Would you care to stretch your legs in the garden with me?"

"I feel much better and think that's a great idea. Do you mind if I ask you questions while we walk?"

Thorne put his hand against her back to guide her out the door and toward the steps. The feel of his palm felt warm and relaxing. Candy suppressed a contented sigh. How easily this man's touch seemed to reduce her apprehension while warming her like sweet mead.

While the expression on his face told her he easily knew how to charm a woman to quivering amoeba status, his verbal response surprised her. "You may ask anything from a man on the night of the 'needing moon', as this is the one evening we are truly your slaves." With a wink he added, "Tonight I am yours to command my Lady."

In that case maybe I could tie him to the bed! For shame Candy.

However her preposterous thought made for a delightful fleeting guilty visual.

"You're so totally hot . . . *umm*, handsome." Good grief, maybe she was better off with the single word commentary she usually gave to men. And no more mead if she was going to blurt out what she was thinking without any filters. "Do all men here wear clothing to show off their stunning physical attributes on the 'needing moon'?"

Well, so much for any conversation filters!

Thorne's smile grew bigger with every word she stupidly uttered. She hadn't seen him so light hearted before. Wasn't it nice to provide him with comedy while she blurted out embarrassing confessions?

That's Candy, always one to please others.

Leaning down to her, she felt his warm breath as he whispered in her ear, "Whatsoever to gain notice from the one you desire. I hoped to please your eyes. Mayhap I did."

He straightened and took her arm. "Women oft tend to dress to show more flesh on this night—to offer more bait to the fisherman one might say." His eyes sparkled with mischief. "If this pleases you, I would always wear such to keep your eyes from another."

Oh dear. He'd noticed she was gawking, awkward but true, and who wouldn't gawk at *that* alluring physique? Celcee was correct—he could be totally charming. Way too charming. Damp panties kind of charming.

With his hand at her back, Thorne began guiding her down the staircase. Not being used to long dresses, or a distracting man who oozed pheromones while at her side, Candy got her foot caught in the hem. She tripped and started to fall.

Thorne simply extended his arm from her back, to around her waist, and lowered her to the landing, as though she was weightless. The incident happened so quickly and smoothly that she almost escaped feeling embarrassed. Almost.

Thankfully he was kind enough to not mention her slip of step as he released his arm from her waist and guided her out the arched side door into a garden area.

At one time the large expanse of garden had probably been beautiful with all types of colorful flowers. There was a large gazebo supported by five columns of stone that had a roof made of flowering vines.

The monochromatic beige landscaped garden was fragrant, but the lack of color left the blooming flowers disappointing to the senses. The place needed color desperately. Even the spirals of lack-luster evergreens (now 'ever-beige') were void of vitality.

It was a travesty how all of the landscape was now in dull shades of graduating tans. Not a hint of pink, coral, yellow, or red or even what should have been predominantly green.

The entire garden's appearance just proved how the difference between a weed and a flower really related to a gardener's sense of aesthetics and nature's use of color. With everything beige, all the plants could all be dead weeds as far as Candy was concerned. The entirety looked terribly anemic from apparent loss of chlorophyll. All the plantings tragically required a transfusion of virulent green.

In Savannah the spring landscape would be ripe with bright blooming azaleas. Spring flowers would be planted in planters and window boxes. How sad to know this land she now stood in was bereft of color to enliven the senses.

Such a terrible and unimaginable loss to no longer see vivid colors, and she wondered how such a thing was even possible. Could it be some dreadful virus? If so, she couldn't chance spreading it to Savannah and ruining that beautiful town.

She let a sigh escape. Undeniably this place was becoming more mystifying by the hour. Much like her interest in the man next to her. Her loose tongue and curiosity took over her better sense. Again!

"Celcee tells me she's never seen you partake of the women at the festival. She seemed disappointed."

This question couldn't be categorized as anything other than being just plain nosey, and certainly not really her nature regarding private matters. At least not until tonight, and curiosity about this man.

Obviously his presence lessened her inhabitations the same as two stiff drinks might. Not that she'd ever had two stiff drinks in a night. Drunkenness was something she abhorred.

He *tsked*. "She is but a child, I prefer a woman. Do you wish to know if I get the 'needing' or are you asking another question?" Thorne's eyes met hers and Candy quickly looked away before they scalded her. Dang the man was hot!

She could have sworn raw lust radiated from those chocolate-colored eyes framed by his long sable lashes. Goodness, how she loved chocolate—especially tonight. By nature, Candy would have never discussed such a personal topic in public.

Like *never. Ever!*

Maybe not even in private. Certainly not with a guy, not even her friend Liam, and definitely not a man the likes of

Thorne. This was entirely too intimate of a conversation for her sensibilities.

But she seemed less restrained as the evening went on, and that was entirely uncharacteristic of her. She kept admonishing herself *to be quiet*. It seemed her perverse curiosity was deaf to good manners.

"Maybe some people don't feel the influence as much and that's why she doesn't know the females you have . . . *um*, been with. Oh my! Maybe I assumed wrong and you're drawn to men. Which is fine of course, although a terrible pity to womankind. I'm so sorry—I shouldn't even be asking such personal questions." Her words became rushed, as she realized they shouldn't have been spoken at all.

Prying wasn't like her. But if this hot guy was gay, she was going to cry at the terrible unjust cruelty.

Please don't be gay!

His feet stopped walking and he turned to her. "Candy I am absolutely not, nor have ever been, a lover of men. I feel the 'needing moon' as strongly as every other male, of this I assure you. In this matter I choose not to be public in my choices and needs. As a ruler, people oft times expect more of you than they have a right to.

"My sister is the opposite . . . she publicly and wantonly shares herself with whomever she chooses at the moment. Her sole concern is the promise of a gratifying release. Levenia knows and cares naught of the men she gives herself to. I doubt she even knows the names or faces of those with whom she lays. Nor does she hold concerns as to if the male is married or unmarried. And though this is not considered ill on the 'needing moon', it settles poorly with me. Should not vows be valued above indiscriminant rutting?"

Thorne's eyes betrayed distress. With a resigned sigh he continued. "Her behavior disheartens me. I want better for her than pubic displays of uninhibited lust. It seems as though she lacks an inner sense of worth, and such grieves me. I have raised her since she was ten summers of age and fear I have sorely failed her."

He turned his head away as if realizing he'd openly shared something personal and obviously hurtful. After he took a deep breath his tone softened and he turned back to Candy. Gazing into her eyes he brushed his fingertips through her hair. His finger stopped to rest against her pulse point and he raised an eyebrow before he spoke.

"You seem much interested in this subject for someone who has never felt the 'needing moon'. The effects can begin early in the day or eve for some."

Thorne wrapped his arms around her and pulled her against his chest, then took her small hand and placed it over his beating heart. The strong beat could easily be felt hammering through his leather vest.

"Feel how deeply my heart beats?" With her nod he continued. "The early effects of the night's promise, and having you so near. Candy, I am hardened beyond comfort, and you surely know how deeply I desire you."

She was so close that no space remained between them making it impossible to ignore the fact that his solid, very swollen groin was pushed against her. Shame on her, but it felt impressive and inviting.

"You tremble, and your pulse quickens. Mayhap you feel the hunger within your womanly core?"

"But I don't want to." Her timid response came out close to a whisper.

How awkward to admit. Could this really be happening to her? It was so crazy. She had a moral compass and Thorne's presence kept spinning it south, to her girlie parts.

"Your eyes dilate as well, showing your physical interest. This frightens you, does it not?"

Embarrassed by his observations and her "interest" as he called it, she nodded.

"I would be gentle, taking time to please you—if you were to consider me." Thorne's voice was deep, filled with a raspy sensuous quality, promising the most incredible delights of the flesh.

The temptation this man imparted rivaled holding imported Belgium chocolate to her lips—the rich aroma, the promise of mouth-watering melting goodness, sumptuous bliss—all too alluring for her senses to ignore.

Her moral compass was failing to keep her on her path. Salivating, Candy unconsciously licked her lower lip.

Your personal code and moral compass, remember?

"Does my scarred face sicken you?" Thorne's eyes searched hers for the answer.

"No." The simple word came out sounding like an elongated whimper, reminding her of how inept she was when it came to being sensual. Was a whimper really the epitome of her sensuality with a man like Thorne?

She added three more words. "Not at all."

"Then tis fear of this night?"

"Yes."

Pitiful, simply pitiful, Candy.

"Why so, when the Moon Goddess makes us as we are on this night? Tonight is meant for heightened physical need and pleasure to be shared between lovers."

The timbre of his voice was enough to convince any woman to drop her drawers, panties or thong. That is, if they wore those here, which obviously they didn't. Of course with a man this hot who needed an extra layer of clothing?

OMG! I'm becoming a total slut!

Finally her brain engaged and began to regurgitate meaningful communication. Or so she hoped. "None of this make sense to me, and I don't know this Moon Goddess. Plus, I don't do casual sex with a man I don't know. That just isn't me, or what I do. I need to know and care about the man. It probably seems really old fashioned, but I don't sleep around or do booty call."

"Sleep around? Booty call?" His eyebrow furrowed in confusion.

In an exasperated tone Candy thought of other euphemisms he might grasp. "You know like 'hitting it', 'giving it up', 'doing it' . . ."

His perplexed expression softened, then a smile curled his lips. "Fucking?"

"*Umm*, that too." She blushed. Raspberry pink was a good color on her, probably how she looked about now. Candy hoped to avoid the all too familiar fire engine red. Not her best look, totally wrong shade of red for her complexion.

"Then 'it' refers to fucking? How strange that sex is called something other than the act it describes." With his heavy lidded eyes and a sigh, he stepped back from her.

"And you have no liking of me, and we remain strangers as well? I regret you feel that way. Then you will likely be holding me to my promise?"

Oh, she liked him plenty and Candy actually felt like they had known each other far longer than they had, making this situation so much more difficult. Finally she forced out a whispered response.

"Please."

Her voice sounded more like a frog croak, not at all feminine or sexy. Unless you were a male frog, then maybe. . . or maybe not. But she didn't want to sound like an amphibian tonight; she wanted to be attractive to the hunter with the gorgeous drool-worthy physique. This was going as well as bubble gum in her hair, and just as sticky and embarrassing.

Kissing the top of her head, Thorne turned to walk Candy back to her room. "How I wish I had not made such a promise. Though I assure you no man will ask a woman of your beauty to do any *sleeping* on this night. Such is not what a man will be wanting from you."

Didn't his statement make her feel like she rocked it?

Once back in her room, he took a quick look around as if making sure it was safe for her and then turned to leave. Candy watched his backside as he walked towards the door with a rolling confident gait.

She couldn't help but admire every last inch of his muscled thighs, tight derriere, broad shoulders and those soft curls at the ends of his hair that begged her fingers to play with them. Although the artist side of her admired his finely crafted anatomy, tonight the female in her more than appreciated his form. She craved it.

Yummy.

When he suddenly stopped, dropped his head forward while tilting his head to the side, she feared he'd actually read her thoughts.

Yep, totally guilty as charged.

A strand of sandy colored hair fell across his face, curling at the end as if gesturing her to come to him. She fought her desire to step forward. As if he knew her thoughts, he directed an enticing warming-to-her-core crooked smile directly at her. That made her feel like melting ice cream—all runny and ready to slide to the floor.

"You need aught Lassie?"

Apparently I do.

Darn him for being so fine, but she steadfastly shook her head no. It took all her control of her neck muscles to prevent nodding 'yes' to him. She prayed her gesture hadn't come out as befuddled looking as her feelings.

As he left the room he instructed her to lock the door lest someone erringly walked in. He also reminded little Ono to guard her companion.

Meanwhile, all Candy could see was that smile peeking from under his lock of hair, showing a hint of perfect white teeth between his very full kissable lips—the feature she found most enticing on his face. You always heard about how a man might be a 'leg', 'boob', or 'ass' man. Who knew she was a 'lip' woman. Come on, what didn't she like about Thorne?

The heat that man generated could cause rampant global warming. No man had the right to be so hot. Certainly it wasn't fair to any female who was trying to resist him, and somehow she doubted any woman did succeed in resisting this man if he set his mind to it.

That man really is walking pheromones.

When the door closed she fanned herself and wished she had an ice cold Coke to help cool her down. How she missed her sweet bubbly caffeine pick-me-ups at moments like this.

'

Chapter Three
Candy

Sounds of music and laughter awoke Candy. She got up, stretched, and felt remarkably renewed. Her legs felt considerably better and her thighs now offered her a truce. Her nap had been refreshing.

While pacing the floor, not sure what to do with herself, she heard a knock on the door. Candy hadn't expected Thorne to return, but he probably wanted to check up on her.

With a quick check of her dress and hair in the mirror she frowned at a rebellious strand of hair sticking straight up. Bedhead at its finest. Quickly wetting her fingers she slicked the wayward piece back where it belonged, then reached to open the door.

Opening it a crack she spotted a handsome man with his hair pulled back and tied with a string of leather. He was nonchalantly leaning against the railing as if posing for a photo-op.

When he turned and looked at her, his eyes traveled from her head to her toes. It was a little unsettling how they lingered uncomfortably long on feminine parts of her anatomy.

"Ah, so you are the little trinket Thorne brought home. I am his close and utmost handsome cousin, Shemmar, and will accompany you. You might enjoy some food and music before the full rise of the 'needing moon'." He quickly pulled Candy into the hall, closed the door, and ushered her towards the stairway.

Shemmar reached for her arm and put it through his. Candy followed his lead down the steps, this time carefully lifting her hem to prevent tripping. The main hall was full of people eating, drinking and . . . doing other stuff.

Candy tried to not look at them as they engaged in carnal activities. If she was into painting orgies, these people presented enough provocative substance to rival Thomas Rowlandson's works.

Oh my, was that position even possible? Seemed it was. Who knew?

Quit looking, close your eyes.

Time to focus on something else. "Thorne didn't mention you to me. So he asked you to escort me?"

"No doubt he was afraid my good looks would make him even less appealing with all those scars."

That hardly sounded like Thorne to her, but then she barcly knew the man. Besides, Thorne's scars only added character to the hunter as far as she was concerned, and she didn't mind them in the least. Actually, they were darn sexy on him. They provided testament to his rugged 'don't screw with me' looks, which made her hormones want to do cartwheels—right into his arms.

The grand hall was littered with tables covered with crisp linens and foods of every kind. Except without their expected natural colors they looked terribly bland, as if the loss of color resulted in the loss of some of their taste.

However, the food's aromas were as expected and she enjoyed the wafts of spices, followed by sweet and fruity smells as well as savory roasted meats. If only the items looked as delicious as they smelled. Every fine chef knew presentation meant everything, and obviously that included the need for color. This travesty of color loss affected so much in this place.

Music soon filled the room and provided a unique blend of sounds, with drums of every size, shape and reverberations. Some were being played with what looked like slender bamboo brooms while others were being beaten with large padded sticks. There were some odd looking flutes as well, and the music carried a hauntingly exotic and erotic quality. The melody reminded her of the song *Team* by Lordes.

Mega-sized pots of the honey concoction were placed everywhere she looked, and it appeared couples simply reached in when they were ready to do the deed. Somehow sticking fingers into the shared large pots of contraceptives seemed less than sanitary to her. Candy reminded herself that in this land she was a guest and had no right to judge.

Still, *eww*.

As they moved through the crowd all forms of bedding became apparent. One large bed was centered directly beneath the domed glass circle of the high ceiling. The sheeting on the bed appeared clean and crisp as if great attention had been given to the bedding. Beige perfumed petals were strewn across it as well. Unlike every other flat horizontal spot, surprisingly no one occupied this bed.

Shemmar leaned close to Candy and she could smell liquor on his breath as he spoke. "That is Levenia's bed, as she enjoys the heightened sexual release when the moon reaches its zenith and shines directly upon her nude body." He was looking up at the transparent oculus.

"She'll have sex in the middle of the room with all these people watching?"

Candy couldn't help be a little shocked by the woman's brazen self-confidence and willingness to be seen so intimately. Then she recalled what Thorne had said about his sister. How he didn't consider her behavior as confidence, but rather a lack of self-respect. Candy tended to agree. Certainly this was something she couldn't ever envision doing.

"Indeed, she relishes being watched when she is absorbed by passion. A shy partner would never gratify her."

The more Shemmar spoke the less Candy liked him. "It sounds like there are few inhibitions between men and women."

"All is allowed, and it hardly impeded my lust when I fucked her upon this bed. It requires a lot for Levenia to beg you to cease, though I was man enough."

Candy was disgusted by his braggart need to share, which seemed to please Shemmar all the more. Was this guy actually getting turned-on by her discomfort?

What a total tool.

Shemmar drew closer to her. "If you are the timid sort, I can take you to a more private room."

She chose to ignore his presumptuous sickening remark knowing she wouldn't be sharing anything with this man no matter what that Moon Goddess wanted. Shemmar would never be her type, not that she knew enough about men to know what her type would be. Except, well maybe more like Joe.

Despite thinking Joe's name, it was the hunter's physique and face that Candy pictured, and the memory of his lips touching her hair that she felt.

They stopped to watch a group of erotic female dancers who wore skirts made from numerous sections of long flowing chiffon. As the dancers twirled the fabric seemed to float and when they lifted their legs it exposed—OMG—*everything!*

She hoped none of their mothers or fathers were here to see that! This place had more exposed flesh than Las Vegas. The entire effect would be more spectacular if the fabrics were in festive colors. Maybe adding a little crotch piece or thong too because this was just too revealing for her comfort.

Looking more closely, she realized that the graceful dancers wore no tops. They were painted with henna artistry forming intricate patterns across their entire torsos. If not for the movement of their swaying breasts, they would've looked like they had clothing on.

Many of the designs used the female's nipples as the center of a flower with entwined vines surrounded the breasts. The skillful application of the henna reflected the many hours had it taken to paint the dye.

Their sensuality was punctuated by the beating of the variety of drums, some as large as the men who beat them, while others were small and hand held. Then a woman's voice was added to the music, carrying a somewhat sensual melody with exotic undertones.

The singer's words were unfamiliar, sounding similar to humming along with the music. The entirety was entertaining and the complimenting graceful movements of the performers could easily rival any spellbinding music video. Probably one rated 'X', considering the over-revealing kicks.

Once the performance was over, the dancers ran into the crowd. Each female was grabbed at by men until one would finally catch the giggling and squealing female and carry her off to a bed platform or even down onto the floor. Some even used the tabletops, simply pushing food to the side. The lovers were having the time of their lives under the influence of the 'needing moon'.

Did they even know each other's names? Nametags might come in handy on these monthly get-togethers.

So many people were wrapped around each other, and hearing their rutting grunts and moans of unbridled lust made her uncomfortable. Those numerous entwined bodies enjoying carnal abandon reminded her of some of the Renaissance artworks such as *Garden of Earthly Delights* by Bosch.

In Candy's case, she didn't feel a need or desire to draw the scene.

Almost all the beds were now being used for more than mere lounging. The space had become a crowded room of covetousness and people were being too intimate for her comfort. But then it couldn't really be called intimate if so public, now could it?

This clarified what Thorne meant. Intimacy wasn't truly possible in these surroundings. This was very public decadence, an orgy by any definition. Some couplings were in groups of three or more, while others were simply two people sharing an urgent primal need.

Some sex looked utterly raw and forceful, and at first that disturbed her until realizing everyone seemed more than willing to consent to what was happening around them and to them. The need for physical release overrode tenderness and no one complained.

The sights became increasingly and erotically awkward, and her moral compass was spinning out of control. Her desire and 'need' was mounting unbidden and Candy couldn't pretend otherwise as anxiety rose to the point where she feared hyperventilating.

No way was she planning to end up horizontal on the floor, in this room and with all these licentious people!

Glancing up she saw the position of the moon. The rim of the culprit sphere was creeping ever so slowly towards the edge of the glass-domed ceiling.

The realization increased her nervousness and the room began closing in around her, suffocating her. This was too visceral for her tastes and she needed to leave *now*.

"I need to return to my room. I'm not going to participate, and this was a mistake."

Apparently Shemmar disagreed, as he held her wrist tightly and drew her in closer.

"Surely you are not so modest? Does so much passion frighten you? Soon the moon shall peak. When it does, the lust within all of these people will rise as well, and coupling will be everywhere there is a spot. Men will be on top, underneath, or behind, it matters not on the 'needing moon'. All is allowed, as this night has no taboos to consenting couples. Even husbands and wives may choose another on this night. We shall stay and enjoy its fervor together, as lovers."

Forcing his lips to Candy's, she tried to squirm away while he wrapped his other arm around her. Hid hand was sliding down her back, grabbing her bottom, pulling her closer. Feeling his body, including his hardened groin, pushed against her repulsed her. She might actually vomit on him, maybe then he'd let go of her.

"No one cares if you fight me woman, as some enjoy playing the game roughly. I have decided I have want of you, and my cousin is a selfish man to bring you to our home and not share."

With his hot and liquored breath against her ear, he added the epitome of insults. "I can tell you desire me as well."

Like hell I do!

Realizing Shemmar's full and sickening intent, and how the concept of 'mutual consent' had left the building, she quickly and forcibly drew her knee up into his crotch.

When he staggered back, shocked at being physically rebuked (and in pain from her gonad assault), Candy turned to run to safety.

Her body slammed directly into a marble column.

More accurately, Thorne's chest.

Her hands had landed against his bare skin where the vest didn't cover. As her fingers met his flesh a humming sensation began within her, something else new and confusing. It required all her self-control to not begin caressing his muscled and honed body. He felt so good.

At that moment Candy conceded she really had a thing for men's chests, she'd become a 'chest' woman. Goodness, such a perfect torso all rippled with abdominal hills and valleys of perfect male landscape. She'd love a deed to this piece of territory. His topography was breathtaking.

Thorne pried her hands from his skin. Like Velcro she didn't want to let go, but unless she planned to dig her fingernails into him she had little choice.

Looking down at her and then back to his cousin, Thorne gently pushed her to the side as he shook his head. "You cause much trouble to me Lassie."

Guilt engulfed her, until he winked at her.

Seeing Thorne standing between himself and his intended conquest incensed Shemmar. He pulled a knife from his right boot; the glint from the metal blade reflecting his intent.

Thorne's expression foretold a warning loudly promising, *"try to take her and you will die."* Everyone but Shemmar heard the silent threat. Seemingly his cousin was deaf to good sense.

Slowly shaking his head, as if the knife meant nothing to him, Thorne addressed his cousin. "I warn you

Shemmar, this will not end well. She is not for you, nor has she chosen to be with you."

The music had since stopped, and all faces were turned to see what would happen next. Occasionally jealousy and lust could lead to a fight on the 'needing moon'. Their ruler was a renowned warrior and would have the advantage. Any man would be daft to threaten him over a female, or otherwise.

A sneer preluded Shemmar's words. "I think she has. You think to claim her when I wager you have not even glimpsed her nakedness, cousin? She seems quite shy, mayhap she teases. A man like myself can remedy her teasing ways."

"Aye, I claim her, and found her nakedness pure perfection. A wager you lose, but you shall not be privy to her in any manner. Put your blade away and pick another. Despite your conduct, most women will welcome your handsome face above them. This female will not be one of your conquests."

Shemmar's hold on the knife tightened as his eyes narrowed. "You are one to speak! Though small, perchance we could share her. She simply plays a game of hard to catch, unlike your sister Levenia who doth never feign to be unattainable."

"Beware your words or I shall be forced to end you, not truly a task I would abhor. Lest you forget, by my mandate Levenia rules over you, as do I. How easily either of us could disavow your leisurely existence, even forfeit your life altogether."

With a chiding smirk Shemmar responded, "I have said naught but what every man in this room knows to be true. Levenia lusts for any large cock. I have heard you are overly well hung. How many times has she enjoyed yours, *cousin?*"

Thorne's fist struck Shemmar in the jaw. The force of impact enough to drop his cousin. As Thorne turned to leave, he scooped up Candy to take her with him.

The gathering of people sent out yells of bravado and clapping as their ruler carried her from the room and towards the staircase leading to the bedrooms. At the top of the staircase he finally set Candy down.

Stupid didn't begin to describe how Candy felt for having been so naïve and needing to be rescued. And then there was the issue of being carried again. If this kept happening she was going to become dependent on having his finely muscled arms wrapped around her.

Not the worst vice a woman could fall prey to, but undoubtedly as habitually intoxicating.

Then she saw red. Literally.

Blood was flowing down to his forearm. "He cut you! Let's get you to the bedroom so I can tend to it."

A smile crossed Thorne's face as he looked down to his arm. "A small cut Lassie. He has very poor aim and is a coward as well. A disappointing relative."

"I don't think it looks insignificant since blood is dripping onto the floor." Using her most determined maternal voice Candy waved her hands to usher him forward.

"Into my room, so I can wrap it." He didn't budge.

Figures. I'll so suck at motherhood, just like Mom had.

He folded his arms across his chest, a glint of mischievousness played in his eyes. "Had I known by a small cut I would be invited into your room, I would have drawn my blade to myself far sooner."

Candy ignored his words and steered him into her room, closed the door behind them and locked it.

She turned and looked up at him. "I don't trust him to not come back, and it seems not *all* men here like to knock." Her accusatory words to Thorne went unheeded, although Shemmar's blatant action didn't.

His anger seethed. "He came unsought to your door? I should go back and destroy him for his insult to you. I thought mayhap you favored his company—his handsome face."

She gave Thorne a push to sit him on the edge of the bed; afraid he might otherwise storm off for a second punch to Shemmar. Then she mumbled, "I think you did enough to his jaw." By his scowl and pinched eyebrows, Thorne disagreed.

There was a large carved armoire to the side of the room and she went to look inside for something to wrap his wound. The contents weren't as promising as she'd hoped. Not really a great deal to choose from and certainly nothing like Band-Aids. No Sponge Bob bandages for her hunter.

Candy returned carrying several items including a wet cloth, ointment that smelled like it would annihilate any flesh necrotizing germs, plus clean sheeting, to serve for bandaging.

Turning around she saw Thorne sitting without his vest, causing her to ogle his now nude and oh-so-fine chest.

Yep, solid as granite with muscles carved finer than any sculpture of a Greek god. A physique like his provided testament to strength and prowess. And now, apparently she'd become a certifiable 'abs' woman. Candy closed her mouth to keep all drool contained.

Eventually her eyes moved to his wounded arm, having almost forgotten about his need for medical intervention. Thankfully the wound was no longer bleeding. Taking her sweet time as she gawked at his chiseled abs obviously meant his knife wound had plenty of time to coagulate. Thankfully the man hadn't bled to death while she was distracted!

Swallowed your drool girl before it slips out.

"I favor this vest and wished it not become bloodied," he said as her attention again moved across his bare skin.

She liked the vest too. She liked the flesh under it even more so.

Hmmm. More likely he removed it just to make me swoon at the sight.

Shamelessly she did consider swooning—right on top of him. Taking a deep breath to steady her pounding heart, Candy began administering to his wound. Touching his skin initiated that humming sensation again. Strangely it made her feel . . . connected to him.

This had been her fault for being so trusting of some man she didn't even know. The result had led to Thorne being cut. Talk about feeling guilty.

What a foolish action, certainly very reckless and not typical of your sensibilities.

As if her guilt wasn't enough—her conscience was more than hasty to add its two cents.

"I want you to know I only went with your disgusting cousin, who isn't appealing to me and even less so now, because he made it sound as if you wanted me to. He's pompous and definitely not a man I would ever be attracted to. And trust me, I'm being generous in my assessment of him."

Thorne's eyes simmered with interest. "And what type man would you favor?"

You.

The words were left unspoken, but Candy knew she was in deep trouble because right now he was exactly what she favored. His sun-bronzed skin warmed her senses and his honed body taunted hers. It was unfeasible to imagine a more comforting place to be than just being held close against his chest.

Your focus should be on attending to his wound.

Thrown back into reality, she tried to rip the sheet with her trembling hands. The darn zillion-thread count fabric didn't tear, because obviously Thorne wasn't the only fine thing in this land—they also had really high quality linens.

Taking it from her hands, Thorne tore off a strip providing a very makeshift bandage. While watching how easily he managed to tear the sheeting with his strength she mumbled, "It was my mistake to trust him, and I won't fall for that again. I try to learn from life's little lessons."

My goodness, did any man have biceps so fine? Maybe she was actually a 'bicep' woman?

Thorne handed her the torn piece of fabric. "How do you manage without a man to aide you, or have you a husband?"

With a sigh she shook her head. "No husband, but I do have a neighbor friend who helps me with epic tasks, such as rock throwing or sheet tearing. You know those usual tasks in a typical day."

Thankfully the cut wasn't so deep as to require stiches. Gently cleaning off the wound, Candy then applied the nasty ointment and began wrapping the homemade bandage.

Aware of how his eyes were focused on her, she was afraid to meet his coveting gaze—afraid of what she felt. This was the 'needing'. Maybe the moonlight from the downstairs sky window triggered it, or truthfully it could easily be this man.

Near enough to smell his unique male scent she wondered if it was from his soap and leather, or his pheromones? Whatever the scent, it inebriated her.

Glancing at the wrapped wound Thorne spoke. "You most likely have many men who would be of service to you in any manner you would have them."

Knowing he was watching her with those hungry eyes just made her more uncomfortable. And just what did he mean by "in any manner you would have them"? Did he think she juggled men like some circus act? Hardly.

"I seldom go out with men." *Boy, talk about an understatement.* "It isn't that I'm not attracted to men, but I don't believe in one night stands. Meaning the man takes you out, expects sex at the end of the night, and then you never hear from the guy again. I want a relationship, not sex with a stranger. Not my thing—never has been, and never will be."

"One time with you would not be enough. I would take you many times. First for the 'need'—then for the 'want' of you . . . do you understand the difference?"

Such gorgeous penetrating dark eyes, they were like decadent bittersweet chocolate. How she loved bittersweet chocolate, and she could swear his voice deepened when he'd spoken those words. Have mercy, but those were really sexy things for him to say.

Where had this guy learned how to be so incredibly panty pooling hot? Feeling ready to start fanning herself to cool down, Candy quickly stopped before he'd see how affected she was. The temperature in the bedroom had raised enough to melt both chocolate and her.

"I think I do," Candy quietly answered.

Hot, hot, hot. I refuse to fan myself in front of him.

After administering his cut to her satisfaction, and with much more care than it probably necessitated, she no longer had an excuse to evade his face. Unless maybe she tied a cute bow over the bandage, which Candy suspected no card-carrying male would tolerate.

No longer able to avoid the man in front of her she spoke of something the servant girl had mentioned. "You know, you hold quite the reputation. Celcee says, 'men pray to avoid Thorne's wrath, while women pray for his love'."

Thorne scoffed as he looked over the bandaging she'd done. "Foolishness. I protect my own, including all within my realm. And though I hope my people hold respect for me, tis not as if women clamor to be at my side. They covet what I can offer them, not the truth of me. What female would willingly chose a man with a marred face?"

It took all her resolve not to jump up and down with her arm waving in the air yelling *"me, me, me"* like a first grader. That scar wasn't anything less than enticing to her female-cheering hormones. Candy glanced down at her feet. And how many times had she already tripped due to his distracting presence?

Since I'm a klutz it might not be because of him. Yeah, right.

As she looked up at his promising eyes, Candy murmured, "I'm in trouble."

This was an embarrassing admission for her. For the first time in her life she felt an unaccustomed longing beyond anything she'd ever felt for a man before. The feeling made her uncomfortable on several levels.

"Aye, I sense thus. You tremble again as well. Tell me, what would you have of me Lassie?" He was stroking her cheek with the back of his big hand.

Erotic warmth flowed through her as she felt herself leaning in to the feel of his flesh. But she needed so much more contact than merely his hand on her face and was beginning to feel a deep aching between her legs.

Looking down, his strained leathers provided impressive evidence of his arousal and need. Those leathers indicated he was very well packaged and she wanted to see and feel what was beneath so badly that it took all her resolve not to reach for his crotch.

Don't you dare girl! He isn't your birthday gift to unwrap. Definitely turning into a total ho!

Her body *needed* him. So this was why they called it a 'needing moon'. Very fitting, because her feeling of 'need' was creating a huge hunger within her and she wanted Thorne to be her repast—and what a fine buffet his faultless body would make. Candy wanted to lick, nibble and taste everything he had to offer, something she'd never been tempted to do with any man.

Take a calming breath, gain control before you speak and for goodness sakes, try to sound intelligent.

"If it's this intense with every full moon how can anyone stand it?" She was certainly finding it difficult and knew her tone revealed her frustration, and for good reason.

He nodded then shrugged. "Mayhap not as demanding as this 'needing moon' will be for me, as already I held great desire of you, and now I want nothing more than to be with you, and inside of you. You must decide soon else I go mad by my 'need' of you Lassie."

"What if we just ignore this 'needing'?"

"A goddess's gift cannot be ignored and never have I tried so hard to fight it. I beg of you to either choose me, or lock me out of your room before I cannot control my lust. Truly my 'need' and 'want' of you are greater than I can endure."

"Do you say that to all the women, because it sounds like a come-on." She'd meant for her words to be joking. By Thorne's pained expression they weren't.

"Candy, I would not speak falsely to you. I find it insufferable to remain so close yet not within you."

She was afraid to meet his eyes again and didn't want to picture him with another female. That amazing chest of his against another woman made a painful visual. Tonight was going to be one tearful night—alone.

"This is really difficult for me, I've never been intimately carefree. I don't want you to leave, even though I realize you're going to need to find another woman."

Was she just being selfish to want to keep him from having his needs taken care of? So it seemed, because she didn't want to let him leave. There was no doubt Thorne was a virile man, and if she was suffering he'd probably be feeling it even more so. By now, he probably had what men referred to as 'blue balls'. Maybe she should take a peek to see?

Good grief Candy, what are you thinking?

She knew full well what she was thinking. The strain in his leathers and that long hardened rod left little to her imagination.

Thorne stood, picked up his vest and headed to the door. "Nor do I Lassie. Tis not by my choice and the Moon Goddess will not be denied."

Closing her eyes she asked herself when she'd ever met a more compelling man, let alone a *straight* guy she could feel so at ease with? A man who heated her in this manner? A man so utterly alluring? A man she wanted to be naked with *without* hiding under the covers? That was a first.

No, no and no, she reprimanded herself.

She couldn't do this. Remember you have a personal code, rules, and a moral compass she reminded herself— repeatedly.

However she couldn't quite let him go either. Her hunger cried out to be fed by this seductive and enthralling man. Inherently Candy held no doubt he could pleasure her until she was rendered completely and blissfully senseless. She heard an inner 'pop'. It was her compass cracking.

Please say yes, her hormones begged. *Rules were meant to be broken.*

Says who? She argued.

Your estrogen! Countered her girlie parts. *He's soooo worth it.*

Okay she couldn't quarrel that.

As she argued with herself she saw him head languidly towards the door. His backside was so finely made it should be on display as a fine work of burnished bronze.

And how many women, or men, would pat his posterior as they walked past a sculpture of him? His bronze derriere would never acquire patina with all the deserving attention it would get. A pat here, a caress there, his bronzed bottom would be polished shiny like a teacher's apple.

And Candy liked apples. A lot.

Oh please, come on! He's impossibly sensual. Just once follow your instincts.

Her instincts had never spoken up before regarding having intimacy with a man. They had always remained quiet little buggers. At least not until Thorne showed up all sinfully tempting while touting his testosterone-laden-physique and wafting with those intoxicating pheromones she was breathing in.

It was difficult for *'reasonable*-Candy' to argue with *'needful*-Candy'—really difficult.

Meanwhile, Candy's intuition screamed at her, yelling how Thorne was the one man not to let go of.

But what did her intuition know? And since it hadn't bothered to speak up before now, she wasn't even sure if her intuition provided a reliable source.

Her female parts cried out with distress as Candy noticed she was trembling. Thorne was like a male version of the mythical sirens luring her to disaster. His pheromones were calling, and calling...

Lordy girl, this isn't the time to ponder the ringtone, just pick up your inner cellphone and answer that call!

Chapter Four
Thorne

His emotional avalanche started yester eve.

There she'd sat, a frightened delicate woman, huddled in the dirt within dangerous terrain.

When her beautiful green eyes met his, his heart quaked. Beholding those emerald depths triggered unexpected reactions. His judgment forewarned he would surely suffocate from the onslaught of such foreign feelings. Breath was stolen from his lungs while blood rushed to lower regions. This was not his customary response to a female.

As if the beauty of her eyes and face had not been discomforting enough, the female's absurd attempt to harm him with her feeble throw of that pebble of a stone had both amused and captivated him. Was he insanely daft?

Apparently.

Aye, the petite woman made him randy for her while wanting to protect her virtue as well.

And on a night of the 'needing moon' could there be a more miserable and impossible combination? His groin was repeatedly triggered by her proximity as evident by his unrelenting engorgement. An iron blade could not be harder.

The sensations this female awakened in him were as distressing as anything Fate had ever sent to his course.

Aftereffects? Aching ballocks.

The truth of it was undeniably simple—his want of her was fierce, he burned for her. When by chance her skin touched his flesh a feeling of anticipation and humming began within him. What would her lips feel like? His cock jerked at the thought of it.

No need to be thinking on that, he reminded his cock, readjusting it again.

While riding back to the House of Rule Candy had been seated in front of him making it impossible to ignore her perfect arse against his groin. Her legs were spread wide across his war-horse, leading to dangerously vivid thoughts. Without a doubt, her manner of dress made it easier to imagine what he should not be thinking upon.

By the goddess, her closeness as she'd ceaselessly rubbed against him—hour after anguishing jaw-clenching hour was both anguish and bliss. Twas a wonder he had any teeth left in his head as surely he had nearly ground them to dust.

How close he had been to spilling seed into his leathers and leaving the stain from it upon her clothing. The female would have thought him a lewd male, and she would have been correct to think so. His thoughts of her were indeed lascivious. Neither within his leathers nor upon her clothing was where he wanted his seed to go. His desire was to be sheathed deeply within her heated womanhood.

Trying to deny this degree of lust on a 'needing moon' night would be ill fated. Thorne had the needs of a healthy man, and on a 'needing moon' those needs became amplified, this night more so than usual. Nevertheless, he had given his word and would remain honorable though a damn difficult if not a nigh impossible task.

Regrettably, Candy's gargoyle was far too young and inexperienced to be much use as a protector. No man would see little Ono as a threat and cease unwanted advances. The burden was left to the very man who wanted her so desperately he would not hesitate to spill blood to possess her. Verily his sac would hate him for this night without her beneath him.

When Thorne said many would want her, he should have been honest and admitted how desperate his hunger for her. And how was he to protect Candy from himself?

To remain in close proximity to this female on the 'needing moon' yet not touch her? By what means was he to accomplish such a task?

He had barely managed not touching her when she was seated against him during the day's travels. Certainly his efforts would be even more excruciating to endure this night under the Moon Goddess' influence.

Aye, I shall have neither teeth, nor sanity left after this needing moon. Only my man parts, and they will loathe me for forsaking them.

By the Moon Goddess' sovereignty this longing for Candy became a warring battle within. Demanding 'need' to feel her flesh surrounding his shaft presented far too much temptation for a mortal man's mind. It necessitated his removal from her nearness to either seek another female or tend to this 'needing' himself. Thorne's body was demanding release, and soon. His sac felt heavy as stone and ached from both his seed and driving desire.

The Moon Goddess, by her very nature, would not be relenting. This night was by the goddess' design and on the fullest moon she governed mankind in her divine manner. It served as a night to enjoy passion and procreate, and none could resist such deific influence. Men jokingly referred to this as the night of "need and seed", as both overflowed by the Moon Goddess' intent.

Craving need could become so demanding that if a woman was not available men might fuck anything they found, man or beast. Such was the nature of the goddess' demand, a driving frenzy until sated and seed spilled.

Thorne had neither been tempted nor debased by use of men or worse and luckily he easily managed eager females. Nevertheless, at times when in the wilds, his hand had been relegated as his sole source of release. Never was it as satiating as a woman, and he would prefer to avoid his palm on this night. An agreeable female could be found within the gathering in the House of Rule, regrettably not the one for which he ached.

Would he be imagining Candy's face while he filled another with his cock?   And would he infuriate the substituted female beneath him by erringly calling out Candy's name in the throes of passion? Both scenarios seemed quite possible, as he could not rid his brain of thoughts of his Lassie.

During his perusal of the crowd in the Great Hall, Thorne spotted his cousin. Having thought Candy safely tucked within her room, he was surprised when spotting Shemmar's hands on her, forcing his body against her.

A flare of jealous fury enveloped Thorne to the point of wanting to slaughter his cousin. To his credit, he had reigned in his temper in front of Candy, only relegating his fist a single time upon his dishonorable cousin's stubborn jaw. Shemmar had crumbled like a dropped egg. How tempting to haul him from the floor and strike him again and again until his handsome face was no more.

Never had Thorne restrained himself so well when angered, however he was well rewarded by Candy's yielding softness as he carried her upstairs. Her head rested against his chest as her arms encircled his neck, and Candy's fingers caressed his hair where it met his vest. He doubted she realized when a small sigh escaped her, though his manhood certainly did. How Thorne wanted this wee female he had found where she should not have been. His cousin would not be sullying her with his mannerisms. No man would. Ever.

Only by Thorne's promise to Candy had he prevented himself from trying to sway her by means that typically won females to a man's bed. Though tempting, he'd refused to succumb to such. He was a man of his word—or so he again reminded himself.

Thorne struggled to neither use his body nor eyes to show her how deep his desire. Repeatedly his cock betrayed him with its own responses and he knew his eyes were fervent as well. It became impossible to effectively disguise his want of her.

At one point Thorne actually considered tempting Candy through the effects of mead.

Aye, the female is obviously conflicted so would not a bit of mead help relax her?

By his pledge to her he admonished such tawdry and selfish thoughts. Tonight he hated his sense of integrity, it did nothing to ease his lust and need. Honor, apparently did little to sate a man's groin.

A poorly made promise indeed, nigh impossible. Fucking hate my conscience.

In truth, Thorne wished for this unique female to choose him freely, or not at all. He tired of women who came to his bed for what they hoped to gain in position or wealth. Such trysts only served the most basic carnal needs, nothing further. He enjoyed fucking as much as any man, yet he'd become weary of pretenses by the fairer sex. There was no 'love' to be had despite the empty words the women forever spoke.

Nor did he ever reply to their meaningless promises of *undying love* and *fidelity*. They knew nothing of him, just as he knew nothing nor held love for them. And never did he promise them anything beyond a single night of shared physical pleasure.

He enjoyed these women as any man might, but that limited the extent of their relationship. None held a hold on him.

Not until this female from another land.

Candy's nearness made him feel an unaccustomed light-heartedness and he easily found himself smiling when in her presence. His Lassie warmed not only his groin, but also his heart and soul—a new sensation, as foreign as she was. And Candy asked nothing from him. No promises, no jewels and no crown.

But Fate reigned cruel, and he had need to take leave now, else go insane from the intensifying desire and 'need'. Before he kissed her, caressed her and took her beneath him. Before he would explore her . . .

"Thorne?" A soft feminine voice called from behind him, making his cock pulse just knowing Candy had spoken his name.

Dare he look into those mesmerizing eyes again? If he did, he was not certain he could leave the room as intended.

Never had he forced himself upon a woman, but this night he felt alarmed he might resort to such appalling behavior. But then never before had he felt such 'need' and craving for a specific woman.

The Moon Goddess could weaken all men, and therefore he turned to glance at Candy one final time. As his eyes met hers, she let her silk dress drop from her shoulders. His eyes followed the trail of fabric as it unhurriedly and gracefully pooled at her feet.

Thorne closed his eyes and when opening them he calmed his breathing, forcing himself to inquire of her. "Are you certain? I will not be able to stop myself Lassie. Of this I know." If she denied him now he might go mad.

Candy trembled, nodding to him as a blush dappled her cheeks.

Sensing she'd never before been so bold before pleased him. Inherently he knew she was not another woman who would speak empty words into his ears to gain wealth and station.

His steps towards her were measured, fearing she might bolt from the room. "Tell me."

Candy needed to be certain of this, and he needed to hear her speak it. Hungry eyes devoured her as they traveled over her breasts and hips and all that was between. Throbbing need made him silently beg to the goddess for Candy to choose to receive him and not flee from this night's passion.

She looked small and unsure of herself, but her coy smiled reached out to him. "Please stay . . . I want you to."

Between her nakedness and words, the moment felt like a godly blessing. Quickly stepping forward and closing the last few steps of distance, he embraced her. Only then did he note he'd been holding his breath, awaiting her response.

Touching her skin slowed Candy's trembling, as though his touch controlled her very existence. Touching her also made his maleness harden further.

This want of her far exceeded anything ever felt before and he would relish taking her as his woman this night.

Thorne tried to slow the demands of the 'needing', so as to do this properly with her. She was petite and he did not want to hurt her in any manner. A woman such as his Lassie needed to be appreciated, not treated like a common harlot to rut over.

Placing his hands to cup the sides of her face, he bent his head to kiss her. The gentle reverent meeting of slanted lips quickly grew into a ravenous probing.

It became a possessive kiss between their mouths as their tongues behaved as two lovers engaged in a teasing and thrusting duel. His breath and hers mingled to become one. Clearly they *both* needed this, as her response was equally heated and demanding. His tongue thrust in her mouth showing her what he would be doing when they joined and a small moan escaped her.

The fresh scent upon her soft skin was unlike what women generally chose on a 'needing moon'. Candy wore a subtle pleasing fragrance—nothing heady hiding her natural scent. This delicate essence fit Candy to perfection, and he wanted to bury his face against her hair and skin and inhale her alluring female scent.

One hand began unlacing his leathers. The other held her tightly within their delectable kiss. Her lips were so soft, yielding, tasting sweeter than any mead in his cellars.

When the kiss ended she began to fall backwards. Thorne quickly grabbed her shoulders and steadied her.

Surprised at her loss of balance, Candy smiled up at him with her startling green eyes. "You kissed me dizzy," she giggled.

"Did I?" He pulled her closer and started another kiss thoroughly enjoying the taste of her as their lips touched.

Beginning with a slow caress, their lips quickly becoming fevered again. This woman was indeed passionate as her tongue sought his and he could feel her body molding against him. Her hunger for him was palatable and he thanked the goddess for this kindness. Candy would be a zealous lover.

Candy's body was pressed so close against his that it became difficult for him to maneuver; yet he would not let go, his soul demanded the closeness. Finally he managed to unlace his breeches with his free hand, and to pull his manhood free from the painfully restraining leathers.

The tight confinement had been far too long and had grown exceedingly uncomfortable. With his leathers resting on his hips, there was nothing he wanted more at this moment than to be inside of Candy. His Lassie was nigh irresistible, and his 'need' and 'want' of her grew with each hammering beat of his heart.

His skin felt fiery and his mind saw only her. Nothing else existed—only the two of them and this moment.

Rush not this female, he reminded himself as he forced him pace to slow. It became a most difficult task with her luscious, naked body facing him, and her obvious arousal summoning his own.

When Candy looked down at his maleness she seemed in awe and gently touched the engorged tip of him. That sent a shudder through him as he sucked in his breath, feeling cool air as it passed his teeth. How could her single touch feel so persuasive? A second touch could be his undoing and he might spend before even getting inside her.

Thorne struggled for better control forcing down his lust and seed. No worthwhile lover would come so hastily before he even touched his female, let alone pleasured her. His Lassie should be savored, not rutted over like an animal.

Their eyes met and Candy gave him a demure smile. "My, my! Your cousin didn't exaggerate on your account. You're definitely a *very* endowed man."

"Do I please your eyes?" She looked eager, needful, and the sight of her perfection almost made him groan aloud with appreciation of her form.

This decorous female with her beautiful eyes drew him to lust for her in a manner never experienced before. Candy was not simply another woman on another 'needing moon' to feed his physical needs. Nay, she felt like much more and he would value exploring her, learning her preferences and pleasing her. He wanted to know much about her beyond how to sate her.

Indeed he wanted to know all of her in ways beyond what other men had known. Ways unique only unto him.

She had not answered; Thorne became apprehensive. He prayed to the goddess that his petite Lassie would not be wary of his size and would choose to receive him without trepidation or regret.

Never would I hurt her.

"Do I Lassie?" This time his question was uttered more softly, but with greater anticipation and fervor for her answer. Her eyes said aye, but Thorne needed her to say she longed for what he would give her.

His need wanted to thrust deep within her core and make her take notice of him. Nay, he would take her gently, but take her well. She would have no doubt he could please her when this was done.

Looking a little embarrassed Candy answered. "Yes, you more than please my eyes and I'd like you to please other parts of me, too."

At her reply any hesitancy he felt vanished and he reached between her legs. A groan escaped both their lips as his fingers touched her folds and the degree of wetness proved her more than ready to receive him. She might appear timid but her body yearned with heated need.

As his breath caressed her earlobe he spoke softly. "So wet and needful my beautiful Lassie, and it shall be my honor and pleasure to sate you."

While kissing her neck, Thorne lifted her up intending for her to sit on his engorged cock, but she did not seem to know to wrap her legs around his waist. This confirmed his suspicions—she was not an overly experienced female.

Nuzzling her ear he whispered to her. "Wrap your legs about me Lassie."

As she did so, he braced his hands under her buttock and eased her ever so slowly down onto him knowing he had both length and girth that would require stretching her. He would not want to hurt any female, but *never* would he hurt this precious one.

By the goddess, she was very tight, so fucking tight that he was fearful, given his size, he might push to the point of pain. Luckily her abundant wetness eased his slow penetration into her.

Will. Not. Hurt. My. Lassie.

Cautiously he filled her while allowing her body to accommodate his size. Her female fleshy heat gradually enrobed him and she let out small moans as if finding his joining with her most pleasurable. How difficult to remain patient with this insistent 'need' plaguing him, but he was determined. No plunging, no thrusting. Not yet.

Will. Not. Hurt. Her.

Too many times he had heard women apprehensively tell him he would be too large, though always he carefully refrained from pushing beyond their level of comfort. He decided half his shaft was ample—he'd not risk entering her small body further for fear of causing pain, or rejection of him. He could be content with how they fit, however, should she reject him—that would make for a painful though bloodless wound.

Surprisingly, Candy seemed most eager for him to fill her and showed no hesitation whatsoever. Her pleasurable sighs hardly suggested the least bit of discomfort as he stretched her sheath to encase him.

While she held onto his neck, little moans escaped her lips—her head dropped back as she neared cresting ecstasy. Slowly he rode her up and down his shaft supporting her hips. All the while he gazed into her flushed face and beautiful eyes until she looked back and spoke in a breathy voice.

"Don't we need to use that honey pot?"

All movement ceased as he let a curse slip beneath his breath. "Wisely so. I find you most distracting." Shaking his head he chastised himself. "Never before have I forgotten use of the honey pot."

Truthfully, he'd always been adamantly prudent in using the concoction. Candy's proximity fogged his better senses as easily as she hardened him. Never had this insensibility occurred with any woman, as he had no plans to erringly father a child.

This time *he* would chose his betrothed mate. Neither by his father's decree, for some political alliance, nor by errant seed would he be ensnared. Thorne wanted far more than 'obligation' if he ever took a wife.

Clearly he remembered his father's words of warning of how in Thorne's position, a babe included the burden of the breast from which it suckled. And how that woman in turn, would demand to share the weight of his crown—or at least equal gold forever lining her purse.

Several times in his youth his father had advised him: "Beware that you do not erringly plant your seed in fertile ground, else you harvest more than you intended to sow. And son, that crop will be your own to tend."

Thorne wanted no bastards due to his lust. Other highborn men might consider their seed so valuable that any woman should feel honored to bestow their issue. Such arrogance troubled Thorne a great deal and seemed exceedingly unfair to the resulting children. He had taken his father's words to heart since his thirteenth year of age, when he became a man. And he had *always* been adamant to never spill without utmost precaution. He would choose the mother of his offspring, not the reverse.

As he lifted Candy and set her down, he regretted stopping when they were both so close to completion. His sac was tight and ready to release and he had not wanted to cease the movements with her legs wrapped so tightly about him. Thankfully his mind was far wiser than his male-minded greedy cock.

"And where did Celcee put the honey pot?"

Candy went to the tray and picked it up, but he took it from her and held his hand over hers as he stroked her delicate fingers.

"So you knew she brought a honey pot?" Candy asked with a bit of accusation and a smile.

"Aye. I am a man with bold confidence and demanding desires, and this night they be named Candy." He gave her a wink as he took the honey pot from her. "Please honor me with this most valorous task."

The mischievous crooked grin on his lips bespoke how much he would enjoy this, and again she rewarded him with her shy smile as she lowered her jewel green eyes.

While Candy climbed upon the bed, Thorne quickly went to open the drapery at the windows overlooking the lower gardens. Sounds of laughter and covetous-ness arose through the openness. He cared nothing of those sounds. Rather it was this night's moonbeams as they crossed the bed to caress his female that he was eager to witness.

When he turned back towards Candy his gaze caressed her perfect body. Never once did his eyes leave her form as he hurriedly removed his boots and leathers.

As he had hoped, the moonbeams gliding over Candy's skin indeed made her flesh sparkle as though covered with dancing diamond dust. She was both perfection and precious, and on this night he would claim her as his most coveted treasure.

This female I choose as mine, and mine alone shall she be.

Candy saw him gazing at her body and started to cover with the sheet. His Lassie behaved somewhat modestly, but somehow he knew she was filled with a depth of desire and passion not yet revealed to him. He intended to unmask it this night.

"Nay, Lassie, do not deny me this. Never cover yourself from mine eyes, as always I will want to see you. You could not be more perfect to me."

Reaching over he gently pulled the sheet from her. Candy did not argue and let her body be savored by his approving eyes. By the goddess, she was faultless, and her skin sparkled as the rays of moonlight enrobed her nakedness. His Lassie was far more than he had envisaged—her womanly figure was truly a blessing from the goddess.

When Candy followed his eyes and looked down she appeared startled at the shimmer on her skin. "Oh, the moonbeams, they make me look . . ."

"Like the precious jewel you are."

Thorne reached into the honey pot with two fingers and drew out some of the thick contraception. As he reached toward Candy she again blushed but opened her legs for him. The softness and wetness of her awed him. Her tight cunny was hotter than any flame, her damp blonde curls teased his lust of her, and her wetness felt like fluid silk. Being betwixt her thighs and feeling her clenched around his cock would feel far more than exquisite. The craving for her was likened to a beaconing candle leading him home on a cold night . . . home between her warm thighs.

First one finger and then a second were slid into her as he spread the honey mixture and stretched her tightness. As he watched her delicate facial features, he took his time with this task, within her and around her opening, knowing where she would be most sensitive. He'd make certain she would meet her pleasure tonight. Repeatedly.

Her breaths came out faster until Candy let out a sweet moan, and her body quivered as she met her bliss. Sliding himself on top of her, he enjoyed her finish as her sheath tightened around him.

At first he used gentle thrusts but when Candy's own hips pushed harder he added momentum now realizing they both desired more. Still, he remained cautious to avoid going so deep as to cause her discomfort or pain.

"Never would I hurt you. If I push beyond comfort tell me and I will pull back."

"No, please you feel wonderful and I want to enjoy your size. Will you let me feel all of you?"

Damn if I will not make it so.

No further words of encouragement were needed for him to push in further and to take her with more force. She pushed toward him as well until she actually met his hilt and accommodated his full size—with lust-filled bliss. For the first time in his life he was sac deep in a woman and found the sensation to be indescribable.

Other women could not take all of him in, but this small female did and relished it. He would not have thought it possible of such a petite woman. What she did not have in experience she more than accommodated for with fervor and desire for him. And the realization made his ego soar as he ground against her pelvis.

She chose me and receives me—all of me.

He held his control to ensure Candy would feel her release of pleasure again before he took his own. Sensing she was close to coming, his thumb touched her bud and his thrusts grew frenzied, demanding all of her heat.

This time her orgasmic release culminated with a loud moan followed by a small cry of her release, further stroking his male pride. His Lassie was letting herself feel carnal pleasure with him, and it made his seed begin its rise. Wrapping his arms under her, he pulled her tightly to him while his seed and pleasure exploded into her tightness.

He had wanted for far too long and his pain was turning into ecstasy as his pleasure pulsated heatedly and deeply into her. Deep arduous sounds escaped him as his head cradled against her neck and he became a most satisfied male. This feeling seemed as if he had waited his whole life for this intensely powerful shared moment with Candy—a newness to him he could only describe as a justly *intimate* moment.

She is truly mine.

Rolling off her he still held her tight so she lay against his heaving chest. He could not let go, requiring her nearness as much as the air he breathed. And right now he needed a great deal of air as their level of spent passion had left him with little breath.

After a few minutes of quiet between them, Candy rose upon her elbow and looked at him with that expression he was recognizing as her uncertainty. Her other hand reached to feather her fingers through the hair behind his ear. No female other than Candy had ever done so, and her tender touch felt—pleasing.

"That was incredible. I—" Embarrassment stole her words and her cheeks began to color beyond what their coupling had wrought.

"Aye, Lassie, a degree of pleasure with no equal. How easily your body responds to me." Her deeper blush at his words made him suspicious. "Has this depth of pleasure never occurred for you before this night?"

Had she never been completely sated before? How could such be when she was so lovely and eagerly passionate? Mayhap she had never before let herself freely feel the passion as she did this night under the Moon Goddess' influence, or were her lovers so lacking? A thought that pleased him even more.

Candy snuggled closer against his chest and body. "Not like that with sensations consuming my entire body. I thought there was something wrong with me or that other women exaggerated about their earth-shattering climaxes. I'm sorry and a little embarrassed about being noisy, that intensity just really took me by surprise."

Truly, she is embarrassed about such?

"There is nothing to be regretful for as I consider such as a measure of how well I pleasured you and now that our 'need' is sated I can focus on my 'want' of you. Now I shall be able to take my time to fully savor you with our next bout. And be assured Lassie, you are absolutely not lacking in any manner."

"You want me . . . again?" A diminutive smile crossed her flushed face.

Beautiful and sensuous woman. My woman.

"Many more times. Did I not say once would not be enough with you? I shall prove my words and greedily take all you will give unto me." Aye, if he had his way she would not be walking from this room, but rather limping from tenderness left by his body.

She looked rather pleased by his declaration and that pleased him equally. Yesterday's hunting trip had wrought far more than simply finding sustenance for the stomach. His Lassie offered him nourishment to both his physical needs and spirit.

Again he wondered if his discovery of her was by the goddess' design? Always devout, he would offer up prayers of thanks for this precious gift he held within his arms.

Candy's hand began to travel across the planes of his abdomen. Thorne enjoyed her sensual touch, which triggered that humming within him again. When her hand dipped further, his languid eyes opened fully and he began hardening. He watched, as she seemed to be learning him. When her fingers traced his shaft he wondered what she was thinking.

Unexpectedly and timidly she asked him if she could study his form. Thorne was taken aback, never had a female asked such a thing.

With a nod he propped himself on his elbows to watch her while bemused on this unexpected request. How curious she seemed as her hands moved along his abdominal muscle planes as if examining every raised muscle and depression his body made. When she reached his maleness she examined his shaft in depth using her delicate soft hands to trace him.

His manhood reveled at her touch, but Thorne pushed back his desire to grab her and show her how his body worked . . . again.

Let her get to know you in any manner she choses, he reprimanded his cock. His cock ignored him.

Once he had reached his full hardened length, she looked up at him and he arched his brow. "If you touch me thus you can expect enthusiasm."

He would swear she held a satisfied smile at knowing how easily she affected him. As Candy studied his sac and cupped him, he wanted to pull her on top of him. Stifling both his groan and desire, he appreciated how rare this moment, and to not disquiet her, else she may never feel comfortable in this manner again. It hurt nothing to let her get her fill at looking and touching him, and her hands felt good on him. Very good! No woman had ever touched him in this manner, as if admiring all of him.

His throaty voice broke the silence. "Surely you have seen men before?"

With a nod Candy replied. "Well, sure, I mean I've sketched male models but not studied them up close, certainly *never* like this. So many textures and . . . You know Michelangelo's sculpture of David really does look like a wimp compared to you," Candy commented as she caressed his shaft. When it jerked at her touch she let out a small giggle. "Especially in regards to the *male* parts. Your body is so beautiful Thorne."

His want of her was increasing and his sac tightening. Who the fuck was this Michelangelo or David? At least she seemed to think the man she was touching was more worthy of her attention.

How many men would he need to displace to keep her attention? A trifling task if needed and one he would not hesitate to tend to. Indeed, he would stop at nothing for her affections. She belonged to him, only him.

Candy looked up at Thorne and gave him a timid smile and sigh. "The artist part of me finds all of your exquisite and perfectly sculpted body and male parts to be fascinating and most *generous*." The smile she was trying to hide made her sensuous mouth twitch. After she let out a sigh she continued.

"The woman in me finds your form *enthralling*, totally *fulfilling*. From now on every other male will look . . . well, inadequate to say the least."

Though he asked her, he realized she'd never explored a man in any manner before and he was gladdened by that thought. Though his Lassie was mistaken if she thought to ever be looking or touching any other man. Never before had any woman shown curiosity of his form, only what he did with it. And of all the things he had been called in his life—and there had been many—*exquisite, fascinating* and *beautiful* were not words ever used to describe him.

Not that he feared he could not measure more than equal to another, as he was well aware of his size and form. He was a taller and bigger man than most in all manner of measure, and valued his strength for preservation of his realm. But to know her curiosity of him, that felt remarkable. Not only her touches and interest, but knowing she was not a brazen female outside his arms. This reserved woman felt enough at ease with him for an intimate moment of discovery. Nothing could merit a more precious complement than knowing she wished to know his male form intimately. Additionally, she found him pleasing.

"No, I've never touched a man. Not really, or not like this. Actually, I guess not at all. I've been more of a hide under the covers kind of girl during intimacy. How fascinating, and thank you for not minding."

Candy wiggled back up to his side and his arm wrapped around her shoulders, to where she fit perfectly.

Truly? Of course he did not mind, what sane male would?

And again she had used *fascinating* to describe him. As a man should he be offended? Thorne knew he had all his male parts, and they were abundant enough to not be overlooked. The look in her eyes did not suggest she thought anything but pleasant (even lustful) thoughts of his body. Nevertheless, what kind of man was described as *fascinating*? It seems that in her eyes—him.

But she had used other words as well and he should focus on those utterances of praise. Certainly he preferred *generous* and *enthralling* to that rather questionable description of *fascinating*.

As Candy's hand traveled across his chest, he could sense she was thinking about something else. He prayed she was not comparing him to those other men or another man from her land, or worse, having feelings of regret.

How would he handle such? Candy was his now, and he would not be sharing her no matter the cost. This woman filled a depth of vacancy within him. A place he had not known existed, or needed to be occupied, in order to feel whole. She felt right to him, and together they felt complete.

When she spoke he felt relieved to know it was her inquisitiveness again. Not talk of another man. A man he would not hesitate to kill to keep Candy for himself.

"Are all men here circumcised?"

Certainly he had not anticipated that question! Again she had taken him by surprise. *Ah, my curious, sensual female.*

With a questioning arched brow and simmering smile he responded. "Are they not in your land, and does my being cut in this manner displease you?"

Candy let out a small sigh. "No, it *hardly* displeases me, I prefer how you look. Not that I've seen many men up close and personal, but I understand not all of them where I'm from are . . . cut. Anyway, I would think a male would prefer being circumcised, but then I'm not a man so maybe I don't understand the big debate. Of course some males are circumcised for religious reasons. Is religion the reason males are cut in your land?"

A smile threatened his face. Indeed she was definitely not a man, and her continuous curiosity, rambling words, and wit humored him a great deal.

"Aye Lassie, as a newly born male tis a holy ceremony. The foreskin is removed as a welcoming of him to the world, an unveiling before the gods of the man he will one day become."

She sat up with her curiosity peaked. He held no wish to offend her with such talk, but when he did not continue she coaxed him to explain.

"The midwife or father removes the flesh and then the foreskin is laid upon burning glass beads in a sacred gold bowl. This serves as an offering to honor the Sun God."

"*Hmmm.* So why is the offering to the Sun God?"

"To gain the Sun God's favor, so the boy will grow up to hold an inner spiritual fierceness likened to fire, and a body born of strength. Both make for traits parents wish for their son."

"I like that you're circumcised although the process sounds painful. I think you look perfect and *most* plentiful. You are a very large man, even with my limited experience I can see and feel that."

With a chuckle Thorne smoothed the strand of hair moving it from her cheek to behind her ear. "I assure you I have no memories of the offering and am pleased to not offend my Lady's eyes nor hurt you by my size. And did I not grow up strong and fierce?"

"Very large and strong. I don't know about fierce, I think you're very kind and giving."

"For that I am thankful, but there are other times as well." He prayed the gods spare her to ever see him when his warrior self was needed. In her presence he smiled ever much, however when provoked, growls better described his nature.

"These moonbeams make me look like I'm wrapped in bling. So why don't you sparkle from the moonlight too?" Candy was stroking his chest and outlining his scars with her delicate finger.

"Only you Lassie." This 'bling' he knew naught of, but she was indeed lovely with the shimmering glow upon her flesh.

Why did she have to see those scars? So many damn scars from years of fighting to keep his lands safe. She must despise the ugliness of them as well as that hideous scar upon his face. How deeply that blade had cut, scarring far more than the damage to his flesh. The memories tied to that occasion had penetrated his soul.

"What do you mean only me? Why would I sparkle?"

How unique this female was. Candy said she was reserved with her affections and he believed her, yet she was anything but when in his arms. How much she boosted his male ego as well. He could almost disregard his scars when she looked at him that way, as if she was blind to his damage.

Thorne enjoyed her clever banter, her curiosity, her everything. Never had a female made him feel so relaxed from burdens or to feel this tenderness he felt towards her. And if he kept smiling his jaw would become sore from it.

She was moving to sit up and he decided this made a fitting time to enjoy her well fashioned, but not overly copious breasts, and those equally enticing perfect pale pink nipples. He wanted to suckle on their peaked perfection until they were hard and swollen, as none of her could be more flawless in size or form to his liking.

Before he'd been too consumed with 'need' to really get to explore her, but he planned to, he needed to. Indeed he would.

"My, my, how inquisitive a woman you are to ask so many questions at such a time when clearly I want more of you. I shall tell you this after I take the time to explore every part of you with my lips and mouth." Again he was hardened to a level of discomfort and his sac heavy, and wondered at his exceedingly quick response to her.

How she makes me burn for her.

"I like that idea, but you did say that on the 'needing moon' a woman could ask whatever from a man. I won't be denied." Candy gave him a pretended petulant expression, which he instantly adored. Was there naught of her he did not find alluring?

"My Lady, I would deny you nothing no matter what moon we lay under. Now lie back so I can begin my long journey of kisses and licks upon your sparkling skin."

So soft and feminine and he craved to taste all of her. A part of him screamed it so loudly he feared deafness from the demand if he did not heed it. His mouth traveled down her body as he methodically enjoyed the mounds and dips along his journey.

Her breasts received his full attention with his teasing tongue and sucking until she whimpered and groaned in a most pleasant manner. The trail along her body continued until he rested between her legs.

Candy looked at him with both surprise and heat. "Does my Lassie like my kisses? Perhaps you desire more?"

She bit her lower lip while nodding.

"I will be tasting my woman," he said softly as he looked from her openness to her face to see her eyes widen. He resumed his journey, keeping his eyes focused on her face.

Intending far more than kisses, he used his tongue to tease her. By her expression and response, this too she'd never encountered before. If she had a lover, the man had done a poor job of partaking in passion with her, and that was a difficult thing to understand. She was too perfect to not be enjoyed, savored, and pleasured. He would relish being her lover.

Her solitary lover.

Such knowledge made him feel as if much of her had been saved for him alone, and he'd make certain she would delight in these many experiences they would share. When her hands clenched the sheets, he knew his tongue would tease her until she cried out with bursting pleasure.

He planned to make her come on his tongue driving her to shattering ecstasy. Then he would lap the nectar she produced just for him. Those kisses, intimate licks and pulls to her feminine fleshy folds led Candy to writhe and cry out his name as she tore at the sheets as he brought her to another climax.

Hearing her call out his name with such passion, Thorne determined to leave a *warrior's kiss* upon her inner thigh. Never before had he thought to do so with any woman, though he had long ago earned a warrior's right to mark any woman he greatly favored.

A primal need to brand her flared within him. Only Candy had ever incited his desire to do such a thing. As he placed his mouth to her inner thigh he sucked upon her skin until it stained with the blush of her blood.

A mark that would stay for several days and warn any man who saw it that she was claimed. Should any man see her flesh so close to her womanhood, then that man was as good as dead.

Seeing his mark upon her tender thigh made his cock throb for more of her, and that led to more use of the honey pot and another round of heightened sex between them. No part of her would escape his attention. Thorne wanted to experience all of her in every manner possible. It would take time, but this woman would be worth every minute, even if it took a lifetime.

As they lay in each other's arms, spent and sated, Thorne knew Candy wanted him to explain the moonbeams and truly his sac needed a short reprieve. Turning on his side and propping on his elbow to face her, he sighed at those big green eyes looking back at him. Such a beauty she was. His hand reached out and stroked her cheek.

Flawless skin. Faultless lover. Fucking perfect female.

He had no plans for her to ever feel another man's lips upon her, nor touch her in any manner. The thought of another male near her was intolerable to him. For the first time in his life he had found a woman he wanted as his own, to keep in his bed, and he'd not be giving her up.

If a worthy man had treasured her he would not have let her end up unprotected and hungry in the wilds. And any lover certainly should have realized she was not sated as she should be.

This one is mine. I found her and I shall be keeping and treasuring her. Any other man—be damned.

A truly rare woman—she was far more valued to him than the incredibly intense pleasure they shared. Indeed she meant more than he had known he could feel for a woman. Thorne had long thought he was beyond caring for another person beyond friendship or a single night of fucking. Two nights with the same female had always made for one too many, as then the woman erringly thought he cared for her, and a queen's crown was within her reach. It had been best to keep interludes to a few hours and nothing beyond, and so he had.

Conflicted emotions made him feel both light-headed and unsettled. Candy was a woman he might come to love . . . had she not already settled into his heart?

Never before had he shared laughter with a woman, and certainly not during a 'needing moon'. Smiled, aye, he smiled in response to a woman's wiles, but never had he felt enjoyment to the likes he did within his Lassie's company.

Her closeness made him feel akin to joyful, something he could not recall if he had ever felt in his life. He felt light of heart, even playful. All thoughts of playfulness had been forced from him in his youth. How strange to feel that way now, when he had thought to never to feel in this manner or depth again. Indeed, he'd thought it a childish trait stolen from his life, no longer of consequence to him. He had been wrong—this felt good.

"I shall tell you of a prophecy told to me many years back, but first I want to tell you how beautiful you are and how much you please not just my eyes but any dream I could ever had imagined of a perfect lover.

"Never have I fully fit within a woman, nor ever expected to. To feel such deep . . . I mean to say your body sates and gratifies me beyond anything I have known. And looking upon you would be a feast to any man's eyes, yet you share yourself with me."

And she asks nothing in return, he thought.

"Lassie, I value your company, and your presence makes for a priceless treasure."

Thorne had known so many women, but never one the likes of this one. Nor had he ever been clumsy or at a loss of words with a female before.

Had he actually been considered a man of charm to women? How he could be so muddled with Candy, he could not comprehend. She obviously affected his senses and words seemed an ineffective means to express his thoughts on this passion-filled night. He hoped his body could convey what his utterances failed.

Candy smiled as if comprehending the words that seemed to evade him as she added her own. "It feels as if every nerve is tingling with desire when you're near me and profound pleasure when you're inside me." She shivered at the memory. "It feels different between us, doesn't it?"

"Aye, Lassie," he whispered with never truer words. He enjoyed the feel of her softness against his skin as she wiggled closer to him, and how his skin warmed hers.

What manner was it that her touch seemed to create that strange subtle humming sensation that flowed through him, likened to a song without music or words one could not truly hear.

This enticing woman was the opposite of him in so many respects, and without doubt she was the epitome of a physically beautiful, fragile, and innocent woman, lying next to an unequivocally hardened, physically marred, not-so-innocent man.

A man who had been forced to rule at a younger than anticipated age—a man who had seen and spilled far too much blood. How swiftly you learn when a knife sits at your throat, and your very life and Kingdom are at stake. An early lesson and well heeded in regards to how too much misspent compassion and trust can lead to great mayhem and loss. And so, he no longer took time to consider before killing to protect his Kingdom. Quickly he'd learned from his mistakes, as the consequences of ignorance were too great.

There were times the weight of his Kingdom's crown was likened to carrying his father across his shoulders, hour after hour, day after day, now for ten winters past. Despite the love he held for his people, the responsibility often tired him to his core.

Somehow, with Candy's presence, the burden felt as if it might become . . . more bearable—lessened.

He promised himself to try not to offend her with his harsh mannerisms. Could he not be polite and caring, though much of his life's responsibilities demanded the other side of him—the callous warrior who bore too many scars and abhorrent memories? Always he strove to maintain peace within his lands and his body displayed the receipts of his efforts.

Could such a beauty learn to care for a man who carried such a marred face, the single scar that could not be hidden?

Thorne pulled a sheet over them, as though by hiding the scars on his body they might disappear. Her innocent green eyes should not have to behold such ugliness. She was entirely too pretty to have to suffer a man of his looks. Still she was at *his* side and had chosen *him* this night. Perchance his face did not offend her eyes ever much.

A low breath left him as he contemplated his words. "Tis far beyond the 'needing moon' Lassie, as this sensation blazes fiercer than even the goddess' decree. Your touch singes me with deep wanting and finishes with untold ecstasy. Only *you* fuel it. Now let me caress you, as I tell you of this glistening upon your beautiful nakedness."

"Aren't you afraid caressing could lead to something more *intimate?*" Candy asked playfully. Her green eyes held a sparkle that harmonized with the moonbeams on her flesh.

"I am counting on such. I want to take you many more times if you will have me." He had never felt the depth of craving for any woman like he did for the one beside him.

Somehow Thorne knew he could easily continue taking her the entirety of the night, and that he would. Their passion would continue to smolder within the embrace of each other's arms, and no night would ever compare, and no other woman would ever make his sac so full.

"My goodness aren't you a poster boy for Viagra," she laughed.

"Who is this boy Viagra, a younger male?" His brow creased. Did she have another man—a younger man? Thorne was twenty and seven summers of age, hardly too old for her. He would not be sharing his Lassie and the man would be most wise to disappear or he'd see to the end of him—one manner or another.

I have claimed her, and she is mine from this night forth.

"No," she giggled, "it's a medicine for men who have difficulty getting," she grabbed through the sheet squeezing his hardened shaft, "like that, an erection."

"Then they have never seen you or they would have no need of such a thing. You keep me solid as any blade. Now hush, and listen woman or I will take you again . . . Indeed I plan to have you soon, nonetheless," he playfully growled in her ear. "But let me finish what you asked of me first.

"As I was to say, years past, my grandmother was a wise woman with many skills related to the influences of the Earth. She knew much of healing, could foretell weather, advise as to where to plant crops for the best yield, and also counsel people who were to me be mated. My grandmother could tell if they would make a strong union, bear children, and always she spoke true. Her services were esteemed and she was a fine and loving woman. Truly she taught me much about the Earth Mother and Moon Goddess and I loved her greatly.

"When our world became faded and almost colorless, like a child's bowl of bland porridge, many fell into a depression. Every day less color, until our souls felt as lifeless as the land looked. Still we survived, as did our colorless crops. One day I decided to ask her counsel on this, and what would become of our world. She told me of this prophecy:

'An unlike female will be offered a choice by the Moon Goddess. She will glisten in the moon's embrace like a precious jewel, and if she choses to lay with you, my grandson, then a precious silver thread will be tied unto your souls. But if she freely chooses another first, on the night of the 'needing moon', or chooses you not at all, we are lost. This female holds the key to our salvation, but I fear the cost will indeed be great.'

"This female can only be you Candy, as you glisten likened to jewels beneath the Moon Goddess' caress. And because you freely chose me, we may yet find salvation from what was stolen from our land. For color to once again grace our realm would provide both a miraculous resurgence of visual delight, and also a gift beyond measure for our eyes and souls."

"That's an interesting story, but I don't see how I can be useful when I don't know anything about your land, or goddesses, or even about your loss of color." "You can be more than useful by climbing upon my engorged 'abundant' shaft, and ride us to completion. I have renewed want of you."

Extremely aroused yet again, he reached for the honey pot while asking with his eyes if she would receive him.

Candy seemed more than interested and Thorne knew he would guide her through pleasure yet again.

With bashfulness and lowered eyes Candy spoke. "I wonder if you'd mind, before this night ends, if we could resume the position we started with, before we were, you know, interrupted by the honey pot issue." Candy sighed at the brief memory. "I've never felt anything like that—it was amazing."

"Ah, enjoyed it did you? I assure you it would be my pleasure. So many ways to enjoy our meeting of flesh Lassie, and I want to experience all of them with you. When I see your beauty and feel your depth of desire and passionate eagerness it causes me to wonder, how is it you seem to know so little of men and pleasure?"

"Teach me," she teased.

With an arched brow he considered her invitation. "I do carry a *little* knowledge and experience of such."

Her bright green eyes widened at his words, making a silent bid to him. On pleasures of the flesh he knew much. No doubt more than he rightfully should, and he would gladly show her all she would favor to know.

He held knowledge of how to stoke a woman's desires, but as to how to stop his burning for his Lassie—it seemed this he did not know. Together they made a very heated flame and he favored keeping it blazing—tonight, the morrow and all days thereafter.

Opening the honey pot he again prepared her. This time two fingers entered her more easily but he still used them to stretch her opening before pulling Candy to straddle his hips.

Slowly he guided himself into her as a groan of pleasure escaped her. Holding her hips, he started with slow movements letting her chose the pace.

Soon she took the lead and Thorne was surprised at her fervor as she pummeled his shaft with a proud smile on her face. Obviously his woman liked knowing she made him moan when plunging against his hilt.

He had been gentle with her, however if she sought to be fucked harder he would give her as much as she wanted.

Wicked, sultry woman.

Candy's confidence and pace increased, until by her face he knew she was ready to descend into a place of deep pleasure.

His finger went to her sensitive bud to send her over the edge, into her fall into ecstasy. Candy threw back her head as her senses shattered and she screamed his name. Never before had his name been called with such a plea of raw hunger and craving for him. That sound from his Lassie made for a most virile compliment. It also provided all the encouragement needed to push his pelvis up hard against her making him come, releasing his hot seed into her.

Both were sated and exhausted—at least for the time being. Damned if she was not the most amazing female. On he morrow, Thorne suspected his sac would be bruised from the slaps against her flesh. Verily, he would be grinning all the more for it.

The Moon Goddess continuously graced them with her glistering beams across their heated bodies, as if the goddess wrapped the lovers in her ethereal blanket. Within the veil of the 'needing moon', they coveted only each other's touch and it felt as if this night had been designed for them alone.

As the night pressed on so did their unremitting desire of one another. But it was far more than simply lusting intimacy between their bodies and shared breath as they kissed. Deeper feelings bound them with a need for partaking of conversation, laughter, and physical proximity.

The tray of fruit left for them provided needed energy. Thorne teased Candy as he fed pieces to her, and playfully she slid the fruit from her mouth into his. They acted with childish abandon. Neither Thorne nor Candy had ever done anything so carefree before, thus this blithe shared time became a new and heady experience.

Playfulness and teasing had never been part of his sexual endeavors in the past. Fucking had been for a sole purpose—physical release into a convenient female vessel. How could he ever fathom his Lassie in such a cold fashion? Indeed he could not.

Candy confessed how when he settled between her thighs, the erotic sensations were so powerful that it felt as if she actually transcended outside her body.

When she told him how the potency of each of her climaxes continued to be greater than the previous, until she felt as though she might faint from the intensity, he understood as he also experienced the same intense carnal influences. Indeed Thorne wondered how his ballocks sustained and his cock remained intact when the physical gratification exploded through him. He likened the experience to a volcano erupting and his cock spewing hot seed into his woman.

As Thorne took a sip of mead, he cocked his head and gave her a teasing smile. "Lassie, on this night your cries of passion go unnoticed by others, but on the morrow you may wish for me to stifle them."

"Oh, my. I'm that noisy? I had no idea, I'm so sorry about that." Candy's expression held seriousness.

Silly woman to imagine he cared one twit what her level of ecstasy sounded like past these walls. She was his woman, and her exclamations of pleasure were fashioned for his ears.

"Truly I care naught. Only if thus would embarrass your sense of modesty. The House of Rule has thick walls, but as you become delightfully and thoroughly enthralled, you also become loud. If I do not muffle your cries of pleasure, I would no doubt need to warn my warriors that your screams and moans are not the result of me causing you harm."

He offered up a knowing wink, while his lips tried to suppress the humor he felt. The hint of his smile was breaking through.

"Myself, I enjoy these sounds you make when I fuck you. Tis by your decision, but on this night, and every 'needing moon' hereafter, I want to enjoy hearing you calling out for me with unrestrained abandon. Your outcries are most pleasing to my ego. Think on it. You have until I take you on the morrow, and indeed I intend to."

When he looked over to the honey pot he noted the contents had diminished while his lust had not. Thorne rang the cord for his servant.

As he glanced to Candy he wondered why her mouth was open as if in disbelief. Did she truly think he would not be craving more of her? Unless she denied him, he would be pleasuring her and himself every chance he got in the days, weeks, and moons to come.

With the knock at the door, Thorne grabbed the sheet and quickly wrapped it around his waist, while Candy covered up with the remaining duvet. He gave her a quick glance, to make sure her nakedness would not be revealed, before he opened the door.

From behind him, he heard Candy let out a sigh. So she appreciated even his quick check on her, or was it his backside that held her attention? The goddess had indeed blessed him with this female who favored him so entirely.

"My Lord, what is your need?" Celcee's head was bowed.

"A honey pot."

At his comment Celcee looked up with surprise at Thorne, and then across to Candy. "Of course, right away, I thought I had left a pot. So sorry my Lord."

As Celcee rushed off, Candy giggled

"These little honey pots are just too damned small." Thorne looked so serious with his complaint that Candy laughed all the more.

With the delight of hearing her feminine laugh he dove onto the bed and began kissing her and playfully pushing his erection through the sheeting against her. "You are going to be so sore. Worse than after riding my war-horse all day long."

"Oh my Lord," Candy mocked, "I have been riding your horse all night, and he is a magnificent stallion. So strong, and so *hung* and so ready to satisfy my needs, which I must say he does exquisitely."

With those words Thorne was eager to plunge into her again, but the delivery of the honey pot interrupted him. Jumping up with sheet in hand, he hastily pulled open the door.

"Thank you Celcee." As he handed her the empty cup to trade for the newly filled cup, he accidently dropped the sheet.

At first his servant girl stared at his enormous erection, then her eyes traveled to the empty cup. She looked over to Candy sitting in the bed and smiled.

"Indeed, my Lord. I see your *need.*" Celcee began to giggle as she ran off, all the while Thorne tried to recover the sheet.

"*Tsk, tsk*, my Lord. All the female servants will be talking about this to no end." Candy said shaking her head but with a twinkle in her eyes. "About your prowess and the enormous size of your *tremendous cock.*"

As he made it back to the bed she grabbed hold of his cock, although her hand couldn't quite encircle the entire width of him. "And I will be so envied by all of them."

"*Envied*, eh? And *tremendous cock* as well. Such bold praises, I think you could not heat me more Lassie."

"As if that was a difficult task!"

That led to use of the new honey pot as well as a new position to try. This time he watched her face in the tall mirror while he took her from behind. Thorne sat back with his calves under his thighs and had her sit on his lap, her back leaning against his chest as he slid into her.

The sensation was very erotic but not nearly as enthralling as watching Candy's face while her tongue ran over her bottom lip. She looked entirely impassioned and when he reached his arm around to touch her, she cried out.

Thorne watched their reflection as he lifted her up and down on his maleness, hearing Candy's burst of completion into a state of bliss made for a perfect coupling. When he was ready to pulse his seed into her, he grabbed her breasts as he lifted to his knees pushing hard into her. Again she screamed out his name as if it was the only word that could leave her swollen lips.

"By the goddess woman, you fuck me dry," he called out as his seed shot into her. Seconds later they were laying entangled in a heap of arms and legs. Candy was filled with his seed and both were filled with sensual fulfillment.

Thorne knew she would be left far more than a little sore, but he could not stop his desire for her and she wanted him equally. Each time they were sated, the hunger began anew. This desperate wanting to be within her and to give her pleasure was not likened to what he ever felt before, and her responding pleasure heightened his own.

Generally on a 'needing moon', spending twice was sufficient for him, mayhap thrice if it had been a time since he had sought pleasure.

But on this night he'd lost count of the times and ways they had enjoyed each other as he introduced Candy to many ways to feel pleasure—enough to deplete the first honey pot and they were making good use of the second pot. Yet his sac kept filling with seed and his demanding desire continued for her.

Never did she deny him, always she received him as if he was the only man she had ever lusted for. Nothing could make a man's chest or cock swell more than such knowledge, and the proof of it was pulsating betwixt his legs.

Utterly spent, and needing to take time to rest, Thorne began to unwrap the bandage on his arm. He was intent to wipe the odiferous and stinging concoction from his skin.

"What are you doing?" Candy inquired in a sleepy voice as she looked up to him from the pillow.

"Removing this uncomfortable wrapping. Rest Lassie, as I will be done momentarily."

Candy pushed herself to her elbow. "You should've told me it was too tight, I had no idea."

"Not too tight."

Now Candy sat up and tucked the bedding under her arms. "Then why are you removing it?"

Thorne was thankful to have unworked all her numerous knots and was pulling layers of the bandage free. "Did the smell not offend you while we fucked?"

"Uh, could we call it 'nookie', or something else?"

Not looking up while he unwound the bandages he spoke. "I think my second cousin has a baby goat she named Nookie or mayhap Pookie? Seems a rather poor choice to call *fucking* something akin to a baby goat."

He was confused why this bothered her. "Lassie, no matter what words they use in your land, I do know *fucking* and we have *fucked* many impassioned times. Another name for the act neither changes what the act is, nor how I spilled my seed into you—repeatedly as I recall—and I will not ever be forgetting how you called out my name and begged for more of me. Why does this seem to be a word you choose to evade?"

"I guess I'm a little shy and it's not considered a pleasant word where I come from."

"You do blush easily, which I find endearing. But how can this act not be considered pleasant to you? I recall your legs wide open for me, and sounds of ecstasy from your lips. You are a beautiful female with womanly needs and desire beyond measure. I find our fucking to be far beyond pleasant."

Thorne had finally found the end of the long wrapping. She had certainly put great effort into binding the cut, much more than the wound called for. Unfortunately, the ends of the fabric were stuck together with dried blood.

A moistened towel would be required to soak the fabric free without tearing open his wound. If it bled he feared Candy would want to administer the wound yet again, so he grabbed a wet towel for the job.

"I almost have this foul smelling wrap off my arm and no longer will I smell distasteful to you."

"Actually you always smell really nice to me. Well maybe not at the wound site, but otherwise you do. And sometimes medicines are like that, you know the worse they taste or smell the better they work."

"And where did you hear such balderdash Lassie?"

She thought for a moment. "My stepmother, why?"

"A fallacy if ever I heard one. I know you thought to be caring to tend to my wound, and I most undeniably appreciated your attention to it. However, I can no longer abide the stench of this, and truly tis senseless to."

Candy's brows creased. He really hated to have to tell her, but he had to, the wound itched worse than a bush of nettles.

"Lassie, that *medicine* was naught, but rather a concoction of finely ground diamond dust mixed in rancid old hog grease, meant to sharpen and polish a blade."

"Oh my God, really? And you let me put it on your open wound?" Her voice was rising with panic.

The last piece of the bandage loosened and peeled from his skin. The flesh beneath was reddened, clearly inflamed, providing proof of being irritated by the not so therapeutic ointment.

"Why didn't you tell me? I'm so sorry Thorne. It looks raw and must be really uncomfortable."

Thorne started to wipe the cut clean. "I spoke naught of such because I would have endured much simply for your touch, even more for a taste of your lips. Imagine what I would have endured to be inside of you. Thankfully you did not require me to suffer beyond the pain within my sac while trying to have my way with you."

Candy *tsked* him while shaking her head. "Very amusing. With you, I'm what men where I come from would call 'a sure thing'. Something that should mortify me, but amazingly doesn't. Guess I'm just too high on endorphins from awesome sex."

"Is that so?"

Taking the towel from him she washed off the remnants of what she'd thought had been antibiotic ointment.

"Geez Thorne, this looks bad. I'm really, really sorry and feel awful about this. What can I do to ever make this terrible mistake up to you?"

His movements ceased. Without looking up he spoke casually as he cleaned the wound. "Indeed woman I have suffered much. Tis a wonder I was not brought to my knees by the pain of it."

As Thorne raised his head, his eyebrows followed. "Have I not warned you how heedless words can convey lewd intent to a man's mind and groin? I wonder how can you possibly repay me for this grievous act against me when you carry no coin? This time I will be taking what you have to offer as trade for my suffering. And woman, the price for amends will be most steep."

Candy giggled as she reached for the honey pot. "Oops, my bad."

Raking his eyes over her he added serious gruffness to his tone. "You do not care to barter on the heavy price I shall extract?"

Candy shook her head.

"I warned you—now you shall learn. In the future you will not be offering up any such respective *bargaining* or *coin* to any man. Restitution requires I take you entirely, piercing you with full deep thrusts, driving hard with my thick length until you scream my name."

As she let out small groan of anticipation he knew he could not hold back to play this game much longer. Pulling her close against his chest, he spoke with a low seductive voice into her ear, warning of the dire consequences she would be forced to endure as he stretched her tightness beyond measure.

"Greedily I shall collect your manner of payment, while loosening my lust upon you and thrusting my cock to my hilt without mercy no matter how much you writhe or beg beneath me. And be assured you *will* beg for mercy from the pleasure I force you to endure. I shall suck your little bud and fuck you with my tongue until you scream my name. Only then will I enter you. I will not subside until the debt and debtor are most satisfied and my seed runs from your tight little cunny to pool onto these sheets. What say you woman?"

He heard her softly beg, "yes."

And repayment began

Chapter Five
Celcee

When Lord Thorne had returned from his day's hunt he appeared far less burdened. Seldom did his expression show signs of true happiness, and she was pleased to see this change upon his handsome face. Evidently his hunt had gone exceedingly well.

Approximately thirteen moons past, Celcee's life had changed when, thanks to the goddess, Lord Thorne had taken her into service. At first she'd been intimidated by his physical size and the fact he held a fierce reputation as a warrior. Not to discount he was also her King.

However, he spoke to her in a kind manner, never demeaning, and had not hesitated to employ her as his personal servant. Since then she had learned the House of Rule was not nearly so overwhelming, as it had seemed, and neither was the man she worked for who treated her honorably.

This job was a blessing, far better than most work available to a young female. Celcee was treated well and enjoyed her work at the House of Rule. Also, she was paid coin in addition to room and board, and all for a fraction of the work required of her at home.

Caring for a single man such as Thorne was far easier than a house full of young children, a hungry and angry father, her worn out mother and bossy older brothers who thought she should ever pick up after them.

Nothing had been more distasteful than cleaning her families outback privy, which serviced four males who forever seemed to have no regard for where they pissed. The House of Rule had indoor facilities and Thorne seemed to have far better aim with his manhood.

Having her own room in the House of Rule signified a great luxury to Celcee and was her first opportunity to have a space of her very own. Nor did she have to share the space or a bed with other house staff.

At home the single room house was occupied with seven others, and although she loved her family, she treasured her new independence and private space.

Moreover, she valued not seeing her father abuse her mother when he drank too liberally, or hearing their arguments, their fucking, or her oldest brother's nightly masturbating. There was no privacy to be found in the one-room house.

Tonight was to be the 'needing moon' and again she wondered if it would be a special night for her. This morning when she looked into the mirror Celcee thought she was becoming a more attractive female. Her breasts were perhaps a bit small yet compared to some, although there was certainly enough to fill any man's palm. However, more would be far better because she wished to look bountiful and imagined men might like a great deal of breast to fondle.

She also took notice of how her body was filling out nicely with roundness to her hips, gaining a womanly look to her figure. Plus her freckles seemed less prominent now and Celcee decided she had nicely shaped lips— hopefully, kissable lips.

A prayer was offered to the goddess in the hopes a handsome man would find her desirable and choose her this night. Now of maturity she felt certain this would be her first month to participate in the 'needing moon'. Yearnings had begun, and she wanted to know the feel of a man. What had been curiosity had grown into a need within her.

Often she fantasized as to who would be her first man, the man who would change her from a child to a woman. Of course she often daydreamed it would be King Thorne, but he would never truly choose her and was always most discrete in his liaisons. Never did he ask for her attention to any needs beyond being his house servant, though she would have eagerly given whatever he asked of her.

Her employer had days when he was brusque, though never did Thorne target his troubles against her. In fact, he treated her better than expected, never with a heavy hand, and ever with respect, and that should be enough.

Truthfully, she had a secret love and lusting for him, but knew he would never be interested in the likes of her. The man was merely her fantasy, as he was with most females who laid eyes upon him. Yet the sight of Thorne always made her sigh and smile.

His muscled body and handsome face looked of perfection to Celcee, and none could ever look finer unto her eyes. At least in her service to him she got to enjoy his brief proximity a few times per day on most days.

Today, when Thorne chose her to serve the foreign woman, Celcee felt honored to be thought worthy to be of service this woman with which he clearly seemed captivated. Such was indeed a boon to her, plus, Lady Candy was likable as well, though her ways were at times most peculiar. No doubt that was because her land was so far away, and a most strange province it must be.

This foreign female spoke in an amusing manner. Never before had Celcee heard of 'fucking' referred to as 'fooling'. How could a man's intentions not be clearly known and anyone be *fooled* if they were being fucked? Did not a swollen shaft between your legs give an indication of what was occurring?

Many words Candy used were confusing, and at times a bit humorous, though Celcee refrained from laughing, thus possibly offending Lady Candy.

Celcee had returned, with what turned out to be a *replacement* honey pot, and thought to faint at the spectacular nakedness of Thorne. Glorious he was! Of course she'd seen her brothers naked, as they lived in a small house, but a man in such a state of arousal—honestly, Thorne was magnificent, and massive, not likely a sight to ever to be forgotten.

Tomorrow she'd enjoy titillating gossip with the other servants. No one ever had need of a second honey pot in a single night and she imagined Candy would be quite sore from Thorne's immense size and the amount of passion they had shared.

Her own 'needing' began surfacing just thinking about it. This might indeed be her night to leave childhood behind, and she was looking forward to the romantic thought of being held in a man's embrace, and hearing endearing words as he turned her into a woman.

As she rounded the corner to the kitchen she saw Shemmar holding his jaw. He wiggled it as if checking to see if it would still move. So it appeared it was not broken after all, for which he should consider himself most fortunate.

"It looks painful my Lord. Should I get you tonic for the pain?"

Like everyone else, she'd heard what happened earlier in the evening and thought Shemmar to be blessed by the goddess, for it to be simply his jaw that suffered. All knew of Thorne's battle abilities and his sometimes quick and deadly temper. Her King was not a man to trifle with.

Shemmar should have known better than to try to take another man's woman, let alone Thorne's. Was it not obvious how King Thorne favored Lady Candy and any man who touched her would become a wounded, if not dead, fool? Her ruler had little patience when confronted or challenged, and as their King why should he?

At her inquiry, Shemmar focused closely on Celcee, as though he'd never taken notice of her before. Being merely a servant, he probably had not. Then he smiled at her. He had a very pleasing face, although she preferred the look of Thorne.

"Celcee you are becoming a woman, are you not? Are you yet a child who needs a man to break her?"

If not for the 'needing' rising within her, she might have been taken aback by his boldness. He was a handsome man, but had a reputation for taking many women and respecting none. Never did his conquests seek him out, not as women did Thorne. Rumors said Thorne was a generous lover. Maybe they meant more than just his size, maybe in other ways as well. Would Shemmar be a caring lover?

"I am virtuous, though I am feeling my first 'needing' with this moon."

"Truly Celcee, a girl of your looks has yet to be plucked. Are the boys of the village blind?"

The compliment made her smile at him. "Perhaps so, as none has yet to approach me."

"Then allow me to be the handsome man to make a woman of you."

Shemmar took her by the hand and led her through the kitchen door into the garden, all the while seeming confident she would not deny him. He was a fine-looking man and had chosen her this night and with her feeling of 'needing' perhaps she should not turn from his advances. He was in fact a relation to the royal House. She could do worse on this night and what if no male chose her?

There were many other couples outside as well, but Shemmar glanced around and picked a specific stone bench. Then he rudely told the couple using it to leave, as he had chosen this spot. His relationship to the House of Rule convinced the couple to scramble off half-naked to finish their tryst under a tree.

He could have chosen any vacant spot and Celcee was surprised by his choosing this spot to take her virginity. This bench seemed so public, not offering any semblance of privacy for what she was going to be giving up.

Nervousness filled her, but she knew Shammar was more experienced than perhaps the entire village. He would know how to do this thing, to bring her to womanhood.

As he pulled Celcee closer he reached under her dress, and eased it off over her head. "I want to see your nakedness. Feign not coyness, as this 'needing moon' the goddess has chosen you, as have I."

Shemmar tore her barrier panties from her and tied them around his wrist, favoring an old custom indicating a sexual conquest. He seemed most pleased with himself while Celcee thought he could have simply asked and spared her abraded flesh from the roughness of the act.

A communal honey pot was nearby for anyone's use and he waved her towards it. "Go prepare yourself, as I will not tolerate bastards from you." Waving her off to the task he began unlacing his breeches.

His words both surprised and disappointed her. She had thought all men enjoyed the preparation of their female. Doing as he said, she then returned and he guided her to the bench.

"Kneel on your hands and knees on the bench as I break you from behind."

Never had Celcee heard this was how a woman was broken, and expected something more caring to happen, like in her daydreams. Admittedly she knew little of men, whereas he knew much of women, so she did as instructed. When he touched her she felt heated. He said she was wet and ready for her first 'needing' to be fulfilled.

Shemmar pulled himself free of his breeches and went to stand at the back of her. "Are you certain you want to be broken, as it cannot be undone, and I will hear no complaints of this deed I endure for you?"

By this time Celcee was no longer certain—even though she felt the 'needing' within, she was also humiliated. Finally she said yes to him, but wondered why. Surely if not for the 'needing moon' she would have denied such a rude man no matter his handsome face.

The Moon Goddess had set her 'needing' in motion, and it was proving intolerable to try to deny the lust she felt. Certainly this was not how she'd thought her breaking to womanhood would be done.

The 'needing' desire to be filled by a man made her wetter, warmer, more needy and Celcee knew she was ready to become a woman. Despite Shemmar's lack of concern or comfort, the 'needing' was now consuming her thoughts. Celcee wanted, and *needed*, to feel the pleasure that women whispered of, and to know of that release while in a man's arms.

His manhood plunged into her with such force that she cried out in pain, yet he did not even consider relenting. He withdrew and repeated the act over and over, as stone scraped her knees and he tore through her maidenhead. Deep and painful thrusting continued until she finally heard sounds she well knew from hearing her father when he mounted her mother—a man's deep grunts and groans from sating his own need.

She, however, felt no such gratification, only the pain of torn flesh to her core and knees. When he spilled inside her, she felt shame at having been so in 'need' to not consider refusing this man who cared nothing of her. But the breaking was done and she could not undo it. A child no more, now her tears would be that of a woman.

When he pulled out some blood covered his shaft but he just tucked himself back into his breeches and threw her dress to her. "Now you are a woman. Are you not pleased as you can brag on how I honored your cunt?"

Tears threatened her eyes but she said nothing. Of course she was not pleased, what woman would be? He had used her harshly with neither any gentleness nor concern for her needs. And why did he keep looking above this bench he'd chosen to take her on?

Finally she noticed he was looking at an open window. It was the guest room Candy was in. Now she understood why he had taken her from behind—so he could watch that window while he broke her. Shemmar cared nothing about her, as this was about his lust for Candy.

Feeling of hurt, anger, and foolish flooded through her. What a stupid girl she'd been. Nonetheless, if he had thought to make Candy jealous, Shemmar certainly held little knowledge of the degree of pleasure Thorne was providing to her. Nor did the hateful man before her know how many times the couple had already thoroughly enjoyed each other.

Shemmar was a poor substitute to his cousin, but in Celcee's mind all men were a poor substitute to her Lord Thorne. Suddenly her broken pride gave way to an inner strength and harsh words escaped her.

"I had thought as Thorne's cousin, you might be at least half as endowed as he, or at least skilled in ways to please a woman. They," she gave a nod up indicating the guest room window, "are coupling repeatedly, and have already required a second honey pot to be delivered. My Lord is like a fierce virile animal with his bitch in heat and they are enjoying their mating profusely."

Just then she heard Candy's passion rising with cries of intense pleasure as she called out Thorne's name and begged for more of him. Thorne's growing masculine climax followed, roaring from the window above them.

Such a male, thought Celcee. *So much more than his cousin could ever pretend to be.*

When Thorne came to completion there was no question about his sensual gratification. The warrior in him fucked like a lion and his lioness returned with resounding roars of her pleasure.

Shemmar's expression of surprise turned to one of anger at hearing those telling sounds spilling from the overhead window. Fearful he might strike her in retaliation, Celcee quickly stepped back from him, turned and ran back toward the house.

Tonight had been very disappointing and painful for her. In addition Shemmar no longer seemed nearly as handsome of a man, as his mannerisms had taken away any appeal she had held for him. No wonder he'd had so many women if this was the limit of his fucking skills, as none would ever choose his return for a second bout. As her first lover he measured poorly and was deemed lacking.

Had she been the cause by not being pretty enough and not experienced at seduction? These thoughts saddened her. But Shemmar was correct—indeed none of this painful experience could be undone.

The next morning, when Celcee went to Candy's room and knocked, Lord Thorne answered. Her Lord looked tousled but wore a brilliant smile, the likes she'd never seen before, likely depicting his delight from his night's pleasures. He wore only his leathers, neither vest nor boots, as if he were still trying to dress. Celcee had never seen him so happy and his eyes sparkled with mirth.

"Ah, Celcee, perfect timing."

"Send her away and return to bed to pleasure me one more time you hunk of testosterone," whined Candy from beneath the sheets.

With a quick look over his shoulder he shook his head while his smile beamed. "So it seems I must care for my Lady one more time. Forgive us for delaying your chores. Come back in a generous half hour and I will have her sated and ready for a soothing hot soak."

"Will you be joining her in the tub my Lord?"

"If I do, never would I leave her, or this room. Draw a separate bath for me. Handle her with care, she means much to me."

"Indeed my Lord I see she does, as you must see she feels the same of you." *And how could she not*, thought Celcee. "She still remains under the 'needing moon' influence my Lord."

"Mayhap she is still drunk from it. She will need something in her bath for soreness when she acknowledges how many times we. . .well, see to it Celcee." Thorne was running his finger across the scared cheek.

Celcee had only seen him do this when he was greatly concerned. "My Lord, is something amiss?"

He looked down at Celcee who was easily twelve inches shorter than he. "I know I have a hard face to look upon, and can be a hard man as well, still she chose me. I have always thought females would lay with me due to my power and wealth as a ruler, yet she does not seem to have full knowledge of this."

Shaking her head, Celcee could hardly believe her King thought so poorly of himself. "My Lord, how you underestimate your worth to a female who sees beyond your markings of courage with such insignificant scars. They do not mar, they enthrall us with visions of your fearless valor. Only men see so shallow as fair of face. I would wager she finds that scar rather appealing."

Indeed Celcee could not see anything but perfection within this great man. What a shame his mirrored reflection spoke otherwise to him.

From the bed came a singsong call. "Thorne, I'm still waiting, what's taking so long? Oh, tell Celcee we need another honey pot, and quickly because I need your *enormous* cock again." Candy began giggling. "Please Thorne, I feel needful."

Celcee snickered. "I would dare say she remains a bit drunk from the 'needing'. I shall bring another honey pot with haste, my Lord."

As Thorne glanced back at his woman, Celcee could see the smile on his lips and the look of adoration in his eyes. She knew what lust looked like—this was far more.

Although happy for the couple, she felt a little jealous as well. If they needed another honey pot, Candy would be lucky if she could even walk this morning. No one needed more than a single pot, let alone two, but three honey pots in a single night? Thorne had stamina worthy of a King. Any man would be envious of his prowess—any woman would swoon at the thought of so much passion.

After delivering another, this time larger honey pot, she left to draw Thorne's bath. Some men wanted their servants to bathe them, often taking liberties as well, but Thorne would not allow her that duty.

He had told her it was not a proper job for a servant of a healthy grown man, as he considered bathing too intimate. To be sure, grown he was, and splendidly so.

Celcee smiled as she recalled that memory from last night, and how it would always be treasured. His sizable shaft was the most erotic thing she'd ever seen.

She returned with a tray of refreshments and to begin Candy's bath. Thorne was kissing his woman as he pulled away telling her to enjoy a soothing soak, as she would have great need of it. Candy seemed hesitant to release him, which Celcee could rightly understand. Thorne grabbed the buttered rolls from the food tray Celcee had brought and escaped from the room before Candy could protest.

"Poor man must be ravenous," Candy said to Celcee as they watched Thorne retreat from the room.

The women looked at each other and laughed.

"It seems he was not easily sated my Lady, and I envy how impassioned he is with you. And truly he has the most *abundant* manhood I have ever seen."

Truthfully Celcee would have expected no less, as Thorne was a man skilled and dedicated in all his tasks. Of course with a woman he would be equally resplendent. But the size of him—certainly that, she could never have imagined.

"Oh, he was sated all right, many, many, many times over. He's an incredible man and lover, and yes he's ginormous and my goodness, how I appreciated every single inch of him. And he has a lot of inches doesn't he?" The two groaned in unison.

"Exactly! And the erotic things. . .I had no clue sex could be so amazing." Candy sighed as a scenario replayed in her mind and a shiver traveled through her.

"Now tell me Celcee, did you experience your first 'needing' last night after all?"

Nodding her head, Celcee carefully hid her expression. She held no desire to ruin Lady Candy's day by reviewing her mistake.

"Do you want to talk about it while I soak? Was it difficult for you then?" Candy gingerly lowered herself into the water, suddenly feeling the glorious soreness in her inner thighs as well as deeper places.

Celcee was generous with the powder to relieve her Lady's pain, which was apparent by how slowly she walked and gently climbed into the tub. Then Celcee added the same oils Candy had chosen the previous day. Her eyes widened as she saw the red mark on Candy's inner thigh.

"He honored you by his claim of you as his worthy female. How I envy you. Someday he may mark you in the old ways with a true permanent warrior's woman marking. This is but a *warrior's kiss.*"

Looking down Candy didn't recall when he'd managed to give her the hickey, but smiled as the proof of his wickedness resting inside her thigh.

"Warrior's markings?"

"My Lord will no doubt . . . one day he may speak of this. Only true warriors follow this custom, and Thorne is truly an accomplished warrior who follows many traditions. How fortunate you are to be claimed by him." Celcee shook her head in awe.

Candy's curiosity piqued, and she decided she would ask Thorne about it later, when they were alone.

Finally she told Candy what had happened with Shemmar. Celcee included details, such as how he had focused on Candy's window, and how he reacted when he heard their passion culminate. Her comment about how Candy had called out for more of Thorne seemed to embarrass her Lady.

The fact that Shemmar had listened beneath their window concerned Candy even more so. It was when she heard what Celcee had retorted back to Shemmar that Candy began to laugh.

"That must have been what we call a ball-crusher to his ego. When I was a virgin my first time was very awkward and not pleasant either. The boy had no skill whatsoever, and it was painful too. Last night's poor experience was the fault of the selfish man you entrusted with your gift. Next time choose carefully and you'll hopefully find pleasure, and trust me with the right man it can be incredibly pleasurable."

A memorable smile crossed Candy's face. "I never knew how intense it could be and how your toes really do curl."

After finishing with Candy's bath water, Celcee returned downstairs and spotted freshly groomed Thorne heading toward the library. He stopped her and pulled her to the side.

"I hold trust in you Celcee and want you to spend the day overseeing Lady Candy while I am meeting regarding political matters. Do not let Candy wander alone, although she may see whatever she desires of the grounds or village. Trust not of Shemmar to be near her. And if you see anything that perhaps bothers your good sense, call out for a guard or warrior. All know you are my servant and will without question care for you and my Lady." Thorne hesitated as he thought before reaching inside his vest.

"Take these coins to purchase all she needs and wants, I will deny her nothing. If you need more, have the merchant bring a bill to me. She must wear a traditional dress, not what she came with, as that would cause unnecessary interest. Clothing, aye, she will need to purchase clothing. I insist you purchase a new dress for yourself as well, to celebrate your new services extended to my Lady."

A pouch of coins was slipped to her, far more than she had ever held before. Indeed her King seemed a most generous man when besotted, though never had she seen him care for a woman before. By the glint in his eyes he cared much for Lady Candy.

"Celcee, why do you have tears in your eyes? Have I been rude or unkind to you? I know I can be a coarse man at times." Thorne pushed his hand through his hair as if regretful for some affront to her.

How his hidden kind nature could be the ruin of any woman's heart. "Nay my Lord, you treat me well."

"You dislike the thought of attending Lady Candy then? I could assign a warrior to do so in your stead, though she seems most comfortable with you."

"Oh no, my Lord, she is delightful, and I feel very honored at your trust in me. Truly, I shall enjoy the time with her."

"You must tell me what saddens you then."

Studying Celcee, his eyes widened upon realizing she looked different today. Her hair was braided, as a woman would wear it on top of her head. She was stalling and not answering him.

His brows pinched, a concerned expression crossed Thorne's features. "Must I command it of you Celcee?"

"I became a woman with the 'needing moon' last night." Her words came out quickly as though to be done with it.

Thorne looked flustered as if this was meant to be female business and not for a man to ask. Still, he seemed to care for her welfare more than a servant could hope for.

"Were you not treated with respect and a gentle hand?"

With discomfort Celcee shrugged, "I chose poorly, and tis not something to be undone."

Creasing his brow and crossing his arms Thorne looked her in the eyes. "Should I kill him for your honor, or simply beat the man senseless for his lack of appreciation of that which you gifted him?"

She was not certain if he was jesting when he looked so serious, but felt privileged to know he cared about her feelings. Not a common thing, certainly not something expected. Straightening her shoulders and raising her head high Celcee addressed his concerns.

"Have no concern of it my Lord. In regards to Shemmar, he will not get within a fishing pole of your Lady or I will call for help, and always, my family says I yell likened to a she-bear with mischievous cubs. Also I carry a knife and learned the use of it from my older brothers." Celcee touched the pocket in her skirt to indicate where she kept it. "May I take leave my Lord?"

Sighing he nodded to her.

Celcee told Lady Candy how Thorne would be occupied with meetings for much of the day, and in his stead she would take her to see whatever pleased her. Although looking disappointed, Lady Candy replied how she wanted to see everything of the grounds and the village. Seemingly this foreign woman had much interest in even the most mundane things. So be it.

When they set off toward the village, Candy had taken what she called her "backpack" as they planned to walk and tour a part of the village first.

Meanwhile, Ono alternated between Candy's backpack and shoulder, or at least when the little gargoyle was not fluttering about exploring nature. Celcee suspected Ono was in search of breakfast. The little gargoyle was such a hungry fledgling.

This reminded Celcee that proper gargoyle padding needed to be purchased. How many times had she seen Candy flinch when Ono's talons bit into her flesh? Thorne would not be pleased to see his woman's delicate shoulder full of gashes. The foreign woman must have journeyed unprepared and without proper padding for her gargoyle and herself. Perchance she had not planned to travel at all? Celcee thought it seemed almost as though Candy had no knowledge of these things, but how could that be?

The walk to the village was full of girlish laughter between them. This woman Thorne had brought to the House of Rule was dissimilar from other royal females Celcee had met. Candy laughed easily and was curious of common things. She also spoke freely and did not treat Celcee as a person of lower birth. Her easy manner and treatment of the villagers as people of worth surprised all.

Thorne's woman had been here less than a day, and already the entire village gossiped about how this foreign female belonged to their King. Indeed it was whispered King Thorne he fought against his own blood for her.

Of course the tales were exaggerated with great details of how the fight took place. Of how Lady Candy was pinned to the floor by Shemmar as he tried to force himself into her, and how Thorne had eviscerated his cousin before throwing his woman over his shoulder and taking her to *his* room. The tale was a bit embellished, but the villagers reveled in the telling of romantic heroics of their King.

Many maidens' faces held expressions of jealousy. This hardly surprised Celcee, as how long had every female dreamed that young King Thorne might choose one of them to someday sit at his side in the House of Rule? Already he was twenty and seven summers of age, and he'd yet to choose a Queen. None could have fathomed some woman from another land, obviously far outside his realm, would finally gain his eye and favor.

This provided grave disappointment to all single females, some of whom had assuredly at one time shared a bed with him, but to no avail. His heart had remained steadfastly closed, despite how they had opened their legs to him.

Candy met shopkeepers with a genuine smile and curiosity. She asked so many questions that it was as if she was but a four year old. Nevertheless, Celcee could not help but enjoy her company. This foreign woman could be described as special beyond compare, well past simply a face of beauty. It was easy to see the cause for Thorne's interest in her charming ways. What male would not find her alluring?

Candy's spirit shone like a nugget of gold amongst scraps of tarnished copper. How rare a thing to behold so humble a woman of worth, yet Lady Candy's soft heart shone bright.

After helping her Lady select dresses, Celcee showed her the traditional gargoyle cross-shoulder-wraps. These wraps, called *para-clo,* were what prosperous women wore when their gargoyle companions attended them. *Para-clo* pieces were padded with a strong thick leather piece resting on the right shoulder. Soft fabric draped crosswise over one bosom, then attached at the waist on the left side.

Lady Candy was intrigued not only by the efficient usefulness of the *para-clo*, but also how pretty the draped fabric pieces looked when worn. "If only they came in seasonal colors and not just dreary basic-beige", she had said.

Three wraps sounded like a reasonable purchase to Celcee, however, Candy balked, saying the purchase of a single *para-clo* was more than sufficient spending of Thorne's funds.

Should Candy's words ever be repeated to Thorne, he would likely be angered by how she thought him to be so poor. Thorne was a prideful male and would not want to be thought of as not being generous with his woman. So Celcee snuck in a second *para-clo* wrap of finer material in with the purchases, paid the shopkeeper with coin and a finger to her lips for his silence. The man nodded, obviously pleased by the sale.

Ono seemed partial to the padded wrap as well, immediately taking to it and sinking her nails in for good purchase. Candy let out a giggle while her shoulder escaped damage. Once again Celcee pondered why her Lady did not know of these things.

The day turned out to be most pleasant for them with Candy stopping when she wanted to 'sketch' something of interest. That 'backpack' contained a bulk of parchment and some wooden sticks. Candy's hand would move the wood piece across paper and shapes formed mirroring what her own eyes saw.

How was this possible? So strange a thing much likened to writing, yet not. There was neither quill nor parchment, as Candy called these *pencils* and *paper*. Celcee watched as tiny homes and trees appeared inside the parchment—a most unusual thing to behold. Flat, though appearing quite real. Surely this spoke of magick. Finally Celcee inquired.

"Is this some magick within you that makes these shapes appear thus?"

"Magic? Not at all, it's called drawing or sketching, an art form where I come from."

Candy's nimble fingers were rubbing across the soft lead adding what she explained was 'shading' and 'dimension' to the drawing. When she seemed satisfied with her 'drawing', her materials were put away, saying she would finish these later.

Despite her Lady's words surely some sort of magick was involved, and Celcee wondered what would become of that home Candy had put into the parchment. Would it disappear? Hopefully not before the family could move out and seek other shelter.

Before returning to the House of Rule, they enjoyed refreshments purchased from a hostelry. Celcee thought it strange that Candy had no experience with hazel wood juice in her land, and how she seemed to savor the common-enough beverage as if some great treat.

When Celcee inquired what they drank in the land Candy was from (since wine did not seem so common either), Candy's strange answers left Celcee confused. What were these liquids *cokes*, *stars* and *bucks*? She shuddered and hoped her interpretation had not meant they drank the blood of deer or bucks. A most peculiar land indeed!

While they walked up the cobbled entrance of the House of Rule, Candy asked to see where the horses were stabled, and mentioned how much she enjoyed sketching the grace of horses.

Celcee had learned to ride a horse when she helped her neighbor's brother with farming for coin two summers back. Horses were costly and generally only ridden by the wealthy or warriors. Even a workhorse was considered an extravagance, though sometimes their services were rented or bartered at harvest time.

The two chatted like long time friends as Celcee guided the way. When they arrived at the large stable they came upon a young man who Celcee introduced as Ram. As the young man smiled his eyes surveyed Celcee, and the servant girl smiled back. It seemed he was most eager to want to be of service to them.

Ram showed Lady Candy a beautiful off-white horse.

"This is my favorite horse, my Lady. She is well trained and though smaller than the war-horses, exceedingly fast," he added, as his hand caressed the mare with evident pride. The magnificent horse had a long and well groomed and partially braided tail.

The smell of the horses reminded Candy of when she'd visited the equestrian center at SCAD and watched Gina ride. The scent was actually rather warm and pleasant. There was no doubt that the beauty of a horse could pull on a female's heartstrings, as they really were one of the planets most beautiful creatures.

"What a stunning horse. What is she called?" Candy was stroking the horse's forehead with both hands while in return it nuzzled her and blew air across her face.

"Now be a nice horsey," she whispered.

"Lightness, because she is quick as lightening and an almost sans colored horse." The very light coloring obviously provided distinguishing merit to the horse. Lightness was beautiful with all the fine lines that made horses such intriguing animals to Candy.

"Would my Lady like to ride her around the arena for me, whilst I clean her stall?"

Ram was scrutinizing Celcee, and Candy wondered if cleaning the already immaculate stalls was really on his mind. It hardly seemed likely Ram had OCD regarding the state of those horse stalls. No, the young man seemed to be thinking more about Celcee in the hay, than hay in the horses' mouths.

After Celcee's cruel experience last night, that girl definitely needed her self-esteem boosted and if Candy could help facilitate that, well, she was all for it.

With the extent of Candy's inner thigh soreness (thanks not only to the hours of horseback riding the day before but also Thorne's added hours of ardently riding her), Candy declined the horse-riding offer. Plus, she'd never *actually* ridden a horse unaccompanied, except at the state fair pony ride, which hardly counted.

"I would love to walk her, if that would be all right?"

Being quite pleased by her offer, Ram got Lightness tethered and ready for a walkabout. As he led the mare into the arena, he explained what to do to give her a good warm-up walk.

Candy wished she could also advise Ram what to do to lift Celcee's spirits, but these things had to run their own course. Besides, she had a horse to walk and had never done that before either. How hard could it be?

As she stepped up and took the lead line Candy waited until Ram had left her to her own devices.

"Now Lightness," she cooed, "this is my first time, so be gentle with me because this is virgin territory, and I haven't a clue what I'm doing."

Lightness tossed her head as if to say she had the situation under control, Candy sure hoped so. Giving the mare the lead she watched as Lightness began trotting around the arena. Meanwhile Candy turned in her own tight circle to follow, soon realizing she could get dizzy doing this.

The horse was unquestionably an animal of grace and Candy studied every flexion of the muscles so she could later replicate this strength and elegance on paper. The horse was showing off with prancing and now sidestepping toward her. Candy was praising Lightness for her dancing skills, telling the mare that the judges had shown their cards—all with straight ten's on them, and how she'd win the golden strut-dance globe award.

That was when it happened.

Suddenly a big beige hound bounded into the training ring and headed straight for Candy.

Everything occurred so swiftly—Candy's terror was instantaneous, followed by her piercing scream.

As the scream escaped from Candy's lungs, Lightness panicked and reared. When the horse came back down, a front hoof hit her on the forehead, knocking Candy to the ground.

Feelings flashed through her mind—petrifying fear, pain . . . blackness.

The groundkeeper's old hound ran over to her prone body and tried to revive her with licks to her face, but Candy didn't move.

The dog whimpered.

Chapter Six
Ono

What to do, what to do?

Ono was flapping her wings distraught at her repeated failure regarding Candy's wellbeing. These situations were so beyond her traditional feline scope of required knowledge. As a feline she had known of little else other than eating, sleeping, playing, sleeping, purring, sleeping and being kittenish. Cuteness fit in there somewhere as well, but Ono was too frazzled to think about it.

Recently all her activities had changed. Now she knew of flying and some hunting. Never had she encountered these strange predicaments when she was a kitten in Savannah. And never had she felt so useless as now. Gargoyles had *duties*, while kittens were only expected to be *adorable*. And, *sigh*, she had been magnificent as Coco. Now she was an inept gargoyle!

I am a hopeless gargoyle. Such a disgrace!

Last night that cousin of Thorne's had abruptly closed the bedroom door leaving her trapped inside Candy's room before Ono could follow them and guard her person. Ono knew it was deliberate as the man's face revealed his ugly intent. Unfortunately Ono had not been fast enough or wise enough to be useful to Candy.

Hateful human with smug grin!

Then, when Thorne came back into the room wounded, Ono felt as though it was partially *her* fault for not being at Candy's side. Luckily Thorne had not chided Ono, as he was too enthralled with her human. The hunter smelled musky and Ono now knew what *that* meant. Thorne wanted to mate—and mate, and mate some more.

He surely enjoys mating!

Sure enough, Candy had lifted her tail for the hunter—repeatedly. Thorne apparently represented a prime alpha-male and had very strong mating instincts and it seemed Candy was in season.

Who knew?

Luckily Thorne had opened the bedroom window. Thank goodness, as that provided Ono the opportunity to rest on a nearby tree branch, because with all those sounds they were making it was impossible to sleep.

Learning to perch and balance while clutching with her new thick talons was a bit awkward and so not kitten-like. In addition she lacked her fluffy tail, which she used to use to wrap around her head and eyes to close out light and ugly sights. How disturbing to have lost that kitten capability, because what she saw below her included more humans—and they were all *mating*!

Ack! These humans were more prolific than rabbits and she wondered how many litters would result from the balmy musky night.

Being a gargoyle was not a career choice she would have chosen. Who knew *she* would be expected to watch out for her person? After all, when *she* had been a kitten *she* was the one who expected others to care for her. And rightfully so—because, hello—didn't anyone remember her ancestor the goddess Bastet?

Ignorant humans, thou should bow before me. Well maybe not while in her present gargoyle form, but certainly in her feline fineness—should it ever returned.

Between this new level of responsibility and her lack of experience, these turns of events repeatedly proved her to be a less than accomplished gargoyle to her companion. Ono actually felt *disappointed* in herself, and that realization alone reminded her she was no longer a cat, because felines didn't even recognize self-deprecating words in their vocabulary of meows.

Why would they?

To think today had started out so perfect with a little flying and then a little riding on Candy's padded shoulder. Ono was pleased her wings were getting stronger now and stayed close to Candy in the village as she figured proximity was expected of her.

Once back at the House of Rule, Ono thought she could explore and maybe find a fresh, plump and succulent lizard. So she decided to stretch her wings a bit. Flying definitely worked up an appetite. Sure enough, Ono spotted an appetizing lizard sunning on a rock when all Hades broke loose.

So much for lunch—I will undoubtedly become an emaciated and underappreciated gargoyle.

Then she'd heard that scream. Ono recognized the source and didn't hesitate to fly back to her person. And now Candy was down on the ground with a big nasty canine licking and slobbering all over her face.

Revolting!

If that dog started to try to hump Candy's leg, Ono was going to teach him a lesson. She was not sure what that lesson would be, but no dog was going to do *that* to her person and get away with it!

Poor horizontal Candy, if she knew what that mangy dog was doing her terror would become even more compounded.

Candy appeared to be dead or possibly playing possum. Her person had never played possum before and was very good at it, unless she was dead. In that case things were very bad.

What to do, what to do?

When Ono glanced to Celcee and saw the degree of panic in her face, Ono decided to seek out Thorne. The big hunter would know what to do. He was smart and strong.

Taking to her wings Ono headed back to the house. No doors were open so she circled the house to find a window to fly in or at least spot Thorne.

What in the . . . all the windows were closed!

Awk, indoor dwelling primates!

She flew to the big window where all those nice smelling leather books were stored. There he was! Big human Thorne seemed in a heated debate with his untrustworthy cousin.

Grrr, she hated that despicable male, and maybe Thorne did, too.

Very smart hunter.

Not knowing any other means to get Thorne's attention, Ono began to thrust her body against the window and flapping her wings while trying to remain airborn. This made for a frustrating and demeaning task, and it appeared as though she wasn't bright enough to know better.

Flap, flap—hit window, slide, *flap, flap*—hit window, slide . . . and of course she gained absolutely no purchase so she kept sliding down against the slick glass.

I look like a stupid pigeon!

One thrust against the hard glass had been so jarring she feared having chipped a tooth as well a leaving her bowel contents behind to streak down the glass. Obviously she couldn't bury the stuff either. This gargoyle form of her knew nothing about litter box etiquette. Although a remote part of Ono's brain found it embarrassing, another part of her said *whatever*.

When Thorne finally got distracted by the noise and saw Ono flapping with all her strength he ran to the window to let Ono in.

Finally! Slow human!

Thorne did not hesitate. "Take me to her."

So with what little strength Ono had remaining, she flew back to the stable with the hunter matching her speed. This human was very fast, and Ono was thankful, as her person had great need of his help.

As Ono landed on a ringside railing she noticed the disgusting canine was now sniffing Candy's crotch!

Really? Did the animal have no shame?

Gag, would the degradation to her person never end?

Bad, mangy, smelly, animal with doggy breath.

Bad dog!

Chapter Seven
Thorne

His cousin was a pompous idiot and coward. Not an ounce of warrior in his making.

When Thorne spotted the torn garment on Shemmar's wrist he knew it was to boast at what had been done to the servant girl—Thorne's servant girl! Thorne glared at his cousin who sat across from him at the council meeting.

Despite Levenia's faults, she would have no such thing as bragging of his deeds. "How young are you Shemmar that you still parade a conquest of taking childhood from a virgin by wearing that? I thought males outgrew such vanity while still in their teen years. Take it off at this meeting and in this house, tis disrespectful of the female. Do you rape and plunder villages as well?"

His sister had many traits, not all that Thorne liked, but she would not put up with disrespect to a female. This, at least, was one thing about which they agreed. What a shame that Levenia did not see how she disrespected herself.

Their cousin dared not argue and removed the under garment from his wrist. All the while Thorne wished he had gelded the man yester eve. By Celcee's demeanor, Thorne gathered she had suffered a poor experience last night. This was likely Shemmar's way to retaliate, not honorably man-to-man, but against a sweet female. How his relative's actions repeatedly disappointed him.

This gathering with the elder advisory council had been called to discuss the increased friction between two villages east of them, both under Thorne's rule.

The advisors consisted of two men his father had deemed as valuable. Thorne did not always agree with their thoughts, but he generally did respect their years of wisdom. Their knowledge of history and past pacts held value since Thorne had not had time to study such before he held the responsibilities as the King.

Malkum of Old, as he was called, was white haired and had a beard he forever stroked as one might a beloved pet. Often the hair on his head stood straight up as if the man had argued with it hours on end, and perchance he had.

The elder had a tendency to speak to himself and never had Thorne known if Malkum was losing his senses or if he indeed talked to spirits as some rumored. There was no doubt that at times the man held wisdom of an unnatural manner and he was well past a century in age. At other times, Malkum of Old simply seemed forgetful. Some said the man was well past a millennium old. This was not something Thorne held as truth, as undoubtedly the gossip had grown larger than the man.

Years ago the elder had taken in an apprentice, a young orphaned boy, seven summers of age. Now the boy, named Webber, had grown to become a young man with good looks and widened shoulders. He had remained ever faithful to Malkum of Old, and while the boy grew stronger, his mentor grew weaker and his eyesight diminished. His orbs were now devoid of color, and milky white as clouds in the sky. Oddly, at times it seemed as if the old man's sight proved to be just fine, yet at other times he truly seemed blind.

Webber was a quite lad with inquisitive eyes, which served Malkum of Old well. The boy had been schooled well in many subjects. Rumor even said that young Webber was even able to do small magicks.

Knowing his people were too easily superstitious, Thorne considered this as unmerited gossip and hopefully not a danger to Webber.

Then there was Allister, a fairly tall, gangly, and overly thin man, that Thorne found to be of little use. His large eyes and hawkish nose were too prominent for his sunken face. The man also had a bad habit of biting his fingernails to the degree that the skin was then ripped off the tips.

More than several times Thorne had spotted the man as he peeled the skin from around his thumb and then ate it. A disgusting habit and always Thorne wondered why his father had held this strange man in esteem. For a decade Thorne had seen nothing in the man to prove any merit. The quiet man seemed to have neither family, nor a woman he cared for.

As Fate would have it, Thorne had been denied time to learn intricate wisdoms of ruling afore his father, the previous King, was murdered.

Surely Thorne's father had known some trait that Allister held that could be of use, other than warming a chair, drinking wine, and collecting a stipend.

This was not the first meeting with his council to discuss the troublesome villages, as this arguing had started and grown into an ongoing feud many years past. As always, the two villages quarreled with unproven accusations against each other until recently when their retaliations had gone beyond merely heated words.

One was a mining town and the other made money from trading, yet they argued over which village was more profitable, which had the most children within their village, which village had the prettiest females, most virile men—the list was long and never ending. The ceaseless bickering was for naught.

Now it had escaladed to include accusations of poisoning each other's water sources. Such would be a very dangerous act, if indeed true. The turmoil was growing and needed to be resolved between the villages. Thorne would not tolerate such childish bickering, as it could lead to death of innocents.

Indeed Thorne was considering taking warriors with him to blacken a few eyes and break a few bones until the villages and their leaders saw the situation with more clarity, or in the manner Thorne would advise them.

That was the point of discussion when Ono was seen flapping violently at the window, which could only mean Ono's companion, Candy, was in harm's way—or worse. He neither hesitated nor addressed the council, simply reacted and followed the little distressed gargoyle to Candy.

When he reached the stable's practice ring, he dropped to his knees at Candy's side and took her hand. She had a pulse, although slow. But how did he know if such was normal where she came from? Last night he had heard the beating of her heart, which was faster due to her 'needing'. This was surely too slow. She looked so small, delicate, and broken, and it made his heart ache as anger welled within him.

Without getting up he roared. "Who is to blame for this harm to my woman?"

Celcee and Ram shamefacedly stepped forward. Each answered, taking on the blame.

Thorne frowned at the two young ones and tried to dampen his voice. "Surely neither of you put this lump on her forehead, Ram? Celcee?"

Ram stepped forward in front of Celcee, and Thorne respected the boy for the brave gesture of facing his King's wrath while trying to protect Celcee. "I asked if your Lady would like to walk Lightness about the ring, since she was so taken by the mare, and Lady Candy said she would."

Thorne looked the boy up and down and saw how his shirt appeared disheveled, as was Celcee's hair. He held no wish to punish them for misspent young passion, especially after what had happened to Celcee last night. He knew full well Shemmar had treated her special day harshly in retaliation.

A crowd of workers and warriors were gathering to see what had happened as they had certainly heard Thorne's thundering anger. Quickly he covered Candy's calves and ankles with her dress, as none should see her looking so undone.

"I see what looks akin to lustful yearning betwixt the two of you, which left Candy in unexpected danger. I shall consider your punishment. Meet me in the library after supper, and pray my Lady will awaken without permanent harm."

Although he did not wish to be harsh with them, he needed to make sure they understood when they had duties they could not dally with each other. If his Lady were severely injured, his punishment would not be lax. His fists were clenched at such a dire thought, and he prayed to the goddesses his Lassie would be set to right.

Hermin, the healer, came running up to see to Candy. He was an older balding man who huffed and puffed from the exertion. The man ate too many meat pies and sweets as evidenced by his girth. Sweat beaded on Hermin's brow, as he verified no broken bones, likely fearing any other prognosis would be ill received.

Though his warriors offered assistance, Thorne declared only he would carry Candy back to the house.

When Thorne placed her ever so softly onto her bed, Hermin told Thorne there was naught he could do. Cool compresses for her head, and wait to see if her brain was injured. Hopefully she would awaken soon.

Thorne considered the old man useless if this was the extent of what the healer could do for her. *Cool compresses.* Any fool could figure that out, after all she had a hoof print the size of his palm on her forehead, and it was profoundly swollen.

With due remorse, Celcee was anxious to help Candy, but Thorne could not consider allowing such until her meted punishment had been served. Despite his fondness for Celcee, he was compelled to follow their system of justice and balances. There had to be a penalty due to her degree of negligence, thereby giving cause to another person's harm. Favoritism was a forerunner to dissent in any kingdom, and he avoided partiality.

Thorne stayed at Candy's side and administered the compresses himself. He fretted whether she was chilled, or too warm. Seeing her so helpless was heart rending and he recognized she meant much more to him than he'd imagined possible. To think he had promised to protect her, and yet here she lay. As he held her hand he spoke softly to her, hopeful his words would be heard and pull her back to consciousness—Back to him.

A servant brought Thorne the evening meal, but the thought of food was unbearable when Candy lay so broken. Finally he rested his head next to her hand, on the bed that held so many pleasant memories. Here she was, on the same bed they had used to enjoy each other so fully the night before. It seemed impossible to comprehend.

Thoughts on her injury became a physical response within him, and felt like spikes being driven into his heart. Each spike hammered by a blow from a heavy mallet, and each blow matched the tempo of his heart. *Thump*—pain, *thump*—pain, *thump* . . .

Thorne brought a perch to Candy's room for Ono, and hooked it to a ceiling toggle. The little gargoyle settled there but seemed as wrought as Thorne felt, as her little wings nervously fluttered. Both waited for Candy to awaken, as they shared feelings of grief and failure.

Finally Candy stirred. As her eyes opened she let out a small cry of pain, then quickly closed them again.

"Let me lower the lighting Lassie. You must be in great pain." He lowered the oil lamps, returned to her side, and stroked her soft flushed cheek.

As Thorne changed the wet cloth from her head yet again, she looked up at him and her expression held confusion. And though her eyes appeared the same green, they were not quite right. Those eyes, her beautiful green eyes seemed recessed. The blow from Lightness' hoof had hurt her greatly. How could this have happened? He wondered what had originally made her scream, thus frightening the horse?

Thorne stared out the window as he waited in the library. He held no appetite of anything other than the numbing effect of drink. Seldom did he resort to what he considered a weakness, but this situation with Candy was too much to contain. Another glass of spirits slid down his throat and left a sweet burn in its wake.

When Celcee entered the room, she was followed a minute later by Ram. As they stood in front of Thorne to receive his judgment, each confessed how they had been negligent to Candy's safety.

Braver than many, Thorne thought.

"Before I proceed, do you have any pleas for mercy or questions to ask of me?" By sheer size Thorne was an intimidating man, let alone when he was angry about something so serious. That fact did not escape him and he often put it to good use. All men appeared diminished when Thorne stood so close.

Celcee had puffy red eyes and it was obvious she'd been crying. "I may neither see Lady Candy nor tend to her unless you give your say. Will she be well my Lord?"

Thorne let a breath escape. "I pray to the goddess she shall be." Candy had been his but a single night. It had not been far too short a time.

Ram took a small step forward. "My Lord, I regret this serious accident but ask for mercy for the horse. Lightness is a good mare and I know not how this occurred."

A nod of Thorne's head indicated his agreement. "I agree, and Candy would not forgive me if the horse was put down for such a thing. However if a man were to harm my Lady I would be less forgiving, not hesitating to remove his manhood and shove . . ."

A deep sigh and a rough hand across his chin eased his tension. "Let me simply suffice, I would extract much pain before his death. I ask you Ram, what do you say was the cause of your distraction?"

Ram looked at Celcee and then looked to the floor. Ah, so he was more of a gentleman than Thorne's own well-bred but disappointing cousin. Thorne respected Ram for his honor. The young man held merit.

"I will tell you what I deem ensued." Thorne looked grim and worn as he took a swallow from his newly poured drink.

"Turn and face each other while I see the truth of it. Now if I were a young man, I might take notice that Celcee is now a woman, and growing into a most shapely body, well-formed one might say. Do you not agree Ram? You have not been blind to her comely face I assume?"

"Uh, my Lord I have noticed and she is indeed pretty."

"And Ram what of her full lips? Do they not call out to be kissed?"

"Most certainly my Lord."

"And did you kiss those lips Ram?"

Ram fidgeted, then spoke up. "I did my Lord."

"How did you proceed?"

"You want me to kiss her again?" Ram looked uncomfortable, as did Celcee.

"*Want*? A King does not *want*. I *command* it."

Ram reached forward and gave Celcee a quick peck on her lips.

"What do you take me for Ram? I saw Celcee's hair as well as your unkempt shirt. No bird-like peck leads to such. Celcee?"

"Yes my Lord?"

"Show me how that kiss was done."

Celcee stepped close to Ram and put her arms around his neck and initiated a deep warm kiss. When she finished and stepped back Thorne again addressed Ram.

"Have you known women, felt the 'needing' calling to you?"

Ram looked confused. "I have my Lord, I am a man now."

"Have you made a female come to completion, to shudder with ecstasy?" Thorne hoped so, if not his plan would fail to be effective.

At first Ram appeared awkward, but then lifted his head, "I have my Lord, although I admit not on my first time."

"Nor did I Ram," Thorne added softly. "It can take practice to learn the makings of a woman's passion and to be a considerate lover."

As Thorne ran his fingers through his hair as he weighed in his mind about the difficult decision of a fit sentence, until he was certain of his ruling. "I have decided upon suitable punishment. Are you prepared to meet it as a grown man?"

"I am my Lord." Ram was now visibly shaking. It was good for the young man to understand there were repercussions regarding his delinquency in duty.

"There is a spare bedroom next to Lady Candy's, and therein you will find a generous honey pot. Go into the room and do not come out until I hear through those walls that Celcee has been fully pleasured, as well as your own needs met. If you feel you did not pleasure her thoroughly, you will need to repeat the task until you do so. I care not how long it takes you to sate her needs, but Celcee will let you know if the task requires redoing, which I suspect it will. You may find it requires several trysts to fully sate your thirst of a woman," Thorne gave Celcee a quick wink, "and her need of a man."

He thought back to last night when quenching his hunger and thirst for Candy had in fact required the entire night. They had enjoyed each other more times than he thought possible—even for a 'needing moon'. Now all that was between them was gone, leaving but a memory for him alone.

My Lassie—how he ached for her touch again.

"In the future, never neglect duty to explore lust. Fulfill your carnal needs before or after, but never when you have other responsibilities. Now go quickly as I plan to lock you in until there are moans of passion and Celcee has been proven a worthy woman to rightfully bed. And in the future you will both make better choices, will you not?"

They answered in unison that they would.

"And do you find this this ruling fair?"

Celcee spoke up as she eyed Ram. "This shall be done as you command my Lord, and is more than generous for our grievous error. We thank you for nothing harsher, although it was your righteous prerogative."

"Go now." Thorne turned from them and looked out the window.

Never had he administered a more perfect sentence for justice, as the two would never let their curiosity of each other interfere with their work again. They simply needed time to explore one another, and neither had shown the courage. Now they had a place and the time to do so. Better judgments would be made in the future, of this he felt certain. Ram held the lust of a man but had used the judgment of a boy, what male could not relate?

Were his own feelings for Candy making him too soft? Last night had shown him the importance of how the right woman could make a man, even one as hardened as him, tender.

Malkum of Old unexpectedly entered the library and looked about as if he had never seen the room before. While the old man meandered towards Thorne's desk he paused as if reading titles from the tomes. "Aye, a most marvelous work of history," murmured the old man.

Thorne wondered why the man was here and what he wanted. "Mead, Malkum?"

"Oh, indeed. Did you call me here to share a glass? How grand of you."

Not his most coherent moment, thought Thorne.

"I did not call for your attendance. Have you perchance something to tell me? Mayhap regarding the villages?" He thought reminding the old man of what the meeting had been about might stir his mind, but by the blank look on Malkum's face, it did not.

Suddenly Malkum of Old's bushy white eyebrows gathered as if in great thought. "I have something of importance to tell you, though it keeps eluding me, much like a young mistress. Oh aye, speaking of young women, how is your fine lady doing after her most awful accident?"

Thorne poured mead and handed it to Malkum before answering. "She . . . I know naught as yet."

"No worry, tis simply a tribulation, although always I thought you were favored by the gods and goddesses."

With a smirk Thorne responded. "How so?"

"You were wrought of a fine body and face, maintain physical strength, wisdom, and a great capacity to love. Are these not blessings?"

Of course the old man was blind, at least part of the time, so he could see neither the numerous scars Thorne carried nor his disfigured face. "Mayhap not as blessed as you think."

"Then you are the blind one my King. If only I could remember . . . You know one day you will seek the advice of that witch. I hear she is as comely as your woman. *Hmmm*, I wonder if she would have a fondness for an old man's meat?"

Thorne's mead spewed from his mouth as he choked on the old man's declaration.

"Now, now boy, no need to drink so hastily. Fear not, your lady will heal. As I was to say . . . what was I to say? You know, once I too was a fine looking young man, and that witch, well I have heard she is fine of figure. If only I was two hundred years younger. Now days all young women run too fast and the old crones run not at all. A man with my virility likes a bit of chase, a challenge to conquer. Makes the conquest sweeter and resulting rewards greater while proving a man's merit as well.

"Pursuing a woman can be likened to a hunt you might say—do you not agree? Though rumor says *you* never have to look far to find a woman who offers herself to you. But this one . . . aye, she is different, is she not?" Malkum shook an old gnarled finger at Thorne. "This one means something to you."

Malkum took a sip of mead before continuing his oration. "The future holds many challenges for you Lord Thorne, but do not let pride rule you as it makes for a lonely, cold mistress. Well I thank my Lord for inviting me for a drink, but I really must leave your company and return to Webber, I fear he gets lonely without me."

Thorne was at best perplexed by Malkum's seeming riddles. "Do you not think Webber needs friends his own age? Mayhap even a female?"

Malkum of Old laughed and stoked his beard. "He has seen this Lady of yours and finds her most fine. But all have heard you do not share and Webber does not need to cross blades with you—much too young to die. When he comes upon the right mate he shall know, as shall you. The heart speaks loudly—far too forthright to be dismissed. I bid good night my Lord."

"And to you Malkum." He shook his head not sure why the old man had come to the library.

At least he had offered some hope regarding Candy, even if the rest of the conversation seemed a bit eccentric. But Thorne remembered his father had repeatedly said the truth would be found between the words Malkum spoke.

Thorne put his glass of mead down and headed up the stairs to lock the young couple into their room.

Then he went next door to face what he dreaded most. His hand hovered over the door handle.

With a sigh he opened the door, to the woman he feared he was falling in love with, and who no longer even remembered him.

Chapter Eight
Candy

She felt confused—confused and dizzy far beyond the confines of typical blondeness.

A man was touching her hand.

No he was . . . he was closing drapes and lowering the lighting in the room. Dang, her head really hurt, her eyes too. Her vision was somewhat fuzzy making it difficult to recognize the man's face. Who was he?

"Dad?"

The man looked back at her. He was frowning. Then she remembered this man couldn't be her father because her father had passed away. This man was younger, taller . . . quite tall actually. And he was hazy, like an angel, only she didn't see wings. Was she dead?

Pulsating pain in her head caused her to whimper.

Death couldn't possibly provide such pain, unless she was in hell. She didn't think she deserved eternal fire and brimstone. If so, what had she done? Gone postal at SCAD? It must have been a doozy of an offense to merit this painful karma.

The man sat on the edge of her bed. That caused movement, which led to nausea and increased pain. When the man saw she was in more pain he let out a small curse then stood up and moved back to the chair facing the bed.

"Lassie, can you hear me?"

Whoever he was, she liked his voice—it reminded her of someone. But who was he? And why couldn't she remember?

"I can hear you, it's seeing clearly that's the problem. Where am I?" Her eyes kept quivering unable to focus. Sometimes her vision crossed and other times it doubled, and felt like someone was playing ping pong with her eyeballs.

"In your bedroom . . . or your bedroom within my home." The man seemed to be having difficulty deciding how to describe the situation. Candy could totally relate because she felt jumbled too.

"I live here?"

She didn't remember moving to this room, and where was this room anyway? Was she in a rental apartment? No, she owned a carriage house. She remembered she'd inherited it, while the main house belonged to stepmom two, Cherry Ann and her son, Todd.

"At this time you do. Lassie, can you see me, because your beautiful eyes look unfocused?"

Looking down at her skin Candy confirmed she was still human and not some furred collie breed dog. His masculine voice really confused her.

"Is that my name, Lassie?"

Thorne began running his hands through his hair with frustration, leaving it all mussed and sexy looking. "Your name is Candy, but I sometimes call you a pet name out of fondness."

Candy looked down at her hands again as the words repeated through her mind—*a pet name*? *I'm from Fondness, where was that?* Sounded like maybe a town somewhere in Missouri, with a population of less than a hundred. Had she ever been in Missouri? She didn't think so.

"I'd like some water please."

Would he bring it in a glass or a bowl? And would she sip it or lap it?

She'd soon find out.

The very tall man rushed over to the pitcher and poured water into a cup, stirred something in it and then brought it to her lips. Her coordination sucked, and she remembered she had a predisposition to be a klutz. Where she reached she didn't touch—like a frustrating game of 'keep away'. Darn these game-playing eyeballs. The tall man had to assist her or the glass would never have met up with her lips.

"This will help nausea and pain as well. Try to drink all of it."

As she finished she heard his comment. "Good girl, you finished it. What do you see about you?" His voice sounded filled with concern.

Good girl, like a dog? *Here Lassie, good girl.* Where had she heard that before? Maybe when she'd been a young girl . . . or had she been a puppy?

"I can sort of see you, when you stand very still. But everything is moving."

Try as she may, the room wouldn't stop spinning, much like a state fair park ride. Maybe like the tilt-o-wheel ride, which made you both dizzy and nauseated. Just when the ride stopped it restarted. Dang, she hadn't even had the chance to climb off the ride and it was starting to tilt again.

"Close your eyes, that may help. Can you describe what you saw of me, so I understand how much vision you have?"

"Well, I saw a very tall hunk of a man who looks like he works out in the gym a lot. Do you work out? Am I right? Because you looked like solid muscles when they weren't wavering, and your body is certainly a 'panty-melt', which is an euphuism of sorts for a piece of meat that is sexy enough to melt underwear in case you were wondering. I just made that up." She giggled and resumed her montage of eloquence.

"Gesh, you're totally sizzling hot with that awesome chest and I'll bet you're packed where it counts too. . . Who are you anyway, and how did I get here?"

Candy was peeking at him between splayed fingers and found him almost impossible not to look at.

Such an awesome male specimen, goodness he was hot!

And she felt . . . tipsy.

He just shook his head realizing the tonic meant to lessen her pain was making her loose of tongue. She said senseless things, and her lucidity was questionable.

Before Thorne could even respond Candy spoke again. "I think I'm going to throw up now."

The following morning Candy tried to get out of bed, and immediately slumped to the floor.

Oops!

For some reason she found her prone position funny and giggled. Obviously her coordination and balance were a teeny-tiny-bit questionable, possibly even impaired. A sweet young and attractive woman rushed to her side and helped her back into the ever-moving bed. The thing swayed like a hammock.

"My Lady, please do not try to move so quickly! Let us restrict your activity to small steps, and with my assistance."

"You're very helpful. Do I know you, because I think I might?" Her vertigo was making her nauseated, and the room was spinning like a top again. "You have pretty hair, but I can't tell if you have four or six eyes."

Celcee laughed. "Merely two my Lady. You had an accident and my Lord wishes that I assist you, and try to help you to remember, if it does not cause you more pain. I am Celcee, and you do know me as Thorne's servant. Meanwhile no doubt you would like to use the privy and bathe, and I already know your favored bath oils."

Candy nodded, quickly noting that was *not* a movement to be repeated, and stifled a groan of pain. "I doubt you're strong enough to carry me and I think I'm too dizzy to walk. Do you have another idea?"

"Would you accept the aid of Lord Thorne, as he is most strong and has carried you several times before?"

"Is he that tall, muscular man, I saw last night?"

She was trying to put the pieces of her puzzled mind into place, but it was as if they belonged in different boxes and she couldn't find the right pieces to even get an outside border started. Boy, she sure hoped this wasn't going to be one of those super-duper advanced five thousand piece brain twister puzzles. Her brain already felt thoroughly battered without further torture. And to think, only forty-nine hundred and ninety-nine pieces to go.

"Aye, most tall, he is your . . . you know each other very well. He has only allowed Hermin, our healer, and himself into your room, until this morning when my Lord said I could serve you again. I truly regret your accident."

Celcee was trying to steady her, but Candy kept falling over on the bed.

Plunk, face plant into the pillow again. That was humorous too, although Celcee wasn't laughing.

"I think I should seek Thorne's assistance. Lie still, and please do not try to stand again. If you become harmed further, I cannot imagine the consequences." The attractive four-eyed girl rushed out the door.

Lying there with her eyes closed, Candy heard a strange noise coming from her left side. Was it cooing or a grumble? When she turned her head and opened her eyes she saw a large bird above her, but it wasn't really a bird. What was it? It was an Ono. No, that was a name. What she did know was that Ono wasn't a threat to her. They were companions—of some sort. And that overbite seemed way too familiar. Was that drool on Ono's chin?

"Ono, I'm a very confused and dizzy dame. I hope someone is caring for you, because I'm sure doing a poor job of it. Please don't turn me in to SPCA."

Flying down to her person's side Ono rubbed her right wing against Candy, and then the left wing, as if marking her. Candy reached to pet Ono's fur . . . or was she covered in feathers?

Her hand missed the target entirely and petted the pillow instead. Cotton! Very fine cotton by the feel. Obviously her eye and motor coordination weren't in sync.

Annoying.

As Candy propped on her side, it brought her dizzy-eye-to-eye with Ono, who oddly kept spinning. Was Ono doing pirouettes? For some reason the thought brought a smile to Candy's face. Imagine Ono in a pink tutu, how cute would that be? Although with those odd legs Ono would never dance gracefully (although she wouldn't ever tell Ono such a sad thing and ruin her self-esteem), still it made for a humorous thought.

When the door opened, Celcee and that tall-hunky-testosterone-laden man walked in. More accurately, he sauntered with a rolling confident gait.

Sexy. Really, really sexy.

Celcee kept reminding Candy that the man's name was "Thorne" not "Pheromone Man".

Pfft, a simple enough mistake anyone could make by the looks of the guy.

The expression on the man's striking face seemed tormented, as though his best friend had died. Maybe in the same accident she'd been in? Had he fallen down a well like Timmy did? How sad. She would ask Celcee for details later. Wait, who was Timmy and what well?

The man *not* named 'Pheromone Man' spoke to her. Although his demeanor sounded cheerful, his eyes seemed to be assessing. "Ah, good morning. I see you are awake and wish to wash up. Will you allow me carry and assist you?"

Hell yeah!

Boy he was really muscular, no wonder Celcee thought he was strong. Candy liked the way he looked—a lot. Dizzy or not this guy was freaking hot and could probably make any woman dizzy. Maybe he was the cause of her vertigo.

She suspected she was smiling way too much when she answered. "Sure, let's give it a try." Having this sexy guy's hands on her wasn't going to be a hardship.

Not at all.

Thorne scooped her up so gently she hardly noticed she'd been lifted. He held her close to his chest. Oh my goodness, this man smelled great, so totally male, and yummy. Those bunched muscles in his arms felt rock hard.

And his chest was just too appetizing from what peeked through his somewhat open linen shirt. Before Candy thought better of it, she tried to wrap her teeth around one of the buttons.

I bet I could just bite those buttons off and see his entire awesome chest.

Thorne looked down at her with a frown, which rapidly turned to smile and lifted brow. "Are you hungry Lassie, or do you have a liking for buttons?"

Actually it was his chest she was trying to access, but he was apparently on to her. Probably best to give up on the buttons, because if she swallowed one wrong, think how humiliated she'd be—especially if she required the Heimlich maneuver to dislodge the thing. She could picture this epitome of masculinity hitting her back as a tiny button shot across the room. Not a feminine or coquettish way to impress this gorgeous guy. Candy forced herself to refrain from a developing a button fetish, but felt determined to see his chest when the opportunity arose.

Containing her loose verbosity proved far more difficult. "I'll bet you have an awesome chest. And look how you fill out your pants, *wowzie*. I'd pay to see you on stage half-naked. Better yet totally naked! But then where would I stuff the dollar bills? I'd make a trip to the bank just to see you strut your stuff."

Thorne and Celcee eyed at each other before he responded. "I gather you gave her more pain tonic? It appears we should use a wee less now."

"Aye, however she speaks more plainly. Neither did she again ask if she is a dog, nor if she came from a sizable litter. Tis a good sign, do you not agree my Lord?"

He nodded his agreement, as this did seem an improvement . . . of sorts. "Candy, with Celcee's help I plan to set you on the privy, then put you into the tub. However I do not wish to offend you in any manner since you do not recall who I am."

"The privy? Like toilet? I don't think so! The female with four pretty eyes will have to manage with me." What was he, crazy? Like she was going to tinkle in front of him. No way.

The sexy man seemed to look as if he thought as much as he glanced over at Celcee with an expression of "I told you so" on his face.

"Then I shall stand you up and Celcee will assist. The room would spin less if you close your eyes." He wanted to help Candy but had to respect that she held no knowledge they had shared more than simply physical pleasure on the 'needing moon'. How it grated him, though he knew she bore no fault.

Celcee maneuvered Candy to the privy and then finally got her back to the tub area. The servant looked apprehensive, obviously afraid she couldn't handle Candy on her own.

"I cannot lift her in or out of the tub, and I fear she may fall."

Thorne rubbed his chin as if he was warring with himself. "Candy, I am going to lower you into the tub, and then after you bathe I shall lift you out again. I will not drop you, of that I can promise."

When Thorne reached to undo the nightgown he had put on her after the accident, Candy tried to grab his hands to stop him. Her coordination wasn't as well defined as her words were. She looked like she was batting at flies, but it was enough for him to stop what he was doing.

"Do I know you well enough for you to see me naked, because although I'd love to see you naked, I'm not sure I should be naked in front of you."

Wow, that had taken a few of those puzzle pieces and shuffled them into that stubborn border. A remarkable start, in fact she'd impressed herself.

His eyebrows furrowed as his deep and sexy voice replied, "We have intimate knowledge of each other. I know every inch of you and find you to be pure perfection. Should you do not hold trust in me then you will have to bathe with this nightgown on. Do you wish for that?"

Gesh, he was *sooo* sexy looking. "Have I also seen every inch of you?" She was becoming most inquiring at this point. "Are you my boyfriend or something? Have we ever 'done it'?"

Melt-My-Panties-Man was frowning back at her and crossed his arms as if not pleased by something she'd said. "Aye, we have partaken of this 'it'. Understand, I am a *'man'* not a *'boy'*. Now, with or without the gown?"

This guy seemed to take his man card seriously, as if there could ever be any doubt. "If you take off my gown do I get to see you naked as well?"

Thorne sighed a he reached up to unbutton and remove his linen shirt. "Will this suffice?"

She couldn't begin to hide the grin on her face. "You know, you could have just ripped it off like other strippers do. Goodness, you have a fabulous physique. Just look at all those abdominal ridges—they'd make Lay's chips jealous. Have I ever sketched you?"

"You have done much with me but I know naught of sketching. Into the water with you."

Thorne dropped the nightgown from her shoulders and quickly lifted and then lowered her into the tub before Candy could even pretend to gather her thoughts. He watched to make sure she would not slide and sink below the water.

"Do you wish for Celcee to help you bathe?"

"I thought you knew me well enough to bathe me? Have we ever done that before?"

"My Lady, nothing would please me more but you are drunk from the tonic and I fear you would consider my actions intrusive once you thought upon them. Or do you remember me now?"

"No, I don't hardy remember myself. Why is the water moving so much? Are we having an earthquake or something because it's making me nauseated?"

"Lassie lean forward just a little and I will rub your back."

As Thorne slowly caressed her back Candy relaxed and the nausea from the movement subsided. Obviously the guy had magic hands, like in some song she knew in the back of her mind. His voice was very soothing to her as well. Oh yeah, 'Magic Hands' was totally sexy even if she didn't remember him, she sure would like to.

This guy was like a very sensuous dream, the kind you hate to wake up from. In her case the dream stopped before it ever got to the *fun* part. Was she prudish, careful or just neurotic? Right now she had no idea because her thoughts were as scrambled as eggs at Sunday brunch. Amazingly, his touch felt very soothing and seemed to slow down the movement surrounding her. His touch was . . . comforting.

"Celcee help her bathe while I talk to her. I want her to stay calm, at least that I can do for her. Candy, one of my hunters has brought back game from his hunt and if you do not mind, I have appropriated some, uh, scraps for Ono to feed upon. As a young gargoyle she requires a great deal of sustenance, and Ono has not left your side since your injury."

"She's a gargoyle, that's right. I'd forgotten. Ono's my little gargoyle." *How about that! A buck toothed gargoyle.*

Geez Louise, her life seemed a little odd. Maybe a whole lot more than a little.

"Indeed, and she will grow in size, although she may always remain a bit smaller than usual. Like you, my petite." Thorne started to nuzzle into Candy's neck.

"Time to wash her hair my Lord, if you would tilt her head back for me." Celcee had water in a cup ready to wet Candy's hair.

Tilting Candy's head and shoulders back, Celcee washed the remnants of stable debris and hay from Candy's hair. Her eyes were closed, and he began speaking tenderly to her.

"You are so beautiful, Lassie. I wish you could remember me, as I will never be able to forget you. How I regret you ever came to harm." His words were soft and quiet against her ear. As he reached forward to kiss her lips, her eyes opened. Thorne pulled back from her, aware by the blank expression in her eyes that she had no idea who he was and why he was bent over her.

"She is ready to be lifted from the tub my Lord. I have towels laid out on her bed to dry her." Celcee stood up and was drying off her forearms in preparation to dry Candy.

Reaching into the tub he lifted Candy out while Celcee wrapped towels across Candy's nakedness. He carried and lowered her onto the bed noticing Candy was quiet—much too quiet.

Finally Candy's eyes traveled up his torso to meet his face. "Who did you say you were again?"

Thankfully her breakfast stayed down. It had been questionable at first. The nourishment from the beige food provided some strength. Plus she felt like more puzzle pieces were sliding into close proximity to where they belonged, slowly forming an image of her life.

Sometimes Celcee corrected the placement of Candy's memory pieces. Other puzzle pieces fit absolutely no-where, although Candy suspected that they really did go into the scenic picture . . . somewhere. Obviously these pesky little pieces of memory had gone joy riding and not returned home yet. When they did return, she'd give them the what-for and then ground those suckers.

Although Celcee had explained to her that no one had died from the accident, Candy didn't actually recall any of the specifics as to what happened. So it seemed it wasn't a car accident either, although Celcee seemed baffled at what Candy was talking about. Then Candy remembered she hadn't seen cars here in this strange land void-of-color. That village she'd spotted when arriving was rather antiquated and hadn't boasted any modern conveniences.

What ridiculous male reasoning! Thorne had forbidden Celcee from revealing any of their personal history, as he was seemingly using such knowledge to gage where their relationship might be.

Huh?

This made little sense to Candy because if there *was* a relationship why didn't he want *her* knowing about it? Male thinking was really confusing, as if from another species altogether.

Despite being curious (and admittedly curiosity was one of Candy's personality traits) she only got to hear about what a great hunter, noble warrior, and respected King this man was. Obviously Celcee revered Thorne as well as having a huge crush on him.

He was so tall, with zero percent body fat and muscles galore. How many times had Candy caught herself trying to get a glimpse of him? Way too many to keep track of, but then come on, by the looks of the guy, what pair of ovaries wouldn't take notice?

This entire secretiveness felt like Thorne was teasing Candy with a Godiva chocolate, holding it just outside her reach. She could salivate at the rich chocolate aroma, but not have a single itty-bitty taste. She wanted answers—a nibble of that decadent milk-chocolate brown-eyed man wouldn't hurt, either.

Candy did carry memories; she simply didn't have clarity about her life since landing wherever she currently was. Past events, like those long hours of waitressing, and how her bosses had always been men with 'beer and nacho bellies' (aka 'jelly bellies'), and how they never bothered to hide their crude sneers regarding her ridiculous name, yes those were clear as bottled water. But what else was she supposed to remember?

One thing she absolutely knew was that this mysterious, hunky-male (whom she sadly couldn't remember) was bestowed with the epitome of the perfect male physique and would be superlative to sketch. Such perfection needed to be committed to paper. Just thinking about him made her mouth water.

Or had she had a stroke and was drooling?

Chapter Nine
Thorne

The sunny dawn offered a new day, new promises.

For others, not for him—this morning he felt only loss and hollowness. Sleep had not been his companion and new day or not, he'd heard no promises regarding Candy's welfare.

Hermin said her injury required more time in order to determine if her memory might return. Thorne thought any fool could have speculated as much. The man's words had frustrated Thorne to no end and strained his patience, forcing himself not to physically throw Hermin out of her room.

Meanwhile, Candy's words made no sense, other than telling Thorne he was tall (something he was well aware of) and whatever her other words meant. Candy had smiled at what she described, like it pleased her, but the tonic in her system made rational thoughts dubious.

It saddened Thorne that she remembered naught of her time here, though she had clarity regarding her land. Or so it seemed.

Celcee had completed her decree and was again attending to Candy. Hopefully the budding friendship between the two women would in some manner comfort Candy. Someday she might even remember the servant girl, though right now that prospect seemed dubious.

His hands pushed through his hair as Thorne felt a rare feeling of helplessness—both uncommon and punishing. How long had it been since he'd taken a meal? Substance would likely add clarity. Thinking that a prudent idea he headed towards the breakfast room.

Levenia was entering the round eating room at the same time as Thorne. Of all days—did she lie in wait for him? He was in ill temper to meet her banter. As usual, she remained in some sort of sheer sleep attire, much too thin for any sense of modesty whatsoever.

Although the thought of Candy dressed in such a thing, within a private setting, would be savored, he loathed the sheerness and lack of covering on his sister. All her figure showed, just as Levenia intended.

"Why will you not dress appropriately for breakfast, sister? You forever show too much of yourself."

"Why does it bother you, when you continue to refuse me even on the night of the 'needing moon'? Never once have you let me show my love of you or allowed me to enjoy your manhood. Tis my greatest desire to prove the degree of my affections." Her eyes raked his chest and Thorne quickly sat down, before her eyes wandered lower.

She makes me feel like a savory meat pastry at the market place.

Again, something that if within Candy's eyes would be to his liking, but never a look desired from his relation. Damn his sister for her constant efforts to bed him, her own brother. Obviously he had sorely failed in her upbringing, a task he'd been required to assume.

"I wish to please you and express my love of you." She began buttering a scone, her favorite breakfast. When she took a bite she moaned and then licked her lips as she looked up at him.

Then please me through silence. Would she never cease her futile attempts to seduce him?

Her efforts were pointless. By his sister's conduct, his sac sought to retreat close to his body as if to find refuge. If she kept to this behavior his sac would likely seek sanctuary directly beneath his heart.

"We have discussed this too many times. Will you never lose such lurid thoughts?"

"But I have love of you and desire you, and what can that tiny woman you brought home give you that I cannot, and do you really find such a female desirable?" Levenia took her second bite relishing it in an obscene manner before adding, "She probably has a cunt the size of a thimble."

Hardly. Candy's silken sheath fit him perfectly, as did her mouth, when her lips slanted against his and their tongues danced with perfect rhythm. Remembering triggered his groin. Damn.

"You are my sister and our flesh will not ever meet in such a manner. You have numerous lovers to choose from. I am neither one of them nor will I ever be. Be done of such thoughts Levenia, they serve you poorly."

And again he was loosing his appetite. Repeatedly she did this and he tired of it. Damn his sister, she could ruin any meal. Levenia continuously forced her desires upon him, though never would he relinquish. The thought of fucking his sister was repugnant to him, 'needing moon' or not. He held no carnal desire for her—never would that change. Why could she not comprehend the difference between brotherly love and lust?

This was by his failing. He had raised her from the age of ten, and now she was now twenty summers of age. Despite trying to teach her the merits of behaving as a subtle female, suitable to her station, she preferred to be provocative—bordering on being a common whore.

Did proper female behaviors require a mother's guidance? That he was not able provide her. Most likely he'd overindulged her whims when their parents died, in his efforts to compensate for their loss. She now thought all her desires should be met and never did Levenia recognize consequences. Or perhaps this was simply her nature. He wished she was more subdued in her sexual interests and showed a caring for others.

Royal families sometimes inbred with each other, but the results were damaged, or weak children. Why she would think to risk such with a child's life, he could not comprehend. Or did she carry hopes to be crowned his Queen? Neither mattered, as he had no sexual interest for his sister and deemed incest as loathsome. Mayhap when their parents died, Levenia's mind was scarred by the shock. All he truly knew was that this obsession of hers was painfully tiresome.

"And that *woman*," Levenia almost spat the word as if a vile thing to her lips, "you brought home for the 'needing moon', was she an effort to taunt me?"

Why did she always think everything was about her? Indeed she had been overly indulged and he had himself to blame.

How was it that bedding of women always came naturally to him, whereas *understanding* them did not? He had enough to consume his thoughts without Levenia's obsessiveness on this topic.

"She is as I said, lost. Lady Candy is far from her home." Entirely how far was another question to which he had no answer.

"*Hmm*, I heard the servants talking and they said you enjoyed this woman many times. In fact, they say you used up the honey pot in a single night. Is such truth or idol gossip?"

Thorne studied his sister. How was he to answer her? To say that was not the truth, because they actually required more than two honey pots with their need and want of each other? Verily, she would be even more jealous of Candy. Never had he been a man to share tales of his sexual deeds, and that most certainly included not telling his sister regardless how she prodded him.

How he wished by the goddess, Levenia would find a good man to love and stop being so promiscuous. Then she would stop wanting what Thorne would never give her and spare him such base conversations.

"What do you care of such idol gossip when we have more important matters at hand? Do you really insinuate I am some floppy-eared animal, hopping and humping all night long?" He was shaking his head at her, wishing she would not pry into matters personal to him. She was pushing too far, trying his patience.

Again.

"True enough, yet gossip tends to have some ring of truth in it in most cases."

Would she never relent?

"Ah, indeed. Like the rumor last spring about the oxen born with two heads. I remember that one well. Such idiocy. Spare me talk of lust during our meal. And pass the potatoes, sister, as I need to eat before the next grueling meeting."

"One final question of you. Is it true you have a genuine fondness of *that* female?"

Thorne let out a sigh. Such tenacity. Another trait his sister held, and right now it sorely irritated him. If ever she found a man to love she would test his fortitude to no end.

"Surely I must I have a deep love of her if the gossip is true. Cease this questioning, and allow me eat in peace."

Thorne would not entirely lie about his feeling for Candy, though he knew he should. It was dangerous for him to show affection to someone who could be easily harmed. Rulers always had enemies ready to take their place, and Levenia was a dangerous woman when jealous or peevish. Long ago he had learned how deep a wound from a sibling could cut. He held no trust in Levenia, not when it came to Candy's welfare.

With all the gossip that seemed to run so freely in the House of Rule, Levenia had to know of Candy's serious injury. Still she had not asked, as she simply considered it of no consequence. Sometimes she seemed as cold of heart as his brother had been. Though he knew his sister did have times of compassion, Marcamus had never shown any regard for others.

His family was flawed. He doubted a woman like Candy would be strong enough to endure them, but he could teach her to be—if she would allow him.

Of course it would matter little should she never remember him. Such a thought ended any pretense he had of an appetite. So it seemed his Lassie owned not only his cock and his heart, but also his stomach.

May as well give her keys to my Kingdom as well.

Thankfully his day would be filled with other tasks to attend to, taking his mind from his sister and the woman upstairs who knew naught of him. He would engage in weapons training with his men.

That would force him to concentrate, else he become skewered during bouts. Right now, that was not such an unpleasant thought.

Did he not already feel as though severely wounded?

Only the sight of his blood was missing.

Chapter Ten
Candy

$\mathcal{D}$ays passed and Thorne's presence was a rarity.

Yet each day he provided Celcee with instructions (something similar to a 'to do list') as to what activities were to be done with his 'ward'.

When Candy finally asked Celcee why he never came to see her if they knew each other, the servant girl hesitated, tears welling in her eyes.

"Oh my Lady, do not tell him I spoke of it, but once you are asleep at night I am to tell him. He comes and watches over you for half the night, and then he slips back out to his own room for a few hours of sleep."

Candy didn't know what to think of that. "Was he to blame for the accident? I don't understand unless he feels guilty for some reason and feels he can't face me."

Shaking her head she corrected the misconception. "The blame was not his, the incident was but an accident and he was not even present. Again, I am not to speak on this topic."

As the week passed, Candy's sight and balance returned sufficiently for her to start to roam the House of Rule. She felt quite capable now, meandering without tripping or running into walls, or at least not more than usual for her.

Sometimes she'd spotted things she wanted to sketch, and with the balmy weather, that romantic gazebo in the garden called out to her inner artist. Today she hoped to manage her coordination skills well enough to draw. Her hands seemed steady and her eyes no longer betrayed her.

More importantly was her need to ground herself with art, and have one constant she understood and could depend upon.

Candy left Ono to enjoy the outdoors, and to no doubt hunt, while she decided to return to her room and gather art supplies. Today was going to be a perfect day to draw. When she reached for her backpack, which she kept under the bed, she felt someone behind her. She turned and expected to see Celcee. Instead a man she didn't recognize stepped forward.

"Ah, Lady Candy. Perchance you remember my handsome face? I am Thorne's charming cousin, Shemmar."

"No I don't, but then I don't really recall much of anything yet. Are we friends?"

Shemmar chuckled. "I thought we were much *more* than mere friends." His eyes traveled over her body as though he knew it well. "We spent time together during the 'needing moon', and as I recall you fancied me." His eyes roamed her body, again.

Candy hated the 'I know something you don't know' grin he'd planted on his face. Her mother had used it often enough, and she didn't like it any better now than she had when she was a child. Of course he knew more than she did—she had amnesia for pity-sakes!

Condescending jerk.

"Well Shemmar, I *don't* recall, and *don't* remember any 'moon' or astrological anything. What made you think you could just come into my bedroom without being asked?"

She didn't like feeling vulnerable, and a strange man barging into her bedroom pretty much spelled trouble. A quick disgusting memory of Todd standing in her bedroom stroking off flitted through her head.

"To act so innocent when we both know women have numerous ways they ask much from a man. Some use their smile, others the sway of their hips. Do you not remember? I surely do." He palmed his groin.

Although Candy didn't remember squat about her time in this place, she knew she didn't like how cocky he was. One thing she *was* sure of was that she'd never be attracted to this man no matter how handsome his face might be. And what was that cupping himself like a Michael Jackson video supposed to do, excite her? It hadn't with Michael and not happening with this 'male-appendage' either.

"I might not remember, but I'm not an idiot. You're insinuating a relationship which couldn't have happened, and I want you to leave."

"You simply forgot the lust we shared. How can you say you did not lay with me when your memory fails you?" He was inching toward her.

With her hands poised on her hips Candy answered without hesitation. "For one, because, I don't even like you."

Apparently he didn't take her response well. She could actually hear Shemmar grinding his teeth. Her mind always thought the strangest things at the most bizarre times, and she was wondering how Shemmar's dentist would feel about his teeth grinding habit. Maybe a mouth guard would help.

"We shall see if you like me better when I am on top of you and nestled betwixt your thighs, for you are surely teasing me again."

Tease? Me?

Without pepper spray, or any weapon for that matter, she was forced to use the only resource she did have.

She screamed at her full lung capacity.

Shemmar seemed startled, and even stepped back for a second. Then his anger-filled eyes traveled her body. He took an incensed step forward, and slapped her.

Hard.

"Quiet woman, or I will not take you gently."

The impact caused Candy to stumble back a couple of steps to land against the armoire. The door handle jabbed into her back and the doors rattled, but thankfully she hadn't tripped and fallen on the bed.

His forceful slap stunned her, and the burn to her face hurt. As she put her hand to her cheek, she felt the heat and sting. Never had anyone hit her before, and it drew her fury. He had no right to touch her in any manner, let alone with violence.

What a total douche.

From behind 'douche' she heard an unexpected male voice. "You will not take her at all. Why is it as you grow older, you neither become wiser, nor learn manners, cousin?"

"She invited me in. The Lady obviously prefers my face. Be gone, and I shall teach her not to tease a man."

Thorne looked at Candy clearly seeing she held no fondness for Shemmar. The woman was frowning and holding her cheek. As Thorne pushed Shemmar to the side, he removed Candy's hand, and saw the redness and handprint from where she'd been struck.

Turning back to Shemmar, his fist hit his cousin's nose, then delivered another blow to his jaw. Not one to waste time, Thorne grabbed his cousin's throat and held a knife to it. Everything happened so fast that Candy hadn't even seen where the knife came from, only that it looked very sharp.

Thorne pressed until blood trickled down Shemmar's throat. "You dare suggest Lady Candy would tease men like some hungry whore in need of coin. Has life become so boring that you have lost all desire to live another day?"

Without taking his eyes from Shemmar, Thorne questioned Candy. "Tell me, has he touched any part of you other than his brutal hand upon your fair face?" With his focus on his cousin, he couldn't see her response.

"Lassie, answer me, or I will take his life for his crime against my woman."

My woman. Had she been his woman? Why couldn't she remember?

"Candy if you do not answer me I *will* slit his worthless throat and be done with it."

Blood welled from Shemmar's throat and trickled down his chest. Fearing Thorne would slice his cousin's neck open right in front of her, she managed to squeak out a timid response.

"He slapped me, but didn't . . . he didn't touch me in any other way. But he did come into my room without my knowing, I'd certainly never invite him in."

"Then should we simply remove the hand which struck you? What say you? Does such sound like a fitting judgment to my Lady?"

Thorne's voice sounded almost eager, the promise of violence in it frightened her. Certainly his knife blade hadn't been removed from its precarious position, and Candy saw another trickle of blood run down past Shemmar's Adam's apple and trickle onto the man's beige linen shirt. Yep, that blade was as sharp as she'd suspected.

Just then Celcee entered the room. "Sounds befitting to me my Lord. My knife is kept very sharp should your own become dull."

Her words made Shemmar fume. "You little—"

"Now a wise man would not say more if he wished to keep his vile tongue," warned Thorne. "*Please* cousin, I *encourage* you to finish what you were about to say." A dangerous smile curled Thorne's lips.

By then two warriors had made it to the room and looked confused as to what had happened, until they saw Candy's cheek.

One warrior spoke up. "Shemmar dared strike a woman, and within the House of Rule no less? Stupid piece of—*uh*, forgive me language my Lady," the warrior apologized while nodding to Candy.

"Aye, the King's woman as well. What an imprudent man you have always been Shemmar," the other warrior added as he shook his head in disbelief.

Thorne's blade dug a little deeper into his cousin's flesh before pushing Shemmar towards his two men. "Take him to the Hall for sentencing and inform my sister I will be there shortly."

The warriors were none too gentle as they kicked and tripped Shemmar repeatedly while leading him away. They told him he was dumber than dung, and must crave death to touch, of all women, Thorne's own female.

Finally Thorne turned back to Candy. "My sincere apologies Candy. I knew he had want of you, but did not think he would dare to try to force himself upon you, or ever touch your face." He reached up and gently touched her cheek. "This problem shall be remedied with proper justice."

"What will happen?"

As Thorne pulled his hand back, his caring demeanor transformed to a commanding tone. "For this offense he will be offered two choices. If he had forced you beyond his hand against your face, the choices would become castration or death. Most men choose death and we find it preferable as evil begets evil, it does not leave a man's soul by simply removing what hangs betwixt his legs. We find our manner of justice to provide excellent determent from repeated crimes for most offenders.

"Walk with me. You as well Celcee." Although Thorne's voice was softer now, his words had without a doubt delivered a polite command and the two women joined him.

When they reached the Great Hall, Candy remembered having seen those three opulent chairs before. Levenia (who Celcee had reminded her was Thorne's sister) sat in the chair on the right. Thorne went to the middle chair. The third chair remained empty. Candy wondered who was meant to sit there.

Shemmar was on his knees in front of Levenia and Thorne, and anger radiated from his bloodied face. Two warriors guarded him, as their broadswords hovered at his neck. They seemed to enjoy taking bites of his flesh by their sword tips, and no one seemed inclined to stop them. Trickles of blood continued to run down Shemmar's neck to his shoulders, as he let out small grunts when the points of the blades dug in.

Celcee guided Candy to the side of the Great Hall and she seemed familiar with what was to come next. At least Celcee's presence was comforting since Candy didn't know what to expect. The whole incident was humiliating, and she wished it over. There went any thoughts for a pleasant day of drawing in the garden.

An older man with a beard stood in front of Shemmar. An aura of wisdom and the bearing of power surrounded this aged man. He wore a floor length beige fur-trimmed robe and commanded the attention of the gathering of people. Candy had no idea where so many people had come from and wondered if they all lived in the village Celcee had mentioned.

"Who is that?" whispered Candy.

"Malkum of Old," answered Celcee.

"On this day, numbered ninety-two of spring, year seven-twelve of millennium Abacca," the old man started in a strong voice belying his age, "a crime of covetousness and antagonism has been wielded against the female Lady Candy, the King's guest at the House of Rule. The complaint is: Physical threat, extended to carnal intent, followed by physical force. Neither held with merit, nor provocation. Lady Candy, please step forward."

Celcee held Candy's hand as she walked her to the front to stand before Levenia and Thorne. This was frightening and horribly humiliating to Candy. Her throat and mouth felt dry. No wonder rape victims often avoided testifying. She could feel hundreds of eyes on her back and wished she could just become invisible. If only Shemmar hadn't sought her out. She had no clue why he had.

Thorne gestured for Levenia to speak. "Is this the man who threaten you, as stated?"

Dropping her head Candy let out a timid reply. "He is."

Thorne's words to her were spoken softly. "Candy, raise your face unto me. This was not your crime, or in any manner your shame." Then his voice rose for the room occupants to hear. "Did this man strike you because of your refusal of him?"

Candy stood straighter. He was correct; she wasn't at fault. She met Thorne's brown eyes. "He did."

Thorne's small encouraging smile helped her relax a tiny bit. Not enough that she ever wanted to go through this experience again, but it felt comforting.

"And have you thought of what justice would appease this insult against your character, and the sting upon your face?"

She fought the insane, but oh so compelling, need to run from the room. "What would my choices be?"

"What would you chose Lady Candy? This reprisal is for your honor. Levenia and I shall judge him separately regarding his dishonor within these walls—against you."

"Well, personally I like to beat the do-do out of him, but I don't think I'm physically strong enough."

With a frown Thorne quietly repeated her word. "Do-do? Ah, you must mean shit?"

With a self-conscious sigh she nodded affirmation.

A small smile met Thorne's eyes as he cocked an eyebrow. "Indeed." He looked into the growing crowd and called out. "Would any present choose to champion for Lady Candy, in the matter of striking this man who affronted her?"

The response was terrifying as man after man offered to do so.

Had she won a local Miss Congeniality contest and not even known? Obviously, they had a strict sense of justice—or they hated Shemmar, or both. When the crowd quieted down, Thorne spoke again.

"I too would be honored to do this for you. But the choice is yours."

"I appreciate the support, I really do, but I'm the one he hit so I think it's best if I just give him a good shot back."

Thorne leaned forward, again speaking for her ears alone. "Candy I know you, and suspect if you do so, you will without a doubt cause harm to your small hand. Choose another for this. You are too fragile and gentle, and have already suffered ever much."

Wow, this guy was actually aware she was a tad accident-prone. He was right, but somehow having some-one else step in seemed wrong.

Celcee leaned forward and whispered into Candy's ear. Candy thought Celcee's suggestion provided an excellent solution to the situation.

"I'll do this, but Celcee will wrap my hand first."

Thorne frowned but then upon looking at Celcee's smile, agreed. "Go then and prepare, while Levenia and I debate our decree."

As Celcee grabbed Candy's hand they rushed off to a small room down the hall, evidently where the servant girl resided. The room was clean and orderly but quite tiny. Opening a drawer, Celcee pulled out a pair of cotton underwear that sort of resembled boy shorts.

"I am a woman now and no need longer have need to wear virgin barriers, and it seems like we might both get a bit of satisfaction, do you not agree?"

She did agree, although not certain what she was agreeing to. Celcee obviously must have her own bone to pick with Shemmar, and somewhere in her memory Candy felt that was true.

When Celcee was finished preparing Candy's hand they rushed back, arriving before the final decree was pronounced.

"Proceed," Thorne nodded, "take as many strikes as required for you to feel righteous, as none will make too many."

Candy had never done anything so cruel before, but if Thorne hadn't gotten there in time, she might have been raped, and that thought not only frightened her, it actually enraged her. She reached up and slapped her aggressor's cheek with all the force she could muster.

Shemmar stumbled back as tears welled in his eyes from the pain. A second later he spit out a bloodied tooth. She'd caused him both pain and humiliation, and knew she should feel remorse. Even though her actions felt justified, they certainly weren't comforting. Considering herself a kind person by character, this cruelty was out of her comfort zone. It left her conflicted.

The two women retreated to the side of the room as Celcee helped Candy unwrap her hand. A square sheet of metal clanged to the floor, which led the observant villagers to laugh.

Thorne smirked as well. *"Tsk, tsk, tsk,* Shemmar. Why do you have tears in your pitiless, spiteful eyes when this small female did not shed any when you struck her fair face? Your punishment has been determined. Levenia?"

"Shemmar, you may choose the removal of the offending hand, or the removal of your thumb on your offending hand plus the addition of fifteen public lashes. You are a wearying man and tis not as though you have not been forewarned in regards to your behavior with females, let alone Thorne's woman. Consider yourself most fortunate that your King did not kill you on the spot, which would have spared us this tedious ruling." Levenia sounded bored and continued, "We declare this sentence as fitting. Which do you choose?"

Such extreme punishment was horrifying to Candy. Although, if he had raped her, it was doubtful she would have cared what they did to him.

She quickly walked back to Thorne and whispered to him. "This seems harsh, really harsh. May I ask for leniency?"

Through clenched jaws Thorne spoke. "You may not. If I were to say you wanted leniency, the village would think they were made a mockery of, and perchance you really did invite this man to your room. Your heart is too kind for the likes of Shemmar's behavior. Now step back. This is not your kingdom to rule."

Celcee and Candy left before hearing the punishment Shemmar chose. Both sounded extreme, but Thorne was correct—this wasn't her land. These weren't her customs to judge.

Later that afternoon a group of villagers gathered in front of the House of Rule to witness Shemmar's punishment.

Candy couldn't help but hear his yelling, kicking and screaming, as he was dragged to the whipping post. Soon the snapping of the whip began, followed by Shemmar's shrieks.

She cringed. Despite disliking the man, the sounds were hauntingly brutal. Candy ran to her room and closed the windows and drapes, hopeful to close off her awareness of his punishment. Those sounds associated with pain were intolerable, and she felt responsible.

A minute later there was a knock on her door and Thorne entered.

Candy didn't want to talk to him. The circumstances of the day were incomprehensible and she felt conflicted about the whole incident as well as Shemmar's punishment. But it was entirely by Thorne's hospitality she even had a roof over her head, so she couldn't really ignore the guy.

Thorne walked over and opened the draperies, then turned to face her. The light from the window showed all the angles of his handsome face, and his expression was full of concern.

"I know you have unwarranted feelings of guilt concerning his punishment. Though by all truth, I merited every right to kill him for his intentions to defile my . . . you. He well knew that, and everyone except you understands such. Believe me Lassie, I was sorely tempted, but suspected you would think poorly of me if I did not use restraint. His punishment was lenient. I fear too much so."

Apparently using his fist and knife was considered restraint. Well, compared to death they probably were. Still he sounded as if he understood her conflict. "How did you know about me feeling responsible?"

He walked around the room touching a table here a chair there, until finally his eyes met hers. "Unfound guilt is like a nagging rash and something I have tried to not scratch the itch of for far too many years. Candy, leave it behind, for if you give in, then guilt, like a rash, spreads. Guilt can become consuming and yours is truly unfounded."

Stepping forward, Thorne placed his finger under her chin, raising her face to meet his eyes. "Understand me. My lazy, womanizing, cousin has been warned before, and if we had not been overly lax mayhap his hand would never have ill-treated your face. I do not wish to see him make this mistake again, as it will likely result in damage to some innocent female and ultimately the loss of his useless life."

"But the screaming—"

"He is ever the dramatic is he not? Think on things he has said to you and consider the truth of it. I am not saying the pain is not real, still fifteen lashes is paltry compared to what my father often decreed—even to his elder son's back. Part of the punishment is public humiliation, as who wants others to think lowly of him, to expose one's shame born from ill behavior?

"Be assured Candy, I had them refrain from the sharpest whips, and no metal barbs dig into his flesh, though he deserved it. Shemmar hears worse from the whips journey through the air than the actual bite to his back. I know this because I have felt *that* very whip upon me while growing up. That strap neither left blood, nor scars upon my back. And even as a child, never once did I scream. As a man, one would expect Shemmar to fare better, despite his loud vocalizations to the contrary."

"How terrible! What could you have possibly done as a child to justify being whipped for it?"

How could any parent be so cruel? Her father had never once struck her, and her mother was too busy smoking to consider it. Later her stepmother, Bitney, was always too drunk to notice if her stepdaughter dared to misbehave.

With a shrug Thorne gave a small innocent and charming smile. "Mostly as punishment for beating my brother senseless."

He raised a finger as if to explain. "Which always followed my brother's attempts to kill me. Somehow my father always overlooked that fact and forever remained far too lenient with my younger brother, never really seeing the truth of him." By the end of the sentence his smile had faded and his jaw clenched.

"Oh . . .Well, I still don't believe a child should ever be disciplined with any form of abuse, either physically or emotionally. And I can't imagine how much it hurt your feelings knowing your father would punish you like that. I'm so sorry."

"Then you truly do understand that the pain of it was not so much from the sting to my back, but rather the injustice of how my father did not rightly see the failings of my brother, only mine own. And I agree, neither shall any child of mine feel my anger by fist, whip, demeaning words, nor by another man's hand through my decree."

"Your mother didn't intervene?" Candy knew she could never let such a harsh thing happen, she'd put herself between any lash and her child.

"My mother followed her husband's every command, as women here do. She did not question him, certainly never publicly. I sense you would not allow or submit to such thinking. Though outspoken, and many times trouble-some, I find your strength of mind admirable—albeit foreign amongst females in my realm."

Thorne was right, she wouldn't tolerate the father of her children mistreating them for any reason. Children had enough baggage to drag around just trying to learn about the world they lived in. The process of growing up was a huge learning curve and should be guided by parental love, not pain or fear.

He headed toward the door. "Try not to think further on my cousin. If he had . . . let me say I am ever thankful you have vigorous lungs." With a little bow of his head he opened the door.

"Thorne?"

Turning his head slightly to her was enough for a strand of his sandy colored hair to fall across his eye, looking sexier than it had a right to. His caramel colored brow lifted as if inviting her to continue.

"Thank you for talking to me about this."

"Always, my Lady."

That small crooked smile of his made her feel much better. And he was correct that none of this was caused by her actions. Shemmar knew what he was doing, and what the consequences were likely to be—she wasn't going to let herself become sucked into victim mentality over this.

Her life here was already too confusing. Certainly she didn't need to add any more puzzle pieces, let alone any guilt that might lead to itching.

Chapter Eleven
Thorne

How oddly this day had come to pass.

Early this morning Celcee had informed him that Candy planned to walk in the gardens today. That made for better news than he'd heard and he was grateful to know she was moving about on her own now. He would have liked to watch over her but had obligations this day.

Like the day of her accident—a stab of guilt sliced through him.

He should have been with her. Nothing would have pleased him more, yet always he'd been taught duties to his Kingdom came first. Damn duties, he wanted to be with Candy.

Regardless of his wants, today was a designated day of reprisal for grievances from the populace. This day he and Levenia would meet in the Great Hall to hear them. Three times in each passing of a moon the two of them would help settle disputes or try to correct wrong doings.

His father had addressed the populace daily, but by spacing hearings to every ten days, Thorne found many disputes remedied themselves. Generally the people presented minor or petty arguments, however as part of his ruling obligation to the people, he offered impartial judgments. And those judgments were upheld. None questioned his authority.

Levenia had looked up from her plush throne as he strode to his own in the center of the three. His tardiness was unusual and she had noticed.

"Brother, you look worse for wear. Do you not sleep?"

Though she held genuine concern in her voice, he noticed her eyes had lingered at his groin. What was wrong with his sister that she would not leave him alone? Could she not care for him as a sister should, instead of pursuing him as some lover he would *never* become?

As he glanced over to her, he took care not to truly focus lest she think he held some deviated carnal interest.

"You look lovely as always. Another new dress I see." She had more dresses than any woman in the Kingdom of Chroma, mayhap within two kingdoms.

Fatigue enrobed him. The past week's passing felt forever long since Candy's accident, although news of her physical improvement gladdened him.

Nevertheless, he felt much the same . . . broken.

His nights remained sleepless, and his appetite sparse. But Thorne held neither plans to discuss his lack of sleep, nor Candy with his sister.

He had not intended to give his heart to that small foreign female. The night they shared should have been a simple 'needing moon', nothing further.

A pretty woman to bed, that was all she was.

A night like any other 'needing moon' with a female and shared flesh.

A physical need, nothing more.

Then why had a single night felt like so much more between the two of them? Why had it caused him trouble breathing, as though he'd been punched in the chest, when Candy did not remember him? And why did he want to hold her close and whisper in her delicate ear that everything would come to right? That he would care for her in all ways, as she became whole again. None of which could he say or do, for she remembered neither his arms nor him—let alone 'them'.

Levenia interrupted his thoughts. "We have seven to consider on this day. Are you ready Thorne? You seem preoccupied."

He noted Malkum of Old sitting at the small desk to the right of them to document the complaints and resolutions in his parchment journal. Then Thorne looked down the length the Great Hall and called out to the guard. "Bring our first citizen in."

Should this man hold a complaint of an ingrown toenail I shall enjoy pulling the entire offending nail from his toe, if not remove the entire foot. Your pain best exceed mine on this day if you expect sympathy.

Thorne realized his thoughts were ruthless, but today was not a day to offer up lame complaints, as he was not in the mood to placate. He would rather be watching Candy's progress and perchance hear her beguiling laughter at some silly thing little fledgling Ono did.

Before the villager had even made it through the doorway, Thorne heard Candy's scream from upstairs and felt a searing to his soul, as he wondered what had occurred.

Without hesitation, he ran across the hall with his booted feet striking the stone floors hard and loud as he climbed the staircase three steps at a time to her room. Never did he doubt the sound had come from his Lassie—instinctively he knew.

His worthless cousin was in Candy's room and had his hands upon her. Overhearing Shemmar's words of threat, then seeing the red imprint from his hand upon Candy's fair face—both actions incited Thorne's need to choke the life out of his revolting relative. His blood felt as if it hit boiling, knowing what his cousin had contemplated. The oxen-arse had assaulted her, no doubt planning worse.

I will geld him, kill him slowly then gift Candy with his shriveled limp cock.

The gods only knew how Thorne managed to control his anger in that moment. Surely his cousin had learned Candy was not for his taking on the 'needing moon'—apparently not. By what manner Shemmar could be so ignorant Thorne could not comprehend.

His fair-faced cousin was forever a slow learner who thought being of relation spared him from obligations and honorable behavior. Royal blood or no, the man was a swine. Thorne may not get to pick his blood relatives but he could surely end them if need be.

The forfeiture of Shemmar's thumb and fifteen strokes to his back shaped the justice dealt. A very lax verdict compared to what could have and probably should have been dispensed. Thorne wished it had been more severe. Death would have done nicely—a slow painful demise by Thorne's hand seemed judicious. Torture sounded even better.

Recently Shemmar had become overly bold in his dishonorable behaviors with occurrences seemingly escalating. Would his cousin never have better sense? It seemed not. At this rate one day his cousin would lose more than his thumb or skin off his back if he did not change his ways. What frightened Thorne most is what his cousin's actions might cost a female.

Wish I had removed his fucking manhood!

Should Shemmar ever again dare lay his hand on Candy, his life would be forfeited. Thorne would neither stop his hands nor knife next time. Twice he had restrained himself for the sake of the blood they shared, but a third time would be the end of it. Thorne had other concerns and could not, and did not, want to watch over his cousin, as if he was but a poorly disciplined swaddled child.

Should have gutted that familial sack of shit and be done with it.

In afterthought he had imagined Candy would be unsettled by the event and the decree, so he went to her room to provide some consolation. Embracing her would have been preferable, but at least talking had been heartening.

To expect more of their relationship was unreasonable, as she did not even remember him, and he still refused to tell her of all they had shared. If she did not remember, then this was how it was meant to be. He truly hated the fickle nature of Fate.

Later that afternoon Thorne deliberated on what was required of him as ruler. Without delay he needed to travel to the villages to address the feuding, already he'd waited overly long.

His concern returned to Candy, and what to do about her. Obviously he could not leave her alone at the House of Rule. Any thought of her being hurt in any manner was unbearable to him, and Levenia could not be trusted. Only the gods knew what his sister's jealousy might fashion in his absence. Thorne could not chance it. He trusted few, and none related by blood.

Celcee, although dedicated in her service to him, could only do so much to protect Candy. Additionally the thought of a young virile warrior sleeping outside his Lassie's door did not offer comfort either. He held no intentions for her to become familiar with any other man.

The man could be a hundred years of age, decrepit, and a lover of men, and still he would not trust that man around Candy. Simply considering her with another made his fists clench and bite into his palms.

All these considerations left Thorne with a solitary choice—simply take her with him. A woman amongst his warriors would make for a trying situation at best. With his decision, Thorne provided Celcee with a list of things to prepare Candy for the journey.

The first was how to seat a horse properly while wearing a dress. Candy could not wear men's type clothing as he'd seen her in when he first came upon her. She needed to show less of her form, and neither look obviously foreign, nor provocative. Should she be dressed dissimilarly would invite far too much notice. That in turn would mean she would be made more valuable to thieves or bandits to steal, sell, or worse.

Instinctively he also knew that wherever Candy had come from needed to remain secreted. He could not say why, only that he knew this within himself and suspected knowledge of Candy's land would be like tinder to a fire.

Celcee was quick to point out that in order for Candy to ride, her skirts would need to be fuller; else she could not seat a horse. Dresses with narrowed hems would never work, and all of Candy's dresses were of that style, such as refined women wore.

Thorne told her to see to it, and moreover, whatsoever would be needed for a Lady about to travel. He also instructed Celcee to have Candy's tiny feet fitted for riding boots. Those flimsy sandals Candy wore would be far from safe in the wilds. The female was already easily prone to accidents and proper foot covering would be required for riding.

Candy would likely be the first female in his realm to have such boots, but the cobbler would tend to the task. Then he reminded Celcee these tasks needed to be done with haste.

Lightness would be the perfect horse for Candy's size, unless some ill memory from her accident spoke otherwise.

Again, he wished he knew what had led to her scream and the horse rearing. The incident seemed baffling and no one knew the cause. However, he could not afford any further setbacks to this necessary trip, and that meant no time for his Lady to become fearful of whatever had prompted her accident.

His Lady? Why did he refer to her as such? He needed to think of her as Candy. Simply plain Candy, although there was nothing plain or simple about that female with her golden hair, emerald green eyes and strange words and phrases, who drew him to constant distraction.

As Thorne scrubbed his hand over his face he recalled how her perfect arse had moved against his leathers and how the sensation had been likened to masturbation—no other man would be enjoying the tempting feel of her in that manner. Nor would any warrior's seed touch her clothing, even by error. No excuse would be justified, and Thorne would show no mercy to any man who debased her.

Obviously she needed to learn to ride *alone*. Visions of Candy riding, seated in front of a warrior, sharing such physical closeness became intolerable. Truly, this made the most sense, as his warriors would have their own hands full with . . . warrior duties. Aye, plentiful warrior duties, he would make certain of that.

The blacksmith, a tall wide shouldered man by the name of Ter-Raul, was employed to construct a gargoyle perch for Lightness' saddle. The piece would provide Ono a place for her talons to gain purchase as they rode.

Only the most prominent women owned a gargoyle, and even fewer owned a mount to carry the woman and her pet-companion.

Ter-Raul had been told precisely what Thorne wanted made, which was a strong, leather-wrapped, wooden gargoyle perch, with decorative hand-carved silver ends. The perch was meant to attach to the front of the saddle. The one-of-a-kind piece was crafted with obvious skill.

When Thorne saw the finished product he'd been pleased and felt it worthy of the pretty female rider and her little gargoyle. He told as much to Ter-Raul, who was as gladdened by the appreciation of his skill as the coin in his pocket.

Such a small token to please Candy should not have mattered to Thorne—the piece was simply a gargoyle aid for travel. Still, when he saw how delighted Candy was with the perch, it had pleased him more than he'd thought possible.

With another obstacle for their journey resolved, it was time to move on, to Candy's riding skills. Ram was told he would be saddling Lightness and helping Candy to mount and dismount the horse, while testing her riding abilities. Again, he gave instruction that this needed to be done with haste, nevertheless, to try and remain forbearing with Lady Candy.

Thorne knew the young man would be utterly focused on the task at hand and never touch Candy inappropriately. Thorne would disembowel Ram or any male should any dared to do so. He suspected the expression upon his face warned all men, including Ram, of such consequences.

Of course all this concern was simply part of his pledge to protect the foreign woman while she was in his Kingdom. And if ever a female needed protecting it surely was Candy. He told others he considered her his ward . . . albeit no man had ever had such a fetching charge.

His sister had scoffed when he had informed her of his pledge, but his warriors wisely held back snickers. Though their rolling eyes did not amuse him.

As if to slow the time frame to begin travel even further, Thorne was informed Candy had *never* actually ridden a horse by herself. He was not really surprised when Celcee told him this piece of news, as his Lassie ever bemused him with strange ways.

Of course, life would be too simple if she had been an accomplished rider and verily where would the amusement be for the gods if things were not challenging for mere mortals?

Mayhap in her land she always rode within a carriage or wagon. Hopefully she could muster the task of learning to ride without coming to harm. It seemed much to hope for, however a carriage would not travel well where they were headed. In addition a carriage indicated valuable cargo within—a risk he would not take. The safer, faster means of travel was with Candy on a good horse, and so Ram was designated to teach her.

The groomsman had been enthusiastic to be of service. Knowing Candy as Thorne did, the task might be more difficult than the young man anticipated. By tomorrow Ram might hate Thorne for the assignment.

Unable to stop himself, Thorne continually found reasons to meander past the area where Candy was to be taught to ride. He wondered as to how this would proceed and how many injuries she might sustain. If Ram valued his life, no harm would befall her.

Firstly, Ram was trying to persuade Candy to *not* feed the horse *before* riding. It seemed providing treats to Lightness delighted Candy to no end. Ram finally told her that rewards were for *after* a ride. She was not to offer any food before the lesson, and Ram had spoken in an authoritative manner.

Candy had acquiesced, but not without a disappointed pout. Thorne wondered who got the most pleasure from those treats, the horse, or Candy who seemed to find great satisfaction in feeding the bites to Lightness.

When Ram turned his back to get the saddle blanket, Thorne spied his strong-willed Lassie as she slipped Lightness a carrot piece she'd hidden in her skirt pocket.

Crunch, crunch, the carrot was gone.

Both Lightness and Candy seemed pleased at their mischievous secret as she stroked the horse's forehead.

Thorne shook his head at her tenacity. A small smile escaped his lips as he crossed his arms and ankles while leaning against the stable wall.

She was both a stubborn and softhearted female.

Next, was seating the horse, for which Thorne held concern. Candy was not as able at these tasks as one might hope. As delicate as Candy appeared, she held no grace in physical doings.

Ram tried to explain how he would interlace his hands and for her to step within—she balked. Ram glanced to the heavens.

Ah, indeed my Lassie is trying to a man's patience, thought Thorne.

"I'll hurt you if I step on your hands, and my boots are probably dirty and I don't have any hand sanitizer with me to loan you." Candy's expression was filled with unwarranted concern.

Celcee and Ram looked between themselves, bewildered at her words, a feeling Thorne knew well. Finally with exasperation, Ram had Celcee demonstrate the process. Celcee mounted the horse easily enough, and dismounted without any mishap.

It seemed doubtful his Lassie would be equally coordinated, still Thorne's hopes were held high.

"See, no harm done my Lady," Ram said, as he showed Candy his intact hands. "Now you try,"

This simple task became otherwise where Candy was concerned. When she put her booted foot into Ram's hand sling, her dress got caught under her boot. She hopped on a single leg and tugged to release her hem. Awkwardly, both lost balance and tumbled.

Ram was wisely gentleman enough to quickly maneuver to take the fall to his back and spare Candy. However, when Thorne saw her *on top* of Ram, the sight almost undid him. Thorne's eyes became focused like a hawk on the two toppled bodies.

Watch your hands Ram and do not consider moving your groin, no matter where her body parts landed to cause pain to your sac.

Unable to stand it further, Thorne walked forward, lifting Candy up by the waist to disentangle the two. He could not truly fault the groomsman, but he also could not tolerate Ram's intimate proximity to Candy. A glare of warning was directed towards Ram before turning to face Candy.

"Candy let me assist you with this task. First, lift your skirt as you put your boot into my hands." Remembering her previous objection he hastily added, "I can wash my hands later, so have no concern."

Thorne just wanted her to get on the damn horse. Cleanliness at this point was of no concern. A single step at a time, seat the horse then learn to ride. Simple.

To keep from stepping on the hem, Candy lifted her dress to her thighs. Thorne groaned—by the goddess, was he being punished? Her naked thigh was so close to her womanly juncture—he well knew what she would look, feel, and taste like. Not a pleasure he'd ever likely forget.

"*Not. So. High.* Lassie *please*, my men will likely split their leathers at such a sight!" *Like I am ready to do now.*

Candy apologized profusely, as she tried to pull her skirting down. With her foot in his hand, she started to tip sideways, but Thorne put his leg against her to keep her from falling over.

"Now up you go, and grab the—" Too late.

Thorne saw she'd hung herself sideways across the horse, floundering to grasp hold. Of what she was trying to grab he could not guess. This folly left her head hanging mid-air on the other side of the saddle—whilst her fine backside met his face.

Stifling yet another groan he was wishing his manhood was moved a bit to the right to provide more comfort due to his hardening. This woman kept him harder than any steel blade.

Truly the deities detest me, as they show no mercy.

"I don't think this is going to work," Candy said, her muffled voice coming from the other side of the horse.

The sight of her was both humorous and tempting.

If she keeps wiggling her arse in my face I will be shamed as I come in my leathers. Like some randy young buck surrounded by a herd of does in heat.

"Nay", thinking on words he'd heard her use, he amended his. "No Candy, tis not a desirable means of travel," Thorne shook his head then he added softly, "though it does provide interest to my eyes."

And a deep desire to fuck your perfect arse.

As he grabbed her waist, he lowered her back to the ground. He was careful not to brush her against his eager erection. Candy appeared frustrated, a feeling Thorne was familiar with on several levels.

"Why can't I wear slacks or leathers like you to ride a horse?"

"Candy, women here wear dresses not tight trews that indicate what is beneath. My men would find your figure most distracting. There are dangers on any road of travel, and that kind of clothing would cause extra notice."

"Well, if I ever ruled a place like this I sure would want to have some changes in the dress code and fashions. Have you ever tried to maneuver your legs with five pounds of fabric holding you captive? It's total mission impossible."

"I have not, and I clearly see your complaint, what is more, now tis not the time for renovations of tradition. What we require is an important journey ahead. Now let us try once again. This time I will simply lift you by the waist, you adjust your skirting, see if that prevails."

As he lifted her, Candy was able to move her skirt enough to get seated while not show her thighs to anyone. She looked rather pleased with herself.

"Well done Candy. This is the manner you will mount and dismount." Thorne slipped her foot into the stirrup.

"Then I guess I'll require someone strong to assist me."

"So it seems," muttered Thorne. Then he looked back at Ram. "Now teach her to ride, and remember she could fall if you do not take extra care. No more injuries." He walked away and back into the shadows.

Celcee followed Thorne. "My Lord, why are you not pleased, as she is now sitting facing the horse's head and not the tail? Seems like progress over what could have resulted."

He nodded. "But she requires a man to help her seat the mare."

"Still tis a beginning, and surely the warriors will be willing enough to offer her help."

A frown creased Thorne's brow. "True enough, a beginning, but to what? And as for 'willing enough' I fear that is all too true."

Thorne turned to head back toward the House of Rule, unable to watch what foolhardiness would occur next. Just as he was about to turn the corner he heard Candy.

"*Ick*, is this horse poo-poo on the bottom of my boots?"

This was yet another example of the language barrier between their lands, because to him she'd stepped into just plain old horse shit.

Though Thorne tried to maintain physical distance from Candy, his eyes sought her out. Even her most mundane tasks fascinated him. Nothing she did was less than captivating.

How she moved, the manner in which she ate, and the angelic way she slept with her golden hair spread across the pillow while her pouty lip plumped . . .

The woman was likened to an obsession to him. Time again, he found his hunger for his Lassie led his feet to eat a path towards her—to be near enough for his eyes to consume her.

Warriors who were overly attentive towards Candy would not travel with them on this journey. No need to bring extra trouble, as Candy's proximity would be enough to contend with. Indeed Candy was a friendly female, one quick to offer kind words, and his men liked her all too well.

Not that he ever saw her flirting or even seeming to recognize their attention to her. It was as if she knew neither of her beauty nor her effect upon men. Still, he did not need to encourage a relationship by being careless. Thorne told himself it was to protect her from warriors who by nature could be rough and hardened men.

A lie he told himself overly often.

Thorne directed Celcee was to show Candy how to use a knife for basic defense purposes. Although he did not expect his Lassie to become exceedingly proficient with a knife, some basic skills would make him feel better. No journey was undertaken without dangers, and if Candy could at least look as though she could defend herself it might help discourage trouble.

Celcee came to Thorne with her head downcast. Alas, Candy had a fear of knives. A very great fear it seemed.

Truly I must have offended some goddess to merit such a troublesome female under my roof.

Given this news, Thorne decided Celcee should bring Candy to the practice arena, as he would conduct this task. He knew of knives and women, did he not? Certainly he had years of experience with both. Knife throwing was a skill Thorne enjoyed; he could best any of his warriors.

As to women, certainly he'd known many and he could use his charms to maneuver Candy past her fears. This would merit a simple and straightforward task for a warrior of his reputation.

As easily done as stringing a bow.

He was throwing knives as he waited for the women to arrive. Always his throws met the focus of the target. Of course he'd learned this skill at a very young age and certainly he'd practiced a great deal. It had required several years of practice to become as accomplished as he was now.

Thorne considered it a modest task to achieve—know the blade, note the wind, spy your mark, then throw. The ability had become second nature to him. He could easily teach this female the basics.

When Candy and Celcee arrived, he saw the look in Candy's eyes, how she recognized his excellence as a marksman. Her expression of awe made a part of him savor her reaction. It made for a small thing, a prideful thing, a hopeful thing, to him.

He began replacing his knives back into his wrist braces, at his waist, and inside his boot sheaths. When Thorne turned his attention to Candy, both her beauty and apprehension were visible. This fragile female should not travel the wilds with him, yet his choices were too few. If truthful, he wanted to watch over her to keep her safe and would die to protect her.

Verily, his wants went much deeper, but at least he could protect her from Shemmar and Levenia. And what if her memory came back? What would happen then? Of that, he held a need to know.

"I didn't know you carried so many blades." Indeed her eyes were rather large with wonder.

I carry more steel for you than you know Lassie. Thorne gave her a small smile before he turned to his task.

"Now, remember Lassie, the pointed end cuts, but you are safe from the blade when holding the handle properly."

Candy rolled her eyes at him as though to say she knew how to use a knife. How he wished that were so. Still he remained patient.

"First, let's have you chose a knife from these which are laid out. Choosing the correct weapon for the job is essential. Check how it feels in your small hand."

He put her hand on a handle, but she seemed hesitant to take hold of the knife.

"This is for your defense. We will be on the road and sometimes there are dangers, though my men and I would always protect you. Still tis best to be prepared."

"If the purpose of the knife is to help protect me, well, how about this knife then?" Candy had picked a knife with a twelve-inch blade. The thing was easily the length of her forearm.

"Uh, Candy tis a bit large and probably would be taken from you too easily for that very reason. Remember this is not to slice a loaf of bread. Perhaps a blade a little smaller, likened to what Celcee carries?"

Thorne wanted to be gentle with her and not seem overbearing. He was trying not to act as a ruler or warrior with her, simply a man who would teach her how to protect herself.

Bah, more like a lustful man who wants to pierce her with that hard piece of steel betwixt my legs.

"I think I need a bigger blade if I'm going to scare someone with it." Candy was holding the knife by the wooden handle as if the thing was a dead rat that she detested having seen, and now was dangling by the tip of its disgusting tail.

She is simply a bit apprehensive. Patience.

Thorne shook his head at her. "So be it, try to scare me with the knife, let us see where such leads."

Finally Candy took hold of the knife handle, Thorne corrected her grip.

"Very good. Now hold on tight and show me you intend to fight me off. Pretend I am a big and fierce man who has come to steal you away in the dead of night." He followed with a threatening growl at her.

Unfortunately, that made her shake and lose her hold on the knife—it clattered to the floor. Thankfully it had not pierced her foot. Perhaps he had been a bit too frightening.

Will never get her back in my bed if she fears me.

He would soften the scenario. "And if I am simply a small and skinny bear that has entered your tent to grab food?" Thorne suggested.

"Well then, I'm sure we have leftovers to spare. Poor thing, I certainly wouldn't stab you." A look of compassion crossed Candy's face.

Of course not, she would want to hand feed the damn animal!

The woman exasperated him. She was not going to be good at this, time for a different approach. He walked out of the practice arena and spoke to one of his men. After a few words of discussion a plan was devised.

Suddenly the warrior ran into the arena, growling fiercely as he wrapped himself around Celcee, as if to wrestle her to the ground. Quick to react, Celcee threw him off her with a fast turn and held her knife in front of her.

"Excellent. This is what I want you to try Candy. Can you do such?" Thorne asked, hoping she could.

Candy nodded and seemed to prepare herself for the idea of an attack. This time Thorne took the role of aggressor, but did not run into the arena. Rather he waited until she'd turned toward Celcee, as if wondering why nothing had happened. Silently coming up behind her, he wrapped one arm across her mouth, grabbed her waist with the other, and picked her up.

She tried to scream and kick him, he just held tighter and whispered to her. "Do you not have a knife to defend yourself pretty maiden? I think I should take it from you and drag you back to my village, where no doubt I will have make you my sex slave. Imagine all the things I will do to you once you are bound to my bed."

At that Candy dropped the knife and began to laugh until he uncovered her mouth.

"What do you find so amusing? I could have dragged you away and had my way with you and you did not even attempt to defend yourself." He felt confused by her response.

Worse yet, did she consider the thought of him fucking her laughable? This female was maddening. Perchance he held no knowledge of females outside the bedroom, or certainly not in regards to Candy.

"Come on Thorne, that was funny. Besides I didn't want to hurt you." Candy was still giggling as Thorne picked up the knife while shaking his head. Even Celcee was covering her mouth as if trying not to find the scenario amusing. If Candy truly thought she could muster the skill to harm him, then his ego was going to suffer with male disgrace.

Forbearance, he reminded himself unclenching his teeth.

"I still advise a smaller knife, but go ahead and try to touch me with this large one." He handed the hilt back to Candy.

As Thorne stood in front of her he heard the rustling of a crowd of his men who had gathered to watch. A few were laying bets whether or not Lady Candy would be able to draw blood from their leader. As if such was likely to happen.

Only if by pure accident on her part I fear.

This skill was important for Candy to learn, and the warrior in him began to act intimidating, as he circled her in a semi-crouch. He kept reaching forward as if to grab at her, while tapping her here, and there, showing Candy he could easily reach her.

"You are dead, again dead, and dead as a spring flower buried beneath winter snow. Dead, and again dead, you have met your end, dead. So easily you die woman, tis not even sporting."

He kept touching and mocking her lack of defense. Finally Thorne even slowed down his movements to give her ample opportunity to try to strike him.

She was becoming aggravated and disliked being pronounced "dead" and he wondered if she would ever become peeved enough to try to defend herself.

By the goddess I hope she will. She needs to learn some means of self-protection. With her beautiful face and perfect form no man would hesitate to take his want of her.

Eventually, Candy seemed perturbed enough to raise her knife in both hands, high overhead. Then she struck down at him.

Thorne easily caught the metal blade between his palms and pulled it from her, as simply as if prayer beads. Candy looked stunned.

This had not gone as he had planned, and she still did not comprehend how serious of a matter this was.

"Had I been a very large and still loaf of bread, I would have surely succumbed to being sliced by your brutal knife. You strike down toward me as if to stab a squash. Your purpose is known and your movement takes far too long. An element of surprise can be a lifesaving benefit. Again I say, this knife is too big and therefore easily taken from you. Lassie, *please* try a smaller blade."

He should not have let her choose, as she did not understand the merits of knives. But he had been trying to coax her gently. Too gently it seemed.

Her eyes scrutinized the knives on the table and then looked back to Thorne. "You pick one, since obviously I only know how to use a knife to cut produce."

This time Thorne did. With great care he checked the weight of a few knives, then handed her a knife with a much shorter blade. "This is much lighter in weight and a well balanced knife, yet will cut deep enough to kill."

"Good grief, I don't want to kill anyone."

"Not even to live?" He let out a sigh.

Having Candy accomplish the use of weapons appeared fruitless. "Then peel apples with it, but keep it covered by the leather strap and within your skirt pocket, as Celcee does." Thorne turned to leave.

"Ow!"

He turned towards Candy as Celcee spoke up. "Simply a tiny cut my Lord, she will be fine."

Of that, Thorne was not so sure. She would require a warrior assigned to her or no doubt she would end up falling off a cliff or setting the entire camp on fire.

How did this woman manage in her own world? And how was he to manage with her in his? Furthermore, why did he even think to want her in his world, as she was most troublesome?

After the knife incident, Thorne decided they would leave for the villages early the next day, before Candy became anemic from some sort of unanticipated blood loss causing her to be too weak to travel.

Their first destination on this journey was to meet up with his dwarf friend at his treetop home. Thorne would see if Ripple would be willing to travel with them. His friend was a good companion for such a mission and was bequeathed the gift of knowing people's thoughts and intentions. At times Thorne suspected Ripple considered it more akin to a curse. Either way, it was both a unique and purposeful gift.

When Thorne first became King of Chroma, he soon learned that he had become very popular with a great many people—all most eager to be helpful. Or so they informed him. However, few could be called *friend* when you were King, and he certainly would not expose his back to these newfound *friends*. He trusted Ripple explicitly to fight at his side or his back, and the dwarf was a long time prized friend as well.

Ripple was a valuable asset, and you would not wish him to be your enemy. Though a dwarf, he was a truly deadly warrior who knew your next move, and excelled in archery. His knife skills were commendable as well. Only his stature was lacking.

No secrets were kept from the little man once Ripple touched your flesh, and it did little good to try to lie to him.

He once said if a person's soul was balefully sinister then physical contact might not even be required, merely a need for close proximity. Evil carried a dark aura that spoke to Ripple's mind in an unrelenting and punishing manner.

The dwarf described this type of encounter as most distressing, saying his stomach and bowels would purge, as if in doing so he would rid his mind of those foul and disgusting thoughts from such a malevolent man.

When asked how so many thoughts of others felt, Ripple described the sensation as "thousands of crawling, biting bugs within his head". He confessed it had taken him half his life to learn to shut out unwanted noise and information.

Blessing or curse, it certainly provided a rare talent, and Thorne knew no one else who carried such skill. More than a few times the dwarf had saved Thorne's hide from harm.

Thorne could not imagine the kind of burden his friend bore. Then again, did not every man carry his own weight upon his shoulders and mind?

Certainly Thorne did.

Chapter Twelve
Candy

Candy understood the purpose of this journey. What she didn't fully understand was why *she* was going along.

Celcee had explained how at this time, it was safer for Candy to be on the road with Thorne than within the walls of the House of Rule. Really . . . so being in the wilderness was safer than in a lush residence with real feather beds?

Apparently Levenia didn't relish Candy's extended stay, and Thorne couldn't depend on controlling his sister from a distance.

Two of the House of Rule residents had already 'unfriended' her and they didn't even have Facebook here.

Okay, maybe she could understand Shemmar's negativity toward her (with the missing thumb and tooth issue) but he'd initiated the problem. Plus it was just a single tooth he could blame on her, and it probably didn't even show since it was a molar. Besides, he didn't smile much anymore.

Such thoughts sounded cold and unlike her, until she remembered that heated sting against her cheek.

Taking city-born-and-bred Candy along on this journey meant she was obviously going to be a hindrance to these seasoned fighters.

Imagine day and night being surrounded by a group of brawny men.

Wait a minute that sounded sort of fun.

Thinking of this upcoming adventure (*ha, ha, more like grueling camping in the rough*) triggered anxiety. Some people smoked or drank to relieve life's stresses, but drawing was her self-medicating form of Xanax and right now she felt in need of a therapeutic dose.

That led Candy to set herself up on the steps in front of the manse doorway of the House of Rule. With her drawing pad and pencils she began the general shaping to the grand double doors, and then followed with the carved details. It didn't take long for her to become completely absorbed in her art.

Each door depicted a twelve-foot tall torch-like structure carved into the most unusual wood she'd ever seen. The wood grain was unique and distinctive with linear lines that curled at intervals. She couldn't imagine the type of tree or the massive size it must have been for each of these pieces to be harvested and then carved.

At the top of each carved torch was a shape symbolic of flames. Oddly, they weren't carved in a manner to depict the grace that matched the rest of the door design. The flames held the boldness of sharp angles reminiscent of Art Deco. She found the doors to be an enjoyable challenge to replicate, as she tried to embody the depth and perspective on paper.

The light was starting to fade, and the sun began setting, when it occurred to her she was feeling hungry, and someone was standing behind her. As usual she'd been in her zone and oblivious of her surroundings.

Turning her head she saw Thorne staring down at her drawing and then looking up to the door, and back to the pad again.

"Well, what do you think? Does it look like the entry to your House of Rule?" Candy had her head tilted trying to critique the drawing from another angle. When Thorne didn't respond she looked up at him.

Without looking at her he answered. "I have never seen this before. How is it you do this thing on parchment and make it seem so like what is in front of you?"

Candy felt pleased by what she thought might be a compliment. "You're good with knives while I can reproduce what I see on paper. You know, these entry doors seem familiar to me."

"I am skilled at far more than simply knives Lassie. Do you remember something from when you first came here?" His voice sounded deep and promising.

She shook her head. "No, actually they seem familiar in a different way. Like I've seen something related, but separate. Well, they certainly are beautiful doors. My friend Liam would go bananas over them."

"This man you speak of, he enjoys eating fruit? Sometimes your words make little sense to me."

Candy smiled. "It's just a silly expression that means he would find these doors incredible. He loves old and unique buildings."

Thorne was looking down at the drawing as he asked his next question. "So he is of importance to you?"

"Very important. He's a good friend and we attend the same art school." How did you explain things like SCAD when this place didn't seem familiar with such concepts?

"This male is your lover?" Thorne still stared at the drawing as if it would somehow morph by his sheer will without the need of a pencil or eraser.

Candy giggled. "Definitely not. We're close friends but not with any fringe benefits. What I mean is, Liam doesn't find me attractive in that manner. He's like a brother to me."

Thorne shook his head. "He is a fool if he does not choose you to grace his bed. But if you say he is more of a brother to you, then I hope he makes a better brother to you than mine own was unto me."

Candy tilted her head toward Thorne and lowered her voice. "He's gay so he shares his bed with men." She could have sworn she heard him let out his breath as if in relief.

Thorne quickly changed the subject. "Then this is a form of some magick within you? It seeps from your left hand, which I find strange." Thorne inched closer to the sketch, crouching down to touch it.

"Definitely not magic. I'm not sure I'm even that talented at it, but I love doing it. We call this sketching or drawing. I don't understand why you don't have more artistic things in this land of yours. Sculptures in the gardens would look amazing. And by the way, I'm left handed so this," she held up her left hand and wiggled her fingers, "is my dominate hand for most tasks."

"You are a most unusual female Candy. Do you have other of these drawings, and if so may I see them?"

She couldn't help but notice the muscles of his thighs and the proximity of his muscular arms as well. Thorne would make such a perfect specimen for a class of art students to appreciate as they sketched his powerfully built form.

Well, that was if every female, and most of the males, could focus on their work instead of his hauntingly sensuous pheromones. That man's sensuousness could boggle your mind.

No doubt Liam would go apeshit at the sight of him. Funny how just a minute ago she was starting to feel chilled, but Thorne's proximity certainly had a way of warming her sufficiently. Similar to a hot flash, except she was pretty sure she wasn't going into menopause at twenty-one.

"I did a few sketches in the village. This one is where Celcee's family lives, and this is the— "

"Old tree by the well. Aye, I recognize it. Be wary, Candy, as some might think you a demon, or worse, for being able to pull these things from your finger tips." Thorne sounded concerned but not as if he actually believed it himself. "How long have you been doing this with your hands?"

Without thinking she blurted her answer. "Since my mother abandoned me."

She had never told anyone that and now she'd just revealed a very painful part of her past. Something never discussed because she kept it walled up and refused to dwell on what had happened. Mothers didn't just leave like hers had. They were supposed to love their children, not abandon them. Nobody wanted to feel disposable.

Thorne was silent for a few moments before speaking in a softer voice. "A mother deserting her child is unfathomable to me. Then this thing, 'drawing', thus provides a means to comfort yourself?"

Candy nodded. "I was always alone, usually in my bedroom where I wasn't considered a hindrance. By drawing and using my hands, my mind could take me to another place . . . a peaceful spot, to somewhere without emotional pain, and where anything I drew seemed possible. I've . . . I've never told anyone that before."

And why was she telling him her sorrowful secrets?

As he stood up again, Candy noticed *her* eyes were lingering at *his* crotch level. Definitely not a place she should be looking. But since she was, she saw his leathers were form fitting and maybe it was her imagination, but she could almost picture what was underneath. Of course she didn't really know—how could she know? Still she pictured something spectacular with the feel of satin at the tip—a very intimate memory.

Maybe another puzzle piece? She hoped so.

Quickly she pulled her eyes away, feeling guilty at her speculation and heated response to his proximity. She began packing her pens, pencils, and sketchpad. When Candy uncurled her legs to stand, she began tipping backwards, and fell back against Thorne's chest.

He grabbed her waist to steady her. She could swear his warm breath tickled along her neck as she righted her awkward footing.

"I'm sorry, I think I was in one position too long and my foot isn't working yet." Because usually she was utterly graceful—right!

The hunter released his hands as he stepped back from her. When she turned to face him, she saw his look of distress and pain, as if she'd stepped on his foot when she knew she hadn't.

"Are you okay Thorne?"

When he spoke the softness of his voice had been replaced with the steeliness of a man in command. "We leave early in the morning. Make certain Celcee has you prepared for travel. Good evening my Lady." He turned and started to walk away.

"Please, wait. I have questions for you."

He didn't turn but he did stop. "What kind of questions would you want of me my Lady?"

"Well, where we are going, how long will we be traveling, are we really camping outdoors in the dirt or is there a Hilton we can stay at? Those types of things."

Yes she liked the look of his wide shoulders, and his muscled back was mighty fine, and his gluteus appeared to be rock-hard, but that didn't mean she wanted to converse with his back or his 'hard as a boulder' derriere. Why didn't he turn around to face her?

When Thorne spoke he answered without any hint at annoyance, although he still hadn't turned to face her. "Many of these things depend upon conditions during travel, and I am no soothsayer. Likely we will travel a few weeks, or so I suspect, but I cannot know for sure. This 'hilton' I know nothing of, and suspect you jest, as you commonly do, is that not so? You will be treated well and have the privacy of your own tent at camp, and I will have a warrior assigned to you. Is this enough to quench your curiosity?"

"I suspected the hotel was pushing my wish list. And I have no choice?"

"You are correct, in this you have no choice." Thorne had resumed his walking without even turning back once to see the tears in her eyes.

She called to him again. "Couldn't Celcee travel with us?"

Again he stopped but didn't turn. "One female is enough distraction for my men, two comely females would no doubt be chaos in the making. Any other inquiries?"

He was speaking to her with his back facing her. "Has anyone ever told you you're kind of bossy?"

Thorne's shoulders tightened, his head rose higher, and his imposing nature unleashed. "By your tone these words denote an unfavorable thing. Understand woman, what I command is respectfully followed, and without question. This I have earned not only through my position, but also by my blade and mine own spilled blood."

His head dropped forward and tilted to the side. "Though *you* seem to not fathom this, and *you* can be a most stubborn troublesome female. Heed me well, as my orders will be met for the safety of my warriors and Kingdom. How different your land must be for a woman to challenge the Kingdom's ruler—one she feigns not to even remember. How brave you are to tax that man's patience when you do not even share his bed. There will be no more questions my Lady." He began walking away.

"But I really don't remember." Candy said softly as she wiped the tears from her cheeks. Whether he'd heard and discounted her words or not, she felt hurt. Why did his opinion matter so much anyway?

She called out, "I'm sorry, I didn't mean to sound disrespectful, you've been very kind to me, and thank you for the riding boots." Thorne probably wasn't listening, but she said it anyway.

"You will have need of them." He answered while he continued on his way in silence.

So his hearing was just fine when he wanted it to be. Men and their selective deafness! Obviously it was a universal pandemic.

If he hadn't walked away Candy had a lot of question she would've liked answered. Such as why he seemed to avoid her when they supposedly knew each other? And why did he have to be so damned tempting that she craved him like a chocolate bar during PMS? And why did he always smell so manly—in a good way?

Those were a few of the many questions she would have been eager to ask, but she didn't have the nerve to follow him, especially now that he seemed agitated. Besides, whom was she fooling? She'd never really ask him any of those things. What a ninny she was to want this man's attention, as if a man like Thorne would ever be interested in her anyway.

And why should I care so much what he thinks? Still, she did.

This whole traveling in the rough with 'I'm the Boss Man' was going to be difficult on so many levels. She'd gladly settle for an RV park with facilities versus a stinky, small, sticky and claustrophobic tent. Did they have mosquitos here, and if they did were they massive like that sensual man? And was there a repellent like maybe Raid or Off she could use? For the mosquitos, not the man, because unfortunately, she already seemed to effectively repel him.

Had she already learned something about bugs and the use of some kind of leaves? Her memory was almost sure she'd learned . . . something. If she could remember it would be a godsend.

This dreadful journey was going to proceed and she absolutely detested camping. Candy prayed they wouldn't have to resort to eating powdered eggs for breakfast. They were the grossest food item ever. Memories of limp undercooked bacon chunks mixed with scrambled rehydrated eggs, and cold Spam slices (with the icky gel still clinging) reminded her of the camping trip with her father when she'd been twelve. The worst summer ever.

Her father had called it "an adventure".

Candy had called it *miserable*.

Chapter Thirteen
Thorne

Thorne questioned his sanity.

The very female he was trying to forget was traveling with him. He held hopes that this mission would ease preoccupying memories he was forever tamping down. His mind argued: how was he to accomplish such a feat with *her* so close? His quarrel retorted that this excursion would force him to focus on his role as the 'warrior-King'; thereby keeping his thoughts from the part he'd played as 'Lassie's lover'. His inner self scoffed.

At predawn his gear was readied, he was impatient to head out. The weather was mild, however soon to grow too warm for comfort. This time of year the nights were cool, yet became too hot during the peak of the day. They had much territory to travel and Thorne wanted an early start to cover a good distance before setting up camp.

Five skillful warriors had been chosen for the journey, as well as young Beckum, whom all called 'Bec'. The lad wanted to serve as a squire-man and was but fifteen. Still, Bec could fight well enough and had begged for this opportunity. Remembering when he was the boy's age and wanted adventure in his life, Thorne had given in to young Bec's request.

The boy's parents were eager to see their son off on an excursion with their King, while Thorne prayed young Beckum would be returned to them no worse for the wear.

Generally Toemus served as Thorne's squire-man during travel. The man had several skills beyond being a good warrior, as Toemus seemed to know when Thorne had need of something yet was wise enough to stay away when his King was of ill-temper or sought solitude. And though a quiet warrior, Toemus seemed most perceptive as to what was about them.

Also, the warrior did not get drunk and foolish with whoring, which his other men did as frequently as allowed. All these things made Toemus a good squire-man for Thorne. In spite of this, on this trip Bec would try his hand at the job.

As they rode their horses across the terrain Thorne's thoughts went to Candy. She rode on Lightness in the middle of the group of warriors, the safest place to shield her.

Able had been assigned to attend and protect Candy. The gangly warrior had a nose too big for his face and ears that were likewise. But Able was a most honorable man with matching strength. Very strong if the need arose. Truthfully, Able's strength often deceived people and the man oft won coin through wrestling challenges when they stayed in villages.

His warrior would never dare to offend Lady Candy in any manner. It simply was not within Able's nature. In fact, Thorne suspected that Able even treated his hired whores with the same respect the man did his mother.

When Able informed Candy he was her warrior to mistreat as she would, she giggled in that feminine manner she had and seemed most pleased by his sense of wit. Thorne heard them laughing at times, which should have been a comfort to know Candy liked Able.

Unfortunately—it was not. The more they laughed the quieter Thorne became.

While watching Able help Candy onto Lightness, it felt like a fist to Thorne's gut. An irrational response, as the warrior was simply helping her seat the mare. Thorne knew from experience that lifting her onto the saddle was the single option for success, so what had he expected?

I expected not to feel angered by it.

Realizing he needed to avoid watching their actions if he planned to remain sane, Thorne unclenched his fists, and rode on.

After a couple hours of travel he heard Able whistle signaling a need to stop. Thorne knew it was most likely for the woman's private needs. These interrupt-ions would slow them down, however nothing could be done as females apparently had remarkably small bladders, and she was a wee female to boot. He did not expect her to suffer for that fact. These stops just reminded them she was a female, as if he or his men could ever forget.

All his men had been forewarned to dare not move from their horses and to keep their eyes forward until she returned. Thorne would not tolerate embarrassing Candy with meandering eyes. He well knew she was attractive to the eyes of men, and her face and figure were not things he could change. However his men's behavior towards her, well that he could easily rule.

By nightfall they had traveled a fair distance and were more than ready for camp. Thorne had commandeered a man who served as cook and wagon master to maintain all supplies and any problems related to the horses. The seasoned, and darker complexioned warrior was called Ero, a shortened version of Erontious, which the man forbade any to call him with the threat of being fed food that would cause them hours of suffering and regret. The warriors believed Ero's warning, as the man had never been accused of suffering from a sense of wit.

Ero enjoyed traveling the roads and always volunteered to do so. Some men said it was because his wife and five children gave him no peace, while others said he simply was cut out for fighting, not farming. Either way, Ero was an asset and a decent cook as well. He did wonders with whatever game they found while on the trail. Ero said the trick was in his secret seasonings, which he brought with him and refused to reveal to any who asked.

With the horses cared for, the men were ready to partake of a hot dinner and a small amount of ale. Ero knew his job included rationing until they came upon a village to restock, as the two wagons could only carry so much food, drink and supplies. He also knew Thorne did not favor a drunken warrior. As King, he expected much of his men, and all understood. Thus, the men's beverages were well monitored, oft times with the wine watered down.

Able had maneuvered Candy to sit near the warmth of the fire, and had brought a blanket for her to sit on. She thanked him and smiled reservedly at the other men. Unfortunately, the men smiled back. Thorne had never seen his warriors so engaging and could rightfully do little about that.

Candy remained shy, even uncomfortable, with the men and newness of her surroundings. Furthermore, she was not eating from the plate of food Ero had handed her. Candy needed to eat, as she was already so petite and fragile.

"My Lady, how fare you with the riding?" Thorne asked as he threw kindling into the fire. The firelight seemed to make her eyes take on an even deeper green, reminding him of the distant memory of how lush grass had once looked on a dewy morning. The sight also reminded him of her eyes looking into his when he'd entered her, a thought his cock would have done best without.

She looked up at him. "I'm doing okay. Lightness is a fine horse and Able has been remarkable. I'm sorry to be a burden and slow all of you down."

"A burden I would greatly accept," Victus called out while he stabbed at a piece of meat on his plate with his knife.

"Aye," another men added.

"Why did we not get to draw lots for her care Thorne, as any of us would shoulder such an immense burden?" The chuckles from the men made Candy blush.

"I will be her protective warrior tomorrow, what say you Lord Thorne?" Bear was a big and gruff man, but only jested at questioning his King's decisions. He would never act against his ruler.

"I say," responded Thorne, "you had better eat or you may loose some of the girth you carry and become scrawny." The men chuckled, even robust Bear adding his deep rumble.

Looking from one warrior to the next Thorne added, "I know you chide me in this decision only because she is so comely. Knowing you men as I do, I feel certain that if I had brought a haggard old woman with breasts sagging to her waist and rotten teeth you no doubt would remain equally chivalrous in your intent. But Able is my choice despite your generous offers."

Thorne noticed how Candy just stared down at her bowl of stew, and understood her obvious discomfort at being the focus of the conversation. She might be friendly and talk to his men, but never did she flirt with them, lead them to think she was interested in being bedded by them, or show affections. He was thankful for such—very thankful. How unfortunate if he should be required to slay any of his warriors.

Victus would not let the matter rest. "You chose a face she could easily refuse. Mayhap to make your own face look less marred to her?"

A hush went through the men. All ceased eating. This made for dangerous ground and Victus should not have spoken thus to his ruler. That scar was never spoken of.

Thorne looked at Candy and then back to Victus. "I could ask Lady Candy who she prefers, but it matters not, as I have chosen well on her behalf. And you cannot best Able's strength. On the matter of my face, well remember Victus, though you are handsome, I can change that very easily by my fists or the tip of a blade. Do you challenge me to do so?" Extruding a deadly calm, his voice had spoken clearly with promised danger.

There was not a man amongst them who did not know of Thorne's knife skills or the outcome, should Victus pursue the matter. A silence was maintained while both men stared at each other before Victus answered.

"Of course not, my Lord, forgive me as it was a thoughtless thing to suggest. Though you have to admit Able has been favored with this duty and a man can envy him. Shall we toast to a countenance most fair?"

When their ruler lifted his mug of ale to join the toast all the men breathed freely and joined the salute to Candy as she blushed deeply.

Now Thorne would have to watch Victus closely, and they had only begun the trip. His warrior wanted what was not his to have, and that was something Thorne would not tolerate.

Candy seemed unsettled by the conversation, and wandered off—no doubt in need to attend to personal functions before retiring. Able kept his watchful eyes on her path, though wisely did not follow her, likely realizing she needed time for privacy. Indeed Able made for a good choice for Candy's wellbeing and Thorne was glad for that decision.

How could Thorne make the situation of a lady surrounded by so many hardened warriors more comfortable? True, they were all on their best behavior while she was near—none of the men dared be lewd with her, and more than once a jab to a man's ribs had reminded one of his men of the female's presence. They limited aggressive language and neither a belch nor fart passed within her presence. The men even tried to refrain from manly forms of scratching, all for which he was most appreciative. But was she comfortable? Thorne thought not.

"Eeekk!"

Candy's screech was piercing as she ran toward the campfire. Thorne quickly stood noting how she batted at her skirt like it was on fire. Yet he saw no flames. Ono was flying behind her trying to catch up to Candy's shoulder.

While stomping her booted feet in a ceremonial kind of dance a dark and robust spider fell to the ground. By now all the men were standing with their daggers drawn ready to encounter whoever was threatening the woman.

The spider turned and raced back toward the bottom of Candy's dress. Screaming ensued, this time an octave higher. All the while Candy resumed jumping up and down.

Did she plan to stomp it to death?

Candy was stumbling back from the eight-legged pest, which seemingly only sought refuge—unfortunately beneath the screeching female's skirt. Thorne could understand favoring being beneath Candy's skirt, but admittedly it was not a place for the spider to dwell.

Thorne drew a small knife from his gauntlet and with perfect aim he pinned her three-inch stalker. Walking over to it he looked to Ono, who was now perched on Candy's shaking shoulders.

While Ono looked a little guilty, Candy held a look of terror.

Her voice trembled. "I really hate spiders."

Such was evident.

Thorne crossed his arms as he looked at Ono. "Have you been playing with your food again?"

By the manner Ono hung her head and drooled on Candy's shoulder it told the truth of it. Shaking his head, Thorne spoke. "Candy, be still and close your eyes for me and I shall dispatch it."

And by the goddess, the woman actually did as he said. Obviously she would have done much to be rid of the spider. As he picked up the slender knife, which held the impaled the spider, he let Ono grab her prized morsel and fly off. Thorne slid his knife back into his wrist sheath.

"You may open your eyes now, Lassie, tis gone and there are no others."

Candy's eyes were wide with horror as if unconvinced as to how many more might be surrounding her.

He felt both sorry and amused by the incident, though he did not wish for her to be terrified. It was simply a spider after all, and had he not been an exceedingly strong and brave warrior to save her from a single harmless spider? While he might find it somewhat laughable to think upon, obviously she did not.

"I really hate spiders," she reiterated.

"Aye, we all heard your displeasure my Lady. Ono is but a fledgling and will learn better than to bring you her treasures. Most likely she was just proud of her find." *Or wanted to share it,* which he did not mention to her.

She was not very sympathetic to her little gargoyle at the moment, and continued to check the ground about her. "I hope there aren't other spiders that big, because that one looked like a giant tarantula to me."

Out of nowhere the previously reserved Toemus spoke up. "Nay my Lady, that was but a wolf spider and when you consider we have scorpions and—"

His speech was cut short by Thorne's *"Silence or I will end you in a painful manner"* stare, while Bear's big hand closing around Toemus' neck. Bear guided Toemus from the fire all the while mumbling about "of all times to decide to speak to a woman."

The incident had disturbed Candy sufficiently and she decided to retire for the night. Thorne signaled Able to check her tent before she retired and his warrior's nod confirmed understanding—no spider would escape his eyes.

Able was a most adept warrior and well understood his King. The warrior also seemed to somehow understand Candy, which did not sit quite so well with Thorne.

While Thorne sat by the fire thinking upon the woman, he found such thoughts only confused him further. She was quite clever, yet disastrously fragile. But most of all she was foreign to this land and knew naught of it. That made her seem like a stray baby lamb and easy fodder for hungry wolves or men. This foreign female both frustrated him to wit's end and hardened his cock until he felt the pain of it—Repeatedly.

Such thinking served no good purpose and Thorne decided to go to his tent to retire. Sleep was what he needed, not thoughts of a female who did not remember the night she spent in his arms—the only night he had ever slept with a woman at his side, let alone in his embrace. He could still remember the scent of her hair and skin . . .

Outside his tent Thorne found young Bec waiting, pacing in front of the deer hide doorway.

"I am going to retire Bec. There is no need for you to be awake this late hour, squires require sleep as well."

The young squire looked sheepish as his booted toe kicked at the ground.

"Was there something you wished to speak to me about? Come in then." Thorne entered his tent and turned to the young squire-man. "What troubles you?"

Bec looked up at Thorne then glanced around the tent. "Your Lady neither shares your tent nor bed."

Thorne had little need to be reminded of what his mind and body knew so well. "She is not *my* Lady."

"As you say my Lord, though your eyes never leave her," Bec added as he shrugged his shoulders.

The youth spoke honest words, words Thorne did not want to hear. And was it so obvious to others?

"Have you not seen how she is clumsy and not used to this kind of life? She comes from a different land. I am solely concerned for her welfare while within my Kingdom."

"So you say my Lord. But still you are a man with needs and I would be most honored to attend to those needs."

Thorne stopped mid-stride.

By the goddess. He had not expected this.

And to think he had thought he was going to have to explain about Candy being more like a custodial ward to him and so forth . . . Obviously not.

Since Thorne's youth, men had occasionally eyed him with carnal interest. Though not nearly as often since seventeen summers of age when his face became marred.

Generally men were prudent enough to recognize that Thorne held no interest in bedding males, thus leaving any lurid thoughts wisely unspoken in his presence. Now this situation with Bec . . .

Before turning to face his young squire-man, Thorne grabbed the bottle of mead from the table and took a swig, and then another. Liquor was not going to ease the conversation, though he wished it would. By the goddess how he wished it would.

"Sit down Bec."

As Bec sat on the chair, Thorne turned and offered him the bottle. This would not be a dialogue Thorne would enjoy, but remained required nonetheless.

"A most generous offer Beckum, but there are a few problems with such. Firstly, I carry no want of what a man has betwixt his legs. I solely desire the gifts of a woman, her scent, touch, the entirety of her. Moreover, when a lover touches your body it provides you one type of pleasure, but when that lover has touched your heart . . . well, then you do not seek another in your bed."

Had he actually said such words? Still they felt true enough. And now spoken he admitted having no desire for the flesh of any female beyond that of Candy. Considering she did not remember him, the thought of abstinence did not bode well. He would soon forget her and all would be as it had been with pretty but irrelevant females in his bed.

"And so Lady Candy has touched your heart?" Bec looked disappointed. "Still, she is not here now."

Thorne snickered. "Indeed sadly she is not, but on my mind . . . always."

Was she in his heart, because damn she never left his thoughts. He would forget her, would he not?

"Do not assume offering your body is part of a squire's duties. No sexual favours are expected from any male or female who serves me."

"Twas a true offer. I hope you do not think poorly of me for it." The squire-man's shoulders slumped, and Thorne felt sympathy for him.

How much courage it must have required to ask your King such a thing, and then to be rejected. With a sigh Thorne answered the young Bec.

"Nay. I have seen many good warriors who prefer the company of a man. Your penchant does not measure your merit. Now get some sleep, as tomorrow will present another long day."

As Bec readied to leave the tent Thorne stopped him with a hand to his shoulder. "I wish for you not to speak of this to the other men."

Bec nodded his understanding. "I will not voice my desire of you."

Thorne cleared his throat. "Actually, what I wish you not to speak of is *my* desire for . . . *her*."

With a grin Bec shook his head. "All the men already know such. Truly I am the only one who does not covet your Lady, though all the men know she is unquestionably your woman."

As the squire left Thorne took two more swigs of mead. His men knew?

Fuck.

Chapter Fourteen
Candy

Her tent was surprisingly large. Large enough for her to stand in instead of crawling on the ground like some disgusting cockroach. Right now anything moving that low was particularly disturbing and her eyes quickly scanned the canvas-covered floor. Thankfully the surface wasn't dirt like she'd expected. There was even a woven rug, making the space appear less rustic—less spider infested.

Instead of a moldy smelling sleeping bag, the tent contained an elevated sleeping pallet. It was about a foot and half off the ground, adding a better sense of being away from all forms of undesirable crawl-life. The thought of that horrid spider still made her skin creep. But for a tent, this wasn't half bad.

When she said good night to Able, he kicked at the beige grass by the doorway while he looked down.

"Good night my Lady. If you have need of anything, call out to me, I will be close by." He turned, left the tent as he safeguarded that the animal hide hanging across the doorway closed snugly behind him.

Unsure what that was about, she was too physically exhausted to contemplate his actions. Ono was already napping on a chair back and Candy was feeling totally fatigued as well. It had been a very long day. Once she lay down on the pallet, sleep was immediate.

The night was quiet and she wasn't sure why she'd awakened. The lantern next to her bed was turned low and only gave off a hint of glow, but it was enough to spot Ono now asleep on an upper support bar of the tent. Her silly tail was wrapped around her body and Candy heard what sounded like tiny snoring sounds. Maybe gargoyles were kind of adorable after all.

She was feeling the need to go outside for fresh air and decided not to wake little Ono, who had added spiders to her expanding menu selections. They were probably high in protein, but still *disgusting*. Imagine those legs! All eight of them! A shiver traveled down her spine at the thought. The space in the tent suddenly felt too close.

Stifling.

Claustrophobic.

A compulsory need arose for open space, fresh air and earth beneath her feet. Candy thought to just stroll about the campfire and enjoy the openness and brisk night. By staying close to the campfire she'd be safe enough and couldn't get lost. Even as a blonde city girl she could manage that.

As she slipped past the hanging door flap, she tripped and fell. Something large, moving and alive was under her sprawled body, trying to maul her. Amid her screams, the large beast beneath her kept grabbing at her and snarling. Her arms and hands kept hitting it, trying to get it to let go of her.

The animal was big and fought as she beat on it. Her legs were wound it that darn skirt with a thousand yards of confining fabric. She felt like a mummy trying to get loose, drowning in a sea of fabric as she tried to escape. Unable to see in the darkness, she just kept hitting, scratching, and yelling, wishing the thing would let go of her. She finally got in one good kick before getting further entangled in skirting.

Hearing the commotion, the entire camp came alive. Thorne was the first to arrive, pulling her up and out of the entanglement as her fists continued to fly. She was still swinging when Thorne caught her wrists and held her still. Candy began trembling, and when she looked down she saw Able holding his face.

My God she'd been hitting and kicking poor Able. How in Hades was she supposed to know? She had no idea he was sleeping outside her doorway and on the cold ground.

With a furrowed brow Thorne looked between his battered warrior and Candy. "Tell me Candy, did Able try to have his way with you, is this why you two are wrestling, or were you two enjoying foreplay?"

Candy tried to regain a bit of dignity as her shaking hands smoothed her skirt and then put her hands on her hips. Filled with anger at his sordid assumption, she stomped on Thorne's booted foot.

Ow! Dang it, even the man's booted foot was made tougher than it should have been. Did his toes do push-ups? They sure felt like it. Cow puckie, now *her* foot hurt and Thorne just looked at her like she was bonkers.

"Why yes, of course, Able and I were having such hot sex that we rolled right out of my tent. What do you think of me Thorne?" Her anger and fear ultimately surrendered to tears.

Candy hated how her gender had such unstable tear ducts—a DNA issue due to that 'XX' chromosome. Of course because males were missing that shirtsleeve worth, it turned their second 'X' into a 'Y' chromosome. That explained why they had hearing discrepancies, as well as other cognitive deficits. As she pushed her tears back, Candy willed herself not to be a crybaby, even if she had earned every right.

Thorne looked over at Able and realized the man was fully dressed. His warrior appeared to have suffered quite a few blows, as well as several scratches, to his face. Candy had her clothes on and her face held no signs of any lustful pleasure. In fact she looked angry, tearful, and humiliated beyond measure. As he turned to his men, Thorne gestured with his head that they should return back to where they had been.

A few were chucking at Able's expense saying his job had been far more hazardous than they had given him credit for. Able was told to leave them and attend to his wounds while Thorne guided Candy to the firelight to see if she'd been injured during the melee.

"Are you all right Candy? Tell me what happened?" Sounding sympathetic, he was looking over her face and arms as if expecting to find signs of being equally battered. Thorne even checked her hands, including each finger. Despite the size of his hands, his touch was with one of deliberate gentleness.

One of her fingernails had broken off and she suspected poor Able would come across it somewhere in his skin or hair. Luckily Able had held back and hadn't attempted to defend himself, and therefore she suffered no wounds other than to her dignity, which was sufficiently bruised. However, counseling for PTSD might be indicated—maybe for poor Able too.

"Well, I got up and needed some air. I had absolutely no idea Able was sleeping across my doorway and I tripped over him. And of course being so graceful I can't imagine how that could have happened. When he grabbed me I thought I was being attacked, and heaven knows what poor Able thought. It really scared the 'come to Jesus' out of me because I thought some kind of wild animal was mauling me—and all I wanted was an open space and fresh air."

Candy was trembling as tears continued to threaten her eyes. What was wrong with them—didn't her eyes realize she was trying to be courageous? Dang, those wimpy 'XX' chromosomes had major shortcomings.

Thorne pulled her to him and gave her a hug. "Tis all right, no harm done Lassie, just an unfortunate misunderstanding. Of course I would keep your tent safeguarded, I should have told you such. *Shhh*, do not cry, please Candy, do not cry."

As his hand traveled across her back the trembling eased, she began to relax against the warmth of his chest.

Maybe 'XX' DNA wasn't so bad after all, if it succeeded in getting spectacular muscular 'XY' arms around you.

The uncharacteristic softness coming from Thorne was a little surprising and his masculine, yet compassionate, touch was as calming as a hot cup of chamomile tea. She could almost feel herself dissolve against his body and it felt comforting and almost familiar. Then she felt him tense and step back from her.

Her delicious cup of tea had gone cold!

"I will stay with you until you feel at ease," he said while guiding her to a fallen log where he indicated they could sit. "I know this trip is hardly comfortable for you, and if possible I shall return you to your own land after all this business between the feuding villages is settled. You have been braver than expected and . . . Please, let us talk of something other."

They sat silently for a minute just looking into the fire and listening to the crackling of the blistering wood. Whether it was the flames or his proximity that warmed her was debatable. Candy spoke first.

"Will you tell me something about yourself? I'd like to hear about you if you wouldn't mind." Candy found him to be a fascinating man and she was wondering about this monochromatic land as well. In fact she had an entire Google search worth of questions begging to be answered.

"I would rather learn more of your world on this night. Tell me about this place of learning you attend," Thorne countered.

And so she did. It was a topic she could easily talk about, while trying to explain about her major and what she wanted to learn to a man who had no knowledge of any of it. The concept of 'art' was as foreign to him as this land was to her. Surprisingly, Thorne was an attentive listener and asked thoughtful questions with genuine interest. She had talked a good length of time before realizing she was probably sounding homesick and likely boring the poor man.

"Now," Candy said, "it's time you tell me about you."

Thorne frowned, as if unable to comprehend what she would want to hear. "What would you want to know of me?"

My, my, where to start?

The 'three questions' social icebreaker came to mind. "Tell me three things about you that I don't already know, and I'll do the same."

"Is this a type of game?" He took a large branch and broke it across his knee before tossing the pieces into the well-established fire.

The sight of his muscles cording in his forearms almost made her forget what they were talking about. Goodness the man was fine. She'd always appreciated muscled biceps and forearms. It was probably the artist in her, or maybe the 'XX' chromosomes again.

Taking a moment to think, she answered. "Sort of a tit-for-tat game. I'll answer three questions for you if you answer three for me, so I understand you and this land better. Of course you get to know me better, too," she added hastily.

When he nodded she began, "I'll go first." She was thinking furiously. So many things she wanted to ask and yet only three opportunities.

Hmmm, make them count Candy.

"Your land wasn't always beige," Candy waved her hand around to make her point, "and you remember color, so what was your favorite color?" Okay that sounded lame, but it wasn't like she could ask something too personal. This wasn't Match.com.

"Green. Now I ask, is that not so?" Before she could reply he asked his question. "Do you have family or someone likely worried at your disappearance from your land?"

"Only a single word answer of 'green'? Really? That wasn't much of an answer to my question." She was disappointed and needed to phrase her questions in a manner to squeeze more information from him. He was being a typical, not easily forth-coming, type of guy.

He shrugged. "It sufficed, and I find I have a growing fondness for that color. But you have not answered my question." His eyebrows arched waiting for her response.

"No, I really don't have family. My father passed away early this spring and he was all I really had that I call family."

"I am sorry Lassie. Then no others that wait for you?"

"Hey, that makes up another question, and it's my turn." Candy feigned petulance.

"Ah. Woman did I not word the question to include family *or* someone?" Thorne held a smirk on his handsome face. The man caught on fast.

"Alright. I have my friend Liam, but I'm not really certain of anyone else. I've always been kind of alone. I mean I have friends but . . . probably only Liam."

Cherry Ann could care less, unless she thought to somehow inherit money by Candy's absence. Would Joe miss her? Maybe. At this point Joe seemed far in her past and they'd only known each other a short month. Oddly she felt like she'd known Thorne for a much longer time.

Was she mistaken or did the flames highlight a piece of a smile on Thorne's face? Nope, there really was a smile on his handsome features and a charming dimple too. Candy started to fan herself.

Too hot, way too hot!

"Do you find the fire too warm Lassie? Should we move?"

Did this man have a clue what he did to her hormones, or no doubt, to any woman's hormones? It felt like high-octane fuel injection in a racecar. Her engine was revved up with nowhere to go. Geez Louise, she was way too warm.

"No, no I'm fine." -*When had she become such a liar!*- "Okay, question number two. What is your favorite sport or hobby?"

"Sport? Hunting?" He seemed perplexed.

Of course they probably didn't have hockey, golf or baseball, and no TV, certainly no Internet games or even porn for guys to watch, so, she nodded.

With a feral grin his eyes met hers and his voice took on a deep timbre. "I enjoy tracking. Always I find what I hunt, sometimes even that which I did not seek." His eyes ran over her before he looked back to the fire.

Why did that sound way more sensual than any 'sport' should?

"O-kay, y-your turn." The fire felt even hotter now. This man could probably make any female smolder, because she certainly felt a sizzle with his close proximity. His pheromones were no match for her, and that unfair advantage was one she could hardly comprehend, much less resist.

"Mayhap you have become too warmed?" A teasing crooked smile seemed to say he knew his influence on her.

"I'm fine." *What a liar.*

Thorne looked into her eyes as if he could see the answer to his next question there.

"Do you remember . . ." he paused as if to reconsider his question. "Do you recall when I found you and Ono?"

Candy hesitated and a small crease crossed her forehead. "Not clearly. This whole thing is like a massive bizarre dream to me. That seems to bother you as much as it does me. Why?"

"I wish for you to have clarity of your time here." He looked like he meant it, still she wondered if that was the entire story. So often it seemed like his few words meant far more than simply their face value.

Candy changed her position on the rough bark that was digging into her thighs and bottom. This wasn't the most comfortable spot and she'd prefer sitting on a pillow, or on Thorne's lap. Although with his solid muscled thighs, maybe his lap wouldn't be any softer. What if sitting on his lap gave him a hard-on?

OMG, you are so bad Candy!

She forced her thoughts back to the questions. "So is there something in particular I'm needing to remember?"

"Is that your third question?"

Candy thought for a second. "No. The idea is to learn about you not me. Well for me it is, although from your standpoint it's to learn about me, not you. Anyway, tell me about a pet you had while growing up? You did have a pet didn't you?"

He seemed as if he would have had a pet, although she wasn't sure why she thought so unless she was profiling him. Because obviously if you lived in rustic terrain you must have a pet—right? Maybe like a calf or a pony or even a raccoon? But hopefully not a dog—Please not a dog! This was a stupid question, she already regretted asking it.

Thorne nodded his head but didn't look pleased. His eyes focused on the campfire as he answered. "When I was about ten or so summers of age I found an orphaned baby rabbit. Being so young and without a mother, I fed the little fellow, and had love of him. So small, innocent, and trustful, and his fur was incredibly soft. I even brushed him, which he favored. I should have known better." Thorne became silent.

"Whoa, don't stop there. Please continue."

By the look on Thorne's face it wasn't good. He glanced to Candy's face as if searching for something and then looked back to the fire.

"As you wish Lassie. One day my younger brother came to me with a smile on his face. He looked so proud and asked me to come see what he had done. He took me to an area behind the barn and showed me."

Thorne broke a branch, using much more force than required, and tossed it into the fire.

"My pet rabbit was nailed to a tree, with one nail holding each small foot. The rabbit was still alive, shaking with fear, bleeding and suffering while my brother laughed. Marcameous suggested I kill my pet and give the animal to the cook to prepare for our dinner meal." Thorne's eyes had narrowed, and his jaw now had a tic.

"A rabbit's scream is a most heart wrenching sound from such a wee creature. Though it felt like betrayal, and was most difficult to undertake, I ended my rabbit's suffering. Then I released his tiny spirit to the Earth Mother and let flames return my pet to the ashes of the Earth and bosom of the Earth Mother. It provided an honorable burial rite for my pet.

"I prayed to the goddess that one day my innocent rabbit's spirit would be reincarnated into a large strong animal, and eat my hate-filled younger brother, chewing on his bones as he screamed in fear and pain as my poor rabbit had."

Thorne looked up at her with a strange macabre smile on his face. "Then I beat my brother until he could not stand, his jaw was swollen, and his teeth loosened. Thus I prevented my brother from any thoughts of chewing on anyone's pet at our dinner table."

When Thorne saw Candy's pained expression he gave her hand a squeeze. "The loss was indeed sad, but I soon learned my brother would sacrifice anything I loved for his amusement, a truly brutal lesson. Our head cook, we called her our *neemis,* meaning like an aunt or someone devoted and beloved by the family, somehow had learned of my brother cruel endeavor.

"Not as though it was his first, nor unfortunately, would it become his last foul deed, as my brother possessed a cruelty I could never fathom. Nonetheless, that night at dinner my brother could not chew—a well-deserved gift from my fists. So our *neemis* gave him a soothing savory hot broth to sip. Only Marcameous got ill that night—ill enough to be bound to his privy and bed for two entire days. Thus making for a bit of extra revenge, even if not by my own hand."

The story horrified her. What a cruel thing for Thorne to have to endure. So far, from all she'd seen or heard of his family, she seriously wondered if Thorne had been adopted.

His brother really did sound like a hateful little psycho. Maybe Hannibal Lector had somehow traveled here and left a bit of his deranged DNA to father a Hannibal Junior. And to think she always thought having siblings might be fun.

"Why in the world would he do such a hateful and cruel thing?"

"Ah, Lassie," he shook his finger at her, "is it not my turn?"

Even though she'd hoped to learn even more, he'd shared something very private and obviously hurtful, which amazed her. Thorne had entrusted her with his painful memory and Candy knew it wasn't easy to share those kinds of inner scars. It was easier to hide from them than to acknowledge they existed. Yes, the ugliness faded some with time, but the hurt never really disappeared.

"Yes, it's your turn, go on and ask."

Thorne looked contemplative. This was his last question and he seemed to want to make the most of it. "Tell me something I know naught about you. Mayhap something few know. An uncommon thing."

"Tricky aren't you?"

Candy stared into the fire thinking. What could she share that wouldn't be so personal to cause her pain? He'd shared something private, something others might consider a sign of weakness. However, she didn't want to go that far or have the evening end on that note. Finally she decided on confessing one very guilty pleasure.

"I've never known a man anything like you and I find you to be like chocolate."

Both sensuous and totally addictive.

Thorne narrowed his eyes at her response. "Chocolate? I know naught of this, though you mentioned it when I first met you. I thought it a food." He pushed his hand through his hair as if confused. "Such an answer leaves much unsaid and does this response speak ill or in favor of me?"

Candy smiled at him. "Your questions are used up and I think I'm ready to try to get some sleep."

Thorne seemed taken aback by her quickness to end the game, however she wasn't about to go into specifics with this man and confess her addictions. She wasn't even sure what her feelings for him were, other than heated and confused.

As he walked her back to her tent his palm rested against her back, and the sensation she felt went beyond calming warmth. When they reached the tent, and by the way he looked down at her, she thought they'd share a good night kiss.

The smell of him was divine, tempting, masculinity personified. Their lips were close enough to feel his warm breath as it teased across her cheek.

Then Able walked up looking rather sheepish, and the moment was gone. Sullen Thorne was back. Talk about poor timing!

Able couldn't have waited another minute or two?

She wanted her kiss—*fiddle sticks.*

"Good night my Lady," and Thorne turned away. There was nothing more, just the simple and abrupt good night. What a let down.

Double-dang it.

"Thorne."

He stopped and tilted his head in that sexy manner of his as a lock of sandy colored hair fell forward half covering his chocolate colored eye.

"Chocolate, it's a very good thing."

Surely Martha Stewart would agree.

He nodded and kept walking back to his tent. At that moment of frustration, she really wanted to stomp her feet. But if she gave in to such childish behavior she figured Able would question her sanity, or search for evidence of another spider.

She just didn't know very much about men, and the reasoning as to *why* Thorne had pulled back escaped her. So what had led to his quick and blunt goodnight? Maybe no rules fit with a man like Thorne. Certainly her experience with men was too limited to offer any reference in these matters.

But she'd thought his perfect looking full lips would kiss her, and what a disappointment when he'd pulled away. She touched her cheek where his breath had caressed her skin. The feeling had felt like so much more and Candy already missed that kiss she thought was hers.

She recalled one of her father's philosophical phrases: "Candy you can't miss what you never knew or never had."

Dad was totally mistaken, because she really missed that kiss!

Come morning, Thorne completely ignored her.

She didn't understand and decided not to even attempt to mention the pleasant discussions they'd shared the previous night.

Or her stolen kiss!

How ridiculous to even think this handsome, sensual guy, might care for her. After all, she was his albatross on this journey, nothing more. He probably hadn't been going to kiss her anyway. Maybe he was just checking to see if she had a scratch on her face, right next to her poised lips. Totally frustrating.

Able was in good spirits despite numerous scratches and several bruises, for which Candy felt totally mortified. The warrior would not hear her apologies, which he referred to as "such a trifle matter". Before long they were again talking as friends while he told her the names of types of trees and pointed out small animals they as they rode.

She couldn't help but wonder what other kinds of creatures this land might have, since they obviously had gargoyles. So far, nothing looked too foreign to her except the lack of color. Of course the color void was very significant.

Ono seemed content to ride on the custom saddle perch and watch the world pass by. Sometimes she would fly off only to return a little later with drool dripping down her chin and a full, rounded tummy. At least she fed outside of Candy's view; well, most of the time. Candy was very thankful that Ono didn't requiring her to procure those disgusting meals.

One day passed into another as they progressed across the beige landscape. While Thorne generally avoided her, the other warriors were friendly and quick to answer when she asked them questions.

Except in regards to her forgotten memories. She could not figure out why no one would tell her more, but that particular topic just seemed to be taboo by the ruler's decree. And that ruler was Thorne.

Since it was her memory loss, why was it being kept such a big secret from her? Still, asking those questions never led to answers from the men. In fact, nothing seemed to silence them faster. Thorne had been correct when he said none of his warriors questioned him.

As they rode along, Candy found it interesting to compare the differences in each of the warrior's personalities. They all shared pride in serving their respected King and it was evident each was a deadly and dangerous man to confront. Even while talking to her they kept keen eyes to the surroundings as if always perceptive for the dangers of the unexpected.

The most handsome of the men, other than ruggedly handsome and pheromone-laden Thorne, was pretty-faced Victus. That warrior had a perfect photo cover-ready face, wavy shoulder length hair, enviable long lashes and prominent cheekbones. His generous smile was charismatic as well.

Regrettably, the warrior seemed obsessed with his own good looks and no doubt would be a man who hogged the bathroom mirror, the hair mousse, your best tweezers, not to mention the sacred 'Clarisonic' facial brush. Plus, a guy like Victus would never think to put the toilet seat down. Ever.

Besides, the man shouldn't ever be prettier than the girl—it was just plain wrong. Ultimately Victus was too 'pretty' for Candy's tastes. In Savannah, a guy that handsome would likely turn out to be gay and Liam would be all hot and bothered over him.

The world was entirely unjust.

As night fell, and they all waited for Ero to serve the evening meal, the warriors practiced with knives or arrows. Even though Victus was a very good marksman, he was by no means the best of the men. No, that honor went to—drum roll—Thorne. Hands down, Thorne was an all-around, awesomely skilled man. She drooled over him as easily as Ono did her lizard gizzards.

Watching the grace and strength of his muscled arms as he drew his bow, or the accuracy of his knife throws, was enough to warm her girlie parts. Who would have thought archery and knives could be so sexy? Apparently they were, because her ovaries were forming a cheer squad.

Thorne, Thorne, Thorne...

Then there was Bear, a huge man with a broad well-padded back, which reminded her of a grisly bear, hence befitting of his name. She suspected that under his shirt was a burly, hairy, man who could probably use some major waxing or laser hair removal treatments. Candy felt sympathy for the man's huge war-horse, as Bear probably weighed close to four hundred pounds, if not more.

There was no doubt among the camp that Bear was the strongest. Of course, he could probably crush a man with his weight as easily as his large hands. Despite his size, Candy suspected he had a gentle side, as he always seemed good-natured if not a little timid around her.

Her assigned warrior, Able, was a calm man—as though nothing could faze him. He was also a great deal stronger than his appearance let on. The warrior was tall, but not as tall as Thorne, and not by any means handsome. Still you couldn't help but like him with his quirky smile that always showed his chipped tooth, and his easy manner.

Able effortlessly helped her on and off Lightness, and considering the amount of potty breaks she required, he got quite the workout. He made for a good riding companion, easy to talk to and she felt safe with him. Still she would have preferred Thorne's company once in a while, but ironically, no one ever asked for her opinion.

Candy had little interaction with the young reserved Bec or with Toemus, but both seemed as dedicated to Thorne as did all of his warriors.

It was obvious Thorne both deserved and earned his men's respect. All his warriors were well attuned to the silence of many of Thorne's commands—by what his eyes said, as well as his hand signals—words were seldom warranted. The ability to command through silence impressed her. The man was truly a natural leader, one his men eagerly followed.

Today Able told her they were meeting Ripple, who was supposedly a clever little man who had many talents. What fascinated her most was when he said Ripple lived in an actual tree house.

How much fun would it be to see and sketch that dwelling, and wouldn't Liam find it fascinating when she could one day tell him about it? And when would that be? So far Candy hadn't seen any sign of Savannah on the horizon.

If she did, Savannah would appear vibrant green, not this constant monochromatic beige in front of them, behind them, actually surrounding them. She suspected her home wasn't in this realm, dimension, or whatever, and wondered if she'd ever see her carriage house again. With a sigh Candy realized she might never return home.

She hoped Liam was watering that finicky fern of hers. Coco was forever chewing on its fronds, and as a result the plant was always threatening to die on her no matter how much she pampered it.

Chapter Fifteen
Ripple

His erotic dream ended abruptly.

Thus left his sac full, and Ripple in misery. With a groan, he stretched and his engorged cock rubbed against the sheet. Another groan escaped him knowing he had no time to attend to *that*. The dwarf was aware of the pending arrival of warriors as clearly as he knew unquenched lust left his sac aching, and he needed to piss.

There was little need for his eyes to see what was coming his way when he could easily read the thoughts of others. Wiping the sleep from his crusted eyes, he yawned and tended to his bladder. Time to get his arse moving.

The dwarf sensed his ruler's nearness and prepared for the encounter. Perchance this time he would outmaneuver Thorne, though since childhood he never had.

As Ripple dressed in leathers, a cotton shirt and boots, he reflected on the man he much respected, which could not be said of many rulers. Seldom did he and Thorne visit, since the dwarf did not frequent travel to the House of Rule. On some 'needing moon' nights the House of Rule provided the most convenient manner to sate his lust with a female, and always he was welcome by his friend.

Then again, too many people meant ever much noise in his head, which resulted in things he wished he'd neither heard nor seen in his mind. Add a bit of drink, and his brain became bedlam.

At fifty-and-a-half inches tall, Ripple had the same body parts and sexual appetites as any taller male. Luckily his manhood had not been stunted, only his walking legs. Some females did not want to lay with a dwarf, though many found his height had certain carnal advantages when providing pleasure.

He chuckled at the thought, as he did enjoy the taste of a wanton woman. Ripple adjusted his cock a bit for more comfort. His cock seemed to be reminiscing on the pleasures of the female form and reminding him how long it had been since enjoying a woman's flesh. Damned long, and that dream had ended too soon.

Ripple paused and sensed five men . . . nay six, there were six counting old Ero. Only one young warrior was unknown to him. Ah, and a female as well. By each man's thoughts they found her most comely, though their desires spoke of much coarser things. Ripple chuckled at how these men shared his appetite for a shapely woman.

His curiosity grew as to who this female was who had besotted so many admirers. Thorne never allowed a camp whore, so she was not there to pleasure the men. More the pity, but then, who was the pretty who traveled with his friend?

As he turned his thoughts to Thorne, he found his friend's mind to be a complete jumble of confusion regarding this female. So many emotions in Thorne's brain caused a hitch in Ripple's breath. Sifting through the chaos he focused solely on the female who his friend was desperately trying *not* to think about. Of course the more Thorne tried not to think on her, the more he did.

Aye, so that was the way of it. Ripple saw their past, how a night of passion had been followed by an unfortunate accident. Now her memory of Thorne and their time together was hidden from her.

Strange—uncommonly so, as was seeing his friend suffering over a female. This was a first and would have been worth a good chiding if not for the amount of distress Thorne felt regarding this woman.

Ironically Thorne could take his pick of females who lusted for him as a man of power, or for his reputation as a warrior—even without his disgustingly tall and impressive build, which could make any woman swoon at his feet—but he wanted *this* female. The very female who could not remember a single 'thrust worth' about the heated night they had spent together. A terrible blow to Thorne's male ego, though twas not by the woman's fault she could not remember.

Still a man would like to think he left an impression in the woman's mind, not just his cum betwixt her legs after a night like the one those two had shared.

Ripple shook his head. He would need to meet this female and see for himself what kind of woman could get under Thorne's tough skin. There had never been one before, and this should be most interesting.

As Thorne and his warriors drew closer to the tree house, Ripple simply watched from an overhead branch in a nearby tree. He prepared for the challenge he played with his warrior friend. Due to Thorne's distracted mind, this time Ripple might actually win.

Abruptly, Thorne stopped his horse. His men held back and became still. They understood their ruler's movements and intent. Several had seen what was to come from previous occasions. Able warned Candy to remain silent and the warriors quietly glanced between themselves.

Deadly silence ensued.

Without warning Thorne leaped from his horse and managed a tuck and roll across the ground before he came to his knees. He reached forward with his knife tightly held between his hands.

A *swoosh* was instantly followed by a clink against metal.

An arrow had been loosened, but Thorne's quick blade deflected it. The King swiftly dispatched the arrow by slicing it in half before the fledged wood even touched the ground.

The chuckling dwarf jumped down from the tree and the two old friends embraced. As Thorne got up from his knees and began dusting the dirt off his leathers, he shook his head at this dangerous game his friend felt the need to play.

"In your service my Lord." Ripple gave a quick bow of his head to his friend.

"Appreciated, friend." Thorne reciprocated with a nod.

"Damn Thorne, when will you let me win?" complained Ripple.

"Always I have detested this dangerous game you insist upon," retorted Thorne. "Once I let you win there will be no further sport in it, as I will wear your arrow in my heart."

Ripple leaned forward and whispered, "Too late I fear, your heart is already pierced and bleeding, by way of a woman no less."

The dwarf walked over to greet Thorne's men. With the exception of young Bec, the other men were already known to Ripple. Ero was well known, as they had shared several memorable journeys with their King.

Walking up to Lightness, he gave an exaggerated bow to Candy. "I am Ripple, a small man with a history of many big deeds and an even larger—"

Thorne coughed to interrupt him. "She is Lady Candy, and you know such. Do not speak in any manner to offend her. Tis not by her doing you do not go to a village more oft to partake in the pleasures of a woman."

Wearing a wicked smile, Ripple reached forward to take hold of Candy's hand, kissed it, then turned it over and quickly licked her palm. Candy seemed a little taken by surprise, but did not look repelled, instead she seemed curious by his abrupt behavior.

Now she'd forever be committed to his memory and he could read her thoughts at a greater distance. He knew Thorne was not entirely pleased, but his friend also knew Ripple did not travel with people he could not follow through their thoughts. Ripple's strange gift made life impossible for a man who might plan treason against the King. And the dwarf liked knowing who the enemies were, especially since they were all far larger men than his self.

By the curt reproach, it was obvious Thorne was mindful as to what the woman's ears heard. This told Ripple even more about the relationship between his friend and the beguiling female. Indeed she was a beauty, and one with green colored eyes as well. Ripple planned to learn more.

"Forgive me my Lady. I am but a small man with wicked thoughts. But you, Lady Candy are indeed lovely, and if these men do not please you, and provide to your every need, I might prove to be most useful. Tis simply a heart felt offer." Giving Candy a wink, he backed up to bow again.

He could easily sense the fury within Thorne, and though Ripple considered it amusing, he did not want his warrior friend to knock him into the next kingdom for it. Thorne was less than amused, though it appeared Candy was holding back a grin.

Apparently his friend was most possessive of this female, though Thorne seemed to keep denying that he was more than a little enamored with her. Indeed, Ripple could sense Thorne wanted this female beyond life itself, his heart ached for her. He may as well put on shackles and hand the end of the chain to Candy, as she owned him, even if the man did not know it as of yet. Neither acknowledged the strange bond.

Interesting since the King had never taken such notice of any woman before, or certainly not past a single hour or two of trysting. This female, however, consumed his thoughts and by what Ripple saw in his inner eye . . . aye, Thorne's groin as well. In truth, his friend had *not* partaken of another female since that night. That was unheard of, as Thorne was not known for doing without the comforts a woman provided.

Always some female offered her body, and though discrete, Thorne oft partook of what was extended. Ripple did not fault that in the least. A man had needs, which the dwarf well understood.

Sensing Thorne's thoughts and aching sac, Ripple quickly pushed that ugly sight from his mind's eye before he became blind. His own ballocks were enough to worry over, as far too seldom did Ripple seek out a woman for release. Of that Thorne had been correct. Unfortunately,

Ripple's hand usually served as his mistress. So much so, he should probably bestow his hand with a girlish name.

During the King and his warrior's respite before resuming their journey, Ripple asked Lady Candy if she might be interested in seeing his home. She lit up with curiosity like a small child having been given a gift.

Even though Able insisted he go up the ladder first, and check for Candy's safety, he ended up at the end. Ripple assured Able his home was safe, and since it was *his* home, they entered "by *his* rules". The response from Able was a deep frown and an obscene gesture, thus warning Ripple that Candy was to come to no harm and treated well, or else.

Ripple smirked and ignored Able's distress as he motioned for Candy to go up the ladder, he followed closely behind. A fine little arse on this woman, no wonder Thorne had such lust for her. Ripple liked all aspects of a woman, and this one was well proportioned.

The tree house was constructed of split logs with fretwork trim, and Candy told Ripple the place had a quaint 'gingerbread house' feel. A tree grew right through the center of the house and Candy said it was "ingenious". Ripple could sense how well she thought of it. Ferns and moss grew and spread across much of the shingled roof, while the lush tree canopy above finished the landscape of his aerial home.

Candy exclaimed with glee regarding the fine workmanship, and because Ripple had built the home with his own small hands, he felt his chest swell with uncharacteristic pride. She told him how extraordinary and fanciful the round windows were, and continued on, and on, at how well the house functioned.

For some reason every word of her praise warmed him beyond measure. No wonder Thorne was drawn to her, she had a generosity within her soul that could warm the coldest of hearts. What a delightful female!

Although Candy could stand up straight, lanky Able was bent over in order to maintain his position of guarding her. Ripple considered that both amusing and a compliment, as Thorne considered Ripple's small male stature a threat to Candy's virtue. It took little to see why Thorne had sacrificed his heart to this woman. What male would not? And those precious jeweled eyes. Where had this foreign beauty come from?

Ripple followed her thoughts and could reprise how Candy saw him.

-*He's probably half the height of Thorne-*

Humph, indeed the warrior King was a tall brut, but that seemed an unfair exaggeration.

-*Nice looking face and not at all troll-like-*

Ripple snickered at her thoughts. She had worried he'd be a troll? Amusing female. He was thankful he had shaved lest she think him some ridiculous gnome.

-*I'd thought perhaps he'd be a coarsely bearded, ugly, old hobbled man, with warts, and who carried a battle-axe-*

Truly? He wondered where she'd garnered such a silly misconception. He carried an abundance of deadly sharp knives in addition to his bow. All of which he was quite adept.

No battle-axe for him, as they made for an awkward weapon to yield, especially at his hindered height. No sane dwarf would be inclined to use such an instrument for war or self-defense. Additionally, an axe would require close contact with the enemy, a disadvantage a small-statured man did not wish to encounter for obvious reasons.

-*Like his gold hoop earrings and his body is fit-*

Which seemed to mean something akin to skillful. Aye, he had skills, many he would be most pleased to share with her, but Thorne would castrate him if he even spoke these salacious thoughts aloud.

-*He has brownish hair with attractive curls any woman would love, and a mischievous grin to his mouth-*

Well, true enough regarding his mouth. Everyone knew he was often too coarse of speech and blunt in his remarks. He would like to show her other things he could do with his mouth.

She saw much, certainly more than most females noticed of him. How rare she was to see past his stature.

As he left the tree house, Ripple pulled on a chain attached to a pulley system. The wooden ladder folded upon itself four times before it finished flush against his front door. No man or beast could easily happen within his tree house with it gated in such a manner. The chain remnant was hidden within a tree crevice. Ripple brushed his hands together, then mounted his horse.

He used a double stirrup system, with one above the other in order to seat his mount. His father had come up with the idea when Ripple got his first horse and he had used it ever since.

Once atop his horse, he pulled the straps to adjust the stirrups so they would not rub against the animal as he rode. This provided a quick and simple solution that made life a little easier, since he did not have a stable hand at his beck and call to assist his stunted legs.

His parents had always encouraged independence and this system provided that. Although he could not muster a horse the likes of Thorne's huge beast, at least he rode a true horse—not a pony, likened to a child. After all, he was a man despite his lack of stature. Even during his childhood, his father had never considered putting his dwarf son on a miniature horse or pony. His father made certain his shorter son understood how to live in a world far taller than his stature.

While growing up Ripple quickly learned his strengths and limitations, though others sometimes thought to ridicule him for his lack of stature and some also thought him lacking of intellect. That was always their mistake, as he was clever, had a sharp tongue, and sharper blade, and was more than proficient using both. If men did not choose to give him respect, he had ways to 'encourage' that they did.

His father had often commented on how Ripple's courage and determination had far outgrown his common sense and height.

Once the warriors were saddled and ready to resume travel, they continued to ride several more hours. The goal was to make it to the village called Grasslands. The village had few trees but was known for an abundance of fertile meadows, which were filled with what had once been green and golden crops of grains.

Now the field's color was likened to dirt, even though many of these grasses yielded bountiful food grains, including wheat and barley. The land had remained fruitful despite the lack of color, and the people did not go hungry.

Accommodations within the village would make for a more pleasant night for all. By reputation the mead was good, and the females better, something Ripple would like to verify for himself as both could provide comfort.

The dwarf pulled his horse next to Thorne's war-horse so they could easily talk. "The villages you inquired about are indeed in turmoil. Their bickering has become aggressive. Worse yet, and closer to the House of Rule, there is now talk of a group of raiders. These renegades strike the farms to the far west, and leave little for the family to recognize—as who knows a mother's innards from the father's? Tis far more than simple robbery, they leave ruin and merciless slaughter. You face a dilemma— raiders killing innocents, or villagers fighting over falsehoods?"

Both required his attention and Thorne did not like having these added dangers during the journey while Candy traveled with them. He had brought few men, not expecting trouble from renegades.

"And who leads these raiders?"

"They say an outlaw by the name of Sin-Sum. Some tell stories of him being a half-demon by the Under Earth Master's seed, filled with hatred and empty of compassion. Others even say none can kill him. Do you know of him?"

Ripple hoped Thorne knew something of this man because no one else seemed able to provide information beyond tales of speculation.

"I have heard his name and how he ruthlessly follows no man's laws. Never have I encountered him. If he bleeds he can die. Nor have I seen any creature live without his head attached. How many follow him?"

Ripple shook his head. "Of such I know naught. But if we capture one, I would soon see much of their secrets. Now tell me of this fetching female you brought to travel with you. Why would you do such a poorly thought thing? Your men rightfully have eyes for her."

"She needs my protection while in my lands, nothing more." Thorne offered nothing further aware Ripple would scoff at any declaration of her being his 'ward'.

Ripple cared naught if the King was reluctant, he would have his answers. He lowered his voice to keep the other men from hearing.

"You expect your ruse to be believed by me? She is much more, in fact a 'child of the Earth' by what I discern, and I noted her beguiling green eyes. From where cometh this beauty of yours?"

"A 'child of the Earth'? How can you know this, and what does such mean?"

Ripple thought about it. "I am not certain . . . yet. But she has some connection to the Earth, this I do know. Now tell me what knowledge have you of her."

Thorne told him what little he knew of Candy, careful to avoid speaking of the 'needing moon' night they had spent together.

Though a dwarf, Ripple was neither a clown nor fool, and nothing could be hidden from him. A point he felt the need to remind his tall friend.

"*Hmm*, she was surely greedy for you on the night of the 'needing moon'. *Ah*, two entire honey pots? Insatiable wench."

Thorne gave Ripple a dangerous look, but upon reflection admitted the problem. "Truly we were like two parts made whole. We physically fit, and fervently came together as one. The feeling was unlike any I have ever known, and now she carries neither memory of me, nor that night we shared."

Although the dwarf already knew the truth of it, he was curious as to Thorne's response. Not wishing to dander his friend, he carefully considered his next words.

"And you have want of her . . . as your own?" Did his friend even know his own desires?

Through gritted teeth Thorne replied. "She is *mine*. I feel this to be true."

"Ah, she does have some pieces of memory. I can see thus within her, although these confuses her. Be patient, and be assured she seems to hold great interest in . . ." chuckling Ripple continued, "all of you it seems. Her memory is on a cusp. One day it will come as surely as you *came* into her." Ripple was laughing at his joke.

Today Thorne did not seem to share his sense of humor.

Still Ripple continued to push his luck. "By the goddess, you rode your woman hard, such stamina, and I thought only a dwarf could be so virile." Ripple laughed and rode off before Thorne could backhand him. Then he called behind to his friend.

"We shall not make it to Grasslands today nor the morrow. I feel trouble lies ahead. Perhaps you will burn off your aggression and frustration with fighting, if fucking is not in the stars."

Ripple sensed trouble as easily as a man could feel a turd stuck in his arse. And just like an obstinate turd hanging halfway in and halfway out, progress would likely be slow and subject to the whim of the gods.

He detested how the fucking deities forever played with the lives of mankind without regret, as though unfaultable. Aye, this excursion was going to be likened to one difficult turd to dislodge.

In truth—regarding the path of Thorne and Candy— shit was on the way.

Chapter Sixteen
Thorne

His knife was drawn, readied at the man's throat…

Thorne shot upright—sweat beaded his brow. With caution he took in his surroundings. As he regained his bearings a groan of realization escaped. Same empty tent, same empty bed, same fucking dream.

Thorne fell back on his sleep pallet. Always the dreams were about Candy and a faceless lover. He was losing his mind over the small female who haunted his thoughts worse than an unrelenting ghost. If ever she took a lover he'd end the man and feel at peace for it.

By day he worried about her safety and comfort. Did she eat or drink enough to remain healthy? At night his concerns altered. Was she warm, safe, in bed, alone? Candy plagued his thoughts, and it felt like a consuming illness eating at him.

He required a distraction from her.

Decidedly this morning he would leave camp early to hunt. Fresh game would be appreciated and a diversion was needed to clarify his thinking. He informed Toemus and Ripple he would catch up to them before mid-morning and headed off on his war-horse into the wooded terrain.

Alone.

Early dawn granted him to witness a wistful, veiling haze that hovered a few inches above the dewy ground. The mist provided an enchanting opaque curtain, one that would soon be raised, as the Sun God stretched his warm and lighting rays across to awaken Earth. These sights conjured poetic thoughts—by the goddess was he becoming a damn female!

Hunting, a *manly* task, involved blood and death, not prose fit for a female. Still, Thorne knew his Lassie would be delighted to see such awe-inspiring changes as the trees and landscape became visible to the eye. If she saw this she might want to do a 'drawing' of this ethereal scene. Always he'd admired the benevolent gifts of the Earth Mother, but when beside his Lassie, his vision seemed to have become even more focused and appreciative. She saw things differently, and now, to some extent he did as well.

Then he cursed himself for thinking of *her* as *his*—of thinking of *her* at all. This morning of solitary was to hunt, to escape her feminine lures, which he continuously suffered. And thus far he was doing an irksomely poor job of it.

He refocused on the task of hunting. Dawn provided an optimal time to trail unaware prey.

Aye, dangerous prey—a most masculine task.

His horse was skilled; barely making a sound as it ambled through the dense, dewy forest.

Condensation dripped off branches, sometimes to land on Thorne's face or body, but going unnoticed. In his hunter mode, Thorne held a singular focus and purpose.

The birds quieted. He stilled.

There was a rustle . . . low, in nearby brush. The sound was too weighted to the ground to be a stag; most likely it was a wild boar or feral hog. Either would make fine eating for his men, and no doubt, Ono would enjoy some fresh tidbits as well.

Placing a steel-tipped arrow to the longbow, he reined his war-horse to stand fast using his knees to govern the steed. Though his horse would not panic, Thorne knew what he hunted likely had tusks, and would be dangerous, certainly not an animal to be taken without caution. The animal's defensive tusks could maim or kill, so his arrow must hit true, killing before the boar could charge and reach his war-horse's legs.

He heard sounds of dirt being pushed by cloven hooves. The animal was scenting the damp, earth-fragrant ground, while pushing his snout in search for food. The beast let out a low, feral grunt. It did not realize it was being hunted. Not yet, but it would soon. Thorne dared not move or he risked attack. Nor did he choose to lose the perilous beast he hunted.

Remaining as quiet and still as possible, he waited to face the challenge of the hunt. Several louder grunts signaled him to the spot where the beast would likely exit the brush. A furious squeal rapidly warned him of the boar's awareness and pending vicious attack.

Loosening his arrow, another speedily replaced it, as he focused on securing the kill. The first arrow went through the boar's eye; the second hit the neck and spine behind its brain. The boar crumbled dead at the feet of Thorne's war-horse.

Had the beast had not been dead his horse would have ended the animal's life with his powerful hooves, but that made for a poor risk to take. His trained horse was far too valuable to risk a possible injury.

He dismounted his horse and bent down to confirm the kill. A good and merciful kill, for which he gave thanks to the Earth Mother for this gift of plentiful substance. He released the spirit of the dead animal back to the goddess' blessed bosom.

Adrenaline from the hunt had provided a temporary but welcome diversion, and satisfaction knowing his warriors would eat fresh meat tonight. Thorne felt certain he could slip little Ono that remaining eyeball as well, of course only when the beautiful and squeamish Candy was otherwise preoccupied. A smile curved his lips at the thought.

Those tusks were a good ten inches long and showed how dangerous this boar could have been to the legs of a horse or man. These could easily be traded for healing balms when they came across a dwelling where they might find a healer or witch.

The hide would go to the leather tanner to trade. The gift of an animal's life meant not being wasteful, and he never wasted what the blessed Earth Mother provided.

That large boar easily weighed a close to three hundred pounds, and Thorne regretted not having brought a second horse for game. Another example of how he was not well focused, due to that female with the captivating green eyes. With a hefty heave, Thorne got the dead boar over his war-horse. He dared not burden the horse with additional weight and risk breaking the horse's back, so he began walking to meet up with his men.

Luckily he'd not gone far when Ripple showed up with another horse trailing behind him. "I felt your need for a second steed and by luck, we had not traveled far from where you hunted. A fine kill my King."

Thorne smiled back at Ripple. "You are a useful man to have around, but ever should you take a wife she will keep no secrets from you."

"I am but a dwarf, no female would consider marriage with me. But better I should know the woman's thoughts than she know my wicked ones."

"As if you were ever closemouthed regarding your thoughts of women. You speak as unabashed as a whore holds her legs wide," chided Thorne.

They were riding back in silence when Ripple spoke. "Go ahead and ask, for I cannot stand the constant biting of your questions within my brain."

"Ask of what?"

Ripple rolled his eyes at Thorne. "*Humph.* Ask of your woman, as you full-well know."

Thorne let out a sigh. "Does she remember aught of the night we shared?" How desperately he wanted Candy to remember and his voice betrayed his sentiment.

"If she did, you surely did not expect her to suddenly run to your crossed arms and declare so, did you?" Ripple looked over at Thorne and could see the man was suffering.

"Be at ease, she remembers some. Patience is needed, as she is most conflicted and confused. A new land and lover, these are both unimaginable to her. She has little knowledge of men and finds her sensual thoughts of you most puzzling to her senses. But be assured, you most definitely have her attention. How that woman appreciates your body is almost enough to embarrass even me." Shaking his head at his friend Ripple added, "Never have you been a patient man."

Ripple was correct, never had he been patient, and even less so in regards to Candy. So she had been looking at him. He oft thought perhaps she was, but seldom did their eyes meet.

Sensual thoughts as well? Thorne felt his heart lighten ever so slightly. Would she one day remember, and if so, would she be his again? Or would Candy run the other way because she'd neither intended to give herself to the 'needing moon's' influence, nor to a scarred man.

It might be for the best to pretend nothing had happened on that night of shared passion. Easily said, however he was having a difficult time convincing his cock—all thoughts of her heated and hardened him. Such had been so since he first laid eyes on her.

As their horses caught up to his men, Thorne stopped abruptly, seeing his saddled warriors in an enclosing circular formation. As Thorne pushed his steed forward he saw what was within their surrounding circle. There stood a filthy, barefoot man, reaching his hand forward, towards Candy who was seated on Lightness.

Thorne quickly noticed the man was covered with oozing boils, no part of his skin remained unscathed by festering pustules. The clothing upon the beggar's back was dirty and torn, having been worn for overly long and neither having met water nor this man's inclination to use it. Grimy, greasy, hair hung in strings on his scab-covered scalp, while the man's beard was matted and resembled a rat's nest more so than facial hair. Obviously this man shunned the use of water even when he came upon as stream.

Sudden realization of what this man embodied struck Thorne—fear emerged. This could not be! Not within *his* terrain!

"Nay!" Thorne screamed.

Quickly remembering she used the words 'yes' and 'no' he called out again. "*No Candy.* Back up Lightness, and do not touch that man. He carries a pox by a witch's hand."

Ono launched from Candy's shoulder, now hovering between the beggar and her person.

"Back Ono. Do not let him touch either of you!" Thorne's shouted words were so commanding that Ono flew back to Candy's shoulder to await further instruction.

How he wished Candy would be so compliant with his orders. She could be stubborn and should she not heed his words . . . Thorne felt ill at the thought.

The warriors parted their horses to let their King ride closer to her. His war-horse moved forward and he saw Candy still remained too close to the filth before her.

"Lassie, pull back your hand. I beg of you, come to me."

Goddess, I beseech, make her heed my words.

Candy looked at Thorne and back to the beggar. Thorne could see her confusion and conflict. His Lassie's heart was too generous and she did not comprehend the danger in front of her.

In Candy's eyes she'd simply see a hungry and dirty man and she would want to help by giving him food. This foul, festered, man would take more than food if given the opportunity, and in return pass on the pox. Thanks to the gods, he saw she was mindful to his words.

Candy had become frightened by Thorne's extreme concern and tried to get Lightness to back up, but she was unsure how. Had anyone told her how to put a horse in reverse? She didn't recall if they had, and it wasn't like there was a driver's manual in the saddlebag. This seemed like a poor time to learn what to do. Backing up really should've been covered in *Horse Rider's Ed.*

Gently pulling back on the reins, she tried scooting her bottom back and forth in the saddle praying Lightness knew what that meant, and hoping the horse didn't think she wanted to lunge forward instead.

Thankfully, Lightness took a step back, but the skinny beggar followed by stepping forward. She felt trapped.

Ono flapped her wings unsure of what to do for her person, and Candy felt likewise.

Now what?

Since this man was dangerous to her and Ono, what about poor Lightness? She glanced over to Thorne trying not to let her panic show, but doubtful she'd hidden it.

Thorne kept his narrowed eyes on the man, barely sparing her a glance. He signaled for Ripple, who had worked his way closer, to take Candy. Thorne's readied arrow let the man know the consequences if he dared move forward again.

The dwarf rode next to Candy and pulled her from Lightness onto his horse. His horse was experienced and knew how to handle commands far better than young Lightness.

Ripple easily backed up his horse and got Candy out of harm's way and Lightness followed his example. Ripple gently slid Candy down to the ground and told her to stay put behind them.

Thorne's attention turned to the ragged man. "If you move toward her I *will* end you. You thought to touch the female? She is not yours. In fact, never again will you touch a woman, nor shall one touch you. Since the pox was set, you are meant to travel an empty road, one vacant of solace or companionship."

The diseased man lowered his head although his eyes stayed fixated on Candy. He watched her movements like a hawk spying a field mouse, with entirely too much eagerness at the morsel before him.

With eyes focused on Candy, the diseased man spoke. "I only wanted the touch of another human. I find it lonely without the contact, and a female . . . it has been years without enjoying such a sweet smell, or touch, and she looks sweet indeed, and unwed as well, as none called her wife."

Livid at the beggar's words, Thorne retorted, "Wed or not, you know your touch will pass on the pox as part of your curse. Yet you dared think to touch my woman?" He had not meant to call her his woman, but again the words were spoken and could not be undone.

"I was hungry for her touch and she offered me food and kindness. Was it in error to want so little?" The man covered with signs of the pox continued to stare at Candy with a sick longing.

Sucking his breath between his teeth Thorne answered. "Aye, is that not why you carry the curse, because you do not know the *error* in your choices, and what is yours and what is not? Tell me your name and crime."

To receive a pox curse could only mean this man's ruler had not sentenced him to a punishment befitting his crime. Having escaped justice forced the family who had suffered his harm to seek retribution. Desperation for justice was sought through a witch's hand and in the form of a curse.

This man was *not* from Thorne's realm, as no witch's curse was needed for fairness in his lands. Honesty, equality and fairness were his personal codes of honor as a ruler. He would not tolerate less. Where this wretched being was from raised an entirely different issue.

The beggar shrugged. "I am a simple man named Gill, and I only took what the girl offered to me. She desired me, and used her female ways to entice me, and then when I gave her what she begged from me she cried otherwise. I was unfairly accused."

"No witch puts a pox on a man for simple lust. What is the truth of this? Ripple, can you tell without his vile touch?"

Now that Candy was safely behind them, Ripple rode forward to Thorne's side. "Aye, the stench within his soul speaks all too loudly to my mind's eye. This foul man, named Gillese, took the innocence from a child."

Once Ripple's mind sifted through the foulness of the man's thoughts, realization and disgust widened his eyes. "The girl was but two years of age and had no 'female ways' as she was but a tot. He is perverted with his lust and thinks children crave him as a man. Such thoughts still enthrall his boil-covered, and ugly fucking cock."

Ripple glanced back at Candy. "Sorry my Lady. Be glad you cannot see it, an ugly enough sight to make you wish yourself blind."

Looking back at Gill he continued. "His urges are as filthy as his body. This pitiful excuse of a man should not have suffered a pox, rather he should have been castrated and then crushed like the filthy cockroach he is." Ripple spit to remove the taste of vileness from what he'd seen. The sensation felt like black corrosion upon his tongue.

With a smirk the beggar looked up. "Still if any man dares kill me, the curse will carry to him, so you cannot. Look to your men. Is this not why they stand bewildered like stupid lambs not knowing what to do? Let me touch her just once and I shall go on my way. She will suffer neither my lust, nor this unfair pox I carry."

The dwarf pulled an arrow and notched it to his bow. "Indeed she shall not. You are mad, cursed, and you nauseate me, a difficult feat to accomplish. The curse does not pertain to a mere *dwarf,* so no pox can be transferred to me. I never believed that fucking wives tale anyway."

Ripple shot his arrow directly through the beggar's heart. "And now you are dead. A long past due task complete." Ripple put his bow away and wiped his hands on his leathers as if a simple dirty task had been completed.

Thorne turned to his men who looked stunned. "Burn his remains, but do not touch him directly, and do not even consider asking the Earth Mother for release of his foul spirit. The truth of his crime sickens me."

Murmurs of agreement rose from his men.

"Undoubtedly he carries fleas and lice as well so wash well afterwards. Bring nothing of his to our camp. Neither his name on your lips nor a flea from his body."

When he turned to Candy he saw her eyes were enormous. Regretfully, she had seen the criminal put to an end. Yet if the beggar had touched her, Thorne knew the man would not have been sated by Candy's hand in his, even if the pox did not transfer.

He had held firm that the sorry excuse of a man would never touch his Lassie. There was no means he would have allowed that, and if Ripple had not killed the poxed man, then the foul man would have died by Thorne's hand. Ripple had simply beaten him to the necessary task.

Tears filled Candy's green eyes, but she blinked them away trying to hide her feelings. "I thought he needed food and clothing."

"Ah, Lassie, you are ever innocent and have a pure heart. What he sorely needed was to be dead. I regret your witnessing such."

"I don't understand."

"Seldom is a witch called upon for the task of retribution. It means this was the only resolution the parents of that poor girl could manage within their kingdom. For some reason, that man escaped punishment for his crime. Tis the making of a poor ruler to let such a heinous criminal roam freely with his manhood intact so he can repeat his shame."

Shaking his head in distaste Thorne continued. "Such would never go unpunished in my land. This 'Gill' surely traveled across the sea, and thus makes me wonder how a man carrying a pox gained travel privileges."

"Maybe he was very wealthy or related to the ruler, or they hid him in a cabin away from others."

Candy couldn't imagine such a crime being overlooked either, but the concept of dirty politics was something she knew existed across the world, so probably here as well.

A frown furrowed his brow as he reflected about her answer. "Possibly, and I shall need to consider such. I know this land across the water and thought better of their king. Are you all right? You must have been frightened though you acted most brave."

Of course she would have been frightened. Thorne had been so as well, but his fright was in regard to her.

"Nothing a bottle of wine won't help." Although her words were in jest, her shaking told the truth of her degree of distress.

Likely she'd never seen a man die before. Candy was trying to be courageous and he was proud of her efforts, nevertheless, her shock seemed to encompass her, and there was nothing shameful in that.

"We could not let him harm you or another, as was his intent. This had to be done, as he was an evil man."

Were his words going to be comforting in any manner? She was now in a different land with different rules—could he not offer her something more?

Mayhap he should, but acknowledged he knew little of such situations with females. He was solely accustomed to bringing a woman to pleasure, not tears. Candy looked very small and fragile and this situation made him feel awkward and useless. Should he dismount and hold her? Would she let him? He wanted to, but feared facing the memory of how soft and yielding she'd felt in his arms.

"Do you need comfort?" Thorne asked her softly.

Candy looked up at him as if considering her answer. "I'm not a child, I'll be fine."

Her body betrayed she was not. By no means did he consider her a child, and certainly she was braver than he imagined. Thank the goddess, she'd pulled back when he told her to, but he knew she was avoiding the truth.

"As you wish." Thorne rode away wishing she'd been forthcoming. Then he could have had an excuse to hold her close, despite how it would pain him when he had to let go.

Thorne joined Ripple and thanked the dwarf for his proficient use of his arrow.

"Twas nothing, and you had already procured a most fine dinner for us so it seemed the least I could do. Why do you not console your Lady? You should be holding her as we speak."

Thorne shook his head. "She denied the need."

Ripple looked him in the eyes. "Have you lost all sense? Seeing a man die is not a simple thing to a female's eyes. Did you think she would not be unsettled by such a thing?"

"Was I to jump down from my horse and wrap my arms about her despite her words?"

"And I thought you well-versed in women and means to charm them. Obviously a myth."

"Apparently I have no charm or sense whatsoever when it comes to *her*."

"So true, my Lord. If I had known you were not going to console her I would have. You are an irrational man to let such an opportunity pass, but I shall not. If you will not comfort her then remember another male will, and today it shall be me." Ripple kicked his horse into a trot and headed back to Candy.

As usual, the little man was correct.

Would he never get it right with Candy? How could he forever be wrong with his Lassie? All had been right until that confounded accident.

When Thorne saw Ripple talking to her, he tried to avoid looking. The dwarf was no doubt bragging over his deed, although it truly looked as though he was just being kind to Candy. His friend embraced her.

Damn dwarf would do anything to provoke his King and to touch Candy. Still, better Ripple, his friend, than Victus, who was, it seemed, his rival.

This entire incident and the need to destroy the diseased body required a longer part of the day than expected. If the man had not had the pox, Thorne would have been tempted to leave the perverted beggar for the animals to decimate by beak and claw.

However he'd take no chance in harming the Earth Mother's own. The man's soul, if he had one, did not deserve a proper burial pyre; nonetheless it was best to make certain his remains could not taint another.

They moved on to make camp at a spot far enough away, with the wind in their favor, so as to not smell the burning puss-filled body of the beggar. Nothing could mask the pungent distinctive stench of burning flesh. Thorne also wanted them far enough away to keep Candy from thinking about the incident. As if such was possible.

As usual, Ripple had been correct, they would not make it to Grasslands for the night. So much wisdom and foresight for such a small-statured man—though the dwarf never seemed to recognized his full value as a friend or man. Thorne regretted his friend's self image, as Ripple was truly a man with a big heart, and keen brain, despite his blunt tongue.

Surely one day a woman would appreciate all the man had to offer and settle Ripple down to become a husband, perchance with many children wrestling with him in play. That would be a sight Thorne would love to behold.

Ero dug a fire pit and began roasting the wild boar. Of course Ono was quite pleased with the remaining eyeball and a few other select offerings Thorne had slipped her, outside of Candy's view. It made Thorne smile to know at least he could please Candy's young gargoyle easily enough. If only it were as easy with her.

That evening, despite the savory smell of herbs on the roasting boar, and a bit of mead, the entire camp felt unsettled by the day's events. Talk was sparse, but none mourned the dead man—it was the poor abused child was what they felt sickened over. Never again would such happen by that ill minded man.

A pox on a man was a rare occurrence and as the King, he should have been notified that a poxed man wandered within his realm. Why had he not been forewarned? The thought bothered him greatly. Was the truce between the kingdoms weakening? He needed clarity on this, as the renegades were threat enough without worrying about a war with the populace of Grangore.

Today had ended with Thorne feeling drained, but he thought on how the morrow would be a far better day.

As it turned out, it did not bode for a better day.

Rather the day was full of dark ominous clouds and grumbling thunder. The wind and weather threatened to break open the skies and drench them to their chilled souls. The temperature dropped, the humid rose, easterly wind battled against them, and the weather slowed their progress to a pitiless walk.

The plains outside Grasslands Village offered no welcome to the travelers. Nor did the flat terrain offer reprieve from the harsh blowing sand and swelling dust clouds, which required the horse's faces and eyes be protected with blindfolds. The riders had their faces covered as well to protect against the fierceness of the abrading dust. Only gauze covered eyes showed beneath hooded oiled dusters.

When the harshness of the elements started, Thorne had checked on Candy foremost and found Able had done well in covering her delicate skin with his duster and her face and green eyes had been wrapped with gauze. By wrapping Candy in his too big duster, the situation left Able unprotected from the elements. It was then that Thorne realized he'd not considered the need for a duster for Candy, something he would remedy as soon as possible.

Thorne removed his own duster and ordered Able to wear it. Able wanted to protest but knew Thorne would not let one of his warriors suffer when he did not.

Little Ono was clutched against Able's chest, under now under Thorne's duster.

It should be my chest that protects her companion. It was not, and he would be unjust to complain of such, however the duster was *his*, and the little gargoyle would scent *him* while being protected from the abrasive elements.

Rain would be welcome to dampen the airborne dust, swirls of blasting sand, and to improve visibility. Rumbles of thunder only taunted them, while sand laden winds tore at any skin unprotected from the weather's wrath. Thorne wondered if he had offended any deity and was being castigated, thus resulting in this a brutal change in weather.

By early nightfall they finally reached Grasslands Village. They barely escaped the wrath within the dark skies, which opened to dump torrents of icy rain and hail upon them. Added threats from numerous, and luminous lightening strikes, and angry thunder, encouraged everyone to rush into the inn to avoid getting soaked, pelted, or worse.

A young stable-hand aided Bec to quickly move the horses under cover to care for them. The smile on Bec's face indicated he would most likely spend the night in the stables, well pleased with the company he would be keeping. Thorne would make certain food and blankets would be sent out to both of the youths.

Upon inquiry, the innkeeper told Thorne there were three rooms available, in addition to one the whores made use of. When the man offered the King his quarters, Thorne declined. The innkeeper had his own family to care for and Thorne would not have them displaced. This would make for crowded quarters for his men, though more room than a tent, and far drier.

Thorne agreed to pay for all the rooms available, with the largest room for his men, another for his Lady, and then the smallest one for himself. He did not like to sleep in the company of his rowdy men when they were drunk, and no doubt tonight they would also use their coin for pleasure as well. The lustful grinding grunts of a man on a woman did not make for peaceful sleep. It would only remind Thorne of his own unfilled desires—and his Lassie down the hall.

The men's spirits rose with the warmth of the inn and the aroma of hot food. They were hungry and had an overly large and tasty meal in front of them, as the inn's keeper's comely daughter was also a fine cook. There would be no rationing of food on this night. Everyone seemed to be enjoying the abundance of food, liquor and the few females who offered to provide carnal services.

Even the youthful innkeeper's daughter seemed infatuated by the sight of the muscled warriors. No doubt even she would enjoy being plucked on this night given the inviting smile on her face. Thorne wondered which of his men would be the one to take her. Perhaps Toemus, if the smile the girl gave him was any indication. That was, if Victus' fine face did not stir her first.

Candy remained very quiet as she ate and then moved to sit alone by the large stone fireplace. Thorne looked at her sitting over there and thought about what Ripple had said, about how she had interest in him and was starting to remember. He wondered if such was true, although Ripple had never told untruths, he was simply too direct in his speech to ever bother to lie.

His Lassie might have forgotten the feel of him, but never would he forget the feel of her—her silky slickness and tightness as he repeatedly slid into her. And that memory pushed blood downward to harden him, while he silently cursed him cock for this constant response to even a memory of her.

One of the inn's women set her eyes on him. She no doubt recognized him, though he was certain he'd never bedded this woman before. He watched as she worked her way over, slowly, seductively, and wondered if he could get Candy's attention by feigning interest in another.

The wench's blouse was exceedingly low and showed almost her entire ample bosom. What did not show from above could be seen through the sheerness of the fabric. With those rounded hips, the woman no doubt had serviced many men through the years.

When she put her hand on his shoulder, Thorne pulled the woman onto his lap. She was not really the type of female Thorne would choose, unless he had too many carnal needs and few females to choose from, and much to drink—an unlikely combination for him. Without a doubt, she knew how to use her body to pleasure a man—by the looks of her, too many men.

If Candy saw this encounter, and if she really did find him of interest, then perhaps she'd express a bit of jealousy. Thus proving she cared somewhat for him.

The woman's arms wrapped around his neck and her bosom was now eye level. Though she was lovely and generous of form, Thorne preferred a female with a bit less. Too much breast made him feel as if he was bedding a cow instead of a delicate woman. He preferred Candy's breasts. They were perfect, as was all of her figure.

When the female offered her services without requirement of coin, he laughed as though the whore had said something exceedingly cleaver, but in truth he had no desire to have her at all. He had no want of what this woman so brazenly offered, only his desire for his Lassie.

As the woman leaned in for a kiss he obliged. But as soon as he spotted Candy heading upstairs toward her room, he tried to push the female from his lap and thought to go after her. Although to do or say what, he had no idea. But the harlot would not let go of him as she dug her fists deeper into his vest.

Trying not to be harsh, yet be rid of her, Thorne pressed coin into the palm of the wench's hand. "Not this night. Here, take this coin and find another man."

She became enraged and would not let go of him. "Am I not fine enough for you, my Lord? I have the same opening between my legs as any other woman, why will you not have me?"

Her voice was getting louder, and the smell of the liquor perfumed her breath in an undesirable manner. While pounding on his chest, her voice escalated further and bordered on a shout. "I wish to lay with you, can you not tell? Why have you embarrassed and deceived me?"

Now she was scratching Thorne's arms and anywhere else her hands met his flesh. The scorned woman had become vicious. Thorne held no want to physically harm her, though seemingly she had no such considerations regarding him.

Victus and Able pulled her from him, though she'd now added kicking to her angered response. Finally, they pulled the woman beyond kicking range of him, but not before she landed a blow to his shin.

"I would gladly partake of your fine womanly assets," Victus told her, as he struggled to keep her hands from doing further damage to the King.

When she saw Victus' face, she softened and was almost singing her words. "So you think you can you pleasure me, handsome warrior?"

"Indeed. Shall we give it a fucking try?" He began to lead her upstairs to the room the men shared. Victus grabbed a bottle of mead as he passed the bar and held it up to salute his King while using his other hand to grab the female's arse. By the giggles from the woman, it was apparent she had easily managed a change of heart regarding her desired partner.

The other men clapped Thorne on the shoulder and joked about the whole incident and how for once Victus' good looks had been useful to their King.

Ripple sat down at the table with his little arms crossed and shook his head. Leaning over to Thorne he whispered, "Such a foolish action my Lord. You would have done better to spend your kiss on the woman you desire, not the one you do not."

The following day was as dreary as Thorne's mood

He kept considering the words Ripple had spoken. His foolishness could not be undone, and he'd reacted like a young boy trying to get a girl's attention in an inane manner.

Even worse, Candy had not stayed in the room because of it, and now probably thought he frequently sought harlots and whores. To think he was said to be alluring to females, to simply crook his finger at one and she would follow him to his bed.

Thorne doubted that Candy would respond in any such a manner, as she'd made it clear she was not easily won to sexual favors. Nay, she would most likely scorn his assurance and have none of it. Although on the 'needing moon' she had been completely his for a single passion-filled night, and never once had she refused his lust for her.

Certainly it was not the scar upon his face that brought women to his bed, but the power he wielded and the wealth he could offer. All wanted to become his Queen, yet none ever met his appeal to make them so—until this foreign female. Candy saw beyond his crown, in fact she did not seem to see it at all. On the night of the 'needing moon' they had only seen each other.

If only he could forget about her and that night. Were there not many women as fair of face?

None held a candle to her inner and outer beauty in his eyes.

Had there not been other women he had enjoyed on a 'needing moon'?

True, though none whose heart and soul lighted the flame deep within him . . . never had he felt as he had with her—truly intimate, undamaged unto her eyes.

Other women could be passionate . . . why did he continue to lie to himself? For so many years, other women had been measured and found lacking. Candy had no equal, with those enticing beautiful green eyes, eager delicate body and pure spirit. Forgetting her would be as simple as forgetting to breathe.

And therein was the problem, because he would not ever be able to forget that night, or the feel of her against him, or himself within her. A groan escaped him at the memory.

This has to cease.

His realm required his full attention.

That accident that robbed Candy of her memory had robbed him of something he desperately wanted and needed, and now he must learn to live without it, again. Surely he could manage without that frustrating and clumsy female—the one who was much trouble to him.

Thorne let out another groan. He adored the trouble she presented, though only the goddess knew why.

These thoughts are driving me mad.

Why was it that what she could not remember, he could not forget?

How the goddess must be mocking his lust for a woman who wanted naught of him.

Enough!

His obligations regarding the twosome village's unrest demanded his attention. His cock would have to wait.

The matter of how to prevent war should be his focus, not the small delicate female with the emerald eyes, delicate shoulders and . . .

Once more Thorne pushed her from his thoughts.

This morning the sky had cleared and everyone seemed more lighthearted—except him.

As they rode out of the village Thorne caught sight of Ripple riding next to Candy. They were talking a great deal, but about what Thorne had no idea. That little man had best not be boasting about his virility. No humor travelled through Thorne's veins this day.

Once when Candy glanced up it was at the same time as Thorne watched her—their eyes met. When she smiled at him, he quickly turned away.

Thorne wondered what she remembered, and if that was what Ripple was discussing with her. Probably not, as the dwarf, no doubt, was filling her head with tales of his adventures and sexual prowess.

Seemed the wretched little man could be damn charming by the way Candy laughed. And what did she find so amusing? Ripple didn't make Thorne laugh overly much.

Damn dwarf was entirely too entertaining.

When they reached the river, they found the water was far too deep and the current dangerously swift from the recent torrential rains. This was as Thorne had feared, and he was not happy to see confirmation of an overly swollen riverbank and rapid currents. Crossing would be folly.

So many obstacles were delaying this journey to maintain peace, and now this. Did the gods and goddesses strive for his land to war internally? These delays made him question the deities' intentions, as truly haste was not within their scheme.

Thorne knew they could not wait day after day to see how long it would take before the water calmed and receded. They would need to climb high and use what was oft called the 'gap bridge'.

The atrocity was a good ten hands by ten high and crossed a dangerous deep gorge. At this time of the year the ravine would contain deadly currents far beneath the suspended wooden passage. As much as he hated to admit it, this was their only available option in order to avoid further loss of travel time.

As he informed the warriors of his plan, they glanced between themselves. Most men knew the reputation of the bridge. This was not a trail taken by choice, but one only chosen by need. Many men had been known to soil themselves while crossing this suspended bridge. Thorne held no doubt his warriors would follow his lead, as undesirable as it was to contemplate.

The narrow ascending trail toward the bridge was precariously slow to travel. With the two wide wagons, many stops were required to remove large stones from their path. The process seemed unending as the wooden wheels struggled. They would move forward several wagon distances and then again stop to prepare the trail. Men took turns clearing the road, a process that was slow, dirty, and backbreaking.

Sometimes the horses were used to help drag larger boulders away. This made a task these horses were neither bred nor trained for, and all the men regretted using their steeds in that manner. Without oxen, there was no other choice. Fate seemed determined to set a burdened trail as she tested their tenacity.

The blazing sun beat down relentlessly, as though the Sun God took offense to their decision and sought to punish them for such foolishness. Indeed it would take brave men and blinded horses to transverse the 'gap' once they reached it. Still Thorne never doubted his warriors' bravery. Always they did what was necessary.

As they climbed higher, the increased altitude led to cooler air. Deciduous trees became scarce as heartier hemlocks and pines emerged. Soon the stubble of stubborn, gangly pines began to grow tall and narrow.

The air thinned, and the burden of the trail caused both men and beast to labor noticeably as they sucked air into their lungs.

Thorne signaled to his men to walk the horses and for Able to have Candy ride in the wagon for this part of the journey. Candy argued she could walk as well as any man, but Thorne gave Able and Candy a warning look, indicating he'd not abide discussion.

Able knew to watch Candy else she might succumb to her own clumsiness or be stricken by altitude sickness. It was obvious any harm to her would warrant Thorne's wrath. That meant Able sternly relegated Lady Candy to the wagon and forced her to drink water.

When she tried to argue, Able asked if she really disregarded him so much as to want to see him suffer for it. By his meaningful glance to Thorne, Candy became convinced Able was correct. Riding in the wagon was a better choice.

As Thorne watched the interaction, he determined Able to be far cleverer than he. Certainly Able manipulated Candy more easily. Mayhap he should take lessons from his warrior, as his own skills seemed lacking when it came to this woman.

Obviously Candy was not used to the strain of this kind of travel, and Thorne again wondered what her home was like that she knew so little of the wilds. Was she was sheltered within a home by some man? She denied anyone waited for her, but what if she had forgotten?

This made for poor timing to think about such when he had a challenging task ahead, one, which required his full attention. He forced his attention back to the obstacles in front of him, as there were many to be met.

Every time rock or gravel tumbled down the precipice, the men would stop and pray the trail would hold for another thousand years. Thorne, however, worried little regarding the trail along the rocky cliff. It was the integrity of the much-aged wooden bridge he was uneasy about.

Eventually the exhausting rocky terrain opened to a plateau, which appeared to welcome them with the promise of a brief reprieve. Sparse grasses grew and boulders were plentiful. This final piece of terrain would soon terminate at their dangerous destination.

A single-stranded contorted pine tree grew outward from the ridge, as if reaching through the air pointing a crooked arthritic finger to their destination. When they finally ascended the last patch of the trail and came upon the 'gap bridge', all the men stared mutely across the hazardous expanse.

None wanted to speak of it, as no man wanted to cross. The bridge was made from an abundance of thick hemp ropes and weathered wooden planks. Although the pieces appeared to be tied together securely, the profound depth below the bridge was daunting.

Water churned and spit foam like a mad animal, roaring as if defying any to test its mettle. Surely no sane man would be so imprudent. But these men were warriors, and 'sane' was not within their training.

The sway of the bridge when they crossed would be no less thwarting. Never did this bridge stand still, as always the bridge wavered in the winds that pummeled through the gorge. Sometimes the din from the wind and water was so loud it required yelling at the man standing next to you for any chance to be heard.

At least on this day they had no significant mist or fog to contend with while crossing, although such would have disguised the deadly turbulent waters below. No matter what the day was like, never did any man want to cross this bridge. Each would pray to his favored god or goddess before taking his first step off solid ground, and put his faith onto the splintered, swaying planks, below his feet.

This task needed to be done, and Thorne was not one to ask his men to risk what he would not himself, so he blindfolded his war-horse and gently walked him across. As a war-horse, the animal did not panic easily, and despite the sway of the bridge Thorne easily handled his trained stallion. When he reached the other side, he tied his steed to a tree and headed back across, as Toemus started forward with the next blindfolded horse.

His warrior had a gift for calming horses and that was much needed for this task. One by one, Toemus walked the horses over while speaking softly to them, managing to avert their fear from the thunderous sounds of the swift and roaring current below.

One wagon was too wide, which necessitated it be left behind after the items were transferred to the smaller wagon. Taking the remaining wagon across was slow and meticulous least a wheel catch on the ropes. More than once Thorne caught himself holding his breath as he watched the ordeal. After the single wagon and the rest of the horses had crossed, it was finally time to take Lightness across.

The youthful filly was the least experienced, and therefore, she remained last. Should Lightness spook, the other horses would sense it, which would have made for a risk they could ill afford. Even though his warrior used his soothing manner with the filly, Lightness stopped mid-bridge and stomped the boards. One cracked and a piece of plank broke free.

Over and over the broken board turned, as it sailed through leagues of air, and plunged into the depth of the ravine. In finality, the plank smashed onto a bulky boulder, which refused to be budged despite the torrent of angry water that battered it. The wood piece shattered into mere splinters to be washed away and forgotten.

Meanwhile, the rapid current carried entire tree trunks and did not so much as notice the addition of tiny debris being added to its long and swift journey down stream.

Everyone remained hushed as they watched the board turning end over end to be consumed by the ravenous ravine. It might have been insignificant to the turbulence below, but the men above took wary notice. No one could survive such a fall, or those wrathful waters, and the men knew it. The warriors looked at each other, none wanted to go next, yet none wished to be a named a coward either. Only a man unworthy of his stones would waver.

Thorne had enough to worry about without added troubles, but Ripple came to him and spoke. "Your Lady refuses to cross the gap."

"Do not refer to that troublesome female as 'my Lady'," he retorted as he watched young Bec volunteer to cross next. The young man had ballocks to be sure, and Thorne was proud of his fortitude. The other men were hailing young Bec's fearlessness and they would soon follow suit. None wanted to be bested by the young squire when courage was being measured.

Meanwhile, Ripple stood there with his short arms crossed over his muscled chest and tapped his small booted foot, Thorne realized this was not a time to argue with the astute dwarf, whom he had long considered a friend. He turned his attention back to his new problem.

"And why will she not cross?"

He had instructed Able to aid her, as his warrior was stronger than he appeared, and if a problem arose on the bridge he would not panic. Able, like all the men he had chosen for this journey, was dependable and would serve Candy well.

"She has a great fear of heights and the bridge swings in this cursed wind. Terror fills her eyes."

Ripple seemed to show more compassion for this woman than Thorne had ever thought the little man's abrasive personality could hold. In fact, all of his men seemed to be overly fond of her, which further irritated Thorne. Was she making his warriors too soft, or were they hardened with lust for her? This was a thought he wished he'd not had, and certainly not at this time. Did they not have enough troubles without adding a female to them? Thorne turned away from Ripple and cast his eyes over to the deep and dangerous chasm before he spoke.

"We must cross, as the alternate route would easily add another seven days of travel. And in that time innocent blood could be spilled over trivial matters between the villages. Only Candy and the men remain now, we must continue."

"Have you considered what you find to be trivial is not so to others, my Lord? Nonetheless, your Lady will not budge, and has tied herself to the larger wagon we are to leave behind."

Thorne laughed while shaking his head, and wondered what the female would do next. "Has she truly?"

"Not so, but she thought to, only could not find a rope. I wanted you to consider your actions afore you reacted in anger. You oft hold a temper, my Lord."

"I will talk to her then, though I do not see how I will be of help calming her."

Ripple shrugged his small shoulders. "You likely underestimate your charms. But do not go to her angry or she will bolt back down the mountain, of this I know. And she truly lacks grace and no doubt would be injured—at the very least."

With a heavy sigh he nodded. If Ripple said such, it would occur, and she did seem prone to accidents. He would speak with Candy and see if he could talk sense into her.

And what if she failed to see reason? Thorne let out a sigh, *aye what then warrior-King?*

Chapter Seventeen
Thorne

As he approached Candy, Thorne signaled Able to leave.

As hard as Thorne tried, his eyes could not help but take notice of the female, and admittedly her form pleased him overly much. He was determined Candy would never know the effect she had on him, as she remembered nothing of what they shared, nothing of him. He'd not let himself fall into those deep and astonishing sensuous eyes again.

Had his father not warned him twas best not to be vulnerable when a ruler? By his father's words: "Those you love become responsibilities to you and opportunities to your enemies. Better to bed many than to let your love for a single, vulnerable female, be known."

Aye father, tell my heart and cock of that.

"Candy I hear you will not cross." Thorne was trying hard not to look at her heaving bosom. She was scared beyond what he'd imagined, and he felt his heart soften a little. Only the tiniest bit however, as his goal remained, and that was to get her to cross the damn bridge, fear or no.

Her eyes dampened but she held back tears as she straightened her shoulders. "I just can't, it's so high and that raging water. . .it's too frightening. I'm sorry, but I can't do it."

Thorne clasped his hands behind his back to keep from embracing her. He had to get her across the bridge. Slowly he circled around her. From the back he could look at her without her seeing him do so. Standing there he spoke softly to her, with his lips nearly brushing her ear as he inhaled her sweet scent. Damn, that alone hardened him, but he could not help his reaction anymore than he could not breathe.

"Lassie, we have a great need to cross and it must be today if we are to try to prevent blood shed, and I know you would wish none harmed by a delay. Even then we may be overly late. Able is strong—has he not served you well with Lightness?"

Her voice trembled. "He's a good man, but I can't cross, I'll fall and die."

"Nay, no, he would not let you fall. If not Able, then maybe another of the men?"

"You want me to pick another warrior to walk me over that old rickety wood-and-rope bridge? Really? Any one of them?"

Stubbornness overtook her soft face as she frowned at him. She did not believe he would allow her to place her trust in another of his warriors. "In that case, Victus seems very strong and seems to care for my well-being."

Thorne grimaced. He had surely lost his senses choosing Victus for this journey. The warrior had his eyes all over Candy and was overly handsome. None would deny he had a perfect face, a face most pleasing to females.

"Not Victus." Thorne had no intentions of putting those two in such close proximity. "He is not nearly strong enough. Possibly Bear. . .Would you trust him to cross with you?"

An obstinate look crossed her face as she turned and glared at Thorne. "I guess you don't really understand how terrified I am, now do you? You think some strong man at my side will keep me from seeing and hearing the treacherous water that could kill me . . . if the fall didn't? Do you think I'm deaf and blind?"

Her voice had risen. Candy was angry now—a more purposeful emotion than fear. She would most likely hate him for what he decided he must do next.

"Woman, you test my tolerance sorely and are verily much trouble to me." With his declaration Thorne easily threw her small form over his shoulder, and began to carry her to the edge of the bridge.

She was kicking and screaming all the way, calling him a brute, a bully, a Neanderthal, the name-calling list went on. The rest of the warriors were trying to suppress their humor at the site of her strewn across Thorne's shoulder.

Meanwhile, Thorne was trying to ignore her pert wiggling arse in his face, while she pounded her fists against his back. Aye, those small fists of hers felt more likened to a good massage to his back muscles than Candy's attempt to make her displeasure known.

He stopped at the edge of the bridge, set her down, and gave her a stern look.

"Will you be carried thus, like a sack of grain, or will you let me carry you close against my '*Neanderthal*' body while tightly secured by my '*brute*' arms? The choice is yours. But know this, you *will* cross, and now. At this moment the level of dignity and comfort is your choice."

Candy looked past him, ready to bolt, but Thorne was too fast and scooped her up into his arms. Holding her tightly against his chest so she could not move. He shook his head at her.

"We cross now Lassie. I will hold you tight and you must trust that I have far better balance than yourself." He heard her whimper of terror and softened his voice further. "*Shhh*, trust me. I would never let you come to harm. Now close your eyes, we will soon meet your young gargoyle, as Ono has already crossed and awaits you."

With her eyes closed, he began to walk slowly to keep the sway of the bridge minimal despite the buffeting wind. He began to speak to her tenderly as he took each step. "Candy, listen to my voice and nothing else. Once, when I was a small child—"

"It's hard to picture you as a small child," her voice interrupted him.

Now this was the female he knew, inquisitive and with spark. "I was not always seventy-seven inches in height, for which no doubt my mother was grateful whilst birthing me. Nevertheless, as a child I wanted to live in a tree house, much like Ripple does.

"How much fun I thought, to live within the treetop greenery, as then we had a world full of bright colors. I asked my father if I could request the groundkeeper to help me with such a project and he said I could. This is the same man, by the name of Reeves, whom we still have today—although now he is much aged and has a helper. A good man, a gentle man in most things, though strong of hand if a child misbehaves. Not that *I* ever did such a thing."

Although her eyes remained closed, Candy let a bit of a smile escape her inviting lips as she murmured, "*Umm hum*, of course not. I can't imagine you being a bit of trouble as an adorable little boy."

Thorne could not hide his smile at her playful words. "Reeves taught me the use of wood and tools, as I was ever eager to build my tree house. He taught me about many types of trees as well. The tree selected needed to be of strong wood, not brittle under the wind, and with big limbs for the weight of the tree house. Finally we found the perfect old oak, which Reeves said was probably nigh a hundred years old. Such a grand tree with strong and wide branches."

Thorne stopped, stepped to his right, sidestepping the loose and broken plank, before he moved forward again. The wind pushed against him, as he held steadfast with Candy cradled against his chest. He felt a bit alarmed as he realized had she tried to walk this bridge alone she would have likely succumbed to the force of the wind, being so small and of little mass.

He became thankful for her paralyzing fear and that he carried her instead—hardly a hardship. Always when their bodies touched he felt a humming within him, which he ill understood. Those traces of humming coursed through him now, providing pleasure in an unexpected, unmeasured manner.

Ah Lassie, why are you not mine? No other man could need your touch greater, or treasure you more.

He looked at the length of bridge still ahead and focused on keeping her calm and safe, "It took me well over two full moons of time to build that tree house, as it had to be done in my free time, not during studies, chores, or arms training."

"You had arms training as a child?" She sounded almost relaxed now.

"Of course. After all I was nine years of age, but that makes for another story to be told no doubt at the next bridge we encounter."

When Thorne looked down at her face her green eyes w met his, it weakened his resolve. Nay, he was a ruler, not a boy with an over abundance of hormones. She held no memory that night, and he had an undertaking to complete.

"Close your eyes so you can picture my story," he said gently.

How she affects my inner stability and makes my heart stumble.

Taking a deep breath he continued. "The tree house had a rope ladder, which Reeves also taught me to make using hemp. The process taught me the art of knots and gave me more than a few calluses and new blisters as well, but the ladder turned out to be sturdy and functional. The roof was truly the most difficult part to construct, with hides tightly stretched across the beams, and then covered with fitted wood shingles.

"I was most proud of the work my hands had fashioned. My tree house even had a deer skin at the doorway, proudly one from my own hunt." Thorne's feet stopped and he lowered her to the ground.

He wished he didn't have to let go of her, wished she remembered, but mostly wished she wanted him like he did her. But wishing was for children who had not yet learned that life was not so simple. A harsh lesson he'd learned all too well in his childhood, and one he would never likely forget. The gods and goddesses were no doubt too engaged to consider a single man's selfish wish.

"I'd love to see your tree house and draw it if you wouldn't mind."

Candy was staring at him with those mesmerizing intense eyes.

How she steals my breath.

"It no longer stands as my brother burned it down." She could be the ruin of him. He needed to move beyond that night they shared for his own sanity. A ruler needed clarity, and Candy confused his senses.

"What an awful accident, you must've been devastated." Candy had sincere sympathy in her green eyes. How generous her heart was to think it to be an accident.

"Hardly an accident, he had intended to burn me within." Pain crossed Thorne's face. Obviously this was a memory he did not relish, though he spoke on. "How disappointed my brother became that I did not cooperate and die."

The look upon her face displayed sympathy. Was he not King, and as such needed nothing from her? Had he not ruled competently without this troublesome small female he was dragging about?

"Are you telling me your own brother tried to kill you, because of a tree house? What is he now, a serial killer?"

"I know naught of where or what he has become, but no doubt he is causing pain wherever he might be. By his actions I learned a memorable lesson."

Thorne turned his attention to the horses as he undid their blindfolds. They needed to get their sight back now that they were on solid ground again, or at least until the next challenging part of this excursion.

Candy took his arm. "That's a terribly sad story Thorne. What kind of lesson could a boy possibly learn from something so tragic?"

He removed her hand from his arm as his words came out, "How quickly things you love can be taken from you."

Chapter Eighteen
Thorne

None regretted leaving the gap-bridge behind.

With the precarious crossing behind them the warriors gladly partook of a small meal, joking amongst them before resuming the journey. Stress had led to big appetites, and fear had been replaced by hunger, while laughter helped to slacken tension.

Their path soon began to descend as they rode several miles beyond the 'gap bridge'. The path widened with increased sprinklings of tall pine trees amid the brush. Just when the trail seemed almost pleasant, Thorne readied his men for the cavern they would pass through.

Not as daunting as the bridge crossing, still it was not going to be a comfortable part of the journey either. How he detested this damn cavern and remembered it all too well. At least Candy would have no need to worry about tumbling to her death.

His men would be walking through the earthy tunnels, as the cavern height was insufficient if on horseback. Truthfully, at points the war-horses and Bear, would barely skim through the width of it. To keep fear from overtaking the mounts and causing them to rear up, again he ordered that the horses be blindfolded.

Their reins were to be secured tightly so the horses' heads so they could not raise enough to meet the height of the ceiling. None wanted his mount to scrape itself along the roughness of the tunnels, or panic the other horses.

Only at the center of their trail would there be space high enough for easy passage, as there the ceiling easily rose thirty feet or more. At that point they would not be lingering within that deceiving portion of the cavern, and he hoped to pass quickly without incident.

No sooner had he prepared his war-horse by blindfolding him and limiting his head and neck leeway, when Ripple approached him. As Thorne tightened the tether in place he glanced to his friend.

"Have you tended to your horse Ripple?"

The dwarf looked downward at his leathers. "Sadly not. Our camp truthfully has need of a whore or two for that task." Ripple looked up to see Thorne's smirk knowing his ruling friend never allowed whores within the camp and too often villages were ever far apart.

"You did not come to complain to me about your want of a woman, because if so, it humors me not."

Ripple nodded in agreement. "My lack of a woman humors me not as well, truly it pains my sac. I am here to once again be the bearer of news regarding *your* fine Lady."

Thorne let out an annoyed sigh before he turned his full attention to his friend. "Aye, and what news would that be, and why cannot Able handle her this time?"

Setting his hands on his hips, with his head cocked to the side, he studied Thorne's reaction. "As if you did not enjoy holding her close while crossing that miserable 'gap bridge'. I am short-statured, yet you did not offer to carry me!"

Noting Thorne was duly out of patience, Ripple relayed the problem. "Candy is threatening to stone Able to death and has accumulated a small stockpile of rocks at her ready. She seems most determined."

With a tightly suppressed smile Thorne's finger crossed to his lips, as he shook his head. "Then he has naught to worry about, as she has dreadful aim. What complaint does she hold?"

"Ah, so I see you have been privy to her throwing skills, or lack thereof." Ripple snickered.

"She says the darkness of the cavern means there will be things to the likes of which she calls 'disgusting creepy-crawlies'. Your Lady seems to imagine quite vividly from what I have seen of her thoughts. How she imagines such horrid things I cannot comprehend. Also, she justly requires some comfort, as this is all foreign to her delicate nature."

"Comfort? That woman—" Words to describe his frustration eluded Thorne. Why was it this single female tangled his thoughts and tongue and troubled him so?

"That she is, as surely you have seen her fine figure. Moreover, I am most willing to sacrifice my health, perchance dying from an errant stone, to get close enough to comfort her my Lord, if such is—"

"Such is my responsibility. I shall try to talk sense into her. Have Toemus take my war-horse with his own, as no doubt Candy will be a handful . . . or two."

Ripple quickly stepped in front of Thorne. "Are you certain, as I truly do not mind the thought of comforting Candy so that you may focus on other more pressing Kingly matters? Seeing that she is so troublesome to you."

The King's eyes narrowed. "Do not push my friendship little man. She is under my protection and 'tis my duty to care for her well-being." Under his breath Thorne mumbled, "Troublesome though she may be."

As Thorne strode to the back of where his men were preparing the horses, he heard Ripple's laughter and words. "Aye, a most fetching burden you bear, my Lord."

Damn dwarf.

But his friend was ever honest, almost beyond tolerance. Nor could Thorne forget Candy was a woman— indeed the most stunning female his eyes had ever beheld and the sight of her always called out his want of her. No doubt this would not be an exception. Mayhap he should tie down the 'horse' at his groin before nearing her, else his want of her again be brusquely apparent through his leathers.

This female from another land was not malleable when she set her mind. How strange that seemed to Thorne, since women in his kingdom, other than his sister, always capitulated to his words without argument, and seldom did women argue with their men. As troublesome as Candy was, he found her temperament and intellect most fresh and appealing. Though only the goddess knew why at times such as this.

Fucking dwarf would look for any excuse to wrap his arms around Candy. Ripple may be a short man by stature, but he was entirely a man in all ways of men. Including lusting for Candy, which the man hardly pretended to conceal. If Ripple was not his true friend, Thorne would have killed him by now for his taunting demeanor and lewdness towards her. Between his friend and his Lassie, Thorne felt certain his sanity was being put to test . . . and he was sorely failing.

Thorne saw her standing with her hands defiantly locked on her hips. Her left fist held a sizeable rock. He had to stifle a smile. She was a sight to behold with her golden hair blowing in the breeze and her face set in determination. However, behind those green eyes he saw fear. His inclination towards the humor of it was lost, realizing the level of her fright.

"Not any closer or I'll throw these rocks, and maybe at least one will hit you." Her words were spoken with a resolve he well believed.

Well, at least in that she would indeed *throw* the rocks, not that she would *meet* her mark. Not as if he could not easily stop her before she even raised her arm for the throw. But Thorne had heard a slight tremor in her voice, and her hand clutched the rock desperately, the size of which could do harm, if it actually made its way to her target—doubtful though that was.

With a sigh, Thorne crossed his arms over his chest to show her he was not going to grab at her. Still she did not seem any more at ease. Truly, he did not wish to put more fear into her, and knew she could be most strong-minded if pushed.

What words should he speak to her? Never had his father told him what you say to a distressed female. If Thorne ever had a son, and *if* he ever learned the secret words to ease his Lassie, he would need to pass on such valuable knowledge of what he'd learned.

If Candy was but one of his warriors he would simply beat some sense into the man. There was neither any part of her that resembled a man, nor would he ever touch her in any harsh manner. He let a sigh escape his lips as he focused on how to get this woman to resume their journey.

"You would throw rocks at those who have protected you? Not very gracious of you my Lady." Thorne found it difficult not to be amused as he shook his head at her. "Obviously you have forgotten you lack such skills. Now tell me what it was that caused you to be so fearful."

Candy seemed to be staring at his arms crossed over his chest, though why he could not fathom. He held nothing within his hands, yet she stared as if he held her interest. Was she remembering something of him? Had the look of fear within her eyes, been replaced with something warmer, mayhap even sensual? Or was that simply what he wished to see?

This female had much to learn if she was ever going to be able to defend herself, as her eyes forecast her emotions too easily. Never would she dupe an enemy with the honesty within her green eyes. Eyes that now focused on him far more than the rock she held.

How easily she had become distracted, and he was not sorry for that, as long as it was *his* body distracting her. By following her eyes, his arms and chest seemed to have captivated her notice. But when he took a step forward her hand rose to take aim. So much for wishing this could be done easily.

Thorne shook his head at her. "Lassie we have not all the day to think on this. Tell me, what is the problem?"

"Spiders." The single word was sufficient to explain everything as far as Candy was concerned.

This time Thorne did let out a laugh. He knew he should not have, but all this because there might be spiders was incredulous to imagine. Yet he well knew her fear and quickly tucked away his humor and removed any trace of it from his face.

With glaring eyes and clipped words, Candy fumed at his response. "What? Aren't you afraid of anything?"

Indeed he was—his feelings for her.

Thorne collected himself. "We must pass through the cavern or return to the 'gap bridge'. Considering why we are on this slower-than-sap journey we need to move forward with some sense of haste. Will you not trust me to keep you safe from harm?"

He watched her face closely to see what she was thinking of doing. Would she try to hit him with the rock clenched in her fist, or would she see reason? Candy was a woman, unlike any he knew, so what man could possibly guess what she would do next? Even in bed she had surprised him, but then it had been in a most pleasing manner.

Candy motioned with her chin as she spoke. "Have you been in that place before?"

"Twice. The cavern is dark, damp and carries a most vile odor. Of such I will not lie. Yet never have I been attacked by *spiders*." He did not elaborate that any insects had most likely been eaten, or he would never get her to come with him by her own willingness.

"Just because you're really big, muscular, plus obviously fearless, doesn't mean you should belittle my fears."

By her expression Candy actually looked as if he had hurt her feelings, something he had not intended. Now he felt like dung. Obviously he had yet to learn the secret of what to say to a distressed female. He would well remember that laughter was not what they wanted to hear. Or at least, not his Lassie.

"I am not trying to demean you, I just do not know how—What will make this easier for you?"

She looked around at the vacant surroundings. "Can't you just leave me here?"

Thorne creased his brow and scratched his chin, as if contemplating her ridiculous suggestion, as he regarded at the surrounding terrain. "And by what manner would you survive? How will you eat? How much food should Ero leave with you? I think you are ill prepared to defend yourself. What if a band of fierce, hungry, wolves descends upon you?"

This was doubtful given the altitude, but her eyes got bigger as if frightened by the prospect. He continued on, "They would likely be famished and you are but a wee defenseless morsel." When she began to look around with panic he felt regret at causing her to become so fearful.

"No, my Lady, I fear such is not an option and you must be reasonable with your requests. There is much I would do for you, but leaving you here to die is not within me. I brought you with me on this journey to protect you, and of that, I will continue. Let me guide you through, as I have not let you come to harm, have I?"

Nor would he ever. Thorne hoped she would trust him to safely lead her; otherwise he needed to resort to dragging her screaming body through the damned cavern. He could not wait forever for her to decide to agree, as his people were warring between themselves.

When Candy nodded and dropped the rock, he felt relieved that she would entrust him. But when the sizeable stone fell and hit her sandaled toe, she let out a small grunt of pain reaffirming how inept she was with routine tasks of life. Wisely he withheld his smile as he extended his hand to her.

"This journey requires you wear your boots Candy. Aye, yes, they get a bit hot, but they will serve you far better. Pack the sandals away."

Candy nodded and quietly placed her small delicate hand within his large one. If he had been Ripple, he no doubt would have placed a kiss upon her feminine hand or a kiss to her bruised foot. But he was not, and more the pity for that.

So much for charming the Lady—Still, she had accepted his offer.

When Thorne walked her back to the entrance of the rocky entrance, his men nodded as they started to line up. Never in his life had Thorne needed to take time out to cajole a female for anything inside the bedroom or out, yet this woman required much of his time when he should be travelling with haste.

His patience with her surprised him, as truthfully he was not known for such a quality. None had ever accused him of being an overly enduring man.

As he turned to Candy and bent down to reach for the hem of her skirt, she jumped back from him. "Just what do you think you're doing anyway?"

All his men quickly turned to other monumental tasks—all but Ripple.

"He is trying to keep the bottom of your skirting clean. The cavern floor will be full of—"

"Mud," interrupted Thorne giving Ripple a glaring warning to not be so forthcoming.

Ripple looked between Candy and Thorne.

"Indeed my Lord, I shall take my leave. Toemus attends to your steed and Able to Lightness." The dwarf retreated.

Thorne returned his attention to Candy. "Do you wish to keep your hem from being soiled? I will not be offensive with my hands."

He already knew every inch of what was under her skirt and fought to keep his body from thoughts about such a treasure. If his focus could be turned to what lay ahead, mayhap he could avoid her influence on his male anatomy.

When she nodded, he resumed pulling her skirt to one side and tying a knot in it. Her hem was now raised several inches from the ground by his doing. At least it would not be dragged trough the worst of what was to come, but the boots she now wore would require a good washing afterwards.

Ono flew up to Thorne and landed on his shoulder. "Ono, you will ride with Ero, in the wagon. *Do not*, under any circumstances remove yourself from that wagon, as it is dark, the ceiling is low and you could come to harm." Thorne leaned in close to Ono's tufted ear hoping Candy would not hear. He gave Ono a scratch under her chin. "Drink *nothing*, eat *nothing* from within. All are poisonous little one."

Ono bobbed as if in agreement and Thorne trusted she understood. Gargoyles were smarter than most people took for granted. On this day he prayed Ono would follow directions better than her companion usually did. Thorne watched as Ono flew to Ero's wagon before he returned his attention to Candy, as she also needed a bit of instruction.

"There will be an echo within when we reach the tallest part of the cavern. It would be best to remain silent, so ask any questions *now*."

"I don't have any questions. But stay really close in case of spiders."

Thorne nodded and began the lead through the entrance. Bec followed next carrying a small torch with one hand and his horse's restricted reins with the other.

Candy gripped Thorne's left hand and arm tightly. "Shouldn't you have lots of armed men in front in case we run into bears or something?"

"Always I am well armed Lassie, and there are no bears within." The feel of her holding on to him reminded Thorne of their one night together when she was about to come to completion. He felt himself becoming aroused and was thankful for the darkness. This female really did seem to control his manhood beyond all sanity. Maybe he should just cut it off and give the damn thing to her.

"How do you know?"

Thorne looked down at her and saw her trepidation. "Trust me, there are no bears within this cavern."

Candy seemed satisfied with his response—for a solid fifteen seconds.

"Why not?"

Thorne was confused. He had been contemplating the journey ahead and trying not to think of her closeness. And now she was asking some kind of question. Again.

"Why not what?"

"You said there were no bears. Why not?"

Had he not asked her for questions *before* they had started through the cavern? He had hoped for quietness as they traveled through this space, mostly for the sake of her comfort. Could she not counsel her tongue just this once?

"The dragon ate them." He had answered before considering any possible consequences of his words. Her reaction solidified the extent of his error.

She stopped in her tracks and Bec, not realizing it, ran into her backside. Thinking it was an attack of some sort, she cried out and turned to run. Thorne quickly grabbed Candy about her waist and pulled her to his body. The last thing he needed was for her to run backward or trip as she ran into the darkness. The sooner they were gone from this place, the better.

"I am sorry. I should not have said such a thing." Although now that she was clinging to his chest, perhaps they had not been such unwise words after all.

He enjoyed the feel of her closeness and that subtle humming. All people had need of the touch of another, but hers felt like rain upon parched land. His need was desperate, though he wished it were not so. And like rain against crazed thirsty earth, he absorbed the feel of her deeply. Before Candy, he had not known he had a thirst, a thirsting only she could sate.

Ah Lassie, how I miss your touch.

Her words were audible, though muffled against his chest. "I'm going to die in this strange place aren't I?"

"Nay, no. Candy my words were meant as humor. Everyone in this land knows we no longer have dragons. None has been noted in two eras. Often this is said to calm frightened children. Parents tell their children that the monster they fear beneath their bed is no longer there because it 'was eaten by the dragon'. Children then feel safer."

Her small fists pounded against his chest, yet he cared not. Any touch from her was better than no touch.

"That isn't even funny, and I can't imagine how it calms children when it should give them nightmares," she cried out as she pushed away from him. "I should be walking next to Victus, I'd bet he wouldn't try to scare me."

Ah woman, your words cut deeper than any steel blade.

He had not meant to frighten her, and by no manner would Thorne allow her to travel at Victus' side. Truthfully, she would most likely be *more* frightened if she knew Victus' coarse thoughts of what he would like to do to her. His warrior was rumored to not take women gently. Thorne had heard many times over of Victus' enjoying great roughness during his exploits with the fairer sex, though truthfully no woman seemed to complain of it. Still, obvious bruising had been noted on those females the morning after his warrior's lust was slacked.

Why had he ever let a warrior with such a handsome face on this journey? A poorly thought out decision as the man was not even the *best* at any one feat, although truthfully this warrior fought well enough to remain alive. However, the warrior's sword and knife certainly were not as skilled as many others. Likely Victus simply charmed his way out of death's path. But if the fair-faced warrior dared to try to take Candy in any manner, he would die for it. Charm or no.

Thorne's jaw was clenched from thoughts involving his warrior, and tried to relax before grinding his teeth to nubs. This time when he spoke to Candy, he chose his words most cautiously.

"I shall be more considerate of your unease in my land. I truly did not mean to frighten you." He was thankful for her silence as she nodded and they continued to walk. It lasted a full minute.

"Your land really had dragons?"

Would she never cease?

Thorne leaned in to speak low. "Ask me when we are not within the caverns. Soon the echo of any voices will be most uncomfortable to our ears and will lead to much trouble."

"And then you'll tell me about the dragons?"

"Candy! Silence!"

He did not wish to seem harsh knowing she was both inquisitive and afraid and that her talking was a means to take her mind off fear. However, once they reached the high ceilinged grotto her voice would cause intractable problems. Truthfully he should gag her, as he feared she might scream and all manner of hell would erupt. But he did not have it within him, and she would probably never forgive him if he treated her in such an ill manner.

"Sorry," she whispered.

Thorne nodded his head while putting his hand to her shoulder and gave a light squeeze. Then he ran his hand down her back until he rested it at her waist. It felt as though she had taken a soft breath and relaxed some by his touch. If touching her was all it required, he could lessen her fear most easily. Slowly he ran his hand over her back as she then leaned against him as they continued walking. Ever so gently he continued touching her back, relishing the feel of her beneath his hand knowing her skin was under her bodice. Soft, feminine and flawless. Thankfully she was now less anxious, while he, on the other hand was throbbing with desire.

This woman was not from any world he knew. He probably should not have been surprised she was even ignorant of dragon lore. All small children of his land loved tales of dragons and their wondrous brave deeds. What child did not fancy having their very own dragon?

Certainly as a young boy he had wished for a strong and ferocious dragon at his side, as he imagined himself one day becoming a great warrior, the type of legends. Although, of course, that dragon never came to be, the childhood dream had inspired many, many hours of training in the practice yard. Those hours lent themselves well to his future in defending his Kingdom.

As he thought about the female he now held so near, Thorne wondered if he could ever return Candy to her own land—to say goodbye as he let her leave his life to carry on her own. It made for the right thing to do, though the very thought caused physical pain within his chest.

While the Fates might decide the journey each man walked, if she was not on his path, he knew naught of how he could continue. If she returned to her home, her parting would take a part of his soul with her, and Candy would never even know of it.

Often he prayed to the goddesses for good fortune for his people—prosperity of crops, peace, good health, happy marriages, children for those desiring fertility, and so forth. Never before had he considered being self-seeking, to ask regarding to his own need or want. As King it would be selfish beyond all measure, and he'd not been raised to put his desires above his people. Still, for her...

This kind of thinking was useless. She remembered naught of what they had shared. Gone, like a breeze, were the abundant words they had spoken as they learned more of each other's lives, between times of shared physical bliss. He remembered the laughter and gladness felt merely by her presence, her delicate touch.

And those tingling humming touches between them— all that and so much more encompassed that magick filled night. A night of rare familiarity, seemingly a blessed emotional and physical intimacy, except now forgotten. Best to never reflect on it again. If only he could forget. Yet he could not, and she could not remember. Undeniably, Fate could be most punishing.

Quickly he discounted those memories and sought focus on what was ahead. The jagged stone surface could easily scrape the flesh from man or horse. As the tunnel began to descend, the air about them cooled and drops of cloudy, mineral rich moisture sometimes dripped from the ceiling.

Deeper they walked along the cavern walls, and with each step Thorne regretted what they would soon endure. If a more repulsive place was within his domain, he'd yet to discover it and prayed he never would. This cavern seemed more akin to the likes of the Under Earth Master then anything created through the gods or goddesses design.

Damp, dank air soon culminated into a foul stench, which intensified with each step as they crossed the slick cold stone floor. Unfortunately, this foretold how the apex was nearing, and any man who had traveled here before was not looking forward to this passing. Those unknowing would soon never forget.

It had been many years ago, still he remembered the first time he'd seen the huge hollow cavity with its ebony, majestically elevated ceiling. The top beheld a small opening of about twenty or more inches. The opening let the sun and seasons enter to fall upon a grotto of fetid water on the slickened floor beneath.

Upon first eying the mountainous cavern, it seemed magnificent, but then the reality of the cavern and the odor hit like a hammer to an anvil. The glistening, slimy floor held all manner of decay, and all sense of beauty was robbed from those who entered. How he wished he could spare Candy from the impending assault, which would soon cloy her sight, smell and mind.

Thorne pulled her closer and put a finger to her lips to remind her to be silent. And just as he had once raised his head and thought the black cavern exquisite, he saw how she fell for the illusion as well.

Then she choked as the smell stole the air from her lungs and strangled any desire to draw in another punishing breath.

With a firm push he tried to get her to move forward, to quickly get past this place. But of course, as was typical, she was not so easily moved. Likened to a stubborn and wondering child she sought to understand what her eyes beheld, to make sense of it.

As Candy's questioning eyes scrutinized the space, Thorne knew the instant she saw what was upon the slimy floor—within the pool of water. He needed to caution her, but just as he whispered, "do not scream", her fear had already consumed her.

Candy screamed.

Gone was the small delicate female at his side, as this was unquestionably the scream of a banshee!

The ensuing echo was deafening as the sound reverberated throughout the cavern as though a chorus had screamed. Echo met echo, and yet it continued through the vastness with a cacophony of agonizing noise.

An enigma to this cavern as the echo multiplied as if being chased from wall to wall. A single echo becoming two, two became four, four became eight, and so on it went multiplying as the scream circled the cavern space. The men covered their ears as the intensity assaulted them.

"Down," shouted Thorne, hoping his men already had such sense. And his command also repeated throughout the cavern with deafening clarity.

Down . . . Down . . . Down . . Down . . .

He grabbed at Candy as she tried to pull away to run. Little choice was left to him but to tackle her to the floor beneath him.

"*Oomph.*" As Candy hit the floor air was knocked from her.

Thorne kept his body protecting hers, quickly covering her mouth with his hand to prevent any further screams. Damn her, would she never trust to follow his words? Did she hold no trust that he would protect her? Foolish woman!

The air above their heads became a maelstrom of blackness as the flurry of thousands of webbed winged mammals left their roost. They were greatly disturbed and confused by her echoing scream and his bellowing command, which followed. Their razor sharp teeth could slice open even the toughest animal's hide and Thorne deeply regretted their disturbance for the sake of his men and their steeds.

For once Candy did not struggle, whether because she had fainted or his heaviness upon her, he did not know. At this point it mattered little.

As Thorne's eyes glanced at the floor in front of him, he saw brittle and broken bones, cleaned free of any marrow. No doubt his Lassie had also spied this when she'd let her fear engage her lungs. Or perhaps she'd seen the rodents gnawing on the dead flesh of the more recent, decaying, unwary travelers. The coarsely furred critters had wisely scurried off to find sanctuary in crevices when the thousand bats had descended. The rats would not be feasted on this day, as Thorne and his warriors would suffer in the food chain in their stead.

Regrettably there were no places for the horses or the warriors to seek refuge. They would to be descended upon until the bats either left through the top opening (unlikely with it being daylight) or they calmed sufficiently. It would take time for their frenzy to settle, and until then all the group would suffer for it—all but his female, who he would shield with his own body. Thorne could not stomach thoughts of her skin being sliced open and her blood lapped by these creatures.

As Candy struggled to move beneath him and he loosened his grip on her mouth. "Do not scream again," he whispered.

She nodded as best as possible considering he weighed her down.

Very quietly she said. "I really need to make a nature call, and your weight isn't helping."

Truly she was pinned beneath his large body and he easily weighed over twice what she did.

And she needed to piss? Did the Fates really disfavor him this much?

Thorne knew Candy was already mortified at her admission, but he would not remove himself from her while the mammals flew. He tried to raise his weight from her somewhat, taking more on his forearms. At least in this manner she might feel less pressure but remain covered.

"Isn't helping," she mumbled.

"Then piss, pee, or whatever you wish to name it," he hoarsely whispered back. "Tis far cleaner than what we lay upon and the men shall never know of it. But I shall not be letting you up as yet."

He heard her wince at his words.

"A natural function Lassie, I care naught of it." And truthfully he did not care what she did as long as she remained safe. The thick layer of bat guano they lay in was hardly going to be made any the worse by a bit of urine.

When he felt her ready to say something further he *"shhhed"* her gently and rested his lips to her neck. She stilled beneath him. He would have kissed her neck, but knew it would cause a rush of blood to his lower regions, and she would easily become aware of the hardness pressing against her.

Thorne focused on the bat guano to mask his responsiveness of what was temptingly beneath him.

As suspected, it took a good length of time before the majority of the bats regrouped upon their roost. Knowing how sensitive their hearing was, Thorne feared any sound could get them agitated again, yet they needed to move on, and with haste. The bats had settled in numbers, still many flew as if searching for the perfect roosting spot. This was as calm as it was to get and they needed to move on.

Very slowly he stood and helped Candy up. He put his finger to her lips to remind her not to make noise. When he turned to his men and nodded they slowly rose as well.

When Thorne's attention went back to Candy he saw her staring at the pool of water.

There were two bodies silhouetted in the dark water, each suffered from varying stages of decay and rodent consumption. Only bits of dry hair remained on the skulls, while skeletal ribs still carried remnants of decomposing flesh that steadfastly held bones together.

The sinew of what had once been muscle now served as torn, tattered and stringy pieces of rotted nourishment for undiscerning vermin. Men's clothing lay strewn to the side, as if the idiotic travelers thought to bathe here. They must have been sot by mead to be so heedless.

Clearly these ignorant men had known naught of the poisonous nature of this pool. Why anyone would think such an odiferous spot would hold safe water defied all common sense. Again the effects of too much mead influenced all reason, and obviously their sense of smell as well.

Now their corpses fed the rats, and in turn the rat's blood and flesh fed the carnivorous bats that lived within this deceiving cavern, their domain. Thorne had no desire to remain within the feeding frenzy as fodder and nudged Candy to move forward.

As quickly as possible, they hastened through the cavern. At one junction they passed a crumbling skeleton while rats scrambled and squeaked past their feet. Candy had gasped. Thankfully she'd not stumbled over the bones, although her skirt hem had caught on one jagged edge from a broken rib cage.

She started to panic at seeing part of a skeleton attached to her skirting. Thorne quickly deployed a knife to free her skirt, and they hurried past the remains of another unfortunate soul.

Finally the tunnel ended and they reached sunlight. The fresh air led everyone to inhale deeply, to purge their lungs from the onslaught their senses had been forced to endure. The new openness in their surroundings was appreciated by all of the warriors and horses. Once Ero uncovered the little gargoyle, Ono wasted no time flying to a nearby tree to seek fresh air as well.

Candy quickly pulled away from the group and rushed towards the tall, thick bushes to evacuate her bladder, possibly her stomach as well.

Thorne went to weigh the damage his men sustained, and to the sliced hide of his war-horse. As he stroked the wounded hide on his horse he regretted the wounds. This could have happened even without Candy's scream, which he well knew from previous experiences through the cavern. Her fear had been honest and he could not fault her.

When she returned and saw the men attending to the cuts on the horses and themselves, tears and regret pooled in her eyes. Although filthy and stinky, she didn't have any cuts and felt guilty at having screamed.

How painfully evident she'd been the cause for the bats to swarm over them. And now the men were wounded. This was her fault and it weighed heavily on her.

Ripple went to her side. "They are blood drinkers to be sure."

"It's my fault, I-I'm so sorry, I r-really didn't mean to scream." Words became stuttered with her confession as she fought back tears.

"Nay, you just beat me to it my Lady. You saved me the humiliation of letting my lungs scream out like a little girl, so I am utterly thankful to be reprieved of such an unmanly act. That cavern is enough to frighten and sicken anyone, let alone a delicate unsuspecting female."

Candy tried to smile at Ripple, but failed miserably. "I know you're just saying that to make me feel better. I'm not sure it's helping, but you usually make me smile. Do those bats carry rabies?"

A mischievous glint filled Ripple's eyes. "Given the chance, I could do much more than provide you with a small smile."

Then a serious look crossed the dwarf's face. "I doubt they carry rabies, as the swarm seemed quite healthy. There were no dead bats on the floor of the cavern."

Of course he did not elaborate that the rats might well have consumed any deceased, webbed-winged creatures. They had seemed most robust, certainly not ill.

"I certainly hope they don't pass rabies with their bites." She well remembered going through the series of shots as a child after the dog incident and prayed these men wouldn't be subjected to the same. Actually they probably didn't even have rabies treatments available to them. Even more guilt raked her.

"The bats do not truly bite. Their teeth are sharper than a warriors blade and they slice the skin so they may lap up the blood." When Ripple saw Candy's expression he regretted having told her this. Hoping to lessen her horror he added an explanation.

"None really feel it when it happens, as the bats provide a numbing when they slice the skin open." By the look on Candy's face, Ripple thought his added words had not improved the situation.

While Thorne walked towards the two of them, his eyes scrutinized her thoroughly, up and down. Then he circled her. "No wounds? For which I am most grateful."

Thorne could see she was eyeing him as well, but he already knew the back of his arms had been sliced many times, so he stayed facing her. She needed to see neither his torn leathers nor bloodied skin. Already he saw the feelings of guilt her eyes beheld, and wished not to add to it. The cuts would heal very quickly as they did not go deep. He wished to change her focus.

"Ripple, you look as though you were spared. Surely your small stature was to your advantage."

Looking a little awkward, Ripple explained he'd hidden under Thorne's war-horse. There was no doubt the dwarf was clever, and to take refuge under Thorne's stallion showed bravery, as the man could easily been stomped to death. With a nod Thorne instructed Ripple to help Candy get to the creek so she could clean up.

Then he spoke to Candy. "You will require a change of your dress as well. Leave this one behind, as the smell and stains will never wash out."

With a tightened jaw Thorne cautioned Ripple, "Pay heed, escort her only. Her task does not require your assistance."

He heard Ripple's snicker. "A pity."

As Thorne turned to leave, he heard Candy's gasp. Damn, he had forgotten about his back. Without turning around, he continued on to the supply wagon.

True to his nature, Ripple interceded. "Have no concern my Lady. He has lost much more blood in the past and no doubt will again in the future. Truthfully, what man would not bleed freely for the likes of you? Verily I feel rather amiss not to be blooded so that you would look upon me with such concern. Now, let us find water to remove the layer of bat shit from you."

When Ripple saw Candy look down at her dress in surprise, he laughed. "'You are a mess my Lady. And the smell is not your usual sweet scent."

"I'm covered in bat poop?"

Ripple cocked his head as a smile curved his lips and his nose scrunched up. "It reeks of bat shit to me, but name it whatever pleases you my Lady."

Thorne stopped and turned to watch her go. His friend steered Candy toward the brook of clean water that ran down from the mountainside with towels in hand. Thorne shook his head. How troublesome this female was, and yet how he wanted her more than seemed possible.

A few minutes later Thorne was meandering close to where Candy was washing up, eager for his turn at the clean water, when he heard her yelp. Rushing through the brush he found her looking panicked, standing wet and wrapped in a towel.

Ripple had heard her as well and came running on his short legs. "What is amiss?"

Thorne shrugged as they eyed Candy. She looked rather pale and he became concerned. "Are you harmed in some manner?"

"I'm pretty sure a snake just bit me."

Giving Ripple a nod of his head to look for the snake he then asked Candy to describe it.

"Well if I'd seen it I'd know for sure it was a *snake* now wouldn't I?"

Obviously she was perturbed.

"Show me the bite while Ripple tries to locate the reptile who would dare to bite your fair and tender skin."

"Are you trying to be funny, 'cause that bite hurt?" Candy looked a bit peeved and Thorne tried to give his expression full seriousness.

"Nay, Candy it has been a most challenging and long day. Now let me attend to this wound in case you were bitten by a poisonous snake."

Not likely, but possible with the way the day was going and her predictability to draw harm to herself. If the had gods favored him and she had been bitten on her pert cute arse, he would relish the need to attend to her aggrieved posterior wound.

Candy turned to indicate where she'd been assaulted, on the backside of her right thigh.

Thorne scrubbed his mouth with his hand as bent down to inspect the injury.

Meanwhile Ripple returned and held the dead offender by the tail. "Not to worry my Lady—"

"Indeed," Thorne gave Ripple a warning glare, as he spoke to Candy, "worry not, as *I* shall attend to *you* and suck the venom from your thigh."

His small friend suppressed his mirth with obvious difficulty. "Aye, I see you will be in most capable hands. Meanwhile I shall inform the men that washing will be delayed whilst their King attends to this difficult undertaking. Be most wary my friend, we would not our ruler to succumb to the Lady's venom."

Candy's brow furrowed looking worried. She tried to look over her shoulder, but unable to see the bite. "Is it really bad, like, am I going to die or end up with necrotic tissue falling off my thigh?"

"Not likely. I shall make the smallest incision and draw the vile venom out. But I shall require you to be still."

"Well please hurry," she added, "I don't think I want to die wrapped in a towel."

"Tis a most delicate task, I shall use my smallest blade. Would you prefer to lie down during this?"

"Maybe I should, you know how I am about knives."

Indeed he did. Thorne quickly laid a towel out for her to lie face down upon. As those shapely naked legs hardened his shaft, he bit his tongue to stifle a groan of appreciation.

"I guess it's good Ripple found the snake. What kind was it?"

"*Shhh*. This requires much focus and quiet. Now the tiniest of cuts—I will try to keep this from hurting ever much, or leave a scar on your fair flesh."

Meticulously he drew his fingernail slowly into the 'X' shape across her unbroken skin. In truth the garden snake's bite was little more than a mosquito bite. "Was that overly painful Lassie?"

Her voice betrayed her nervousness and she kept her eyes squeezed tight in dread. "No, just knowing it was a knife was the worst of it. Does it look all green and gross?"

"Nay, worry not, it looks most curable. So brave you are Lassie. Next I must draw the venom from the wound, then

I shall attend to the tissue above the bite, as the poison ascends towards the heart. Ready?"

Candy nodded, keeping her eyes closed for the ordeal.

Putting his mouth above her bite Thorne gently sucked her skin as he moved his hands along her thigh, kneading flesh as if monitoring the flow of venom. The towel barely covered her arse and he was most tempted to push it up a wee further.

When he heard Candy let out a little moan he left his lips where they were, ceasing all movement—except for a jerk within his groin.

"Are you doing well?" By the little sounds she was making, his Lassie was doing *very* well. She sounded needful and he was most prepared to oblige.

"*Um-hum*, I think so. Did you get everything you needed to?"

Oh nay, there is much more of you I have want of Lassie.

"Perhaps just a little more, to be ever cautious." How tempting to place a kiss behind her knee, a sensuous point he'd learned on their single night together.

Again he set his lips against the spot and licked before he again sucked upon her skin while he kneaded her calf and thigh. When she let out a small sensuous sigh, it caused Thorne to smile. What he would do to get her back into his bed.

"There, the blood is clear and I shall wrap this for you." A reddened round spot showed where he had marked her flesh by sucking the blood to the surface. It made him smile knowing she wore his temporary warrior's mark as his woman. Though she'd never know of it.

"You know, I thought Ero usually acted as the camp medic."

"I was nearest and the venom was headed to your heart. Would you have preferred his attendance?" As if he would let any man so close to her nearly naked form and female sex.

"Oh, no—not at all. You seem most accomplished with your hands and mouth . . . I mean you seem to know how to handle these things."

If only you remembered what I can do to you with my hands and mouth.

"Never have I heard complaints. I will wrap this and you shall mend with nary a scar."

Just then Ripple showed up with bandages and healing ointment. "Ah, my Lord, it appears you have done a keen job here. I truly admire your quick thinking in this situation." Ripple left the supplies and walked off chuckling.

"Why in the world is he laughing? This could've been fatal!"

"Who is to say what makes that man see humor in the manner he does? Let me help you up so you may dress before the men come to wash."

"Thanks. You know you really are the kindest man."

Thorne bent his head in gratitude, as well as to hide his face and his stifled grin. 'Kind' was hardly what he had been. 'Randy' was a far more accurate description. He must be taking after Ripple to have contrived this false deed and to have garnered her gratitude as well.

Still he did not find regret in his actions. Her flesh under his hands had felt as the woman he remembered, and Thorne held no remorse at making this opportunity to touch her silky skin, even if by doing so constituted deception.

Chapter Nineteen
Candy

$\mathcal{Y}$esterday, the word *fear* took on new proportions. All of which contradicted Candy's previous conviction that 'outdoorsiness' couldn't be worse than she'd imagined. How wrong she'd been, because absolutely nothing in her mind could conjure anything like yesterday's events.

Right now the thought of powdered eggs cooked on a mini-propane stove, set on the tailgate of a Buick station wagon sounded pretty safe, sane and sanitary.

Any form of cavern exploration was removed from her bucket list. Oh, yeah—it had never been on it. She'd now seen what could happen to spelunkers, and it wasn't pretty!

Admittedly if she had to suffer such horrifying events she was thankful to have the company of a steamy-pheromone-laden man at her side. He was the best sigh-worthy distraction a female could ever hope for.

The day had been totally exhausting both physically and emotionally. Had she been in Savannah, it would've definitely been a day to deservedly treat her to a pint of Ben and Jerry's Rocky Road. Totally apropos considering what she'd endured.

One pint. One spoon. All hers—every last lick.

This was by no means Savannah, so no ice cream, no chocolate, no showers and definitely no color, other than perpetual boring beige.

The revised travel plans pivoted their trail to head back to where they would've been if they could've crossed where originally intended. One wagon had been left behind because the wheels had been too wide to safely—

as if such a word could honestly be used—cross the 'gap bridge'.

Even the smaller wagon barely made it down the cavern tunnels and sometimes required being tilted to squeeze through narrow slimy walls. It seemed as if they kept hitting obstacles to slow them down. Of course, *she* was one of those burdens they often contended with.

While the men were attending to the horses, repacked the wagon, and bathing, Candy found she had time to herself. She looked around to find a to place sit (carefully checking it was uninhabited first) and to sketch. She found the perfect, flat, not-infested-by-anything rock.

Since Ono was dozing next to her, she thought to try using the little gargoyle as a model, but the next thing she knew it had actually become a drawing of Thorne—bare chested. Well, why not, because his form made the most interesting composition.

Candy envisioned his pecs, deltoids, biceps; even scars on those tanned abdominal elevations. What a stunning male he was with his strength, power and sensuality. His face held strong pleasing components, with an air of commanding confidence, which was easily reproduced since she saw him daily.

High cheekbones and penetrating chocolate-brown eyes showed he was focused on a task at hand. Every aspect stood firmly in her memory. Lush lashes framed his expressive eyes. Of course, his full, lush lips were impossible to forget.

Thorne's features were truly attractive and memorable and with her pencil in hand she easily replicated his face onto her art pad.

Candy was finishing a little shading on a dip in his clavicle when someone reaching over her shoulder, and grabbed her art pad from her hands. Startled, she looked up and saw Thorne frowning as he stared at the drawing of himself.

When he looked Candy in the eyes, his melted, chocolate-colored eyes reflected what seemed to be agitation. He actually hissed through his teeth at her.

True, he held a bit of a feral and almost animalistic sensual bearing, but *really*, hissing? Wasn't that a little extreme?

"What? Come on it isn't *that* bad." She felt perplexed. This was the occupational hazard when doing portraits, because people saw themselves differently than others, artist included. But Candy knew the likeness was very good despite his obvious distaste.

Thorne looked around then grabbed ahold of her hand, and quickly pulled her up off the rock and out of the camp, away from view of others.

"What's wrong? What did I do? Thorne your grip's too tight and you're hurting my hand." Her distress at his roughness caught him off guard and he dropped her hand before he crushed any bones.

He pushed her back against a tree, as if to keep her from running, and held the drawing in front of her. As Candy compared the likeness of him on paper to the immense warrior in front of her she didn't know how she was supposed to respond. She had no clue what he was seething about. And seething he was, it really wasn't that bad of a portrait!

"What? I don't know what you want me to say." It was a good likeness of his handsome features, so why should he be insulted?

"This," Thorne was pointing to the drawing he'd shoved into her face. "This. Me. You—you bound my soul within this parchment?"

For a second she thought Thorne had been reduced to *her* usual single word responses. Candy started to realize his concern had nothing to do with the quality of her work. "I only wanted to do a drawing of you. I didn't realize you would think anything adverse about it."

"This drawing, it looks much like me—is it not so?" Thorne was still fuming with distress. "Why would you do such to me?"

"I didn't do anything to you, I just like how you look— you're pretty darn tempting to sketch. I didn't know you'd be offended just because I like your body, um, I mean because I wanted to draw your physical form."

Thorne crossed his arms and leaned forward to look closely into her eyes. "I see naught of my soul within your eyes, where have you hidden it? Should I search your body or does it reside within this parchment?"

Although the part about searching her body sounded tantalizing to Candy, he was obviously not flirting with her. By his tone, he was deadly serious, and angry-Thorne was a little scary.

"Twiddle winks! I didn't touch your soul. I swear it. We do this all the time where I come from, and it means nothing other than to duplicate a person or an image you find very pleasing to your eyes."

He looked down at the drawing. "Pleasing? This cannot be what I look like unto your eyes."

She looked at her drawing and back at him. "Why not? You're gorgeous and I think it looks very much like how you look."

"The scar on my cheek is too small." His finger traced the scar on the drawing.

"You seem to think it's bigger than it actually is. Could it be, that over time the wound healed to became less of a scar? Maybe now it's more of a psychological scar, rather than a physical one. I certainly don't consider it marring to your handsome and alluring face."

Questioningly, he looked up at Candy. "You deny having stolen my soul?"

"I swear Thorne, I haven't stolen anything from you. It's simply lead from my pencil put upon this paper, like the house and tree I drew before this trip. This must be a superstition that you have here. But if you don't believe me, ask Ripple. I think he will tell you that I'm telling the truth, and you still possess your soul."

At least she hoped Ripple would back her up regarding this. He didn't seem superstitious to her. But then neither had Thorne, so she felt unsure about just how much doggie do-do she was treading in.

She tore the paper depicting his likeness free from her art pad and handed it to Thorne. "It's only paper and pencil. Take it and do what you need to do with it. I'm sorry, I didn't mean any harm."

As she closed her sketchpad she felt very disappointed she'd given away such a good sketch of him. She would've loved to keep that drawing which depicted his strength, not only of his body, but also the character within him.

He took the paper and walked away, while she watched his masculine rolling gait. Now that was something fine and impossible to portray on paper. Candy noticed how his backside would be equally fine to draw. But heaven only knew what he would insinuate if she dared to draw his derriere.

They had resumed their tedious, long, journey when Ripple rode up to Lightness.

He leaned in close, and spoke to Candy. "You are as lovely as the sun rising to begin a new day my Lady. Alas, if only we shared the Sun God's opening grace of warm rays across our naked bodies whilst we awakened in each other's arms."

Oh good grief. She knew he was just flirting without actually expecting her to respond. Candy smiled and shook her head at the small man. Still she didn't want to encourage this line of thinking.

Ripple's ever-teasing banter continued without reprieve. "How you fill the carnal dreams of men, and disappoint them when they waken finding an empty bed and their seed spilled other than where they had dreamt." He let out a sigh as Candy rolled her eyes at his poetic nonsense.

"Nevertheless, I have need to speak with you about what came to pass this morning with Thorne."

She nodded in agreement that something should be said. The event had certainly ruined her morning, as well as Thorne's, and she'd never meant for that to happen. And it was such a good drawing of him too! *Dang*.

Ripple scoffed as he shook his head. "This realm has many strange ideas regarding what makes for right or wrong. Many I do not adhere to. And why should I, as I am simply a dwarf to many, and not truly a man. Oft times, these ideas seem an absurdity to me, such as their sexual freedom on a 'needing moon', which you will soon remember, yet they remain priggish in other thoughts.

"Most of these discrepancies simply need to remain behind closed doors between lovers, and others need not judge. Why should any man care what titillates another as long as he does not cuckold with another's wife? Now, back to these 'draws' you do."

"They're drawings or sketches," Candy corrected.

"Of course they are, I wanted to be positive I held your attention on this matter. Thorne told me how your hands replicate likenesses on parchment and he showed me this '*drawing*' you had done of him. Personally, I think his scars are *much* more prominent and mayhap his eyes should look cruel and beady, and surely he is less muscular—"

"His scars and eyes are fine, and his muscles . . . Ripple, you're teasing again, aren't you?"

"Indeed, I enjoy your company too much not to. You know you are not so much taller than myself, surely no more than twelve inches. We could fit quite well during coupling, do you not agree?" Ripple's eyebrow arched in a come hither manner.

His joking made her laugh, despite trying not to. "Shame on you. You're incorrigible, and what would your mother say to such behavior?"

"Ha. In my youth, she once told me how I should be home by midnight, as the only thing open after that would be a woman's legs. I found I savored the rewards of staying out past midnight, but I digress.

"I believe there is no harm in your pencil to parchment, but many would think it evil if you duplicate their face. They might wrongly think you have their soul at your mercy. Perhaps tis unwise to draw other men however, you may do *drawings* of me. I will gladly shed my clothing so you may include the best parts of me." Ripple was wagging his eyebrows at her.

Laughing and shaking her head, she now understood why Thorne had been so distraught.

"How can I undo this with him?"

Ripple snickered as he waved his hand as if of no concern. "He is wiser than to let a superstition frame his beliefs, and I trust he actually liked this likeness you did, as he put it inside his saddlebag for safe keeping. Thorne mentioned you said you found his body pleasing. His words were repeated with a smile upon his lips. Thorne will come to his senses, of this I know. Nor can he hold you to blame. But when you told him you stole nothing from him, you were grievously in error my Lady."

Candy was taken aback. "No, I swear I've never stolen from him."

The small man rode off laughing as he called back, "Nay, you stole everything. Fear not my Lady, as you will have the opportunity to return all ten-fold, and you shall. Believe me, you shall indeed."

The following day was hot, muggy and sticky.

Candy felt miserable. Rivulets of sweat dripped down her face and left a salty trail. While she traveled along the dry and dusty road she couldn't help but daydream how wonderful it would be if they were to camp near water. How heavenly to be washed clean by cool water. In her world, showers were daily, sometimes twice a day with the Savannah humidity. Not so here in the wilderness where those niceties were just sought-after memories.

Not only was she covered with grimy dust, but she also felt down right gritty, and her skin felt parched. Able kept forcing her to drink water to keep hydrated, but her skin wanted more than what went down her throat. Plus, drinking warm water didn't cool her down at all. Besides, she really disliked lukewarm beverages. But ice cubes were a foreign concept here. Yet another thing she missed about Savannah.

She wondered what Thorne would think of ice cubes. Candy let her mind wander as she pictured tracing an ice cube across his chest as it left a trail of melted drops to cling to his taut muscles. Now that brought a smile to her face, but did absolutely nothing to cool her down.

When she looked up and saw Thorne at the front of their convoy, it reminded her how 'Pheromone Man' seemed to be keeping an extra wide berth from her. Not as if she understood his rotating moods anyway.

Candy hated to admit it, but 'Pheromone-laden Man' really got under her skin. She kept thinking about certain pieces of memories as they flitted through her mind. That and the fact he was so enticing. Really, a man like Thorne shouldn't be out in the open to ogle and distract women. He should be tied to a woman's bed, naked and for intimate observation.

Shame on her, but that thought was very appealing.

Dang, but the man looked way better than any male had a right to, and he just attracted her to him in ways she couldn't quite understand.

Face it you're in over your head with a man like Thorne.

And since when had she become the kind of female to be so fixated on a hot guy she hardly knew?

Apparently, since first seeing that prime cut of male flesh.

Mid-day, Ripple again pulled up to her horse and relieved Able. Candy always found Ripple to be entertaining, and he made her laugh, so she was glad for his company on such a slow and sticky—beyond nasty—day. The scenery had long ago become too monotonous-beige to care.

In order to bear the heat (with all those thousands of yards of fabric called a skirt) Candy had hiked the fabric as high as modestly possible and tucked it under her thighs, careful not to reveal herself.

"How fare thee my Lady?" Ripple was doing a gentlemanly bow from his horse, obviously trying to lighten her thoughts from the dusty road and turkey roasting weather, including how her inner meat thermometer had long since read 'over done'.

"Oh Ripple, I want a bath so bad. What I wouldn't give for a cool stream, or better yet, a lake to cool off in."

The dwarf's eyebrows lifted. "Truly? And if such came to pass what would you offer?" As his eyes slid to her bare legs, the sparkle in his eyes and a lifted brow didn't hide how his comment was intended.

"Has none warned you how your reckless words provoke lustful thoughts in men? Thoughts as to what manner of coin men intend to barter with considering a comely female such as you?"

Candy frowned. Had she heard this before? No, she didn't think she . . .

"Aye my Lady, your memory. Heed it well, as I am not known to be a gentleman, and though a small-statured man, I have very big desires."

"Ripple, you always joke, but I'm miserable and would love to soak in cool water." Candy swatted away a belligerent fly.

"Who is to say I am joking? Mayhap you do not take me seriously due to my short stature. Candy, forget not, I have a man's needs. Offer only what you intend to make good on. Still, I may indeed be able to encourage setting camp by a lake this night, though verily I dare not collect from you in any manner.

"Regard your words my Lady, beware and set no cost in a man's mind. Any man daft enough to dare take even your lips would pay dearly with flesh and blood. But even at the cost of my valued tenders, I would almost consider any part of you worth it." He wasn't smiling at his last words, which she found disturbing.

Blushing, dumbfounded and embarrassed, Candy cleared the dust from her dry throat. "Well, if you carry any influence regarding that stubborn man, please use it." Her hand again swatted the annoying fly.

Ripple reached for his knife and with a flash the fly was smacked by the blade. The nasty insect was history.

Impressed, she smiled at him. "Thanks, that insect's been tormenting me for quite a while."

"A small thing my Lady, and your smile is reward enough for this grand deed of valor I took upon myself. I shall inquire if we may indeed stop at Lake Walla for this night." Ripple gave a quick nod of his head and rode forward.

She could see him talking to Thorne. For a second Thorne glanced back at her. There was a slight frown on his face, but she couldn't tell if it was because the sun was in his eyes, or if she'd somehow offended him, again— which certainly seemed easily possible. Given the grueling sun and heat, no doubt her body odor was plenty offensive even from here.

Two hours later they stopped for camp at a beautiful pool of crystalline clear water. So this was Lake Walla, she could hardly wait to get into the water. But when she looked over at Thorne's bare arms as he unsaddled his war-horse, her desire to cool off was diverted. Those muscled arms were entirely fine. In fact his biceps inspired her for what she decided to do next. This was totally unlike her, but an imp named 'Temptation' had clawed into her mindset and was feeling daring. Maybe even a bit coquettish, who knew she had it in her? Must be the result of some type of heat stroke.

Approaching Ero, Candy asked to borrow a shirt explaining how her dress would wrap around her legs and be too heavy when wet and how she really wanted to spend time in the water. She was miserable enough to resort to whining, but luckily didn't have to go that route. Ero nodded and started to look in the wagon for a shirt. Meanwhile, Candy picked one up and asked to borrow it, suspecting it would work quite well for her needs.

Ero looked over at Thorne who was busy with the men, then back to Candy with a smile and wink. "Aye, my Lady. Might be useful in a roundabout manner."

She quickly put aside whatever Ero meant by his cryptic words, the water was beckoning her. With the shirt and towel in hand, Candy rushed to the sandy bank of the lake's edge and looked for a place to change. The blissful sensation of bare feet on the sandy soil felt cool and refreshing.

The shirt was made of finely woven soft cotton. Luckily it was so long she could take the back and pull it through to the front to form a tie. This would keep the shirt in place and not float above her head in the water. With the sleeves rolled up she was ready to enjoy the coveted water.

Candy waded waist deep to wash the dirt from her face and hair. The coolness of the water felt like heaven, energizing and rehydrating. Totally what she needed.

Then she spotted a small island further out. The small piece of land had weeping willows that dipped to the water's edge and looked welcoming. She'd love to explore that small oasis, but then looked back to the camp.

Thorne glanced over his shoulder at her while he helped unload tents from the wagon. He'd removed his vest. Sweat glistened off his chiseled and bare chest, as rivulets trickled between the ridges of his abs. When Thorne brushed his arm across his perspiring forehead, his abdominals clenched and showed off every toned muscle.

Holy Moly!

That chest could be used as inspiration to sculpture some virile Greek god! When he leaned forward to unload more supplies, she saw his back as his shoulders rolled and muscles flexed. Her eyes traveled to his narrow waist and hips. Not that his bulging arms were any less spectacular.

Actually, all of him was breathtaking. And yes, that drawing she'd done was spot-on. This man was perfection personified and could serve as any artist's muse, or a woman's most erotic dream—Preferably both, because Candy positively believed in duo purpose function.

Never before had she ever contemplated what she thought to do. But in the spur of the moment Candy decided she absolutely, positively, eagerly, needed a swimming lesson—in Thorne's arms.

She hoped he knew *how* to swim or this was going to be really awkward. Where she got such courage to try this, she had no idea. A smile curved Candy's lips, knowing she shouldn't, *she really shouldn't*, but some little part of her brain seemed controlled by that 'imp' with a Thorne fetish, and really . . . what could it hurt?

Mischievous imp.

Gradually she waded into the deeper water to where the land dropped off and water went to a greater depth. Looking back, she saw Thorne was still glancing her way, between pulling supplies out of the wagon.

Stepping off the ledge she let herself sink down into the deeper, darker water. She held her breath and counted to thirty. Then she came up for air, as she thrashed water and gasped for breath.

Yes, here I am, panicked—drowning—please notice, you incredible hunk of testosterone and muscle. The little female needs you. Yes over here, see the splashing?

While making significant splashing noises and itsy-bitsy screams; she heard a commotion on the beach.

Finally. Well take your time why don't you! Why not stop for a bite to eat as well. Maybe a beer?

Suddenly Thorne shouted to Bear, who was the closet warrior to the water edge.

"Not only can I not swim my Lord, but I fear to sink," Bear yelled back sounding panicked.

Victus started to remove his boots and vest. "I can swim, I will get the woman."

In a flash, Thorne was barefoot, in the lake, and rapidly swimming towards her as she sputtered, spitting out water. Just as he almost reached her, she dropped below the water again. He screamed her name, then dove down and pulled her to him.

Ah, his chest. She was against that awesome chest of his. Wait—she was supposed to be panicking not drooling.

Candy started to squirm and thrash while clutching to him. He held her tighter.

"Tis fine Lassie, I have you. Nay, no, do not grab my neck . . . or my nose or I shall not be able . . . Candy let go of my ears. Calm yourself, you are safe."

"Oh, Thorne I was so—*cough, cough*—frightened. I had no idea the water was so—*cough*—deep."

Tightening her grip on his broad shoulders she wrapped her legs around his waist. *Ooh,* that felt down right intimate, and shame on her for liking it. A lot!

He carried her to shallower water. "What did you think to do in such deep water?"

"I wanted to see the island." Candy didn't loosen her grip. Goodness, he felt good, and she loved the feel of his bare and totally ripped chest.

Once in shallower water Thorne told her she could let go now.

"Are you sure? I'm still frightened. Maybe I should hold on . . . until I feel safer."

"The water is not so deep here, see? Why did you not just walk around to the inlet?"

Because then I wouldn't get you in the water with me, silly boy.

"Really? I didn't realize you could walk to it" —*because I'm totally blonde*— "you're a really good swimmer. Would you teach me? I mean, think what could have happened if you hadn't saved me. I might have drowned, and I should probably learn to swim. Don't you agree?"

Please agree.

Thorne looked conflicted and hesitated. "Never have I heard of a woman who could swim. Not even all my men seem versed in it. Are you certain you want to learn?"

"Well, if you're too busy maybe one of the other men? I think I see Victus at the edge of the water. Maybe he swims." Candy knew full well that Thorne never wanted Victus near her, although she didn't really understand why. The warrior had always been kind enough to her, but it always seemed to really agitate Thorne if that warrior spoke to her. She gave a little wave to Victus and thought she heard Thorne growl.

Yep, sounded like a growl to her.

Thorne looked to the beach and then back at Candy.

"He is going to be most busy. I shall take on this task. It makes for a good start that you do not fear water, but always know your limitations Lassie."

Oh trust me, I do. And 'task' . . . hardly!

Thorne proceeded to begin the swim lesson with basic floating and set his arms out under her as he had her spread out on the water surface face down. He was telling her how to breathe by turning her head up and out of the water as he lightly supported her body. "Breathe in . . . now out through your mouth, good, breathe in . . . and now out . . .

Sputter, sputter, cough.

Yeah big-boy, support my body while I learn.

With his arms lightly supporting her body she almost did forget to get air. Plus she was pretty sure that under the water she'd seen a long solid mass that pushed against his wet leathers. She was pretty certain of what she saw, and Thorne didn't seem to mind this 'task' so much after all.

"Now kick your feet. Nay, no, not in the air, in the water, aye, yes that is . . .that . . . uh, that is very good. You learn fast." For some reason her swim coach seemed a little unsettled.

She'd just traveled over his hands and knew he'd felt her breasts as they passed his fingers. The feeling had been tantalizing for her as the tips of his fingers had brushed her nipples.

Candy knew she shouldn't be doing this, it was atypical and daring, but it did seem to engage him into conversation of sorts. Or so the 'imp' kept telling her. Sure, this swim lesson was all about dialogue. Maybe braille, because the touch of his hands certainly filled her head with all kinds of unspoken words.

"Like that? Did I do all right? Should I try it again? I think I should try doing that again." She repeated her breathing and kicking across his arms. The sensation was sinfully good and the 'imp' in her unquestionably loved Swimming 101.

New swimmers needed encouragement to be successful and Thorne was generous with praise at her accomplishments. She anxiously waited for what he'd teach her next, and hoped he wanted her to repeat what she'd just learned. Practice makes perfect, and his hands had felt *perfect* on her.

Was she learning too fast? She needed to be less adept, slow down that learning curve. "I could try it again if you want?"

Given the tightness of his jaw, he wasn't going to have her repeat this part of the lesson anymore.

Aw, come on. What a shame. Didn't she need more practice?

"Uh, mayhap you should learn to float on your back next. Stand up and lay back. I will support you until you feel comfortable."

Following his instructions she floated on her back feeling his hands supporting her bottom. When he slowly let go, she looked into his eyes and saw he was staring at her breasts. This was far more fun than she would've thought, but since when had she become such a devious female with such boldness? Blame it on that devilish 'imp', because this positively wasn't her.

Yeah, she could float just fine. Too bad he figured that out so quickly as he stepped back from her.

Shoot, she'd been too adept of a student.

"Now what?"

"Lassie, this shirt is . . . when wet . . . I think you should turn over and try the arm strokes next. Stand again, and I shall show you how this is done."

She tried to mimic his masterful arm strokes in the air. And who would have thought? Arm strokes were *soooo* much more difficult than they looked! It was all she could do not to blink her innocent green eyes at him as she pursed her lips in defeat.

"I just can't get it." Candy knew her attitude sounded full of frustration, after all, wasn't she?

Thorne went behind her, put his hands on her arms, and moved them together. "Like such, now cup your fingers. Keep trying, tis something you can do Lassie. Aye, like that. Now try it with your head in the water. Do no forget to raise your head to breathe. No, Lassie, you *must* breathe. Watch me."

With rapture she did, and his masculinization was stunning. Bunched muscles worked effortlessly as he cut through the clear water with his strokes. Such strength and grace, as his body glided through the water almost silently. His form wasn't perfect, but darn close.

Of course when Candy followed suit, it wasn't nearly as refined or smooth.

Or quiet. *Splash, splash, splash.*

Hey, she was a beginner right? Flopping around and needing some 'hands on help' was expected and appreciated. Very appreciated.

His hands felt so good that she could swear she felt tingling to her toes. This man had serious mojo working for him and she felt like putty being molded by his touch. If he continued to distract her, she might actually drown.

When her lesson was disappointingly over, she waded back toward shore. Suddenly her legs were pulled out from under her. Candy suddenly dropped beneath the water, felt her arms being pulled back, and quickly found she was in deeper water. As she got her feet back under her, the water went up to her armpits. Thorne was in front of her with crossed arms and a pinched frown.

She wiped wet hair out of her face and stared up at him. "What was that about?"

His mouth was set in a grimace. "You appear unclothed."

Candy looked down to make sure the makeshift swimwear was still tied. "I have a shirt on."

Thorne let out what sounded like a grunt. "Indeed you do, tis wet and you appear *undressed*."

"Oh! As in *naked*?"

With narrowed eyes, his head slowly nodded.

"Oops, that's not good." Candy crossed her arms over her bosom. "What do you suggest?"

The allure of the refreshing cool water meant she hadn't thought this out well. She certainly hadn't counted on showing her goods to the entire camp.

"I shall bring you a towel to cover yourself as you leave the water. My men do not need to have eyes on you . . . it would be overly tempting. Or did you wish to show yourself to them and incite lust and fighting amongst my men?" Thorne seemed cautious in his response. Almost, but not quite accusing her.

"Of course not!" This man infuriated and confused her. Had he really thought she went through all this for someone else?

When he brought a towel back to her he said, "I would have thrown it, but somehow I distrust you would have caught it." His words sounded clipped, then he retreated back to shore.

She wanted to yell out how his wet leathers were pretty darn revealing as well, but she was too much of a coward. Still she got a good glimpse of his wet backside and the sight of his leathers plastered against his thighs and buttock made her smile.

Really nice ass-ets.

Candy wrapped herself in the towel and went to redress, all the while she wondered what he'd meant when saying somehow he doubted she would catch the towel. As in she was too clumsy? Or did he mean she wanted to be seen? Who knew, because by all that is holy, she had no clue. Men simply weren't part of her knowledge base, as proven once again by interaction with Thorne.

With her hair now wrapped in a towel, she started to untie the bottom of the shirt when she heard a noise behind her. She turned and saw Thorne. He was leaning against a tree, with arms folded across his bare chest, and his ankles crossed. The man looked so nonchalant, as if he wasn't intruding into her personal space.

Now she really did feel naked with the way his eyes roamed over her wet, clinging, makeshift swimsuit.

"You startled me."

"I came to retrieve *my* shirt."

"Oh, really? You want *this* wet shirt because you don't have any others? Sure, I'll take it right off, as soon as you turn around."

Did he really think she was going to just drop her drawers for his half naked awesomeness? Not that she had any on, but that was beside the point. He always seemed so confident. That sensual look in his eyes, his handsome face, and an expression as if he knew intimate secrets about her—all made her shudder.

"And why should I turn around when I have already seen *through* my shirt?" Thorne now held a belligerent smirk on his face.

Smart aleck.

"Because I asked you to, now please turn around."

Thorne did as she asked while she speedily peeled off the shirt and threw it at him. She surprised herself at how the wet shirt landed so perfectly—right on his head. What were the chances that would ever happen again?

"Happy now?" She'd slipped the dress on without even bothering to dry off, suspecting he'd turn around at any second despite her wishes. And he did.

He turned around and his eyes followed her every move. It made her feel like he was indeed a hunter and she was his prey.

"Why is Ripple laughing at me? What is it he knows that makes me so humorous of a subject?"

Candy stopped her in her tracks and blushed. "I don't know. Did you ask him?" The words came out faint, even to her ears. Did Ripple know?

Thorne was holding the wet shirt as though it was his favorite, and maybe it was, how would she know?

"I did."

Candy pulled her boots back on knowing they'd feel hot, but necessary. "And what did he say?"

Thorne looked her in the eyes. "He laughed harder. I know that dwarf and I do not like to be laughed at when I do not know the cause of it."

"Maybe he was laughing at how silly I looked in the water, flopping around and trying to learn to swim."

"You did not appear silly . . . you looked . . . you did well, exceedingly well, and it took courage on your part. Be prideful of your success." Thorne turned and walked away.

Well, the lesson had been short-lived fun, and an enticing event.

Thorne had even remained encouraging during her swimming lesson, which made her feel a twinge of guilt. But sweet mercy, the touch of his hands had been the most sensual thing she'd ever encountered.

Now if Ripple kept his thoughts to himself, she might be able to talk Thorne into a second swimming lesson . . . Or maybe she was pushing her luck. If he ever found out the truth, he'd be hopping mad, but the feel of his hands on her had been totally worth the risk. Indeed, 'Pheromone Man' might require a new moniker—'Magic Hands Man'.

Chapter Twenty
Thorne

A small knock sounded against the tent's doorway beam. Thorne did not bother looking up from the map outstretched on the table. Likely it was Toemus, telling him the evening meal was ready.

Always his regular squire worried that his King ate too little, and yet Thorne had not succumbed to starvation and found the over concern to be humorous. Toemus seemed to behave more like a mother each day, no doubt soon to check behind Thorne's ears.

"Aye Toemus, I can smell the cooking."

When his warrior did not respond Thorne looked up from what he was studying and saw her. She looked soft. Tempting. Unsettled.

"Ah, Candy. What is it that you need?" As always, her beauty was alluring, and her eyes captivating. How easily he could become a prisoner within their depth. So petite, and fine-figured woman, but not his woman it seemed. How bitter the reminder every time he was so close. Did he not have more important matters to attend to at this time?

Truthfully—he did not.

At the lake he had been overly tempted by her closeness, as his hands relished every touch of her delicate skin. Plus the utter sheerness of the wet shirt had made him harder than wood for her.

By the goddess, how he wanted his Lassie beneath him. Every night he dreamt of how intense his fervor when betwixt her legs. Awakening without her in his arms was punishing. Knowing she held no memory of their passion—that was devastating.

Ripple had asked why he did not simply seduce the woman he wanted. What he felt was more complicated than merely desiring a physical melding, he wanted more from her. She needed to remember and decide if he was the man she wanted, or had it simply been from the intoxicating influence of the 'needing moon'.

She'd not indicated any memory coming back to her. But at the lake, whilst in the water, he could have sworn she held a heated look in her jewel-colored eyes. He shook himself from such wishful thoughts.

"May I come in?"

She was looking around his tent as if expecting to see another warrior, or perchance a woman?

Damned if he could tell what she thought, as his words to her were oft ill spoken and poorly received. The woman confused him and her presence robbed him of his crown. For when she was near he felt like a befuddled young man, hardly the King he'd been for the past ten summers.

Candy could be so shy, though unbridled when in bed with him. So female, yet having an inner strength, so . . . everything he wanted.

A sigh of resignation escape him. "Yes, of course. We are alone if such is what you are looking to know."

"Well, I was wondering . . . "

Get it out woman! Her nearness was driving him to madness.

"Umm, isn't this night going to be a full moon, and here we are far from the House of Rule, and well, all these men and no females . . ."

Thorne frowned at her. "Your question then?"

Aye Lassie, you are a conundrum to my senses.

"Do you mind if I sit to discuss it with you?"

Thorne's tent had one chair, which he was clenching to while leaning on. He gestured her to the fur-covered sleep pallet. As she moved over to sit on the very edge of his bed she began to pet the softest of the furs.

"Did you, uh, harvest all of these skins?"

Thorne decided to sit on his chair because seeing her on his bed was liable to cause his manhood to become an embarrassment.

Fucking too late.

Already his cock betrayed him. He could not abide the thought of her knowing how much he desired her when the feeling was not reciprocated. The water at the lake had hidden his lust for her, but here, in his tent—the table and chair would have to suffice.

By the goddess, his sac felt heavy, aching, and the Moon Goddess was readying the 'need' within him. As if he needed that extra burden when he was already incited with lust for his Lassie. This night was going to be most difficult to endure.

The hunter casually shifted his position for greater comfort as he shrugged. "Yes, the softest you are touching, was from far north and . . . Surely did not come here for stories of my hunts. I am busy, so please tell me what you came for."

Busy? Aye, more likely trying to keep my thoughts off her.

How he wished she had come for him, but knew it was not so. How splendid she would look, laying naked upon that fur with her emerald eyes full of want for him. Suddenly his illusion was broken as she blurted out her concerns.

"Your men have no women for tonight. Is that going to create a problem?"

Ah, the crux of why she was here.

"What do you care of how my men handle the 'needing'? Surely you did not plan to pleasure all of them?" Thorne's vitriolic response made for a strike at her. Before his mouth closed he regretted his abhorrent words. She could not help her loss of memory, and none of this was by her doing.

He was a donkey's arse.

"What a degrading thing to suggest. What have I done to make you think so poorly of me?"

Easing back on the chair he looked at her and those beautiful green eyes. Damn, he had hurt her feelings with his words. It was not his nature to be cruel and he could not comprehend why he'd struck so foul a blow. Why could he not let himself be kinder to her? The influence and thoughts of tonight's 'needing moon' had made him exceedingly overwrought today. He knew he'd been curt with his men today.

"You have not, my Lady. This has been a long day and I should not have said such a demeaning thing to you. I truly regret my ill-spent words and hope you will forgive me."

With a deep breath he tried to address her concern. "Perhaps there is a single warrior you could choose for this night? Since you do not remember, I warn you, the 'needing moon' will be a powerful thing to try to ignore. In fact, despite your intentions, it may be nigh impossible to ignore the influence of the Moon Goddess on this night."

Candy seemed to be picking at the fur, obviously uncomfortable with his words. "Will I be safe from your men?" Her words came out soft, not accusing, although possibly holding a small amount of trepidation.

Last 'needing moon' Thorne had made her an ill-fated promise he found impossible to fulfill. Could that be the reason the gods had punished him, taking her from his embrace?

A pledge he'd not repeat.

"Well that is a fair question, and much depends upon your own response to the 'needing'. But my men will not rape any woman if that is your concern. If you go to them freely, you will be well used."

Thorne saw she was becoming distraught, so he quickly resumed. "I am not insinuating any such thing, but I am being honest with you, Candy. Passion on this night is a powerful thing and it can make all of us fools."

Especially me it seems.

"However, have no worry about my men. They may decide to use their hands for relief, or perhaps each other, I know not which. But rape is not tolerated within my Kingdom."

"Yet Shemmar seemed ready to force me against my will."

Thorne looked taken aback. "Aye, yes you are correct. But Shemmar has always been senseless and paid a price no warrior would choose, as a hand without the thumb is useless to a warrior. I wonder, if you remember the first time Shemmar mistakenly thought to make you his conquest?" As if Thorne would ever let his cousin bed and debase her. Never!

Candy looked down at her hands and evaded answering him, and then finally looked up at Thorne. "Where I'm from, rape is a fear most females carry and we're careful to avoid risky situations. Tonight seems like that kind of situation."

He looked shocked. "Men commonly force women against their willingness? Surely only during war; and under the rule of a poor leader would such heinous crimes exist."

"It's more common than you'd think. And as a female, it concerns me a great deal."

"Even with the madness of the 'needing', none would dare touch you without your consent. They well know such would result in their castration or death." He could see she was not entirely convinced, even though a slow painful death would be dealt to any who dared to touch Candy in any manner.

Nor would any of his warriors allow her to be taken against her will. Although a man's 'need' might be great, the desire to live would prevail. Why then did he have misgivings? He tried to unclench his fists as his nails dug into his palms. They resisted.

"You could choose a man you favor before the fullest of the moon, and thus prevent fighting amongst my men. Victus favors you and is comely of face to woman."

Why of all his men had he mentioned fair-of-face Victus? Had he gone mad?

Apparently.

The woman before him became incensed.

Candy wondered why Thorne was being a total dick! Did he honestly think she considered sex as casual a matter as buying a new pair of shoes? Some shoes weren't comfortable no matter how awesome they looked. Couture versus comfort often formed a stalemate at best. The two never seemed to mesh.

She was fuming enough to play along with his hateful game. This was not about picking the prettiest kitten from the litter to take home. She wanted to make the arrogant King regret his words.

Candy forced a demure smile to her face as she responded. "True enough, he's *very* handsome and his lips looks *inviting*. He's no doubt a *really* good kisser who slips his tongue between a woman's lips. And I have seen him look at me like he might find me desirable. Imagine how good his masculine body looks without his leathers."

Looking at Thorne's tensed jaw she eased up before he required dental implants. "But then, maybe Victus is a little too vain for my tastes. He would probably find *himself* more appealing than *me*. In fact, I'll bet all he really needs on this night is a mirror."

Thorne bit back a smile as he shook his head. This woman had wicked humor and spirit, a seldom seen trait in females of his land. Always women were granting with him, never did they carry thoughtful opinions. Not so with Candy. Riling him with her teasing in this manner verily riled his cock as well.

Hardening to iron now.

Candy fingered the fur beneath her, as she appeared to weigh the merits of possible partners. This further raised his ire and shaft, which made absolutely no sense.

Aye, continue to rile me Lassie, and soon I will pull you beneath me and show you which warrior you should be with whilst I plant myself deeper than any other man.

"But then of course there's Able," she continued. "A very gentle man by nature, who probably takes a great deal of time pleasing a woman with kisses and touch. He's quite *strong* don't you agree? Strong muscular arms to wrap under a woman as he orgasms." She sighed as if the thought warmed her, while what she really wanted to say was how Able's arms were paltry compared to Thorne's, but she refused to say it. He started this.

Thorne rocked back on his chair, with arms crossed defensively across his chest, and a spiteful glint in his eyes. "*Hmmm.* If you prefer strong, surely Bear is the man you should select. No man here can best his strength."

"That's true. I've seen him spar with others and he is physically powerful. I bet he growls or maybe roars like an animal when he climaxes. He's so huge, I wonder if the size of his," she glanced downward, "is as *large*—"

"Enough!"

Was she trying to drive him into a rage? Foolish woman had never seen him when angry—was she even fearful of his temper? Candy seemed to be the only person not wary of him when he was provoked, and only she would dare to spar with him armed only with words. Never had he been known to be a soft man by nature, and right now he was an exceedingly *hard*, needful man. Survival obviously was a skill she sorely lacked! Not that he would ever harm her, and he would kill any who tried. Thorne took a deep, steadying breath.

"Choose any man you wish for the 'needing moon'. Surely one of my warriors can service and please you." He stood and put his back to her while he tried to rein in his anger.

How dare she think of another man's *size*.

Had he not been adequate for her?

He knew full well he'd been far more than acceptable, hardly lacking. In fact, always with female lovers he was considered to be *overly* abundant in size.

With Candy, they had fit perfectly, as if by a miracle, and she had loved the feel of his shaft as she called out for more. "All of you," she had begged, "harder", she'd cried out with passion when he was reserved. What previous women considered 'too much', she had considered as moan-worthy and took all he offered. And he had given his all in return to fulfill her want of him, and his of her.

A thief named Fate had stolen his Lassie from him. Thorne's fists clenched at the loss of the woman he wanted.

"Perhaps one warrior can," she mumbled as she headed to exit his tent.

"Lassie?"

She turned back to face him, although he still had his back to her when he spoke.

"Once any man's hand passes below your shoulder, I shall cut it off. If any other part of him were to touch you, in any manner, then that too shall be removed. My men suspect this."

His turn towards her was slow, calculated, his head held low, as if to shadow his predatorily expression. Brown eyes slowly rose to meet her green gaze. He held her captive as easily as if he had tied her down. Without blinking or breaking his heated gaze, a knife appeared in his hand. It flew through the air with strength, speed, and accurate intent, and the blade sank into the wood post by the door.

Candy jumped, startled by his violent threat. She tried not to look at the knife blade so deeply embedded so very close to her. He had excellent aim and if she'd been the target he wouldn't have missed.

The guy was obviously making a point, not that she'd ever doubted his skills or fierce power. When her eyes returned to Thorne, she saw his head was now held high. His mouth was set in a tight line. His demeanor had changed as quickly as he'd thrown that knife—from feral predator to prideful King.

"Why would you threaten to do such a thing? I just don't understand you and why you're so angry with me."

Thorne's voice rose to almost a shout. "Aye, true enough you '*forgot*'! Forgot how you chose me with the last 'needing', even after I gave you every opportunity not to do so. Seems you cannot remember that night we shared." He was fuming, his chest heaving.

The influence of the pending 'needing moon' was not comforting either. His brain kept repeating the same disturbing words: *Take her, pleasure her, take her, pleasure her . . .*

Candy's words interrupted his inner mantra. "You once told me a man could deny a woman nothing on the 'needing moon'."

He frowned and lowered his voice. "And how would you know this?"

With a sigh, Candy took a step toward him. "I can remember some things."

"Aye? How much of that night?" His eyes almost pleaded for her answer.

"Not everything, but pieces are coming back to me."

With a raised eyebrow he asked, "And when did this return of memory begin, and why did you not speak of it?"

"When I rode Lightness, on the first day of this journey, it started coming back. Slowly I began to remember things, fragments really. But for some reason the harder I tried to remember, the worse the headaches. When I told Ripple he gave me something to help, but it made me too dizzy."

"You did not come to tell me of this, or ever spoke of the pain you suffered that I might ease it." His voice had softened, and his anger lessened a few degrees. His arms lowered as if about to reach for her, but he did not. He would not. This woman surely played with him. Did she, or did she not remember what they shared?

She lowered her head as she answered. "You seem easily angered all the time. Both you, and my broken pieces of memories, kind of frighten me. Besides, you had those other women you were doing, screwing, or *uh*, bedding, whatever it's called."

"Fucking."

Candy blushed. She'd thought him to be fucking other women, when he had not.

And she'd been frightened? He had not meant to cause her to be frightened of him. Or had he? How would he know? None of this made sense to him. The emotions he felt were as foreign to him as Candy was to his Kingdom.

This wall he had built after his loss of her always remained too weak, and she kept crumbling the structure beneath him. Her physical presence now seemed too close, and felt as though she'd stolen the air from his lungs. It alarmed him, how with such ease Candy's proximity could suffocate him with his emotions. He took a step to the side, away from her, away from temptation, away from more hurt.

Thorne locked his arms across his chest in an effort to shield his heart. Too late, as already his heart and sanity felt as though they were being cut away. He needed to let her go, to let her have her choice on this night. She was no longer his, no reason to think otherwise.

How well he remembered his father's wise words when Thorne had once been troubled as a child: *Let a wound bleed and then heal. But my son, never allow it to fester.*

A wise man should know such and be generous to her. He could be wise. He could be generous.

And he could be an absolute fool.

"Go, choose any man who pleases you. I shall leave camp for the night. As you say, I cannot deny your desires on this night, as it is not within me." When the words had first been said to Candy he'd never intended for her desires to ever be toward another man. Now, knowing she would choose another to share her body with made him feel ill and his head pound.

Candy shook her head at him as she turned to leave his tent. "This stubborn pride of yours doesn't become you."

Pride?

Thorne sat on his bed with his head in his hands. This would be the most trying night in his life. If he left now he could keep from being too close to her when the moon was it's fullest. He would surely kill any man who touched her, despite what he'd said. Why did she not know she belonged to him? This was a cruel game the gods and goddesses played.

Pride? What had he been told about his pride?

He should have been warned that it was a painful emotion to possess.

Thorne got up, grabbed his bedding and a bottle of spirits—any bottle would do. Straddling his horse he head out to deeper woods. Far enough away from camp so he would not hear Candy's soft sweet moans of pleasure while being with another man. Somehow he knew that nowhere would be far enough away to give him peace of mind. But the wine might help with that. He had always thought too much use of liquor showed weakness in men.

Tonight, let drink serve to mask his weakness for his Lassie.

Chapter Twenty-One
Ripple

The woman was distraught beyond measure.

Candy was pacing, hand wringing, and talking faster than a chattering squirrel protecting a stash of acorns. Damnation, for as fast as her words were, her thoughts outpaced them. Her feelings were assailing his 'thoughts' and twisting in his brain—it made his head throb. Would she never finish? Surely soon she would require a breath.

"Ripple, please tell me which way he's gone. He left too fast for me to get someone to saddle Lightness and follow him, and Toemus said Thorne didn't even eat or tell him he was leaving, or where he was going to go, either."

The dwarf stifled a yawn. She was wearing him to fatigue. His ears hurt from the droning of her words, his brain hurt worse still from the constant buzzing of her disharmonious thoughts. There was no doubt between her spun gold hair, green eyes and inviting lips, that Candy was a true beauty, but right now she was an annoying and babbling one. So it seemed she was finally starting to recognize her true feelings towards Thorne.

About fucking time. By now his friend's sac was probably aching with pent up fantasies of Candy. Ripple could totally relate, as his own sac was heavy with need as well, and he also had fantasies about her. Vivid ones. Was there a man in the camp, other than young Bec, who did not?

Although admittedly jealous, Ripple hoped to guide Candy to her fated path, which led directly to Thorne's arms. Enough of these silly games between the two, as all in the camp suffered from Thorne's foul moods, whilst his men withstood lusty hopeful thoughts of Candy. All knew full well she belonged to Thorne—all except for Thorne and Candy.

The dwarf shook his head. "Tis not as though the man is lost my Lady. And why do you torture that man so? Let him be. When you received him on that 'needing moon' you unlocked the chains he kept so tightly bound around his heart. Yet now, you do not nourish the beast you unbound. He has become vulnerable, and wounded, while you pretend to know neither of his feelings nor your own. He may be a stubborn and proud ruler, but this is *his* land, *his* Kingdom, and he is our *King.* Do you not realize such? King Thorne bends his knee to no one."

"Maybe he's too proud," she bit back. "And I guess I don't really think of him as the King. I always consider him as my hunter, or just sexy-hunky Thorne."

And such is the gist of it, thought Ripple.

Both had their pride and both feared the depth of their feelings. They wanted this connection between them to be simple when the gods and goddesses held other plans. The heavenly deities were unrelenting in their games and he could sense his friends were suffering for it.

Tonight the dwarf held hopes for this conflict between the would-be-lovers to end. He cared greatly for both Candy and his friend. Candy knew full well she was evading the point. *Stubborn female.*

Ripple clearly read her thoughts and feelings and knew the truth. Poor woman, her racing thoughts indeed were in turmoil. But all her thoughts always returned like a loyal boomerang back to Thorne. Both obsessed equally about the other. And now she was pacing like a caged animal again, likely to wear though the base of his tent if she did not cease.

He understood her discomfort and confusion all too well. "You seem to forget you cannot hide your feelings and thoughts from me Candy, no matter how much you lie to yourself or to Thorne. Despite what you say, I know you care more than a little for that overly-tall man."

As the dwarf poured himself another portion of wine he scanned her face. She was a truly lovely woman with a fetching figure, although right now, a very conflicted woman.

Thorne's woman, he reminded himself.

"Go, choose another man to lay with for the night. Why concern yourself if another knife is plunged into Thorne's soul? He is well acquainted with the feel of steel against his skin and surely the man has not yet suffered nearly enough. Thorne will learn to toughen his heart again, to sheath it tighter this time so no female can hurt him ever again. And justly as King, should he not be able to handle a little torture?"

Candy looked as though a chastised child, with more than a hint of guilt upon her face. Tonight Ripple wanted her to learn to trust her instincts and her heart. The dwarf planned to give her a push toward the right path, the one leading to Thorne.

"You make me sound cruel and uncaring Ripple."

Her eyes were damp and Ripple wanted to embrace her. But what he truthfully needed was to send her on her way before the night got any darker.

"Nay, you have a big heart Candy. You just need to tend to it. Both of you are suffering. Perhaps you would be willing to take the first step to right this situation? Let him show you his charming ways, as women say he can be most seductive. Although I do not see the reason they think so about that overly muscled man. *Pah*, I am much better looking, and if I stand upon a mountain I am even taller than Thorne. I think his reputation to be a sham—propaganda to keep his kingly popularity foremost."

At last Candy let out a giggle. The woman had the sweetest laugh and it made his heart beat faster. If she belonged to any other man other than Thorne, Ripple might try to win her over and take advantage of her 'need' on this night of pending bliss. But he was wiser, as these two were truly fated; no man or woman could come between them and not leave bruised and bloodied for it.

Moreover, Thorne would fillet Ripple if he dared touch Candy. That thought was enough to dampen any man's desires and deflate his manhood.

Fucking pity, my mouth would reach her sex perfectly.

"But if you go to him, you must be honest. Quit playing this game between yourselves, as it tires me to see and to know of it. He has long been my friend and never have I seen him thus before. And this is destroying both him and our drinking cups. Do you even know how many cups that man has broken with his frustration? Soon we will all have to drink straight from the bottle. Not an entirely bad thing, but Thorne insists we act *gentlemanly* in your presence."

Ripple focused on Candy's face and sobered his tone. "Truthfully woman, he needs you in his life as much as you need him". The two were fated, singular bond between two worlds.

How effortlessly Ripple saw Candy's thoughts and concerns as they skittered through her pretty head— thoughts as clear as any printed parchment. She held concerns regarding if Thorne would have her.

'If' Thorne would have her', ha! My hairy arse!

As if the King would *not* have her. That man would kill twice over any man in his way to get to her, whilst vultures fed from the entrails on the path behind him. Silly woman, there was no bloody *'if'* about it, Candy was Thorne's true mate.

"Go to him, as he is fated to be yours and you his. The sooner realized the easier and healthier for all us fool men who dare to dream and desire you."

She left the tent with instructions to find Thorne, and Ripple sat and poured more drink.

He had known Thorne for many years, actually since their childhood. And in all those years he'd sadly seen his friend face tragedy beyond his years. Never once had his young King dismissed his obligations to his Kingdom, or lost a fight with any enemy. Not since that brutal betrayal when he was seventeen.

Neither had his friend been in love before and this warring with his emotions was taking a toll on Thorne. No matter how many women made their bodies available to the King and his bed, the man had never felt true tenderness for any woman past a single hour of carnal pleasure.

Not until this foreign gem of a woman. This female from another land had easily stolen Thorne's heart, just as she had stolen the hearts of most of the men in the camp. Thorne had been smitten with her—as simply as that. What male could blame him?

This vexing union between the couple seemed to present Thorne his most taxing challenge yet. Life was arduous enough without being fucked over repeatedly by the whims of deities'.

Twas of little wonder Ripple had little use for the gods and goddesses, and they for him, as he was but a mere dwarf. It made for a dwarf's blessing, to be too short to be of any significant notice to the gods.

He suspected the divine deities had set the plights of Thorne and Candy in motion, forcing a difficult road ahead of them. The dwarf could feel it in his bones.

Aye. As surely as dragons breathed fire.

Chapter Twenty-Two
Thorne

Blistering warring flames battled to survive. With stubbornness, the flames refused to yield to each other, as each flame took purchase and greedily consumed the tinder. The fire was meant to provide warmth. It failed to do so—Thorne still felt cold and empty.

Repeatedly Ripple had advised Thorne to apply himself to Candy's female nature. Always women had easily come to him—not so with Candy. He wanted her to remember, to be his again—like the single night they had shared.

A swig of wine.

Drink would dull his senses this night, though that feat would likely require the entire bottle. Thorne now thought he should have brought a second bottle as well. Tonight would require much alcohol to forget her.

Another swallow of wine.

Was he not taller than most men, and kept himself stronger as well, as never again did he want to feel another blade wielded against his flesh.

Despite his bearing, somehow that small woman could easily bring him to heel and make him beg for mercy. How did a wee woman possess such a hold on a man like him? Had he not always fucked, to then quickly retreat, no regrets, no looking back? Physical release—naught more. Nor had he wanted anything more. Damn that woman, what had she done to him?

Another swig.

The sound of rustling of nearby branches caught his attention. The sound came from behind him . . . within twenty-five feet of his camp . . . too close.

Upon hearing the snap of a breaking twig, Thorne picked up his longbow expecting a predator of either two legs or four. How careless he'd been, but now he was prepared. His eyes searched, and his ears listened to identify the manner of threat.

Silence.

And then he heard it.

A *thump* followed by, "Ouch, ow, ow . . . oh crapola and jellybeans!"

Ono flew to the tree branch above him, and looked down at Thorne as if exasperated by the night's events, as the gargoyles little chest heaved. Thorne shook his head as he lowered his bow and headed toward the brush where Candy's distress had plainly been heard.

There she sat on the ground amid leaves and brush.

Thorne fought not to smile at the sight of her so similar to the first time he'd set eyes on her. Hair mussed and arms scratched, sitting in the dirt, only this time she wore women's clothing. Indeed her dress was wound about and above her knees.

Aye, the benefits of women's clothing suited her well. Thorne felt conflicted as whether he should pull her skirt down to cover her, or push it up further and take what he craved. He scrubbed his hand over his mouth shaking off such tempting thoughts.

"Surely you did not ride in the dark alone, reckless woman."

He could hear Ripple's advice in his head. *Need to be charming.*

His outstretched hand indicated to pull her up, and she accepted.

See Lassie, I can be a gentleman.

"I didn't realize I would be so inept, as usual." She was brushing her dress off and righting it to cover her legs.

A pity. He enjoyed the sight of her shapely legs, which led to other feminine body parts. "Were you injured by your fall?"

And I can show genuine concern.

"Only my pride, otherwise I think I'm unbroken."

"Tis not safe for you to ride alone and you should be back at camp." Aye, returning her to a camp full of lustful males on a 'needing moon' makes for the highest order of wisdom!

And it seems I can be a fool.

"With all those men sexed up by the 'needing moon' and me the only female? I don't think so. What ridiculous reasoning on your part to leave me there unprotected on this particular night. What if things got out of control and I was molested, well death or castration wouldn't undo that now would it? And furthermore, I really don't want to hear men having sex with other men." She was shaking her head at him indicating he should have thought this through.

And sometimes I dispense very poor judgment.

"I thought the male you chose would protect you, but I see your own reasoning is more sound than mine. This moon makes men foolish."

Or at least me!

"Boy, that's the truth." Candy turned and reached into Lightness' saddle pocket and pulled out one ceramic honey pot, then reached in again and pulled another out. She stood with one in each hand and confronted him.

"Celcee insisted I would have need of these. In fact the whole side bag is packed full of these strange little pots."

"Once they seemed small, indeed," Thorne spoke softly while trying to suppress a smile.

"You were to remain at camp and choose a man, not travel into wooded terrain. Who let you travel alone?"

His brows furrowed, though he felt less defensive. Still, she should not have been sent unguarded, and on this night of all nights.

"Ripple said if I hurried I'd be safe enough, and he says he's *always* right. He can't be accused of humility can he? Anyway, he told me where to find you. And thank goodness you didn't go further, with me being so graceful and all!

"Anyway, I decided to do as you suggested and choose a warrior, and I've heard you say you wouldn't deny me on a 'needing moon'. These were your words I might remind you."

She was looking around as if for any signs of a female companion. His bedroll remained tightly rolled.

"Of course, if you've already chosen a woman for tonight I'll leave, since I seem to excel at humiliating myself," she was quick to add.

"You would not make it back to camp easily in this darkness, and would likely fall from your horse again, possibly causing yourself unbearable injury—broken bones or worse. Might be wiser if you stayed here, with me. And I have no one else in the camp at this time, though perhaps later I shall take a woman."

And I seem adept at being a total, lying arse.

"You don't have much confidence in me having self-preservation skills do you? You probably think I need a man to help me with everything."

Thorne simply arched an eyebrow.

Indeed, she appeared in need *of a man. Already her nipples peaked, visible through her dress like two tiny berries begging to be sucked upon.* His mouth watered wanting to oblige her breasts.

Candy's arms dropped to her sides as she let out a sigh. "Well okay then. I see you have many women to choose from out in these woodlands so don't let me get in your way. And no doubt, me seeing or hearing you with another female would be something neither of us would find disturbing or embarrassing."

Surely she knows how much I want her—I'll not be begging. I am King, and she is. . .divine. She treats me simply as a man, is that not what I sought?

And such was part of what made her even more attractive to him, as she held no pretentions. Her passions had been for him as her lover, not as a man of wealth or having the power of kingship. She had no curiosity of his crown, only to explore his form.

They stared at each other in silence, neither conceding to their desires.

Finally Candy let out a sigh of resignation, breaking the silent stalemate.

"Look Thorne, I need your help if I'm ever going to remember everything clearly. And I've decided I want to stop feeling so apprehensive and face those memories."

Candy held up her full hands. "And I'm not sure why I have all these silly ceramic pots clanging in my saddlebags. Celcee actually advised me *not* to spread the contents on scones and then laughed."

Looking up, she could see his hand over his mouth. He was either trying to reason the small ceramic pots, or was laughing at her. She suspected the latter but continued on.

"Celcee said you knew what they were for and would show me how to use them when the time came. So why are my saddle bags full of this extra weight, when none of the men have even mentioned use of them to me?"

No man would dare mention them, not if that man valued his tongue.

Thorne's face softened and he was obviously trying to hold back a grin. Still he held his head high.

"First, tell me what you remember. I must know."

"Well, I do recall when you found Coco, rather Ono, and me, you cooked those huge rabbits, let's see, you carrying me up the stairs because I was so saddle sore my legs wouldn't hold me when we got to your House of Rule . . . and then that wonderful bath to clean the grime off . . ."

Thorne shook his head.

"Do not play with me Lassie. You know full well what I am asking, do you not?"

His eyes were heated now. She needed to yield to him this night or he was not sure how to remain sane. For a month of long days and longer nights he had desired her, now she stood before him and the temptation and 'need' was growing quickly beyond what he could suffer. How he ached for her as he swallowed back a groan.

"The 'needing moon', yes, I remember your hateful cousin and being in the great room, and the moon was starting to cross into the glass above, but after that . . . I'm not . . ."

His patience met its limit. He unsheathed one of his knives and slowly drew it across his forearm, near the cut by Shemmar's hand. Never did his eyes leave hers, as he casually returned his blade to its sheath. Blood welled out, and a few drops fell to the ground, only to disappear within the beige grass at his feet.

Candy rushed to his side. "Why did you do that?"

"To remind you of the blood I spilled for you. Do you still not recall, because I think you remember much or you would not have come here tonight? Or did you come to see and use my 'enormous cock', as you called it on that night?"

Indeed, a totally verbally abusive arse! And I thought to charm her?

The moment the heated words escaped his lips he regretted them and felt ashamed. Lashing out at her memory lapse helped nothing. How was it this female brought forth both the best and the worst of him?

Ripple had told him she remembered a great deal now, so why was she was holding back? True, women were confusing creatures, but this woman confused his senses to the utmost and beyond.

Patience, he reminded himself. *Tell my cock that!*

With a softer voice he tried to mend his words. "Candy, forgive my rude and hasty words. I know you are not such a woman. But how can I help your memory of that night when you will not even be honest with me? This game we play infuriates all of my senses."

She couldn't meet his eyes. "I'm so embarrassed, and I'm really sorry. I didn't mean to hurt you, but there are so many parts I'm still unclear about. I promise to be honest and I'd like to try to remember everything. I feel this huge lump in my heart, that I'm pretty sure it isn't indigestion because it won't go away."

Tears started to spill from her eyes, but she quickly blinked and wiped them away. "Will you help me remember, or are you still angry and too prideful?"

Pride indeed seemed to be a foe to his relationship with this woman, and this night pride needed to retreat if things were to be put to right. Malkum of Old's words reminded him of that encrypted warning—a cold mistress indeed. A warm lover was far better than a cold mistress.

As Thorne relaxed his stance, his anger washed away by way of her apology and tears. She was finally being truthful, even promised to be so. Candy seemed to want to share this night they had embraced a month past. Mayhap this was a good sign for them. Had Ripple's advice had been true? Was Candy 'his lady'. He prayed to the Moon Goddess for it to be true.

"I might be able to assist with these." Thorne reached forward and took the honey pots from her, to set them next to his bedroll.

He turned back and held her face between his palms. "Ah, Lassie," he whispered into her hair. "How I have missed your lips."

Thorne bent and kissed her gently, waiting to see how she would respond to him. Candy's passion matched his memory, and her tongue quickly met his.

Her taste was sweeter than the finest aged mead, just as he remembered. His need to have her closer, to be inside her, to mend what felt broken between them, intensified.

As he pulled back from their heated kiss, he reached for her bodice. She began to waver, and Thorne quickly steadied her, holding her to rest against his body.

She looked up at him with a wicked little smile. "I think you kissed me dizzy."

Never had he heard more heartening words. "Aye, my lips have been known to have that effect on you."

Impatience and 'need' quickly replaced restraint. He pulled a knife from his wrist bracer and cut the ties on the bodice of her dress. Candy did not flinch, as she stared into his face as though it was a pleasant sight. How she could stomach his scar he would never understand.

Ever so slowly her dress swirled, flowing over her curves as it dropped ever so softly to the ground, as if unveiling his woman for his eyes alone. There she stood as flawless as he remembered. How could he ever deny this woman anything? This time a groan did escape him.

So perfect.

Her nakedness was presented to him like a gift to his eyes. And his eyes feasted upon what she offered to him.

The moment felt reminiscent to her, and she deliciously recalled his kisses. Even the dizziness seemed familiar. Candy reached up and with her finger traced his lips. "I remember your lips, and how you make me melt," she whispered.

He began to loosen his leathers, while she reached to open his shirt. The 'needing' was taking hold, instincts rising. She was touching his skin, he was touching hers and that sensation felt entirely true, as though they had been lovers for many moons, not a single, passion-filled night a month past.

"Shouldn't I wrap your cut?"

"Twas shallow, only to get your notice. But the wound to my heart was most deep Lassie, and will require much of your attention this night. Perhaps even on the morrow, and mayhap many days thereafter."

"Milking it for all its worth aren't you?" She leaned in against his bare, and smooth chest, moving her hands across him.

"*Umm*, I love the feel of your spectacular muscled chest. I remember the feel, and I've missed this. When you carried me across that dreadful ravine I inhaled that special scent of you, heard your strong beating heart, and was almost able to touch your skin. That's how you calmed me."

"That so? And here I thought my storytelling skills were the remedy, when all I really needed to do was bare my chest to you. Such an easy task had I known. I will keep such in mind for future obstacles." If it would keep her hands upon him, he would never don a shirt again.

"Your story was so sad and I wanted to hug you, but you turned away."

"*Shhh*, speak naught of that now. You must know how painfully I desire you." Her touch on his skin sent that humming through him again. He craved more of her touch, and lower, he needed her to touch him lower. He took her hand and put it against his leathers so she could feel how badly his need for her was.

Do not push her—be patient. Give her no reason to retreat.

Reaching down he touched her feminine folds and felt her slickness. She was undoubtedly ready for him. Hurriedly he finished unlacing his leathers, and pulled his throbbing shaft free. A drop of pre-cum quickly beaded on the tip.

It had been far too long without her, and now he feared he might spend too quickly. A worthy lover needed to attend to his woman's needs before selfishly meeting his own, and tonight of all nights, he wanted to prove himself to her. Thorne tamped down his lustful 'need'. For his Lassie he could make himself wait a little longer.

Slowly, for her.

His body argued, he did not want to go slow.

He wanted to pound deeply into her core and leave his seed deep within her—to claim her.

Slowly, he reminded himself, tamping down his lust.

Candy looked down as she reached to touch the drop that had seeped from his slit crown. Her finger rolled on the tip of him, and she put it to her mouth.

"Oh it's salty," she purred. "I like salty. *Um*, so big too, I just knew you were packed. How could I forget anything *this* stunning?"

At that moment Thorne thought he would surely spend his seed—all over her belly.

I am the first man she has tasted, and by the goddess I shall to be her only.

Looking into Candy's face, she let a modest smile surface.

Ah, she is a paradox: curious, wickedly saucy, yet shy, and on this night I shall again claim her as mine and fill her with my seed. And pray for half a miracle this time she remains mine.

He lifted her to sit upon his manhood, just as he had at their first joining. This time she knew to wrap her legs tightly around him. How he'd hoped for this response. His body was swollen, throbbing with need—need for his woman.

She truly remembers some and hopefully soon much more of our time together.

Gradually he lowered her down the length of him. Carefully, to be certain she was ready to receive him, as she adjusted to his size. She was undeniably ready for him—slick with her liquid silk. Knowing her wetness was for him made him want to hurriedly proceed on to pounding thrusts.

Again he forced himself to slow his pace. He inched her down his shaft a little further, as he wondered how much of his size she would accept. Given Candy's sighs, she really did want him, at least on this night she did. Could anything feel better than being encased in her tight, heated, sheath?

Nothing, absolutely nothing.

Unless she took him fully into her as she had before. He would not push the matter, as this alone was precious. Let her decide.

"Ah Lassie, how wet you are for me," he growled. Was she already moaning? Indeed. And how he enjoyed making her moan with pleasure.

He whispered into her ear while rotating his hips and grinding into her. "Do I push beyond pleasure?"

"No," she panted. "I want all of you. Every. Inch. Of. You."

He laughed as he lowered her the final length of him to rest at his hilt. "All? Like such?"

With a gasp of pleasure Candy replied. "Yes, oh yes," she moaned. "*Hmmm*, we have a lot more memories to retrieve don't we? Please feel free to remind me of every single one."

"With pleasure my Lady, though I warn you, our previous night was very lengthy, full of passion, and we have naught of comfort such as a soft bed."

"*Lengthy* and full of *passion* . . . that sounds just like how I'd describe what's filling me. I bet you know lots of ways that don't require a soft bed, and besides that bedroll looks padded to me."

A throaty chuckle escaped him. "You sound most curious, eager, and needful. Indeed there are many ways I could take you if you so desire."

He could keep her on top of him to spare her discomfort, though by the look in her heated eyes, she seemed to care naught how he took her. It was the *taking* she seemed focused on.

With a cooing sound of delight she answered, "Oh Thorne trust me, I do desire." She smiled in response to his raised brow.

Saucy woman, without a doubt he intended to take her many times before the night's end. Thorne braced her with his arms, while he rode her up and down his shaft. The hair on his arms rose and his body tensed. He was about to come to completion. She was close as well, and he paced his release to meet hers.

The 'need' would heatedly soon take them to task. Thereafter, they could slow to a languid, prolonged, exploration of each other for the remainder of the night.

Aye, fulfill the 'need' then the 'want' of his woman.

His movements stopped abruptly. Already his sac hated him for the interruption. As they looked into each other eyes, each spoke simultaneously.

"Honey pot!" "Honey pot."

Those two small words of remembered exclamation pleased Thorne, even though his sac was not pleased at all. By the end of this night he held hopes she would remember every single delight they had shared on the previous 'needing moon'. Certainly he would enjoy rekindling her memories, while adding new ones.

His Lassie would meet the dewy dawn sated beyond measure, and without a doubt, deep soreness would be felt as well.

Chapter Twenty-Three
Candy

My word!

How had she ever forgotten this gorgeous man's intoxicating touch? Let alone her intense responses as he held her in muscled arms while stretching and filling her so completely? His body provided her the most amazing sensations she'd ever encountered. With him she felt sensual, feminine, fulfilled—but most importantly, she felt connected to him in ways she'd never felt or known exited. *Whole, complete.*

Her bliss became interrupted when she grasped that she wasn't on the 'pill' here.

Need contraception!

"Honey pot", she'd whimpered in unison with Thorne's rugged voice. Dang, now she remembered that was what those silly ceramic pots were for.

Thorne pulled free of her, obviously having far more control than she did. That man's pheromones really did overwhelm her common sense, which seemed to dissolve the moment he touched her.

They really needed to avoid getting so hot and heavy before using that honey pot. Except, just looking at how sexy he was made her *hot*, and a single kiss led to *heavy*, so figure that.

Poor Thorne looked like he was in agony—*so know the feeling, sweetie.* In a flash, his fingers were in the honey pot. Then he deftly, agonizingly, and teasingly administered the concoction. Memories surfaced of how he'd done this many, many times before and how he enjoyed making her lose all control while touching her.

That wicked half smile of his only made her want to beg for more. How easily this man worked her up to frenzy and he seemed to enjoy every deliciously torturous minute of it.

When her knees began to buckle he held a satisfied smile and lifted her back onto him. Slowly he lowered her down on him, in a teasing inch-by-inch manner, and the man had many, many inches credited to him.

By the look in his eyes, he was well aware that he governed her passion, and that was fine by her. After all Thorne was the only man who'd ever stoked it to this degree. He made her feel uniquely desirable. Those hot kisses, the passion, the cuddling against Thorne's solid muscled body and the depth of intimacy they'd shared raced through her thoughts.

Treasured.

That described how she felt with Thorne.

Suddenly memories from that previous 'needing moon' began to replay through her head like a fast-forwarding movie—a totally adult lust filled film depicting their boundless pleasure and delight.

They had laughed, teased, made love. The memories were so vivid it seemed difficult to comprehend how she'd forgotten such a night. Her recollections recreated how he'd positioned her numerous ways for their joining: Straddled over his hips—*yummy*; from behind—*so deep*; under him—*oh the feel of his body against hers*; as they spooned with one knee lifted—*shiver* . . . the flick played on.

The man was a living, breathing, *'How To Enjoy Sex'* manual, and Thorne seemed to know every secret in the book. Holy moly, he probably wrote the dang book!

Once he had her positioned on him, Thorne didn't procrastinate. She was braced against his hips, and he was fully encased by her. No longer reserved, he now drove in and out of her thrusting like a piston working to get from zero-to-sixty in four strokes. He wasn't holding back, and Candy grew feverish knowing his degree of need.

She shuddered as his masculine force took control, and felt heat smoldering in her girlie parts. The look in his hooded eyes told her how much he wanted her, which made for the best ego enhancer she'd ever known.

"Too long I have needed you," he gasped as he plunged deep and his voice grew raspy, possessive. "You are mine, never doubt that."

Wow, maybe she did have some feminine wiles after all. Who knew?

Cresting . . . her climax hit her in epic waves of bliss. He followed roaring her name with his final grinding thrust of completion. The man had sounded so primal it gave Candy shivers.

Both of their bodies were now sweaty and breathless. Those sounds he'd made demonstrated how visceral his orgasm had been. Admittedly, she loved the masculinity of it.

Hugging her close, he kissed her again before lifting her off him. With a smile on his gorgeous face, he unrolled the bedroll and laid her upon it.

"You make me crave you with such deep lust. Did I cause hurt to you?"

"Yes you are a terrible beast, you broke me into shattering pieces of pleasure, for which I'll never be the same, and I'm hoping to experience a repeat."

She beckoned him to join her and he didn't hesitate. Candy quickly snuggled against his powerful chest, as her fingers followed the contours of his honed physique and then to where a spattering line of hair pointed down past his bellybutton to even finer things.

Sigh worthy things.

His lips nuzzled against her ear. "I would have been more gentle for our first joining this night, had I not needed and wanted of you far too long. Each day has been an agony without you, each night—torture. Pray tell me true, did I cause you pain?"

"Hardly. Truthfully, I loved it." Candy wrapped her finger around the damp curl of his hair at the nape of his neck. "I want you to know that while we shared that incredible experience, I began to remember a lot about the 'needing moon' we spent together."

Leaning on his elbow, Thorne looked down into her face as if all the answers he needed were inscribed there. "Did you now? Let us confirm the accuracy of your memory. How many times did we share passion for each other that night?"

At first Candy wasn't sure what to answer, then she looked into his chocolate-brown eyes and smiled.

"Enough to use more than two honey pots full, and still I craved more of you and the orgasms only you can give me. I was really sore and needed a bath with healing salts the next morning. As I recall you made that night the most remarkable one in my entire life. You also broke my steadfast moral compass into smithereens."

"That so? *Humph*, I hardly regret that. That night you were drunk from the effects of the 'needing moon', however, we did indeed exceed in all terms of passion. I only wish you had told me as you remembered. Even the smallest memories would have helped ease me." He brought her knuckles to his lips for a gentle kiss.

Feeling guilty, Candy tried to explain. "Think about it. I would have pieces of memory flash through my head, but how did I know if they were hallucinations? I couldn't very well walk up to you and say, 'Hey I think we messed around and had incredible sex, and are you really hung like a three- legged-man', now could I?"

Thorne raised an eyebrow. "I would have been more than pleased to show proof that I was that man you had memories of. Or are you saying men in your land carry an additional appendage betwixt their legs?"

A laugh escaped her. "You know perfectly well what male appendage I was referring to."

"Ah. Are all men in your land my size?"

"That would be a 'no'—in fact, an absolutely and completely, disappointingly *'no'*. You are delightfully abundant. But what if we hadn't been intimate, can you imagine how mortifying that would have been for me?"

"True, you are indeed a modest female outside of my arms." He waved his hand as if of no consequence. "Tis the past. I hold faith this 'needing moon' will not escape your memory, and pray you will consider me beyond this night."

Candy looked up at the cloud-strewn sky. "Tonight's moon is still hidden by clouds and hasn't even risen close to its apex yet. Have you considered perhaps my feelings for you go beyond the 'needing moon'? How I might find you to be an exceptional man as well as the sexiest man I've known? Plus you're an incredible kisser, among your many other talents and skills."

Holding her close against his loudly beating heart, he whispered in her ear. "Of this, my Lady, I can hope."

As if to prove his want of her, he pressed their lips into a deep kiss that made her toes curl. His tongue seemed to foretell what was to come as it explored her mouth while she melted dreamily against him.

When Thorne pulled back he held a satisfied smile at her surrender to him. Then he asked her another question in regards to her memory.

"On that night we shared, you said I had a 'tremendous cock'. Do you have remembrance?"

"I do! And obviously I was correct . . . Oh my goodness Thorne, I really hope I didn't embarrass you by referring to you like you're just a piece of man-meat?"

"So I am now 'man-meat'?" His lips twitched as if trying to resist a grin. "Interesting words you use. I favor being called 'tremendous cock', as it carries a far more sensual sound upon those soft lips of yours."

"*Umm*, and what you do with your 'tremendous cock' is so much more than simply sensual. And your kisses, *ummm*, those kisses are like decadent rich chocolate truffles."

As he pulled her closer, flesh-to-flesh, no space separated them. "This word chocolate returns again and bewilders me. Is this not food, or other?"

"It's a sweet tasting food, and one of my biggest temptations and guilty pleasures. I love the rich, smooth taste and how it melts in the warmth of your mouth, and then slides down to your anxiously waiting tummy. To me it's sinfully addictive. Like you are."

Thorne's eyes wandered over her face as if trying to comprehend. "Then that night of three questions, when you spoke that I favored chocolate, that truly was a good thing."

He shook his head as if still confused. "I had feared otherwise. Like rain can be 'a good thing' but not something you desire if you are without shelter. I prefer being known to you for my tremendous cock."

"Of course you do, that's a totally male response. I'm surprised you even remember that night of my stolen kiss."

"I have forgotten nothing if it involves my Lassie. Every detail of you is committed to memory. This stolen kiss however, I remember naught of. Who dared this stealing, I shall end his life for such a bald-faced affront."

Candy smiled. "You did. I was sure you were going to give me a kiss—so sure. Then you left me standing there waiting, wanting your lips on mine. I think of that incident as my stolen kiss."

Thorne's lips curled. "You were sorely tempting Lassie and I was hard as wood for you. I pulled away for self-preservation. Perchance I could return the theft of that kiss now?"

And he did. Warm, deep, delicious, like fine imported chocolate melting down her throat. Sensations of warmth traveled past her stomach to lower regions.

Later, while taking time to enjoy the shared serenity of sated snuggling lovers, Thorne's fingers gently stoked her palm and the back of her hand as though memorizing something precious. As if each finger was unique, just because it was hers. She'd never felt such an intimate human bonding with the way his touch affected her. Candy embraced these heavenly sensations.

At times when they talked, this exceptional man gave her peeks into his soul. For a man as strong and proud as Thorne, it had to be difficult to expose his vulnerability.

Candy found it moving, that he would trust her not to hurt him with what he shared. That made for a compliment of the highest order because she didn't think he spoke openly to others. As a ruler it was probably unwise to do so.

She relished listening to the strong beats of his heart as her hand began to follow the indentations of his chest. His scars were like small divots in the granite of his chiseled body, hardly anything less than enticing, proof of both his strength and courage. Would she ever think any man could have a finer physique? *Doubtful.*

Could any other man make her feel so cherished and comfortable? *That seemed impossible. Hair twirling was a nervous habit of the past with Thorne.*

A small content sound escaped her. *Dang if she didn't sound like she was a cat lounging after nibbling a can of Fancy Feast.*

"Lassie, may I ask you of your accident?"

Candy rubbed her face against his chest, performing a very kittenish behavior. She could totally appreciate why cats enjoyed it, especially on an awesome chest like his.

"On this night how can a woman deny anything from the man she loves?"

Oh animal crackers, had she actually admitted she loved him?

Really?

Out loud?

She shouldn't have. He probably wasn't interested in that kind of relationship?

Awkward.

Humiliating.

Distressing.

Oh poop!

She'd ruined everything of their blissful night. He'd probably freak out, ride back to camp faster than the Pony Express, all before she could even get dressed. And she'd be left in this wilderness with only her humiliation and a broken heart to keep her company, the absolute worst companions.

I really screwed up! Talk about dumb blonde!

Thorne broke into her admonishing thoughts as his hand gently lifted her chin to meet his eyes.

"Lassie, look upon my scarred face. Do you truly love *me*, or is it the 'needing' within you which makes you say such things this night?" Thorne was running his other hand across her shoulders, down her back and then up again.

"How could any woman not fall in love with you?" She was embarrassed but answered honestly.

He scoffed. "I am that fine then, eh?"

Candy nodded. "You have no idea."

Flustered by her admission, she realized her confession also made her more vulnerable. She'd had never said she loved a man and should've been more careful, less forthcoming, less revealing—definitely less talky.

Loose lips sink relation-ships. *Dang it all.*

"I'm afraid I was kind of over informative, Thorne. I'm sorry if that isn't how you feel. I mean, really . . . I understand. I realize you have other woman and we haven't really known each other very long, and men hate commitments, plus I'm babbling and . . ."

His finger went to her lips. "Hush Lassie. As to other women, I have shared nothing more than a kiss with another female since first seeing you sitting in the dirt beneath that tree. And that kiss was meant to see if you would show jealousy should I show interest to another. A senseless gesture, as I did not desire more from her, truly not even that. Her lips were not yours, nor was the smell of her pure and sweet, like you."

As he leaned into her neck he inhaled. "Your scent and taste intoxicate me more than any mead ever could, and cannot ever be forgotten—even in my sleep, always I dream of you. When I refused to take more of that woman, I heard many words of wrath. Many not wholesome, and I feared even Ripple might blush." Thorne snickered at the memory as he shook his head in disbelief.

"A woman scorned truthfully is a most unpleasant thing. Much like a mother who thinks her child has become lost or injured and all reason is abandoned while she rages hysterically. Her anger required two of my men to pull that kicking, screaming female free of me as she tore at my arms. In a manner I admit she did get a piece of my flesh as she wanted, but neither willingly, nor by my desire, and certainly nothing from below my waist. Candy, I only sought to gain your attention, to see if it would trouble you if I touched another. A foolish effort on my part, to try forces you to declare if you held any affection for me. I behaved imprudently, to say the least."

"Really, and I thought those scratches were from heated sex. I really hated the thought of you with a female, let alone a skank like her. Knowing she marred your totally awesome arms and that you'd given her what I had dreamed you might give to me, it ruined my night."

Thorne looked at her dubiously. "Then you did hold some caring of me. And what does 'skank' mean? I have not heard you speak of this word afore."

"Well, it means like a cheap, unwholesome-looking woman. A 'ho', *um*, make that a whore, or like a prostitute. I detested the thought of her touching you, actually putting *her* hands on *your* chest, and wanted to rip her hair out for it."

Her words brought a snicker from him. "Jealousy? Ah, indeed that pleases me. I paid her coin to *leave* and Victus took her upstairs to indulge her. Given her violent nature and his preferences, the two most likely meted a favorable tryst. A most humbling set of events and not an encounter I feel proud of. I should never have let you see me act so lowly. Know I am not a man who generally makes use of what we often call 'hourly women' or whores. With you as a lover, no sane man would be so foolish as to ever stray from your bed.

"Now as to commitments, I hardly fear such, as my life is steeped in them by serving my Kingdom and people. As for the commitment to a woman, I would not fear that either, if done by *my* choice and not dictated upon me by doctrine or otherwise. A woman I could treasure and trust with my heart, and a woman who would not be tempted beyond my bed. For that woman I would gladly commit all of me and all I own. As said before, I will not share and would not hesitate to spill blood in order to retain what is mine. I would die for such a woman and kill if another touched her . . . you.

"Truthfully Lassie, you have owned my heart since you looked at me with your beautiful green eyes and threw that exceedingly dangerous rock at me. Impending death must incite my lust because that moment surely did."

"Very funny, smartass."

"Indeed? So you consider my posterior to be intelligent?" A mocking glint showed in his eyes. "Then my heart broke when you no longer remembered or wanted me. And now, my heart *almost* feels whole again. Possibly after we share this lust filled night it will be so, but I fear not until I enjoy a full night of you. Lassie I want you many times over. What say you?"

"I say: I challenge you to stretch and fill me with your 'tremendous cock' again, if you think you're up to it *again*."

A deep rumbling growl of lust vibrated against her ear. "Surely you do not suggest I am lacking? Indeed woman, you have thrown down the gauntlet, and what kind of warrior would I be to cower from a challenge of my virility?"

"A very unfulfilled one," she teased.

Thorne looked all warrior-king-like as he seriously and boastfully retorted. "Then I must not fail in this. I shall not surrender and I will take you until you scream defeat unto me."

After a few giggles, and an abundance of expert and strategically placed kisses, Candy became heated and felt that familiar aching need between her legs.

By Thorne's tactical plan he instructed her to lay face down on the bedding. Then he gave her pert bottom a quick, playful bite before he spread her legs and made use of the honey pot.

Bracing his weight on his arms, he raised himself above her and entered her womanly wet flesh. He pushed until he met the end of her and she let out a moan of pleasure.

Those grinding circular motions of his drove her senseless, as the intense sensations from that angle made her orgasm almost immediate.

A cry of ecstasy escaped as she climaxed while his thrusts pounded into her. This position made it impossible not to respond rapidly, and she suspected he knew that would happen.

Clever warrior.

"*Ach*, you came far too soon Lassie. Not so much of a challenge it seems. *Tsk, tsk,* I shall need to make you come to pleasure thrice to ensure you understand I have won this round as your lover. I will not be leaving doubts."

And so he did, using his magic hands between her legs, he teased her until she climaxed again. Thorne refused to relent until she finally begged for mercy.

Once more he forced her to ride another crest of pleasure while he thrust deeply, and followed with his own completion. His sounds of total satisfaction gave her tingles along her spine. How entirely male he sounded.

Candy didn't hesitate to admit he'd won the 'triple' challenge, and she'd become his 'prisoner of passion'. He had chuckled at that, but it was entirely true. No man would ever be able to compete with Thorne as a lover or make her feel this way—totally satisfied, and so valued in his arms.

It didn't take long before a second honey pot was required. Thorne had been correct, unfortunately these pots only held enough contraception for three or four encounters, not nearly enough for their insatiable want of each other. Those irksome, clanking, ceramic pots had taken on a completely new value and she was thankful Celcee had packed them.

Lots of them!

When Thorne pulled his blanket over them he spoke softly in her ear. "Next 'needing moon' I plan on fucking you on a proper bed."

"*Hummm*, I haven't complained have I?"

"I fear to hurt you."

Candy smiled wickedly. "What you've done to me is far from painful."

While they rested in each other's arms he asked if she would speak of the accident that had robbed her memories. "Do you remember what happened to cause you to scream and Lightness to rear as she did? We must never let such a thing happen to you again."

His touch relaxed her, and again she liquefied against his flesh like creamy butter on a hot English muffin. Yep, she felt herself melting against his nook and crannies of muscled striations. The feeling was delicious.

Thorne's gentle sensuous touch provided her the feeling that he desired and cherished her. That he was pleased she was with him and sharing his life. The sensation made for an unfamiliar feeling of being wanted simply because she was "Candy".

She had felt inconsequential ever since her mother had chosen a cigarette over her. Or maybe even further back in her life, because she couldn't ever remember feeling a sense of belonging like she did when her skin and Thorne's touched. As though she'd found a home in his arms.

Candy knew he wanted to know about her phobia, and the thought threatened their peaceful moment. That horrid memory from her childhood always triggered anxiety, and she could feel herself wanting to pull away from him.

Never again did she want to risk being tossed away, as if she meant nothing. Or worse, be treated as a regrettable inconvenience. Not again! Candy was heart-sore from feeling insignificant—disposable. If he laughed at her, or thought her a childish coward, what would she do? Worse, would he turn away from her?

Thorne tightened his arms around her, pulling her closer as he kissed her hair. She wondered if he sensed her insecurity and fears because it seemed as if he instinctively knew. This was his way of letting her know he wasn't backing away and wouldn't let her pull away from him either.

Push your doubts back Candy. He's a good man and he hasn't abandoned you, even when you've obviously annoyed him to smithereens.

Explaining her phobia would mean she'd have to reveal her hurtful childhood event. Tonight was too special to rehash that pain. She was enjoying the rare closeness she felt with him. No, she refused to spoil tonight.

"You'll laugh at me, think I'm weak, silly and—"

A soft kiss robbed further words from her. "Not so. Tell me, so I might prevent such a thing in the future. As your male I must know these things. And there will be no laughter at your expense. Your pain is mine."

Her *'male',* she liked the sound of that. His words sounded warm and comforting, the way his arms made her feel. As though they belonged together and he'd be there for her when she needed him. And hadn't he been there during her times of terror? She felt as if she'd known him for an extended period of time when in fact it only been a month. But admittedly, she trusted him more than anyone she'd ever known, even more than her friend Liam.

With a sigh Candy resigned to give him a peek into her phobia, enough to pacify him for tonight. "It was a large, hairy dog."

"The groundkeeper's old dog?"

"I don't know who the dog belonged to, but I have an *extreme* fear of dogs, and it goes back to my childhood and this scar on my leg."

As she showed him her scar, he traced it with his hand and then continued upward to more intimate, warm and wet places on her anatomy.

"Did the groundkeeper's dog jump on you, harm you in some manner?" His fingertip was making circles with on her most sensitive spot and then he slowly slipped his finger into her. A gasp of pleasure escaped her, making him smile.

"You know Thorne, it's very difficult to focus when you're distracting me."

"That so? I thought to make you feel calmer while discussing what frightened you. You look calmer, do you not feel calmer?"

Unable to take his teasing any longer she pushed him onto his back and straddled his chest, as though her small body could ever hold his mass of muscles down. But he fell back letting her take command.

"Let me quickly answer your questions so I can ask one of my own. No, the dog didn't hurt me. It terrified me. All dogs do, no matter their size. This isn't a story I want to share on such a perfect night with you. There are far more interesting things to focus on."

Reaching behind her hips Candy easily found what she was searching for. Apparently Thorne was more than ready for additional playtime. Feeling his length and hardness gave her a certain satisfaction, a feeling of empowerment.

Huh, seems like the former shy Candy Cane could easily affect this high-octane, testosterone-fueled, man just fine, and she planned to make his engine roar.

"Then you must tell me another time, as I have need to know more about you and this fear."

Candy nodded. "I promise. Now, my quick question for you, what changed to make Celcee go from miserable to happy after losing her virginity to that cruel bastard, Shemmar? I felt wretched for her."

With her straddled across his waist he'd gained a very intimate view of her. As he circled her nipples he answered her. "By the goddess, you are perfection." He released his breath, as if to clear his mind in order to answer coherently.

"It seems your memory is returning, I am glad to know such. I want you to remember more than our passionate times. Although I am a greedy man in that I wish for you to recall every single moment I touched you—every moan, cry of ecstasy, and every time you called out of my name as though only I could ever bring you that degree of pleasure."

He gave her his half-lopsided, sexy smile again. "I want to be memorable to you Lassie, as it seems I am indeed a most selfish man. In regards to Shemmar, he has wedded parents, so he is not a true bastard. But I think you mean it disparagingly do you not? And of that I agree. My cousin is not an honorable man and I fear Celcee fell victim to his retaliation against me.

"Surely Shemmar must have succumbed to mad-ness to think I would ever surrender something as precious as you to the likes of him. I had planned for no man to have you that night, as by my promise to protect you. Of course, when you chose me I was quick to change my mind on that. How I craved you, then, and every day since."

While he related the story about his pronounced punishment for Celcee and Ram's negligence, Thorne played with her nipples and touched her wetness. He knew her body well enough to tell she would quickly be ready for another orgasm, and planned to harvest it from her luscious body.

Never had he known such a responsive and eager female as Candy. Reaching inside the honey pot he again used his fingers to massage it into her and around her swollen bud.

By the goddess, how he cherished that intense look on her face when she was ready to come. Lifting her onto his more than ready shaft, he held her buttocks. Slowly he eased her down until she encased him, and then with a measured pace pushed her up and down his length. How he treasured seeing her jeweled-green eyes and swollen rosy lips when she faced him in this position.

The choice of pace was left to Candy, which quickly hastened with her heated desire. All the while he'd watched her as if nothing could appear more precious.

Candy rode him with great intent to satisfy them both, which she easily did. They came to completion at the same time with her sheath clenching him so tightly he saw spots cross his eyes. How pleased she looked at making him moan for her, and how pleased he was to find a woman who actually made him moan.

As she rested, totally spent across his chest, he trailed his fingers across her spine. Finally he asked her his question.

"Lassie?"

"*Humm?*"

"Have you a man you care for in your world?"

Candy rolled off Thorne and wrapped her arms around his neck. "Really? Didn't we just share a blissful experience?"

"Aye, such is why I ask. Have you a man?"

"If you mean like a lover, that's a difficult question, and I'm not sure you'll like the answer."

He held her tightly against him. "You are a beauty and I did not expect you would not have known men. Has he pleasured you as much as I?" Desperation filled his voice as he started kissing her neck, one of her favorite erogenous zones as it turned out. Who knew? Obviously Thorne did.

Candy didn't want to discuss this topic, but also wouldn't lie to him so she begrudgingly and cautiously surrendered to his request. Sort of.

"Are you actually going to ask about men I've been intimate with?"

Thorne took her hand and began kissing her fingertips one by one. "Nay, no, Lassie. None matter but the last one, before you came to my land and to my arms."

"I can't see how that's important or why he matters."

"The others before were not worthy or they would not have been past lovers. But the man you had when you came here, was current and therefore held merit to you."

Candy saw his reasoning and actually liked his way of thinking. At least she could avoid rehashing the first two times she'd had very disappointing sex. Still, she hated his interest in this delicate topic.

"I haven't dated or been courted by many men. I was sort of a late bloomer as we call it. And I was *less* sexually active than most females my age. I don't have casual sex with a man for the sake of simply 'getting off', meaning to have a climax. Intense and sating sex, complete with a climax, never happened before you. Go ahead puff your chest out because you're quite the lover."

As if he didn't already know that.

He chuckled. "You think flattery will dissuade my question?"

"It's the truth."

And yes I was hoping for that as well.

Thorne gave her the lifted brow look. Dang it, if he wasn't sexy. She continued. "I did meet a guy, uh, a man, about a month before I crossed to this place, and I did grow very fond of him."

She paused to make sure Thorne wasn't getting angry. Although he remained quiet, he stroked her back with languorous pets. He did that when letting her know he was there for her, and it felt wonderful. No wonder cats purred when petted. Wait—was she purring too? Yeah, that deep thoracic resonating sound could definitely classify as purring.

"*You* have been an exception to my . . . I guess we could call them my 'rules' regarding sex."

Thorne looked confused. "Rules? You truly have rules for fucking? Tis a physical need Lassie."

She'd never considered sex, as a natural physical need, like food, or water, or a physical connection to another. Admittedly, Thorne affected her intensely enough to destroy all preconceived resolutions she'd held. With him 'rules' no longer applied because she couldn't resist his magnetic attraction. He totally confused that moral compass of hers, but that was the nature of magnets.

Certainly a man like Thorne must be well aware of how women reacted to him. 'Pheromone Man' couldn't be oblivious, not with that body of his designed to pleasure a woman all night long.

Sigh, which he had totally succeeded in doing.

"I wanted to be intimate with you even though we'd just met, which is something I've never considered or done before. You're the most enticing man I've ever known and obviously very difficult, actually down right impossible, for me to resist. I was a goner—a moth to a burning flame of desire. You give me mind-altering sex I couldn't have imagined existed, plus orgasms—repeatedly I might add." Shyness surfaced from her confession.

She tried to read his expression and suspected he actually found her words amusing. Here she was pouring out her guilty confessions and he was amused?

Men!

With a small sigh she continued. "It feels as though we fit together, like that sword in the sheath you carry on your war-horse, and I love that sensation."

Thorne smiled that gorgeous male smile of his—the one that made her feel feminine and needy, like she was getting a fever only he could cure. Then he asked what she hoped he wouldn't.

"I enjoy being your *sword*, and agree you *sheath* my blade most tightly, and our bodies create the most superb fucking I have ever known. Now, have you shared a bed with this man you are trying to avoid discussing?"

Busted. The man has skills and knows I'm trying to redirect. Did they teach Psych 101 here?

"His name was Joe, and he was kind, romantic and a considerate man. I thought I might fall in love with him. But the intense feelings I have for you aren't the same feelings at all. With you, they're deeper. Soul deep."

Thorne wondered if Candy realized she was speaking of 'Joe' in the past tense. This was good, as by no means would Thorne let her return to another man's arms. Candy's sexual innocence was apparent and 'Joe' had not been an attentive lover.

How was it the man had not known Candy was not fully sated? She was so easy to please, and her face bespoke the truth of her pleasure.

I shall teach her, as by both love and desire our bodies meet.

Thorne repeated his question to her.

"Why do you ask these questions when I can't change the past? If I could, I would've always chosen you. I'd have waited and given my virginity to you instead of some silly, teenaged boy, who said things he didn't mean just to have sex."

This conversation was making her feel uncomfortable, and Candy wished he hadn't asked these things. But she'd promised not to lie to him, and he wasn't buying into her vague answers or omissions.

No wonder he made a good leader, the man was direct and tenacious to a fault—like a Rottweiler, or worse yet, a lawyer on *The Good Wife.*

With a sigh, Thorne kissed the top of her forehead and kept her wrapped in his arms.

"And I would have relished the honor of breaking you into womanhood while holding you close, whispering only words truly heartfelt. Such is the past, you are a woman now, and I do not hold such a thing as important. Truthfully, breaking a virgin's barrier was never a task I relished. Causing a female that pain seems a selfish act if a man does not hold genuine affection for her, which admittedly I did not. Not until you, and you alone.

"Tell me, how many times did you lay with this man who waits for you, and did you consider him a good lover?"

"Men! Why do you always ask things you shouldn't? This is mortifying." At least to her, although it seemed important to Thorne.

"Lassie, answer me this. My heart has need to know." And Thorne did sound as if it meant a great deal to him.

Ack!

"We had sex three times. Now are you happy?" She hoped so, since she was humiliated. Her face was now glowing that fire-engine-red—not her most flattering color, although certainly one she was familiar with wearing.

"Happy that another man fucked you? That would not be the word I would use. Now, thrice . . . of this do you mean three nights filled with fucking?"

Candy clenched her teeth. "Three. Times. Total."

"Truthfully, merely three times within a *full* passing of the moon? Surely he must be an elderly man then." Thorne sounded skeptical.

Candy laughed. "No, not elderly, but he certainly doesn't have your prowess. I doubt any man does. I'm sure you haven't heard any complaints from the women you've been with, or are *all* the men here so incredibly virile and outstanding lovers? *Hmmm*, maybe I should conduct a survey."

Pulling her closer, Thorne began a tail of kisses, starting at her neckline and moving to her right cheek then to the left. Suddenly he stopped as her words finally sank in and a frown furled his brow. Lust had slowed his senses.

"Survey? These men shall mysteriously lose their tongues before you ask about any such prowess. You shant be conducting any such 'survey' woman. I will be keeping you much too sore for you to even contemplate thus a ridiculous feat.

"I am to be the only man you shall ask, and this is my answer. One honey pot is quite sufficient for a night of 'needing' in my land, including for me. I find it is *you* my little siren, who calls on my desire for so much more. I cannot imagine taking you less than twice every night, even without the 'needing moon', if you would graciously be willing to always share my bed."

"My Lord, how could I ever resist such an impressive offer, but on some occasions I might prefer less sleep and more of you than *merely* two times a night," she teased.

Her comment brought forward a throaty growl. "Then it shall be as you desire. You put forth a hard bargain woman, and you will drain me dry, I am quite certain of it."

Candy grabbed ahold of him and began to massage his responsive hardening. His quick response brought a satisfied smile to her face.

Reaching lower she cupped him. "Yep, I plan to drain every last bit from you. Starting now."

"Greedy woman," he growled.

Chapter Twenty-Four

Naked and entangled, the couple dozed peacefully.

Suddenly, Candy was wide-awake. It was as though an inner alarm clock had gone off and she'd had a cup of espresso to jolt her awake.

Quietly, so as not to disturb him, she propped on her elbow and looked over to Thorne. A strand of his sandy colored hair had fallen across his face and she gently moved it aside.

Such a handsome, compelling man.

The campfire had dwindled, but she didn't feel the least bit chilled. In fact she felt a little warm despite being naked. She smiled thinking how totally unlike her.

Imagine me naked, in the woods, and next to Pheromone Man in all his glory. Who would've thought?

Glancing down, Candy noticed how she'd been sprinkled in diamond dust. Like on the previous 'needing moon', her memory reminded her.

The remembrance was accompanied with a smile.

What a way to make a girl feel special with the shimmer of body-bling.

This color-restricted land really did hold marvels, other than the obvious tall, muscle-bound one lying asleep next to her.

The atmosphere here was so pristine—no smog, or air particulates to obscure the pure midnight-blue sky. However, tonight the moon's face remained cloaked by impenetrable clouds, as if too bashful to unveil itself to the night.

Never had she seen so many stars in the night sky. There must be millions vividly flickering. The star-filled heavens reminded her of fields of wild poppies nodding in the breeze. She stood and turned to marvel at the glorious heavenly site.

Thousands of minute, silver, twinkle lights appeared as though strung across the nighttime sky with abandon. They illuminated and added ambience of otherworldliness.

As she gazed at the wondrous vastness she realized it appeared as though two stars were blinking, as if they were winking at her—first one, then the other, then together.

Obviously her overly fanciful imagination was at it again, but the sight made her smile anyway.

The tranquil night gave way to sensual sensations and a gnawing desire began inside of her. The feeling heightened and became a desperate sense of 'needing'. Needing Thorne inside her.

Now!

This depth of intensity explained why Levenia liked her bed directly under the moon's path. With this heady, overwhelming 'need' Candy could even comprehend why Levenia cared little about who saw her in her feverish state of euphoria.

The phenomenon took over all of Candy's senses, and pushed away other thoughts and rationale. The night air seemed to drug her and caused all her inhibitions to feel . . . undone. The feeling was heady, filled with abandon, as if some powerful aphrodisiac filled her veins. No longer was she just 'needy', now she was bursting with animalistic lust for Thorne. The potency of her instincts was all consuming.

One word roared in her subconscious.

Mate!

Although the moon remained concealed, beams of light defiantly snaked through and teasingly caressed Candy's skin. As the moonbeams touched and caressed her flesh, she felt a burning sensation, which added to the evolving, blazing desire for her male.

The pain caused her to flinch and she looked at her arms, expecting to see redness and blisters from burns.

But what she saw instead was pristine skin, shimmery and unmarred.

Little did it matter how many times they'd been intimate tonight, this intense 'need' made her feel as though their shared passion had been lifetimes ago. 'Need' was demanding release.

Now!

Never had she felt anything so raw, so insistent. A deep hunger tore at her and knew it had to be sated before she perished from painful sexual starvation. Candy thought to lose sanity if she didn't soon engage in sex with Thorne again. The 'needing moon's' call was commanding, and the pain intense.

Sex. Seed. Satiety. Those three words replayed over and over in her head.

Candy dropped to her knees and slipped hand over hand, as her palms grasped the grass beneath them. She crossed the small distance to Thorne's handsome face.

Her tongue wet her lips as an intense desire to lick every part of him coursed through her. Like a thief she grabbed hold of Thorne's cock.

As she squeezed him, she began to pant and cried out, "Thorne, help me, this 'need', oh this 'need' . . ."

He immediately awoke. Candy was clenching his cock, and sounded desperate. No doubt that would motivate any man.

"The 'needing moon'?" He asked with concern while seeming a bit shell-shocked.

She was rocking and whimpering when he took her into his arms. "Tell me Lassie, in what manner should I take you to give you the greatest release?"

Crawling over to a patch of grassy ground, Candy situated herself on her hands and knees and dug her fingers and bare toes in the dingy, dewy grass. The moist ground beneath her felt yielding, comforting, and strangely sensual.

"I think here. Does that even make sense?"

"I will ease you by whatever manner your need."

None of this seemed rational. She didn't care. All she wanted was sexual release to her core, before she lost her ever-loving mind. Thorne needed to hurry.

Candy stretched her arms and chest across the ground and positioned herself with her buttocks tilted towards the sky. Her body rocked as she waited, desperate to be entered by Thorne. *Please hurry, big guy.*

The grass tickled her nipples, and she could swear the blades caressed and teased her, as her breast swelled. Her nipples hardened and a strange thought went through her mind.

Imagine how my breasts would feel when heavy with rich milk and ready to be suckled by a babe.

The thought made Candy shiver. She shook her head to remove such ridiculous thoughts. If only Thorne would hurry, she needed him *now!* She began to undulate her hips as frenzied whimpers escaped her lips.

Urgency! Sex. Seed. Satiety.

Thorne was behind her, his fingers coated with the honey concoction.

He hesitated.

Thorne, why use the honey pot?

It was a rash thought, and why would he even think to skip contraception? Always he used the concoction with diligence.

If you use not the honey pot she will be yours and never leave to go to the other man.

She would not leave him, in that he had to believe. He shook his head as he placed his fingers into Candy to spread the honey mixture. Her sheath felt hot, as if she was fevered. This must mean her body was cycling, ready for his seed. Therein was the problem, the goddess wished his woman to be with child.

It would be your child Thorne, from your seed. No other man would ever put his seed into her again as she would be forever bonded. Bring forth a child to honor me.

Admittedly he prized such a thought, but he had already placed the honey. Neither would he father a child without first discussing such a choice with Candy, and right now she was hardly in a frame of mind to be rational.

She would be amiable to this, with my moonbeams upon her fair skin. Mate with her, as it is meant to be, I will not be denied. Take your female and plant your seed deeply into her womb. Sate your woman while you honor me, your goddess.

With a sense of confusion he looked to the heavens. Just then, the clouds parted and Thorne saw the moon's massive magnificence in the night sky. Tonight the moon had turned deep red—the color of blood.

A Blood Moon! A rare occurrence and such a moon was believed to heightened a female's fertility. Child-less women sometimes prayed for such a moon. Tales spoke of how such a moon could drive a woman insane with uncontrolled needs that could not be sated. Of course these were old women's tales, nothing more.

The unexpected sight of the brilliant red moon, in a land that lacked significant color, was remarkable. He could not deny the Moon Goddess had consigned his Lassie to suffer under her influence. The goddess' Blood Moon was far more powerful than the monthly cycling 'needing moon'.

Tonight's moon foretold a more intoxicating and compelling night, one promising unmeasured desire and fertility. Undoubtedly, this led to the irrational thoughts circling in his head and his woman's pain. No longer did he know if the Moon Goddess was speaking to him or if it was his own drunkenness from the intoxicating Blood Moon.

What he did know was Candy needed a release from the agony to which she was bound. Never could he tolerate seeing her hurting by 'need', or otherwise.

She continued rocking and writhing, back and forth, but when Thorne tried to enter her from behind she was too tight. When he tried to put his fingers back into her, her tightness denied him entrance. This worried him. Once he could get into her womanhood, he knew the size of him would penetrate deeply to fully fill her and quiet her pain from the 'need'. Yet right now her core was too constricted and he could not get in without tearing her, and that he would never do.

"Lassie, try to relax for me, you are tighter than a frightened virgin and I cannot penetrate without hurting you."

"I don't care, I need you in me. I'm already in pain."

"I will not! Do not even ask such a thing of me." Thorne would never purposely hurt any female with his size, and certainly *never* his Lassie. There had to be another manner to ease her.

His hand began to softly stroke her back. When he heard a soft sigh he thought on how to relax her further. With a soft, fleshly voice, he began to speak to her.

"Candy, I love you deeply. I know I can be a harsh man, but will try to measure to the type of man you would desire. A man you can be prideful of. I will provide for you as a man should the woman he loves, and bring back from my hunts the juiciest, most disgusting delicacies for little Ono to enjoy, as we watch her grow."

Hearing a small laugh from Candy told him she was focusing on his voice rather than her aching.

He continued. "I would faithfully spend every 'needing moon' in your bed, and I hope to spend every night by your side as well. Of course simply to warm your feet, as never would I presume to expect sexual favors from you. This I promise, and more if you will have me."

She was starting to relax, so he checked with one finger, then a second. Slowly her sex was unlocking and soon she would ease enough for him penetrate her. Daring not to risk over stimulating her lest she tighten again, Thorne removed his fingers and resumed talking in a low, seductive voice.

"Open for me, accept my love for you, or I will need to prove yet again how I freely bleed for your female attention, and already I carry too many unsightly scars for your pretty eyes to behold."

"Don't you dare cut yourself, I'm calmer now. I want all of you, and hard . . .*ooh*, Thorne . . .*oohh*, yes . . . finally."

He was in her. Pushing hesitantly at first until her core suddenly eased and invited him all the way in and against her womb. Thorne would not refuse such an invitation. This position granted him even deeper access into her. His hilt ground against her pelvis as his sac slapped at her flesh, and she let out moans of pleasure.

After three deep strokes into her, Thorne could no longer control his restraint. The moonbeams shone upon them and his thrusting became faster, harder, building with more force, as he held her hips tightly against him.

When Candy tried to move he would not allow it, and gave her buttocks a firm slap of reprimand as his hands tightened their hold onto her hips. "Nay woman, this night your body is my Kingdom and I rule what is mine."

And she was without question his. By the Blood Moon's decree he had no choice but to take her by any means to prove as much. The goddess demanded he dominate Candy's body, and tonight she was destined to submit to him.

Aye, you are mine Lassie. There will be no doubting it.

Her plentiful natural lubrication meant he easily stroked in and out without causing harm. Again her core tightened, contracting around him as if she would never let him go, which created greater friction between their bodies.

Thorne held no desire to hurt her, only to govern her body. His pelvis thrust without restraint, his demanding want of her so intense it pained his head.

How tightly he seized her hips, allowing no quarter from her. If she dared try to retreat, he knew he would simply drag her back and force her to meet pleasure again, and again, and then fill her until she runneth over with his seed. At this moment his woman was his to control, to pleasure, his to rule, his to fuck.

Mine.

Pounding, pounding—into her core without falter. This brutal need was too great to deny.

Deeper, harder—he heard her groans and whimpers.

Faster—he feared to harm her, and possibly himself.

Ultimately the building sensation turned into unending intense pleasure—pulsating hedonism. Perspiration from his brow dripped onto her bouncing and bruised buttocks.

The moonbeams from the Blood Moon demanded much of them. It seemed as if he would last forever. All the while, Candy moaned constantly with repeated shudders of ecstasy, as intense pleasure pulsed through her. His sac spent an abundance of seed into her core, while her sheath milked him, wringing every last drop from him.

Candy screamed out his name as she reached her final cataclysmic completion. Even as she cried out with her crescendos of ecstasy, Thorne kept forcing hot seed into her, over and over until his cum now ran down her legs and onto the grass beneath her.

Moans from the power of the fervor flooding through his body, escaped him. Nothing could ever feel more powerful than tonight's fucking of his woman, and she'd surrendered all control to him alone. It made for a thoroughly heady, male experience.

Without a doubt he would be left dried up and consider it fortunate to retain two small prunes between his legs after such abuse to his sac, albeit abuse never felt so divine.

The hair on his arms began to stand on end as a tingling arose from the ground beneath them, as if seeking out Candy's body. Muscles trembled and his nerve endings were on fire. Their unrelenting coupling provided an intensely prolonged zenith as waves of gratification rolled through them bestowing pleasure, while stealing their energy.

Thorne's body followed Candy's as she crumbled to the grass, both gasping for breath.

Goddess almighty, never before had fucking become celestial. Indeed he saw stars even though he was facing the damp ground.

So much sensation, so much power—never had Candy imagined anything could be so intense. Thorne controlled her every move while he drove into her. There was no doubt he was taking command of her body as he held her in place under him. She felt both protected and dominated, while being taken hard by the man she craved. Their sexual activity had never taken this turn, and although different, she found this aspect exciting as well.

When tingling warm sensations traveled through her body, she let out a deep moan. Instinctively Candy knew this phenomenon was created from some earth-born current. Her entire body sensed a sizzling throughout. It teased her as the tingling traveled from the tip of her toes, up through her bosom, and out her fingertips. Her breasts felt heavy as if she'd indeed been suckled relentlessly. In fact her nipples felt sensitive, swollen and sore.

She exploded! Her mind, her body—all felt undone. Ecstasy became an unending force so explicit it seemed impossible to survive the onslaught from it.

Finally with no more pain, she felt completely quenched, conquered, and crumbled to the grass. Thorne laid on top of her, equally drained.

Both collapsed from the exhaustion of being so stimulated and then thoroughly consumed. The lovers lay silent as they greedily reached for each other's embrace, as if any distance between them was unthinkable.

Candy began to cry softly against Thorne's chest.

"You are crying?" Damn, he feared he'd hurt her. He had been pounding her so brutally without tenderness or mercy, what was he to expect, if not tears?

Her surrender to you, he heard in his head.

She gave him everything he needed, why would he care about surrender tonight of all night. Why had the goddess insisted upon such aggression? This made little sense and he feared her opinion of his sexual brutality. If he'd hurt her he would never forgive himself. Mayhap she would not either.

Candy dabbed her tears away. "My goodness, it certainly took a lot to get rid of that pain. And that feeling of energy flowing through us, as you gave me the most unbelievable experience of my life, was indescribable."

She shook her head to clear her thoughts. "*That* was so incredible, *you're* so incredible. I had no idea such intensity could happen under the 'needing moon'."

"Nor I. Never have I ever experienced such afore. Are you truly all right? I know I was uncommonly forceful, but I swear by the goddess, it was not by my intention."

His thrusting should have been gentler, not driving into her with such fierce force. Not that he did not have times when he enjoyed hard fucking, but this was too raw and demanding, almost punishing and far more than his delicate Lassie should endure. Without a doubt he left bruises from his hands while bracing her hips, mayhap even from that hard slap to her buttocks.

"I was far too forceful and I swear, never would I mean to hurt you." He added apologetically.

She was wiping the remnants of tears from her dampened lashes. "Are you kidding? That felt amazing and you can repeat that any time you want. I'm not crying from being hurt or displeased, it's just the experience was so . . . bewilderingly rapturous. That was exactly what I needed to get past the pain I was feeling. As though the discomfort erased the 'needing' pain."

Abruptly her confidence seemed to fade. "Goodness, I think that came out sounding like a kinky confession. I've never done any bondage or submission type stuff, so please don't think I'm twisted or something."

Their hearts were still beating rapidly as Thorne pulled her back to him, cradling her sweat-glistening body against his.

"To find a woman who is far more eager and passionate than any practiced courtesan—such a rare gift is hardly displeasing to me. Truthfully, I could not be more pleased with you, and should you enjoy the feel of raw or dominant fucking at times, I am more than eager to provide you whatever you desire."

He bent to kiss the tip of her nose. "Understand this. There is no right or wrong with our pleasure Lassie. If we enjoy it, our pleasure is just. However, never will I have any desire to cause you hurt or harm. The thought of seeing a woman's skin bruised or broken is not within me, and with you, the thought sickens me." Thorne tilted her face to meet her eyes as he resumed.

"If something is offensive to you it will not be revisited. I admit I am open to diversity—mayhap more than I should—but never will I pressure you beyond either emotional or physical comfort. Feel no embarrassment because you like something new or unknown to you and likewise always tell me if you do not."

A mischievous smile tilted his sensuous swollen lips. "And surrendering yourself to me only makes me want to yell out in virile victory screaming from the top of my lungs, 'see what my woman gives unto me—weep with envy'."

The tone of his voice suddenly became serious. "You are a wonder and proudly declare you are truly mine. I will not be letting you go, Lassie. Do not ever think otherwise. I have claimed you and already you bear my warrior's kiss upon your thigh."

Looking down Candy saw a hickey on her inner thigh and smiled. "I think Celcee told me something about how one day you might give me a permanent warrior's woman's 'mark'?"

"Ah, so curious. Celcee spoke too freely of what she knows naught. Perchance, one day."

"Will you tell me about it?" She was dying to know more. "What if I want one?"

"Such a thing . . ." He paused and shook his head. "You have just returned to my arms. This shall not be debated tonight."

"You know I'm curious by nature and now even more so. When will you tell me more?"

His expression warned her the topic wasn't open for debate. That just made her more inquisitive, and someday she'd get answers out of him. Letting out a huge sigh she finally settled in contently against him.

She felt content against his chest and just had to ask. "Will you do something for me?"

Thorne propped up on one elbow and smoothed her hair, which was damp from the heat of her passion. "Always, anything."

"Really? Because you just denied my inquisitiveness?" She added a little pout.

"Candy, some things are worth waiting for. I have painfully waited for you and you shall wait for this. Some choices must be considered with care, as some acts cannot be undone. Now what else do you desire?"

Seemed her pout wasn't effectively coquettish tonight. *Fiddlesticks.*

She stared up into his rich, chocolate-colored eyes. "Will you say those words to me again?"

"And which words would those be? Perhaps how beautiful I find you with your sun-kissed locks and mesmerizing green eyes? Or how you are the most passionate woman I have known with a body made for sating my lust, thus leaving other men to weep with jealousy at my godsend? Or I wonder if perhaps you wish to hear that I love you?"

"You are very flattering with your words, and a girl could easily have her head turned. She might even 'put out', like 'give *it* up'. Wait, I already did! Repeatedly! But in all seriousness, yes, those last three words. I've never heard you say them before and I'd like to make sure I heard correctly." Her heart felt giddy waiting for those three words.

Please repeat them . . . please.

"Put out? Another phrase for fucking I assume. I find it strange that in your realm, you require so many words for one act of physical pleasure, though none say what it truly is." Thorne shook his head as if finding that amusing.

"To answer you, I assure you I have said *I love you* many times over. Admittedly, it was when you were unconscious, though I did speak those words repeatedly and hoped they would bring you back to me. I feared for you and prayed to every god and goddess as I held your hand and spoke those words."

"You said them to me, back then?" Candy thought she was the first to blurt them out. To know he said them first was incredible, elating—perfection!

"Aye Lassie, I have told you many times. Then during my despair from your loss of memory I felt the need to deny my feelings, in order to survive. Truthfully, I shielded them from myself as well. Losing you was . . . difficult."

"But you seemed so angry and distant with me."

With a deep sigh he answered. "I lost you in the accident and I was beyond distraught. Then Ripple told me to be patient as you were beginning to remember and yet you never spoke of it. That hurt my pride. As you said, I am indeed a prideful man and I feared you considered our night of passion not worth mentioning to me.

"A man does not like to think he was such a poor lover as to be dismissed so easily. As if I was only passable to provide a cock for your lust on that single night of 'needing'. Such thinking pained me. I desired for you to have want me yet again and again, without being under the influence of the 'needing moon'. Already I wanted you evermore."

She frowned in confusion.

Really? This sensuous, handsome hunter-warrior-King wanted her—forever? The inconsequential girl with what sounded like a stripper's name, who never put out on a first date?

"Then why were you willing to let me be with another man this 'needing moon'? That makes absolutely no sense."

Thorne held her head against his chest and gently stoked her hair as he spoke. "To let you choose. I meant it to be my gift to you, but it would have been an ill-fated gift I fear."

"An irrational gift for certain."

"I fear so," he stated as if a matter of fact. "For when I would have returned to camp in the morning, and smelled your scent on another, or another on you, or saw guilt upon a warrior's face, I would know who dared to touch my woman. I knew I would kill him with my bare hands, without mercy or guilt. As Shemmar said, I do not share, and so in this he is correct. Sharing is not within me, as you are my woman, and you alone live deeply within my heart."

Her smile radiated up at him. "Then it's a good thing I followed that grumpy man I love, and chose to share myself only with him. Besides, it seems he already knows what intimate things I enjoy."

Thorne, however, was not smiling. "A very wise choice. It spared a man's life as well as my heart."

His hand trailed down to encircle her nipples, first one then the other. "Now in regards to pleasing you . . . *ah*, tis an enjoyable deed. You always respond to me with curiosity and passion, and you seem to delight in all we have shared eagerly wanting to learn more. No man could ask for a more perfect lover, as you give yourself to me without hesitation. And I greedily want all of you. Seems I truly am a selfish King who will not share his bounty."

He pulled her over his chest and massaged her buttocks before he gave her a playful slap. "Bounty indeed."

"I refuse to blush," although she did. "And you'd better not be insinuating that I have a big bottom. Anyway, you were the only choice I would've made no matter how the 'needing moon' tempted me. No one could ever compare to any part of you. I've fallen for you, hunter-warrior. And I'm not referring to my usual, clumsy, trip-over-my-own-feet manner."

His hand touched the scar on his face. "Even with this?"

"Definitely. I don't find it anything less than enticing. It makes you look bad-boyish, dangerous and very sexy." Considering recent events, she quickly added, "But that doesn't mean you should purposely add more scars."

"Aye, I can be dangerous." His Lassie had no idea how dangerous.

Her lips began a trail of kisses stopping to kiss his scar, which led to kisses on each of his other scars. Someday she'd ask him to tell her the stories behind each of these badges of bravery. Right now he still shied away from her notice of them. Somehow she would get him to tell her and she'd be able to convince him that they didn't bother her at all.

"Strangely it seems my scars entice my woman, and I am thinking you find my touch to your liking as well, do you not? I want to take you again Lassie."

"I'm going to be very sore."

"Tonight I will leave your tight cunny sore, and your thighs weak, and be an arrogant man for it. What say you then?"

He gave her a playful wink, which he well knew she'd never turned a blind eye to. Mayhap his charms worked well enough on her, they had just needed a bit of mending—much as his heart had.

"Riding on Lightness tomorrow will feel miserable," she mumbled.

"I shall add an extra blanket to soften the leather against your precious womanly mound."

"Getting on and off the horse may make me moan. My thighs already feel weak and quivery."

"This is good, as it shall serve as proof to all men that I have fucked you well. Let me hear you practice this moaning now as I touch you. Will you receive me Lassie?"

She let out little gasp at his skilled touch. "So unfair, how could I ever say no to you?"

"Hopefully never and a day." Thorne circled her nipples and smeared them with her wet arousal. "They say yes to me. See how your nipples peak for me? I plan to suckle them and taste your nectar smeared on them. Tell me, do you wish me to be extra gentle, no deep thrusting or pounding against your tender swollen flesh? No grinding in circles with my hips? Reserve myself to only half my length this time? What say you, am I to be gentle with my fucking?"

"Where's the fun if you don't do all those wicked things to me?"

A masculine chuckle followed as he set about getting her readied for him. "As you wish." He would leave her sore all right, and proudly so.

Those clinking sounds she'd heard from her saddlebags now sounded like music to her, and the second honey pot would prove to be most useful.

Chapter Twenty-Five
Thorne

As they lay in each other's arms, Thorne tilted Candy's face skyward she could see the now-visible moon. The cloud cover had finally fully dispersed to unveil the source of the lover's uncommonly demanding desires. And like the Moon Goddess herself, the sight was breathtaking to behold.

Now his Lassie could visualize the degree of power the Moon Goddess wielded. Candy's eyes widened and she propped herself on her elbows.

"I've never seen the moon so huge, and never brilliant red like that. That would be amazing done in watercolors. What does it mean?"

"You wish to hear the fable of the Blood Moon?"

"Yes, tell me the story. You know I love your voice when you talk to me. It soothes me, although sometimes your voice is just plain masculine-sexy and gets me all heated, while other times you're all king-like and forceful. Although I'm not as fond of the surly-tempered voice."

"That so? Seems you have thought much on my voice."

"Among other parts of you."

"*Hmmm*, then my story telling while crossing the bridge helped after all?"

"It was all of you. Holding me so close helped a great deal. You obviously have many ways you soothe me. Now please tell me this fable."

"The Blood Moon is said to be the result of an unrequited love triangle between the Sun God, the Moon Goddess and Earth Mother. Sometimes they are referred to as the Troika—the threesome."

Candy interrupted him. "Just how many gods and goddesses does your world have?"

"Many. Now silence, you interrupt my skilled story telling. Many eons ago, Earth was birthed, becoming whole and soon waiting to be populated through the mating of men and women."

Thorne cleared his throat. "Something we have practiced many times this night Lassie. Soon the Moon Goddess became preoccupied with uncounted hours each night watching the lives of mortal men. She observed how men shared passion with their women and how by giving their seed unto them they begot children to populate the early world. One night when the moon was at its fullest, and therefore closest to our world, the Moon Goddess broke the Laws of Nature and visited Earth as a beautiful and lustful woman. Much like you Lassie."

Candy jabbed his ribs and he continued.

"The Moon Goddess was said to have silken hair that went to her ankles. Silvery white and pure as a new snow, her hair moved and glistened as if a gentle breeze forever caressed it. And her eyes were the hue of the purest azure of the heavens. Over time the Moon Goddess became obsessed by that which she had not—she wanted to know a man's affection. This became essential to her, and she felt a great need of a man to fill her womb with his seed. Again, it sounds a bit like you."

Another playful jab to his ribs.

"You are not the best listener are you Lassie? The Moon Goddess wandered the Earth, through villages until she came upon the most handsome man she had even seen. The man she chose looked like a god unto her eyes. Thinking him magnificent, she wanted to be pleasured by him. And she was. It was the first time she had felt a human's touch and his manhood was said to be mighty and his sac filled with virile seed"

Candy smiled up to her storyteller. "Sounds like your 'tremendous cock' to me."

"Now Lassie why do you interrupt my tale? Shall I continue or tumble you again?"

With a deep sigh Candy suggested, "Can I be greedy and have both?"

"Greedy indeed, insatiable woman! Where was I? He was a virile man who was said to have infinite prowess . . . What no comparison to me? Woman, you wound my male pride!"

Playfully Candy jabbed him yet again.

"Ow, you are so strong, no doubt you broke my ribs. I shall be demanding restitution for such abuse, no doubting that. And I greatly favor your manner of coin. Now let me continue. The Moon Goddess promised to return at the next full moon to rekindle their passion. Knowing it was a forbidden thing she had done, she could not stay with him, only visit on the fullest moon when she could easily reach Earth unnoticed.

"Alas, it was by the jealous nature of the Sun God that he interfered with her plans. He had always lusted for the beautiful Moon Goddess and could not tolerate her dalliance with another, and certainly never with a mere human.

"The Sun God threatened her, telling her she must remain in the Heavens, as was her place, and not to return to her human lover or he would divulge her liaison. They argued much about it. The Sun God would sulk and not show his face to Earth for a week of days, then with a flare of anger the he would treat the Earth harshly with heat beyond any the world had known. His anger and jealousy caused much turmoil.

"Meanwhile, the Moon Goddess, having studied the ways of man, now craved for her lover's seed to grow within her so she might also share the joy of conceiving a child of her own to hold to her bosom, and to love. Her decision meant she must risk another visit to her human male, which she freely and unwisely did on the following fullest moon.

"Her chosen male welcomed her beauty and filled her womb many times with his seed until she felt sure it would take root within her. Now she would share the blessed gift of birthing life, as women of Earth knew.

However, knowing the risks from the Sun God's threats to expose her dalliance, she dared not return to see her lover for nine moons—until the day she was ready to give birth, again on the fullest moon phase.

"When the Sun God heard of her mating and conceiving with a human spawn, the extent of his jealousy and grief overwhelmed him. The Sun God had always coveted the Moon Goddess and felt she should rightfully be his. He held the pride of a god and could not tolerate the thought of any *halflings* born from the womb of the goddess he loved. And so he plotted until he found a manner to extract vengeance.

"On her day of birthing, The Moon Goddess bore twins, a male and female and they were said to be perfect beautiful babes, beyond compare. Although she felt great love for her young, her lover begged her to leave them with him until she could return on the following moon, as he also held them dear. She found the thought heart rending but agreed he might have them the first month and then she would have them the next. Admittedly, she knew nothing of the care of infants or the nurture of humans. Her lover swore to care for their babes and for her to return as quickly as possible so they could have a proper naming ceremony for their twins.

"Meanwhile, the incensed Sun God made a pact with the Earth Mother, who had always longed for him as he was considered quite handsome of form. The Earth Mother was equally heartbroken, because by the Sun God's fiery nature, she could not consort with him, as she had so long desired. To do so meant her entire domain, and all life within, would perish—engulfed in flames. The Sun God burned too heatedly for the Earth Mother's domain to tolerate. Such a liaison could never be, nor her deep longing for him ever fulfilled.

"Since the Moon Goddess had done such an unnatural act in the eyes of the heavenly deities, they deliberated their cruel plan to be just. Thereafter for the next month, every night sky was cloaked with indigo-black clouds, thus shuttering the Earth from the Moon Goddess' purview.

Nor did stars light the way to the land below, as the blanket of dark clouds smothered all light.

"By daylight a dry wind filled with sand blew providing cover to the happenings upon the land below, thereby continually preventing the Moon Goddess from gazing upon her babes and the man she yearned for. The Moon Goddess fretted for the next full-moon cycle as she waited impatiently to return to her beloved babes and man.

"Upon the passing of thirty days, and the fullest moon, she finally descended to the Earth ready to be in her lover's arms and hold her beloved twins.

"What she beheld shocked her soul.

"Proof of the Sun God's jealous hand in consort with the covetousness of the Earth Mother's was evident and punishing to the Moon Goddess' eyes and heart. Within her time away, all the crops had withered from unrelenting heat. All water sources had dried up as a result of the pitiless lack of rain and constant dry winds.

"How difficult to believe that her sister goddess, the Earth Mother, had sacrificed her creations, and had allowed the destruction of her land, out of malice and jealousy. How bitter the Earth Mother must have been to condone such destruction to that which she nurtured from her very bosom, allowing herds and crops to die from pestilence. No life remained within the wind battered village, which was now likened to a titan tomb.

"As the Moon Goddess walked through the dry desolate land, she saw only the remnants wrought by death. Once healthy animals were now simply rotten carcasses. Human bodies were strewn carelessly as if broken dolls. It seemed no life had been considered precious enough to shield. How could any living form survive, as did not all life within Earth Mother's domain require water? The Sun and Earth had transpired against the Moon Goddess in an utterly cruel manner. Once she had thought them friends, but no longer.

"Upon opening the door to the small house, where she had birthed her twins and witnessed their first breathes of life, she saw two tiny dried husks wrapped in swaddling.

The same cloth she had wrapped her precious babes in. Her newborn babies, like all this land, had suffered without milk or sustenance.

"Their lives, innocent beauty, and soft cooing sounds had been replaced by mummified silence. What had been done broke her heart. She questioned when the gods had become so cold of heart, so dispassionate, about mankind? Her answer was the heavy silence of death.

"The Moon Goddess never knew what had become of the man who fathered her babes, but no longer had the heart to care. She vowed to never return to the Earth to consort with humans. Nor would she ever let the Sun God reach out and touch her face again, as forever she would turn from him and spurn his attention.

"With a mourning heart and steeped in despair, the Moon Goddess carried her dead babes into the night sky and interred her twins amongst the heavenly stars. In that manner she could look upon them, remember the miracle of their birth, and always remain near to them—to reminisce on what had once been.

"Upon return to her home, she sobbed with great pain in her heart as copious tears spilled from her beautiful crystalline blue eyes. The Moon Goddess continued to grieve until there were no more tears left to fall.

"Eventually her tears ran dry and were replaced with blood, which ran freely from her tear ducts. In time, blood encased her eyes, hands and gown. And then it began to encase the entire surface of the Moon.

"Now all could behold her pain and grief, as she vowed to hide it from none, but to wear it proudly. She might have erred, but was this penance not far worse than her transgression? While she had created life through love and desire, the gods had selfishly smothered life, including that of innocents. Any who looked to the sky would know their Moon Goddess was in mourning. Perhaps even the lover she had known—should he still live—would see her depth of despair.

"Not able to faultlessly extract revenge, as she had broken the Laws of Nature, she decided instead to confer a gift to mankind, for she still maintained a kind heart, although now wounded by her fellow deities. Her gift would signify that which selfish gods had stolen from her. Deities who seemed to no longer understand love, nor the wonder of creation between a man and woman.

"The Moon Goddess bequeathed a gift of lust, fertility, and the undeniable need for mating, on all full-moon nights. And so these are the 'needing moons'.

"So many eons in time, and still she grieves for her babes. When her grief becomes too punishing to bear, she sends a Blood Moon to all women who crave to hold a child to their breast.

"Thus she creates the Blood Moon as a time of intensified passion and fertility, so no man can refuse giving his seed on those nights. Tis said, that if a blood offering is made to her, she bestows twins to the couple in reverence of her own great loss. Despite her painful loss, her heart still shows caring for mankind. And that is the fable of how the Blood Moon came to be."

Candy was sniffing back tears. "How sad for her to lose her babies so cruelly. I can't imagine how she must have grieved."

"Tis but a fable, please cry not over a tale. This was not told to make you feel disheartened."

"Well let's not ever tell that fable to our children. Where I come from, Disney would no doubt make a tragic children's movie from it and everyone in the theater would get their popcorn soggy from shed tears."

"I know naught of this 'disney' nor 'movie'. But of children, this I know. Tell me Lassie, how many shall we be withholding this fable from? If many, should we not get started with the process?" Smiling, he raised his eyebrow playfully and scrutinized her body with hungry eyes.

It gladdened him to lighten her mood. In truth, the thought of her bearing his children pleased him. Never before had he considered building a family with any female, but now, with Candy, the thought was most pleasing. How proud he'd be to see her carrying his child, with her breasts ripe, and a rounded belly.

Though Candy had laughed, and retorted they would have dozens, Thorne knew she was not serious. Still he hoped there would be many so they could one day share much love with their young.

With their talking, laughing, and teasing, the lovers were too engrossed in each other notice the strange yellow slit-eyes staring from the dense woods—eyes that were taking notice of them—of Candy.

From her overhead branch, Ono saw those investigating eyes. She also saw where they focused, as though studying her companion Candy.

The little gargoyle did not think it bode well, not well at all. Those eerie slit-eyes forewarned of dark places where no days were sunny, a place where boundless wickedness reigned.

Fear engulfed Ono and her wings shifted in preparation to take flight to assist her companion, knowing full well she would be outmatched by the being with the spying eyes.

Then the slit-eyes turned upward and met Ono's black gargoyle eyes. A single word summed up the expression in those measuring yellow slit-eyes.

Evil.

Celestial Realm
Luna's Celestial Garden

The Moon Goddess gazed upon the spent lovers as they rested entangled in each other's embrace. A small smile of satisfaction glowed on Luna's graceful face.

Such as serene moment was merely a twinkle in time for the couple, as the proverbial clock ticked forward—towards less enjoyable days and endeavors to come.

A soft sigh escaped her lips.

Long ago she'd learned it best not to be jealous of mankind. Their pleasures were great, but so were their tribulations and heartache.

She would do what she could . . . except, what of the other two deities of the troika? Therein lay the issue.

One might say her cohort deities did not play well with *humans.* The problem was, they *did* play with mankind, while not considering humanity. Often they considered humans as playthings, pets to generate amusement.

Still, the *Creator of All* might not condone such frivolity should this game become too punishing. Regrettably, the *Creator* hadn't been available for council for a great length of time, and although Luna didn't know why, it wasn't for her to question.

And now the Under Earth Master's half-demon child also seemed to be a player in this contrived drama. A manifestation from the Under Earth outside the cursed and restricted domain was unheard of, and she couldn't imagine the consequences.

Luna wondered what role Sin-Sum would play, to what end? Was it merely coincidence? The Fates would laugh at her for use of that word.

Her crystalline-blue eyes surveyed Earth and she acknowledged it was, without a doubt, a habitat filled with beauty. The landscape was diverse, from rocky mesas, to majestic snow-clad peaks, to meadow filled valleys. The waters were plentiful and appealing.

The wealth of this planet was vast. Unfortunately it was also home to ugliness in various forms, as the *Creator* believed balance was the key to any successful design.

Fate had set the lover's course, and it was going to be long, filled with misfortunes and trying for any couple to survive. Luna questioned if the lovers would lose all hope during their journey. She hoped not, but could hardly anticipate what to expect, now that extra players had joined the game.

Maybe she needed to step forward and try to . . .To do what?

Ah, now that was the question, wasn't it?

From my MAC . . .

Dearest Reader,

I want to thank you, valued reader, for trekking on this convoluted journey with Candy, as she stumbles along her path with destiny. Her fated road has only begun. Some obstacles on Candy's destined footpath contain humor, danger, passion, and some even the threat of heartache.

Also an enormous thank you to those who have given me support through my writing journey with this series, which has had it's own missteps.

Live and learn, live and learn . . .

Foremost thanks to my husband, Al, who always supports me in my endeavors. There couldn't be a more perfect or romantic husband, and those neck kisses you provide for encouragement are *divine*—in fact I could use more of your encouragement right about now!

Vicky, my little sister, has offered oodles of support and insight, despite saying she doesn't know me—but that's just her being a brat (I still love her despite that genetic trait, can't imagine where she got it!). Thanks for sharing Will's recollection of his mother's, advice it fit Ripple's personality perfectly.

And thank you Stephanie. You suffered through countless hours of editing for which I'm ever thankful. I probably owe you new reading glasses.

I also have a special fan (aka. our 'work daughter') that could compete with the Sun God for her sunny disposition, and the Moon Goddess for her grace. Many thanks, Srishti for your generosity of heart and support in helping to get the word out about *Chroma Crossing Chronicles*. By the way, your beautiful bridal henna party inspired me as you may have guessed. Thank you for letting me share that experience with your warm and welcoming family and guests.

It's fun to have the opportunity to write about such diverse characters. Thorne is such an alpha-male hottie, while his friend, Ripple, demonstrates a unique and irksome mix of wit and insight. I love them both.

Don't think that the characters from Savannah are to be forgotten. Cherry Ann, Todd, Liam, and Mark Kingsley will reappear later in the story. Each has a part to play in this drama, as their lives wind together like vines in a vineyard. Some of the resulting fruit will be sweet, some sour, and some rotten.

The next book available will be:

Chroma Crossing Chronicles: Book II
Dragon Tear

Sin-Sum will surface from the dark domains and the half-demon has his own agenda—one he hopes to keep secreted from his punishing and malign father, the Under Earth Master.

So pour yourself a glass of mead or wine (I prefer Muscato, thank you), find a nook to curl up in, and read on. And please watch my website for when the soon to be released **Dragon Tear** will be available.

In the meantime, as an indie, I don't have the support or resources of a big publisher so any posted reviews on *Amazon* would be greatly appreciated.

If you visit Savannah be sure to stop by the historic Kehoe House, our favorite romantic B & B and say 'hello' to the great staff.

S. Yurvati
www.syurvatiauthor.com

P.S. Now that the Blood Moon night sky has cleared, notice the twin stars on the cover—a eulogy worthy of the Moon Goddess' twins. Thanks Melissa, you rocked it.

About the Author

S. Yurvati began putting her thoughts and imaginings on paper during childhood, and continued through her college years. After completing her Master of Science degree at CSUN she was hit with that proverbial wrecking ball. *BAM!* Reality set in—she needed to make a dependable living and put her degree to work.

After decades of working in the medical world, life struck her with a much bigger wrecking ball. This one was sufficiently jarring that her husband convinced her to retire and take the time to write. Admittedly, working full-time in a science-based career left her little opportunity for the creativity of her left-handed brain. As soon as she agreed to return to writing he immediately took her to an electronic store and told her to "choose a laptop".

And that led to the beginning of **Chroma Crossing: Book I Blood Moon**.

She has lived in eight different states, from one end of the nation to the other, six with her husband. That doesn't include the stint at Fort McClellan during the heat of summer without air-conditioning. That unpleasant experience was for Basic Training, as the author was one of the last WACs (Women's Army Corp) during the end of the Vietnam era.

Now she resides in Texas with the "love-of-her-life" husband. She says he taught her to be young at heart and is her biggest fan in her pursuits. He might be doing cheerleading with pom-poms as you read this—very manly pom-poms of course.

To say the author has a love of cats is like saying squirrels love nuts (the reference is intentional). The Yurvati's share their large home with six cats, fondly referred to as the 'herd'. You might consider that over the top and they agree, but argue the last two kittens were adopted during a weak moment. Her husband likely cringes when purchasing cat food and kitty litter, while the pet store is happy he is a regular customer, like an annuity for the store. However, the author says felines make very good book critics, always providing a high five with furry paws or commenting with purrs of encouragement.

Made in the USA
Columbia, SC
20 August 2018